THE
WILDINGS

THE
WILDINGS

Book One

of

The Hundred Names of Darkness

NILANJANA ROY

Random House Canada

PUBLISHED BY RANDOM HOUSE CANADA

Copyright © 2012 Nilanjana Roy
Illustrations © 2012 Prabha Mallya

Originally published in India by Aleph Book Company, New Delhi, in 2012. Published by
Random House Canada, a division of Penguin Random House Canada Limited, Toronto,
in 2016. Distributed in Canada by Penguin Random House Canada Limited, Toronto.

www.penguinrandomhouse.ca

Random House Canada and colophon are registered trademarks.

Library and Archives Canada Cataloguing in Publication

Roy, Nilanjana S., author
The wildings / Nilanjana Roy.

(Book one of The hundred names of darkness)
Illustrations by Prabha Mallya.
Originally published: New Delhi, Aleph Book Company, 2012.
Issued in print and electronic formats.

ISBN 978-0-345-81261-2
eBook ISBN 978-0-345-81263-6

I. Mallya, Prabha, illustrator II. Title.

PR9499.4.R89W55 2016   823'.92   C2015-905267-X

Book design by Kelly Hill

Cover images: (cats) © Vectorig / Getty Images and © Ellika / Shutterstock.com;
(bird) © John Powell / Dreamstime.com; (frame) © Azat1976,
(New Delhi) © Mikadun, both Shutterstock.com

Inside cover image © Prabha Mallya

Map designed by Kelly Hill. Map images: (pigs) © Nenilkime, (abstract flower) © Ttenki,
(spice bags) © Macrovector, (cows and tiger) © Annykos, all Dreamstime.com;
(cats) © Vectorig / Getty Images

Printed and bound in the United States of America

2 4 6 8 9 7 5 3 1

For Mara, loveliest of cats;
and for Devangshu, the best of Bigfeet,
without whom there would have
been neither cats nor book.

map of — THE WILDINGS' — **niZAMUDDiN**

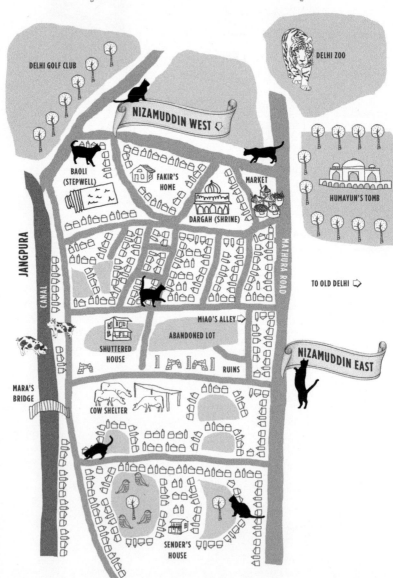

DELHI GOLF CLUB

DELHI ZOO

NIZAMUDDIN WEST

BAOLI (STEPWELL)

FAKIR'S HOME

MARKET

HUMAYUN'S TOMB

DARGAH (SHRINE)

JANGPURA

CANAL

MATHURA ROAD

TO OLD DELHI ⇨

MIAO'S ALLEY ⇨

ABANDONED LOT

NIZAMUDDIN EAST

SHUTTERED HOUSE

RUINS

MARA'S BRIDGE

COW SHELTER

SENDER'S HOUSE

CONTENTS

"Dream the world the way it truly is. A world in which all cats are queens and kings of creation."

—NEIL GAIMAN
"A Dream of a Thousand Cats"

CHAPTER ONE

A New Arrival

Nizamuddin was asleep when the first sendings came, in the pitch-black hours just before dawn. They were so faint that only the bats heard them, as they swooped in their lonely arcs between the canal and the dargah, the ancient Sufi shrine around which the colony's brick-walled homes were tightly coiled. One of the bats chittered nervously as the soft, frightened words reached him, echoing in his head: *Dark. Want my mother. Why are the dogs growling? Why aren't you saying anything? It's so dark in here.*

Then there was nothing else, and the bat soon forgot what he had heard, though when he hung upside down from the ruins near the baoli,—one of Delhi's few stepwells still fed from the depths of an underground spring—slumbering in the pearly light of day, he dreamt of being a hunted creature in a dark, cramped space, helpless against his predators.

It was long after when the second set of sendings came, stirring the post-monsoon air and startling a pariah cheel that was making sorties over the large park in the centre of Nizamuddin West. *"Mara is scared, put me down! Where did my mother go? Who are you? Where are you taking me? Don't want to leave the drainpipe! You're frightening Mara, you horrid Bigfoot!"* Tooth's wings dipped, taking him into a perilously low dive over the rooftops as he shook his head, trying to get rid of the sense that a cat was mewing at him in mid-air— softly, but enough to ruffle the delicate feathers that covered his inner ear. He felt unsettled until his sharp eyes spotted a bandicoot scuttling along the ground, larger and fatter than the local rats, its long snout twitching nervously as the predator's shadow fell over the creature, and the day's hunting began in earnest. By the time he had made his kill, the cheel had forgotten the strange encounter.

The Sender stayed silent after that. There were no cats or dogs in the area at that hour, and the only other creature in Nizamuddin to hear the second sending was a small brown mouse, who sat back on his haunches, cast a worried eye around, and seeing no cats or kittens, continued along his way.

THE DAYS PASSED PEACEFULLY. It was the happiest time of the year for the residents of Nizamuddin and Delhi's other colonies. Summer had gone and Diwali, the annual festival of lights with its menacing fireworks and thunderstorms of noise, wouldn't begin until the middle of autumn. Freed from the summer heat, the cats of Nizamuddin could start hunting again.

Beraal was pleased at the change in the air. She had spent most of the summer in the baoli, liking the tranquility of the disused stepwell, and in the abandoned construction lot where the cats found shelter among heaps of rubble. The heat had been intense that year, shrivelling the flame tree leaves, drying out the red flowers of the silk cotton trees, and the young cat had missed being able to go on long pilgrimages. Perhaps, she thought, stretching and yawning and shaking out her paws, it was time to make the trek to Humayun's Tomb and see what the cats who lived in the quieter parts of its sprawling gardens, undisturbed by the crowds who visited the ancient monument, were doing.

The park was noisy, what with the neighbourhood Bigfeet boys fighting over a game of cricket, and the pariah cheels echoing their quarrel in a treetop battle far above. Beraal ambled off towards the cowshed that sat in the middle of the Bigfeet's houses, settling on the broken brick wall to do her grooming in peace. This was more extensive than normal feline ablutions required: Beraal had long, black-and-white fur that curled silkily down to her paws when it was clean, but it was a magnet for dry leaves, dirt and other rubbish.

She was perched on top of the wall, licking industriously at a clingy spider's web that had attached itself to her paw, when the air around her ears seemed to shimmer and part. *"Woe!"* said a small clear voice right into her ear, *"Mara is worried! Mara is all alone with the Bigfeet! They are scary and they talk all the time, and I do not like being picked up and turned upside down!"*

Beraal almost overbalanced, and had to somersault back onto the wall, an act that did nothing for her dignity. Wild-eyed, her whiskers bristling, her tail fluffing up to twice its normal size, she whirled around on the wall, searching for a cat that was nowhere to be seen. She ignored the small brown mouse who scurried out of his hole, equally startled. The quiet whisper that the mouse, whose name was Jethro, had heard almost a moon ago was much louder, far more powerful than the first time.

Beraal paid little attention to the mouse's squeaks, twitching her silky ears. That voice had sounded so close—could it be in the neem tree? Down near the ground beside the cows? But there was nothing there, and the cat was truly stumped. She stiffened as the dry leaves on the creepers rustled, then relaxed. It was only Hulo, hopping down from the neem tree onto the wall beside her. "What the hell was that?" he asked.

"So you received it too," she said slowly.

Hulo flicked his unkempt black tail lightly in assent. "I'll bet every tom and queen in Nizamuddin is looking for whoever that was—my whiskers are still trembling!"

"I thought it was speaking directly to me, Hulo," said Beraal.

"So did I," said Hulo. "That cat transmitted louder than I can remember any animal ever doing in our territory!"

"And further," said Beraal, as she felt her whiskers tingle. The other cats of Nizamuddin were linking—Miao, Katar, Abol and Tabol from the canal, Qawwali—and the air buzzed with questions.

Hulo's scruffy fur rippled as he listened. "They heard her on the other side of the canal!" he said to Beraal. "Whoever it was, Mara-Shara, whatever, it's a Sender, not an ordinary cat. And what worries me is that it's not one of us!"

Beraal felt her fur standing up, strand by strand. The cats of

Nizamuddin were used to linking across long distances, as all animals in the wild did with their own species. Mews reached only so far; scents and whisker transmissions formed an invisible, strong web around their clan of colony and dargah cats. But linking allowed them only to listen to each other. A true sending, where the Sender's fur seemed to brush by the listener, its words and scents touching the listener's whiskers, was rare. And only a true Sender could link with animals from other species as well as its own kind; the clan, like all clans who lacked Senders, used the mews, chirps and barks of Junglee rather than linking by whisker when they needed to speak to those from other species. From time to time, stranger cats, wayfarers and wanderers from other parts of the city, might breach the web, accidentally linking—but it had been years since the Nizamuddin clan had a Sender in its midst, or had received a sending as strong as this.

Beraal let her tail sink down as she thought about the sending: it had seemed to be coming from deep inside her head.

Hulo and she felt their whiskers crackle as Katar, the tomcat who was the clan's most respected wilding, sent out an all-cats-bulletin across the Nizamuddin link. "Everyone heard that, I suppose," Katar said. A running chorus of assent flickered across all their whiskers, from the bungalows in front to the park where Beraal and Hulo were, right up to the limits where the colony proper ended and the low roofs of the slums, illegal but ubiquitous, took over. "Anyone know what or who—this Mara is? Any recent sightings of strays from elsewhere? Miao, any thoughts?"

Miao was the oldest of all of the Nizamuddin wildings. "We'd have picked up news of any outsiders," she said. "This one must be newly arrived—unusual for a stray this powerful to escape being noticed by all of us. Perhaps Qawwali and the dargah cats know more?" But Qawwali said there hadn't been a whiff of outsiders for many moons now. Abol and Tabol said no strays had crossed the canal, nor had the market cats seen any strangers.

Beraal shared a thought that she'd been turning over in her head. "There's something strange about the way the cat spoke," she said. "Its transmissions didn't just sound foreign—that entire sending was unusual."

"That's because it's not one of us, Beraal," said Hulo impatiently. "Outsiders always sound different."

"That's not what I meant," said Beraal. "There were very clear images, though I couldn't make out what they were exactly."

The link crackled with slow assent. Katar cut in: "Did you see what I did, Beraal? I thought I could see a small, orange blur, hanging in mid-air."

"Something like that," said Beraal. "And who was it sending to? Did it even know it was sending?"

Hulo sent an exasperated twitch along the line. "Whatever it is," he said, "it's a stray who's not one of us wildings, and if it can send so strongly that it almost shook me out of the branches of my tree, I want it dead. It's been years since any of us heard a sending as powerful as that."

"Wait," said Katar. "Miao, who was Nizamuddin's last Sender?"

"You never met her, Katar," said Miao. "Most of you wouldn't remember Tigris, she was before your time. If you're wondering about her descendants, she had none—Tigris had no mates that we knew of, and there haven't been Senders in Nizamuddin since, though we keep an eye on every kitten in every new litter. And though Tigris could send with some skill, the sending we just heard is much stronger. This Sender is definitely an outsider—going by the power crackling on all of our whiskers, an experienced adult, possibly a battle veteran. There haven't been any wildings of that description in the area—we'd have known, by scent or whisker—so it must have come in with a Bigfeet family."

"Then perhaps we should try to find out more about this Mara," Beraal started to say, when Katar gently overrode the link. He and Miao were the most experienced of Nizamuddin's wildings. The colony had no leader, as was the norm with cats, but when all of the wildings had to confer, Miao or Katar would conduct the clan conclaves.

"I'm clearing the link," he said. "Everybody should stay on alert. Look for strangers, listen for any reports of strays who may have come in across the canal, or from the animal shelter. Watch the Bigfeet homes carefully—it spoke of Bigfeet, if my memory is true. Expect to find a large fighter, probably a queen, as Miao says—this cat would have to be an adult of considerable size to have that kind of sending power."

"Katar," said Beraal, "what should we do when we find it?"

"Kill it," said Katar, "if it's not one of us, and especially if it's living with Bigfeet. Beraal, I'll expect you to take a special interest in the execution."

Beraal hadn't expected any other response. Strangers, especially those who lived with Bigfeet, were always regarded with suspicion, and an unknown Sender was even worse. Their abilities set them apart from other wildings, and this one had badly shaken the Nizamuddin clan.

If this was an inside cat, a house cat, killing it might be somewhat more difficult, but Beraal figured she would solve that problem when she got to it. Beraal was the most fierce of the queens of Nizamuddin, and could take on many of the toms. She was a fine hunter—swift, silent and precise—and her immediate concern was finding the stranger who threatened their peace.

IT WAS AN UNEASY NIGHT in Nizamuddin for the feline population. Two more calls twitched through the dark, disrupting prowlers and sleepers alike. *New place smells like new miss my mother new new new, Mara lonely, Mara sad.* That came in an hour after the cats of Nizamuddin had first linked, and set the whisker links twitching all over again. It had been even stronger than the first message, and the fear set all their ears back, sent their fur rippling in empathy.

As she paced restlessly around the park, keeping only the most perfunctory watch out for dogs, Beraal met Katar. The handsome grey tom touched noses in greeting and tried to prevent the small brown kitten who'd been trailing in his wake from tripping over Beraal's paws.

"Me and young Southpaw are going down to the dargah to check the scent trails at the perimeter, just in case we've all missed something," he said. "Miao and Hulo are patrolling the canal—Southpaw, quit playing with my tail or I'll have to smack you again—I'm worried, Beraal, I don't ever remember a Sender as strong as this or as odd. I tried communicating with it, and so did Miao, but we couldn't connect. I don't understand this. I don't like it at all. It's best if we find it and kill it soon."

Beraal wrapped her tail around his, a small gesture of comfort but a pleasant one; she and Katar had mated once, and though neither his kitten nor any of the ones fathered by other toms had survived and they'd had other mates since, she and the grey were quite fond of each other.

"And of course Southpaw has to go along with you," she said, her whiskers gently brushing the young kitten's head. "Shouldn't you be taking a nap, youngling?" Southpaw was the colony's orphan, and so far it had taken the combined efforts of all of the Nizamuddin cats to keep him out of trouble—he had an instinct for tumbling from the antheap into the termite's nest, as the old saying went.

"The sendings woke him up," said Katar, "and I found him prowling the rooftops as though he was on tomcat patrol, all by himself." He didn't need to add that it was safer to take the kitten along. Southpaw could hear the other cats on the link, but his whiskers hadn't grown to the stage where he could send out messages on the link without garbling them terribly. Besides, the kitten's last attempt to patrol the roofs had ended with him tangled in a clothesline, the ropes and wet clothes muffling his mews for help.

Three hours later, the third sending came in. They had almost been expecting it, but it made no sense. It was just as loud, but less fearful. *New, still new, I don't like new—but Bigfeet are nice, Bigfeet make me feel less scared.*

The rooftops of Nizamuddin had rarely seen such activity.

Caterwauling rang across the neighbourhood, causing the Bigfeet to toss and turn uneasily. Lithe ghost shapes padded along the roofs, swarmed down drainpipes and backstairs, patrolled dustbins, swooped smoothly under cars, searching for a Sender who refused to be seen. The dogs whined in their sleep, sensing the crackling of back-and-forth messages in the air; the few foolish enough to try and chase the cats they saw were taken aback to be met with blazing eyes and aggressive hissing and spitting. The cats of Nizamuddin had work to do tonight; they weren't going to let a few curs get in their way.

Out on her third patrol of the night, Beraal sat down heavily on the front steps of one of the houses and decided that she needed to wash for a bit. As her tongue loosened her silky fur, releasing some of the tension that had been knotting her insides, she found it easier to focus on the problem. It was like untangling a very complicated ball of thread—you had to find the ends and pull them out one by one.

Rasp, rasp, her tongue went smoothly back and forth across her coat. *Scared cat called Mara. But if it was a battle veteran, why would it be scared? Because it was in a new—and therefore frightening?—place?* She began to tease the tangles out of her fur. The young queen coughed slightly as she swallowed a knot of loosened dirt and fur—that probably meant a hairball in the morning. Well, it couldn't be helped.

Balancing on three paws, she spread one out carefully, and began tonguing the dirt out from between the claws. *Was it with a new family? In a new house?* Her tail curled around for easier reach, and she began to groom it absentmindedly. *The sendings had grown clearer each time, and so had that unsettling image of a small orange ball of fur, whatever that was. But it didn't make sense. Why would this powerful Sender crash into the wildings' neighbourhood and refuse to talk to them?*

As the first glimmers of dawn came up, Beraal thought she knew what she had to do. She had to find a house that Bigfeet had just moved into. Then she had to find out if there were any large cats in the house. She flattened her ears slightly: Beraal didn't like the idea of going into a strange house inhabited by Bigfeet. And if she found the cat? And if it was the most powerful Sender any one of them had ever seen, and sensed she was there to kill it? Then, she'd see, wouldn't she?

Beraal's first kill had been a cunning old bandicoot rat three times her size, when she was still in her fifth month. That was just the first of many victories. The queen had never failed to make her kill yet, and didn't think she would this time.

CHAPTER TWO

Hide and Seek

The most powerful Sender in Indian feline history took two careful steps forward, sat down on her fur-protected behind then propelled with her front paws, scooted the length of the highly polished drawing room floor, and braked with the assistance of the Persian carpet. This was a wonderful game, Mara thought. She was beginning to settle into her new home. She missed her mother, badly, but the nightmare of the drainpipe and the barking dogs was beginning to fade, and curiosity about her territory had replaced some of her fear and sadness.

The house, which for Beraal or any outside cat would have seemed a confining set of boxes cluttered with all kinds of unnecessary Bigfeet stuff, loomed large to a kitten who had spent her first month under a pile of gunny sacks near the canal, and an entire day holed up in a drainpipe, terrified of the prowling dogs.

Mara had been too scared to explore the house, but over the space of a few hours, she had relaxed. She liked her bed, which was adorned with cool, soft sheets that made the perfect scratching pad for a small kitten. She wasn't very sure what she thought of the Bigfeet—they boomed too much, and often picked her up when she didn't want to be picked up, and didn't seem to understand her at all. But they were gentle, and they were excellent suppliers of fish and milk. And they didn't always interfere with her explorations.

Her whiskers twitched a bit as she attempted to disentangle herself from the carpet, which had unaccountably wrapped itself around her. Mara's whiskers were striking—unusually long, prematurely white unlike the black that most kittens sported, curved at their tips. She kept them pressed down to her face; the kitten had learned early, in her very first days at the canal, that extending them fully would bring the noise and clatter of the world rushing into her mind.

"You're a Sender," she remembered her mother telling her, the day she had opened her eyes for the first time. Mara had been curled up, a tiny comma against her mother's warm flank, listening to the giant purr of traffic on the bridge over the canal. Her mother's blue eyes had been wary, almost sad as the cat washed her tiny kitten's whiskers, making them tingle.

"What is a Sender?" Mara had asked. And her mother had answered slowly: "Senders are very unusual, Mara, there's never more than one in a clan and most of the Delhi clans haven't seen a Sender in more than three generations. Being a Sender means you can travel without using your paws—your whiskers will take you everywhere. And you can see and hear more than most cats can." Mara suckled contentedly, drinking her milk as she tried to imagine what she could hear and see that other cats couldn't. "Even you?" she had asked. "Even me," her mother had said. "I told you, Senders are rare."

They had played patty-paws then, but later, Mara had asked her mother: "What do Senders have to do?" Her mother washed the kitten lovingly. "A lot," she had said. "Senders guard their clans; every clan hopes they will be lucky enough to have one, especially when times are hard. But it's not an easy life—" the mother broke off, not wanting to tell her kitten that being a Sender would mark her as different, that her clan members excepted, most other cats would fear her, envy her, challenge her. "It's an interesting life," she said instead. "Don't worry about it, Mara, I'll teach you everything you need to know." But then there had been the dogs; and then the Bigfeet had found her, and brought her to this new place, far away from the canal.

There had been something odd about last night. What was it? Ah, yes; she'd had the strangest feeling, when she'd been at her most lonesome, that she was being . . . watched. Heard. That a whole heap of other cats had been listening to her.

She wriggled, trying to chase her tail and emerge from the carpet at the same time, as stray thoughts floated through her stripy head. *Miao . . . a wise Siamese cat with gentle blue eyes . . . Hulo was scarred and big, and scornful . . . Beraal was beautiful, deep green eyes, long black-and-white fur . . .* there were many others, but she couldn't make them all out. Suddenly she was in mid-air, the carpet still wound round her—Mara poked her head out and stared into the eyes of the she-Bigfoot. The voice

sounded scolding today, but also amused. Tentatively, still suspended, she licked the Bigfoot's hand.

She was deposited gently on the ground, unravelled from
the carpet, patted smartly on her backside—an indignity, but
well, she'd probably deserved it—and then the Bigfoot settled
down on the ground beside her and began to scratch the difficult spot in the centre of her forehead that she could never
reach herself.

Mara forgot about other cats, strange cats whom she didn't
know; forgot about her plans to go forth on a Bold Expedition,
exploring the house more thoroughly. As her Bigfoot scratched
her head, she leaned forward, her body almost twanging with
ecstasy, and purred, and purred, and purred. Then there was
lunch—milk deliciously flavoured with fish—followed by an
afternoon nap . . .

IT WAS QUITE LATE and very cool when Mara woke up. She'd
been shifted from the cushion on the sofa to a small round uphol-
stered basket that she liked instantly, stropping her claws on the
wicker as she yawned pinkly. Where were the Bigfeet? She padded out of her basket, intending to find the big bed where she'd
slept the previous night, but found that the door to that room
had been closed. Time for the Bold Expedition to begin.

From her position, less than six inches off the floor, the
world was a forest of interesting things. There were chair-legs
and table-legs rising off the ground and becoming platforms
that she would later investigate. There were soft carpets all
over, and she idly tested her claws on some of them before

padding on. One of the rooms smelled nice, all dusty and musty and filled with interesting cardboard boxes that she had started to rip open. And coming through the kitchen doors—oh my, what were all those smells?

Mara sat down and closed her eyes, trying to identify them: they were so rich and so strong that they swirled around her head in a thick soup, confusing the kitten till she shook her head to try and clear it. There was . . . the heavy, brothy odour of garbage coming from downstairs; a scent of many Bigfeet; a sharp smell of iron.

From further away, the mingled scent of dogs drifted in, making her cringe a bit, but there were also cats, and seven different kinds of earth, from gravel to thick loamy mud; and trees, and flowers, and the soapy odour of Bigfeet clothes mixed with the metallic odour of cars. And they were all coming from outside that screen.

She patted the wire mesh door, and it swung open, enough for her to go out. The world held mercifully still, though the smells shifted and changed in a constant dance. The kitten was absolutely silent, squeezing as close to the wire mesh door—the back door of the house—as possible. The perfume of rotting garbage rose up from the narrow lane between the back of the house and the park—it was a holiday for the garbage collectors' that day, so the aroma was richer and stronger than it normally would have been. It was inviting, but Mara hesitated, her tail waving uncertainly from side to side.

This was her first real view of the world. Her memories of early kittenhood were fuzzy. Her eyes had been closed for most of the time that she had lived under the canal. She remembered her mother's comforting flanks, and the way she would be washed until she went to sleep, and the milky scent of her mama's skin. But there had been a frightening period where her memories blurred: the sharp tug at the skin over her neck, where her mother had carried her, the close fetid stench of the drainpipe, the hours crouched inside, her fur trembling as the dogs snarled and circled outside. The last thing she had heard was her mother's low, defiant growl, and then she had waited for hours in the dark, but her mama never came back.

Now that Mara could see and smell the world, she liked it, but she didn't know if she could trust it. The sense of space made her head swirl. But what if she just went out onto the stairs? The stairs were part of the house, so perhaps they were really inside, not outside. The kitten discovered that if she could pretend she believed this, the dizziness went away, and her spinning head settled down. She rested on the staircase, curling her tail comfortably around herself to use as a cushion on the cool steel steps.

CHAPTER THREE

A View to a Kill

From the branches of the mango tree, Beraal watched the tiny orange kitten who'd bounced out onto the staircase with idle interest. It seemed new to the neighbourhood, but then the Bigfeet were always bringing in parrots, puppies, babies, kittens—as though they needed to underline their large clumping size by collecting small creatures for their houses.

Beraal and Hulo had spent most of the afternoon working backwards from the cow shelter, using their whiskers to try and pinpoint where the sendings had come from. The cows, who had lived in the large yard for years after the Bigfeet had constructed a refuge for lost city cows and bulls near the local temple, watched the two cats with interest before returning to their lunch of mango peels and rice straw. Beraal had narrowed her search down to the park, but she wasn't sure whether the Sender would still be here. "If it's a house cat, Hulo, it'll be somewhere in this area," she'd told the tom.

"Perhaps," said Hulo, his tail flicking back and forth dubiously, "but I'm going to go and see if I can find any new scents. That's been gnawing at my mind, Beraal. If we're talking about a tomcat or queen with these levels of aggression, there must be scent markings somewhere in the area." His nose quivered. Just one spray, even if it were hours or days old, would tell him more about the stranger than any of the sendings had been able to. It might tell him how aggressive the other cat was, and would definitely tell him how much territory it claimed—perhaps even where the intruder was located. Hulo rubbed heads affectionately with Beraal and prowled off, careful to avoid the Bigfeet boys, who were playing a rough game of catch in the park.

Beraal used her fluffy tail to cushion her belly against the rough bark of the tree. Her ears and whiskers were tuned to pick up the smallest, tiniest hint that any of the houses surrounding the park contained the intruder. The cat settled in for a long wait, amusing herself by watching the squirrels as they ran up and down the branches, their tails like feathery sails that propelled them effortlessly along. They gave her a wide and respectful berth, sticking to the other half of the mango tree, and she yawned, her eyes narrowing to little green slits as she calculated her chances of killing at least one—very high, if she focused on the tiniest one. It would have the least meat on its bones, but it would be the most easily frightened; fear turned prey witless, causing them to freeze in their tracks, and run the wrong way.

As she waited, she watched the kitten. It was playing with the tip of its tail, and it had a very comical way of going about it that reminded Beraal of one of the kittens she had had a year ago. That one had died young, sadly, falling to a cheel's sharp beak, but it had had a similarly solemn approach to the delicate task of catching and trapping one's tail.

The orange kitten triumphantly pounced on its tail, fell over forwards, narrowly avoided bumping its nose and went tumbling down three stairs before it managed to use its bum as a brake. Beraal found her whiskers radiating a smile at the way in which the kitten carefully checked each paw to see if it was in working order before climbing back up and settling down again.

"That was scary!" a voice said in her head. *"Mara could have gone rolling and tumbling all the way down! And now my bottom hurts!"*

The voice was very loud, and Beraal felt her whiskers trembling like leaves in a storm. She stared at the kitten, and the hunter's whiskers straightened in incredulous fury as it all began to make sense. A Sender who didn't know she was sending, who wanted her mother, who didn't know how to receive signals or understand a cat network—because she was just a kitten, a wet behind the whiskers brat who'd sent an entire neighbourhood of cats into a frenzy.

It was only when the squirrels chittered anxiously, flying up to the safety of the very top of the tree, that Beraal realized her claws were out, stropping the bark, and that she was growling under her breath, her teeth chattering in the prelude to the killing bite. The cat licked her lips and shifted, trying to calm herself.

"And that would have been a long, long way down," the voice continued. *"Oh look—a butterfly! Two butterflies! Maybe I can catch both if I leap up with all my paws out in the air at the same time—oh! mrraargh!—bad idea!"*

Beraal felt her whiskers crackle again as the Nizamuddin link sprang to life. "Our Sender is a kitten?" Katar snarled. "Nothing but a mangy kitten?" Even though he was miles away, on the dusty road at the far end of the canal, his whiskers rang with indignation, and the other cats began to chime in.

The kitten, hopping along a stair, hesitated and looked up. Her wide green eyes, the colour of new leaves in the monsoon, stared straight at Beraal. "Shut it!" Beraal said quietly. "There's just a chance that it might be able to hear us—Katar, I'll get back on the link later. Keep the airwaves clear."

The kitten had her head cocked to one side, and she was giving Beraal a considering look—surprising, thought the hunter, coming from such a little one. There was no help for it. Beraal would have preferred to avoid the risk of Bigfeet reprisal, but this was definitely the Sender.

She stared at the staircase, evaluating the possibility of a clean kill. It wouldn't be easy. She would have to scale the wall below, make the jump on to the stairs without being noticed by either Bigfeet or the kitten. If that went off well, she would still have to make her kill, and the staircase was used quite often by Bigfeet.

Beraal gauged her escape routes; perhaps it would be best to use a paralyzing bite on the kitten's neck and carry it up to the roof to complete the kill. If she got it right, she might even kill the kitten with the first bite. She had done that often enough. And even if she didn't, it was best to get the body out of the way—less chance that her Bigfeet would intervene, more chance that Beraal would make a clean and safe getaway. The dappled branches of a neem tree and the friendly, yellow-flamed branches of a laburnum tree hung invitingly over the roof; it was perfect. And the kitten's attention had wandered; its head bobbed up and down as it followed the flight of one of the butterflies.

Cautiously, since they were so close, the mango tree a distance of three leaps away from the staircase, Beraal began to pad down the branch, towards the kitten, as silently as she could. The young queen didn't want to risk the chance that the kitten would see a strange and much bigger cat approaching her with hostile intent and run for her life. Gingerly, she stepped onto the stairs.

The kitten froze, pivoted and peered across at her. That's done it, thought Beraal, now she'll be inside the house in a flash and it might be days before I get a second chance.

"Rats!" she said crossly.

"Hello there!" said the kitten, scrambling to her feet.

Beraal blinked. The kitten was supposed to run for her life—that's the way the world worked.

"You really are a cat!" the kitten said. "Oh my, your fur's so beautiful! Isn't it scary being in a tree? I would be scared if I was high up in a tree! My mother's not here—she was in the drainpipe with me, of course, but then the dogs came, and then the Bigfeet came—never mind that. This is my first time outside, but I expect you're used to it. I'm not, it makes me dizzy, and I was just going to go inside. My name is Mara, what's yours? Do you want to come over and chat? Please come, there's room on the stairs for both of us."

Beraal felt her head swimming. But there were no Bigfeet on the stairs, and all of Beraal's instincts were telling her that this was the best shot she would get at killing the kitten. She padded up the stairs, evaluating her prey.

"You're the most beautiful cat I've ever seen!" said Mara. "Though honestly, I haven't seen that many. I was born under the bridge over the canal, and then there was the drainpipe, you see. But what lovely fur you have, it looks so soft!"

Beraal decided she'd had enough, this kitten was making her head spin . . . She laid her ears flat, hissed once in warning and let her claws slide out, preparing to spring.

"*. . . why are you making that face? That's really scary! You're frightening me! You're a mean old ugly cat, and you were supposed to be my friend. I want my mother NOW!!!!!*"

Beraal blinked, shaking her head to try and get the noise out of it. Up close, Mara's broadcasting volume was unbelievably loud; it was as though someone had set off firecrackers in her head, and it hurt so much that she had had to stop in mid-pounce.

She became aware that she was being watched by Mara, who had backed up and was within easy reach of the kitchen doors. If Beraal moved too soon, she had little doubt that Mara would dart for safety through the doors. The only question was why she hadn't done so already. The big cat stared at the kitten, puzzled, and found herself looking into Mara's reproachful eyes.

"I wanted to be your friend," said Mara. "It's lonely out here. My Bigfeet are fine, but I don't know any other cats. You were coming up here to talk to me, I thought, and then you started . . . *MEAN OLD CAT! I HATE YOU! I WANT MY MOTHER NOWOWOWOWOWOW!!!!*"

Beraal waited till her head cleared.

"Please," she said to the kitten, "could you stop doing that?"

"*NO! YOU SCARED ME! AND ALL I WANTED WAS A FRIEND! MARA IS SO SAD!*"

Beraal sighed, as the cat network in Nizamuddin lit up all over again with exclamations and protests, the lines crackling from the dargah nearby all the way to Humayun's Tomb on the other side of the main road. Somewhere in her head, Katar was demanding to know why she hadn't killed the kitten already. Hulo was saying he was on his way if she wanted backup. Out on the roof, a Bigfoot head popped up and Beraal knew she'd have to get off the stairs soon, especially as Mara was continuing to yowl at the top of her lungs.

Ignoring the sense that her head had been invaded by a troupe of those infernal Bigfeet marching bands, Beraal decided she might as well take a shot at a kill. She gathered her haunches in, waggled for take-off and, her claws extended, made a powerful leap at Mara.

The kitten was sitting just inside the doorway, her mouth open as she mewed her head off. She wasn't looking at Beraal, and wasn't protecting herself. Beraal rose smoothly into the first arc of her pounce, just as Mara sniffed and moved to the left, to better clean her whiskers.

Beraal overshot, landed in a small puddle of water and found herself skidding in an undignified fashion into the house. She fetched up sharply against the wooden leg of a table and lay there, winded, her eyes closed.

There were noises above her head. Bigfeet voices. They came closer, and Beraal shivered, trying to move her paws, but she could do little more than twitch. From beneath the table, she saw a Bigfoot scoop Mara up, cooing at the kitten and bearing it out of the room. The other Bigfoot was fiddling with the doors, and Beraal shakily got to her feet just in time to see the kitchen doors leading to the staircase being firmly shut. She shrank back under the table as the Bigfoot passed her, and stayed there for a while, her heart hammering. Mara appeared to have stopped sending; there were no further messages, nothing to distract Beraal from the awful knowledge that she was now trapped in a house, at the mercy of two Bigfeet and a kitten she had tried and failed to kill.

THE KITCHEN WAS DARK AND SILENT, and while Beraal could hear the Bigfeet, their voices were muffled and far away. She stayed under the table, her eyes closed, her heartbeat coming back to normal. The house was crisscrossed with Mara's scent patterns, testifying to the kitten's peregrination; without being told, Beraal knew that the kitten was allowed to roam the floors, but not the shelves or the tabletops. The scent of Bigfeet was so strong that it made Beraal anxious, It had been a long time since she had set her paws inside a house.

Her eyes adjusting to the dimness, she came cautiously out from under the table, padding silently to the doors. She nudged them, hard, but all that earned her was a sore nose. The black-and-white cat leapt up on the sink next, careful not to make a noise; but the windows were firmly closed. The only exit from the room led into the house, and Beraal growled deep in her chest—a low, subterranean hum—as she thought of what it meant. The house was not her territory; it belonged to Mara, as every last scent trail told her. The fear of being found by the Bigfeet formed another tight knot in her stomach.

Standing at the door, Beraal did a quick survey. The kitchen opened into a much larger room, filled with furniture. It appeared to be free of Bigfeet and of Mara, and hesitating only briefly, Beraal padded in. Her claws clicked loudly on the wooden floor, and the noise made her freeze. She pointed with her muzzle for a long, long while before deciding she hadn't been heard.

She could almost smell the fear rising off her own fur, and when she realized that her paws were slippery with sweat, she made herself pause and wash, the rasp of her tongue calming her down. Beraal looked around the room, and felt her panic subside, replaced by curiosity.

In the centre of the room was a large carpet, and this she padded over, gingerly pressing her paws down on the surface and reflexively shooting out her claws when she realized it felt like fur. The cat stropped her claws meditatively on the carpet, enjoying the paw massage as her claws stuck into the fabric and were then slowly yanked free. She jumped up on a sofa and almost mewed in shock when she found her paws sinking into the soft cushioning; it was a relief when she leaped onto the back of the sofa instead, and began to walk along its soft but stable length. There were tables dotted all around the room, and these some instinct told her to avoid; she sniffed at a lamp and moved hastily back when it wobbled from side to side.

When she looked at the walls properly, her great green eyes widened. She could see the sky, and forgetting her fear of the Bigfeet, Beraal moved fast, breaking into a run. She leaped for the window, and fell back with a thwack when she hit its glass barrier. Astonished, she put her nose to the glass, sniffing, unable to understand why she could *see* the sky and the trees, but not smell or feel them. The glass was smooth, giving her nothing to work with—no scents, except for Mara's and the Bigfeet's, no tastes, nothing at all.

The fur on the back of her neck prickled and her instincts kicked in before she was entirely conscious that she was responding to the presence of Bigfeet. She whirled, her tail rising, her hackles up, her teeth bared, and then she crouched for cover under a small table as one of the Bigfeet walked past.

The Bigfoot was heading left, so Beraal headed right, her eyes rolling back all the way as she shot into yet another room. The cat's flanks were heaving in panic; all she wanted to do was leave, find her way back to a place where the ceiling didn't press down so heavily on her, where the skies were open, where there were trees and drains to explore, and where it didn't feel so closed, so small.

There were no windows in the room, but there were no Bigfeet, either, and Beraal stopped her headlong flight just before she hit the wall. She turned on the balls of her feet, her claws halfway out, her nostrils flared and her mouth open in a silent snarl; the room stank of the kitten, reinforcing the sense of unease she felt at being in another cat's territory.

Outside on the stairs, the hunter's task had seemed simple enough. But here, surrounded by Mara's scent, Beraal's instincts were kicking in, telling her severely that it was the height of bad manners to attack another cat in its own territory, never mind Katar's orders. If the kitten attacked, she would be on the defensive; it might be smaller, younger and less experienced, but this was its home. Beraal looked around the room, searching for an exit, trying to make sense of her surroundings.

She froze as a tiny orange heap of fur stirred on one of the sofas. Beraal's fur stood on end, and she growled low in the back of her throat.

Mara turned over on the cushion, stuck her paw in her eye, and emitted an unmistakeable snore.

The black-and-white cat sat down heavily on her haunches, her whiskers radiating disbelief. She stared at the kitten, but made no move to get closer to it; instead, she washed the tip of her tail and her whiskers roughly, walking herself through what was a most unusual situation. She was used to cats fighting back, or spitting their defiance at her, especially if they were outside cats in new and unusual surroundings. She would have been able to deal with fear, which would have been a normal reaction for any kitten that had been hunted by an experienced warrior.

But barely ten minutes after being stalked and hunted, Mara had reacted by rolling herself into a little ball and going to sleep. Beraal had never come across any kind of prey that had demonstrated this degree of suicidal unconcern for its own safety.

She tested the air, letting her whiskers probe for signs of the Bigfeet; her sense of space and direction was kicking in, despite the vast differences between mapping the lay of the land outside, which she was used to, and figuring out an unfamiliar Bigfeet house. Beraal listened hard, like a cat at a mouse hole, but her instincts and whiskers told her that the Bigfeet were at least two rooms away.

The older cat licked her paws thoughtfully. She checked her

claws and used the carpet to strop them till they were as sharp as knives. Slowly, careful not to make the slightest sound, she crept forward, moving towards Mara, using the table and chair legs for cover. Part of her attention was on the doorway, her ears cocked to listen for any sign that the Bigfeet might return. But her eyes were fixed on the kitten's sleeping form, and her muscles tensed. One pounce should do it, in Beraal's estimation; one pounce would be enough to get her up onto the sofa, and if she timed it right, she could break the kitten's neck with her trademark sharp killing bite, before Mara woke up or felt the slightest pain. And then she could find an open window or a door and leave this horrible shut-in place and never have to come back again.

"You came back!" said a happy voice. "How nice of you to come back, I didn't think you would, so I took a nap to recover from all the excitement! Have you seen my basket? This is where I sleep at night, it's very comfortable! This is a mouse—a cloth one, not a real one, but it makes a perfect pillow! Would you like to play with my ball? I have a ball and a mouse, see?"

Beraal scrabbled for balance in mid-leap, managed to twist sideways and came down hard on the edge of the sofa with a thump. "Mrrrowwwwff!!" she said involuntarily and shut her eyes. That had been a hard thump; she felt distinctly wobbly.

Her ears were being gently washed, and a small but comfortingly raspy tongue went over the sensitive patch of fur on her forehead. It was so soothing that Beraal kept her eyes closed, even though her mind was scratching at the door, trying to tell her that this was all wrong, that no self-respecting assassin would let the subject of her assassination wash her ears. She opened her eyes, and found herself staring into Mara's upside-down face. The kitten had clambered onto her back and was balanced on her neck, washing her face with zealous intensity. Beraal blinked. This was extremely pleasant, but she felt she ought to protest—Mara had started washing her whiskers now, and despite herself, Beraal let out a tiny purr.

Mara purred back and walked down Beraal's face, making the cat yelp. Before she could voice a protest or growl, though, the kitten had cuddled up to her, and Beraal felt her stomach being gently kneaded by Mara's claws, as the kitten purred and purred and purred.

"I really should—" she began. Mara closed her eyes and continued to knead, her small paws massaging Beraal's stomach in a way that was quite delicious, and that reminded the older cat of the pleasures of having a litter. She looked down at the orange head.

"But you're not my kitten," she said firmly, pushing Mara away from her stomach and getting to her feet. The kitten batted at her paws, and Beraal laid her ears flat and growled.

Mara's eyes grew wide. The kitten put her head to one side, considered Beraal carefully and produced a surprisingly good imitation of the other cat's growl.

Beraal lowered her head, hunched her shoulders up and moved menacingly forward.

Mara lowered her head, hunched her shoulders up and smacked Beraal on the nose with her claws out, leaving a trail of blood and pain.

"My paws and whiskers!" cried Beraal. Her eyes blazed as

she slammed her paw down where the kitten stood, but Mara shot to the right, and she missed by a hair.

"Just you wait, you misbegotten, mangy, rotten little ball of fur," said Beraal, her teeth snapping down hard and missing Mara's tail by an inch. Her nose hadn't hurt like this since she'd got it caught in a mousetrap some months ago, and now all she wanted to do was to break the stupid kitten's neck in two.

Mara was scampering around the room now. Beraal shot after her and found herself scooting under the sofa in hot pursuit. The kitten's bottom wiggled in front of her nose, as Mara tried to find cover.

"Gotcha!" said Beraal, and triumphantly sank her teeth into a mass of orange fur. The pain made her reckless; instead of taking a second bite to make sure she'd snapped the kitten's neck, Beraal shook the furry bundle as hard as she could, slamming it against the wall twice. It hung limply from her jaws as she backed out from under the sofa, the bloodlust fading from her eyes. It was a pity, she thought, the kitten had seemed friendly enough; but the job was done, and perhaps her killing bite had delivered a swift and relatively merciful death.

She dropped the pathetic, limp heap onto the carpet and poked at it with a claw, feeling unaccountably sad inside.

"If you do that," said a voice above her head, "you'd better be careful because he has very long woolly fur and your claw might get stuck."

Beraal spun on her haunches and looked up.

Mara was sprawled out on a cushion washing her paws.

"That was fun, wasn't it? Have you ever tried playing with a ball? It's much nicer if there's two of us, if it's only me then I have to bat it against the wall. I like him, too, but he's only a soft toy. He doesn't bounce very well."

Beraal patted the heap of orange fur gingerly. The scent should have told her what it was—it smelled of Bigfeet, but then, so did Mara. The taste—come to think of it, she'd mentally noted the absence of blood and flesh—was dry and woolly rather than furry. She had expended one of her best killing manouevres on a tattered orange toy monkey with one brown glass eye.

The huntress struggled with a strong sense of discourage-ment. So far, nothing she had tried with Mara had gone right. And there was something about the kitten that Beraal, against her will, found beguiling.

Mara was patting something small and round, rolling it off the bed and in Beraal's direction. Instinctively, the cat batted at it, and her attention was caught when the ball hit the wall and rolled back at her. She padded after it and gave it a good, hard swat. Mara stretched, hopped off the bed and ran after the ball, nosing it back to Beraal. In just a few minutes, the cat was play-ing happily, her tongue sticking out as she tried to get the ball past the orange kitten.

"You're good!" she said, as Mara skillfully dribbled the ball behind the chair legs, using her paws to keep it just out of Beraal's reach.

"So are you!" said Mara, and abandoning the ball, the kitten reached up on her hind legs, rubbing her face against Beraal's whiskers lovingly.

Beraal hesitated, looking at the kitten. Mara's eyes were shut and as she rubbed, she purred, just as she had before. The young queen looked at the kitten's exposed neck. It would be so easy, she thought, to end this now. And then she sighed, her flanks heaving outwards, and flopping down, she began to wash Mara, the way she had once washed her own kittens—starting from the tip of the ears all the way down to the back and belly, to the orange-and-white circles that ringed the kitten's tail. Presently, the sound of two cats purring filled the room.

SOME TIME LATER, Mara showed Beraal the milk bowl, which she liked very much, and the litter box, which the older cat thought was usable, but nowhere near as nice as the soft earth of the flowerbeds or as comfortable as the sand from the construction heaps. Politely, she looked the other way when it was Mara's turn to go, and she used the time to consider the situation, mulling it over carefully.

"Mara," she said when the kitten was done, "what do I smell like to you?"

The kitten, having cleaned herself, came up to Beraal and inhaled the scent of the other cat's fur. "You smell good, like the outside," she said. "Like leaves, and bark from the tree, and you smell keen, like a hunter should, and alert, but also kind."

Beraal looked thoughtfully at the kitten. "I don't smell alien to you? Different from your clan?"

Mara was patting one of her toys around as she considered the question. "You don't smell like my mother," she said, "but I suppose all cats smell different from each other."

"What about your family, Mara?" said Beraal. "Don't I smell different from your family? Didn't your clan cats have their own particular scent?"

She stepped back in surprise as the kitten sent out involuntary distress signals. "I don't have family," said Mara.

Beraal's tail whisked from side to side in confusion. The kitten considered the older cat, and then came up to her, linking whiskers. "This is how it all happened," she said, and Beraal was silent as Mara shared her memories of the drainpipe and the dogs, her mother's disappearance. It explained a lot, Beraal realized; it explained why there was something strange about Mara.

"You don't know what a clan is, do you?" said Beraal.

Mara concentrated very hard on tearing up the carpet.

"Mara, do you know what the difference between inside and outside cats is?"

Mara refused to say anything, though her ears twitched a little. "Do you understand why I was stalking you a little while ago, why any cat from the Nizamuddin clan would try to kill you, Mara?"

The kitten's ears folded back. "No," she said. "It wasn't very nice of you, was it?"

Beraal's whiskers crackled with frustration. How was she supposed to explain basics like the killing instinct to a cat who didn't know the first thing about outsiders and insiders, who hadn't even met her clan, who had no idea about the importance of scent-marks?

"It just doesn't make sense to me," Mara said, curling up on Beraal's paws. "But it would be wonderful if you did explain."

"Yes," said Beraal, "though that might take some time—Mara, were you reading my mind?"

"Yes," said the kitten. "But I can only do that when you're right next to me and if you're relaxed and off guard."

Beraal licked the top of Mara's head absently. This, she thought, was going to be a very long conversation. First they'd have to talk about cat laws, and then she had some questions of her own about Mara's sending abilities, and then—she let out a worried exhalation—she would have to discuss matters with the Nizamuddin wildings.

"We have as much time as you like," said Mara. "My Bigfeet probably won't come in till morning, and if they do, you can hide under the cupboard."

Beraal thought it over. She was stuck in the house for the night, and as uneasy as that made her, she assumed she would be safe unless the Bigfeet found her. Her belly was pleasantly full of milk and egg, and Mara was washing her forelegs in an extremely soothing way.

"All right, Mara," she said. "Now, where shall we start?"

And so the black-and-white cat and the little orange kitten sat there, trading memories and questions, for a long, long time, until sleep overtook both of them. If the Bigfeet had come in then, they would have found it hard to disentangle one cat from another. Tired from the conversation, Mara had curled into Beraal's paws, and her orange fur was inextricably mixed up with the older cat's fur. But the Bigfeet didn't come in, and no sound disturbed the silence except for the very small, barely discernible sounds of two cats snoring.

CHAPTER FOUR

Brawl at the Baoli

Beraal padded along the road that ran parallel to the canal, pausing once to duck the muddy spray from a Bigfoot cyclist who was speeding through a puddle. At this early hour, it was hard to see the black-and-white cat; she blended into the dappled shadows, and found the camouflage useful when she was hunting rats. The call to worship from the Nizamuddin dargah floated in the air; the first prayers of the day would soon begin at the shrine of Nizamuddin Auliya, the much-loved Sufi saint who had lent his name to the colony.

Beraal had her ears cocked, she was listening to the neighbourhood in general, to the rumble and clatter of the morning sounds. She ignored the stink from the canal's fetid waters and the grunting of the many pigs who had made their homes on the banks. She paused a second time, waiting until two rambunctious puppies had run past, their high, excitable yaps fading into the distance.

The cat's progress through the back lanes of Nizamuddin was rapid but cautious. The Bigfeet were unpredictable, and in her younger years, she had once been caught by a pack of Bigfeet boys who had locked her in an empty plastic crate for the length of an afternoon.

They had teased her and poked sticks into the crate to make her jump. One of them had tied plastic bottles to her tail, the string knotted so tightly that it had taken her hours to gnaw her tail free, and the cuts had taken many moons to heal. She had no wish to repeat the experience, and her whiskers, ears and tail were extended and on high alert as she trotted through the butchers' lane, past the fragrance shops, beyond the crowds of petitioners and rose-petal sellers at the saint's shrine.

Beraal shrank back once, as a crowd of Bigfeet children ran laughing through the streets, but she had moved too slowly, and one of them kicked her in passing. The cat miaowed sharply but hurried on; the kick hadn't broken any of her ribs, though the pain was still there as she entered the graveyard.

Beraal allowed herself to rest for a few seconds inside the entrance. The Bigfoot fakir who lived here was fond of cats, and Abol and Tabol would be somewhere inside with the canal wildings—they started the day here, spent every evening patrolling the graves at his side, and often spent the afternoons napping on the gravestones.

The fakir was the only Bigfoot that all the cats of Nizamuddin trusted. His home and the small shrine that he tended was neutral ground. Wildings from all of the clans—the dargah cats, the market cats, even visitors from far-flung Humayun's Tomb or Jangpura—often came here, or went to the nearby baoli, the abandoned, ancient stepwell that only a few Bigfeet ever visited.

Miao, who knew more about the history of Delhi's wildings than any of the Nizamuddin cats, even Qawwali, once said that the dargah had welcomed cats for centuries. The Nizamuddin clan and its allied branches were one of the oldest of Delhi's many clans—older even than the wildings of Mehrauli or the Purani Dilli cats. Beraal couldn't quite wrap her whiskers around the idea of generations and generations of cats living in Nizamuddin through the centuries. But like the other cats, she knew that she felt welcomed and safe at the shrine, sheltered against the occasional cruelties of the Bigfeet.

"Didn't see you last night, Beraal," said Katar, dropping down silently from a giant fig tree. "We had good hunting on the canal banks—found an entire colony of rats."

"Did you get them all?" Beraal asked. Like Katar, she nursed a special dislike for rats: prey was prey, but there was something about the viciousness of rats coupled with the uncleanliness of their surroundings that set her whiskers on edge.

"Most of them," said Katar, reaching across to give her a quick headrub. "One bit Hulo rather badly, but you know what Hulo's like—he took its head off with a swipe of his paw."

The two cats turned; the fakir had come out of his room and was calling to them, a smile on his face.

Beraal ran towards him, her tail up, the pain in her ribs all but forgotten, and Katar followed just behind. The fakir fussed over the two cats. Beraal enjoyed the way he scratched her ears and gently petted her fur just as much as she appreciated the food he set out for them whenever he could. She reached up to thank him, purring as she put her paws on his lap, rubbing her head and whiskers against his tangled locks.

Some time later, the two cats made their way to the cemetery, to find that Miao had already arrived. She lay stretched out on a gravestone. Far above her head, the parrots squawked and scolded, chattering to each other, their conversation loaded with fresh gossip. From the dargah, a slow caterwauling rose into the morning: Qawwali and his brood were clearing their throats. Beraal listened absently, as they issued a rousing set of challenges to the local dogs, who must have wandered into the butchers' lane. Qawwali was adept at the ancient Nizamuddin cat tradition of trading insults.

"So was the famous Sender a very large cat?" Miao asked.

"She's a very small kitten," said Beraal, "and I have something to share with all of you."

Katar linked his tail round hers. "A kitten?" he said. "That's surprising. I really hadn't believed a kitten could send with such intensity. Are you sure you killed the right cat?"

Beraal flicked her whiskers. "I'm sure I found the right cat," she said. "And it—she's a kitten, a very young one with no clan of her own."

Katar's back curved into an arc, his whiskers springing to life. "You didn't kill it, did you, Beraal?" he said.

Miao and Katar looked at her, and Miao's tail started to move slowly back and forth.

Beraal washed her whiskers with great deliberation. "No," she said, "I didn't kill Mara, and I'm not going to. Wait—" she raised her head before the other cats could interrupt. "I know she's an outsider, and she's really loud, but there's something special about her. It's not just that she's a kitten, all of you know I've done my share of culls, but her abilities are unusual, and I think with the right kind of training, we could get her to turn the volume down."

"She may be a kitten," said Miao, "but she has a Sender's powers, and she's not one of us, Beraal. It's dangerous to let a cat that powerful live if she's not of the clan—her mother was clearly an outsider, probably from one of the clans across the canal."

"Mara has no clan of her own," said Beraal, her mew soft but determined. "If we bring her up as a fellow wilding, perhaps Mara can be our Sender. Her mother was from across the canal, but Mara was born under the bridge. Her scent may be different; but wasn't she born among us?"

Miao's blue eyes held uncertainty in their depths. "None of you were alive when Tigris was Sender," she said. "In her time as one of the long whiskers, she scented many kinds of trouble— from the Bigfeet, from intruders, from predators—before even the best of our hunters did. But she was able to keep us safe because she was one of us, and lived with us. Her whiskers trembled for us, Beraal. This kitten with the strange scent who lives with the Bigfeet, who does she belong to? Her mother's clan across the canal? The Bigfeet? Or us?"

Katar stirred, and both queens, the old and the young, turned to the tomcat. "It would have been better if you had killed the Sender," he said. "In the years since Tigris died, there has been little need for a Sender among us wildings."

Miao's whiskers rose. "I am uneasy about the Sender's scent and the power of her abilities," she said. "But my mother and

Tigris told me that Senders are born when the clan is in need; in times of peace and ease, when the mice are plenty and the Bigfeet don't harm us, we need no Senders."

Katar washed his paws, taking in Miao's words. "We have not needed a Sender in our time," he said. "We have been each other's eyes and ears and whiskers. But what you say and what Beraal says has the scent of truth. The Sender was born under the canal bridge, in between us and the clan across the canal. She has a claim on us."

"Rubbish," said a rough mew from the top of the crumbling cemetery wall. Hulo was silhouetted against the light of the rising sun, his ears twitching, a darker patch of matted fur and dried blood on his back testifying to the battle with the rats. "It's not like Beraal to shy away from a kill, and this Mara is an outsider twice over. She doesn't share our scent, bridge or no bridge—and she's an inside cat, a freak who lives with the Bigfeet. Besides, she makes an awful racket. If you won't kill the pest, I will."

Beraal hissed, baring her sharp white teeth. "Hear me, Hulo," she said. "You aren't wrong; but you haven't met her. I have, and I say we should let her live. Mara means us no harm—in fact, she's lonely—and her talents are unusual. If she is not of the clan, she is not a stranger either. If she's an inside cat, that's good for us—Mara's unlikely to ever come outside. We should wait and get to know her, perhaps train her, change her scent even, before hunting and killing the kitten. There's something special about her, and if you wish to go into the Bigfoot house and kill her, be aware that you break into my territory. I may not allow that intrusion."

Hulo's growl rose from the back of his throat, as he leaped down from the wall. Close up, he was an impressive specimen—large, well-muscled, his fur permanently bedraggled and unkempt, but his flanks rippling with power. His paws were twice the size of Beraal's, but the young queen was in no way intimidated—if it did come to a fight, she was faster, and her claws could rip chunks out of his flesh.

She arched her back and spat as Hulo padded towards her, his massive head lowered in warning. Katar moved between the two of them and hissed loudly.

"No fights in the cemetery," he said. It was part of their pact with the fakir.

Hulo narrowed his eyes, still growling.

"I say the kitten dies, Beraal. If you don't do it, I will. It may be your territory, but you were supposed to make the kill, and if you can't, I have none of your scruples."

Beraal let her fur erect; her claws shot out. "I say she lives, and we give her a few moons of grace. I'll train her as though she were my own kitten, from my own litter."

Hulo seemed ready to spring, but Miao intervened, her whiskers bristling. "Settle this the usual way," she said to the tom and the queen. "To the baoli!"

MIAO THREW BACK HER HEAD and howled as the cats moved swiftly from the cemetery to the baoli next door. "Brawl! Brawl at the baoli, come out naaaaaooooowwwwww!" The Siamese cat was older than any of them, and her once bright blue eyes carried clouds in their depths, but her voice was as deep and piercing as ever.

The ground of the baoli was dry and pitted, with a few puddles of green, slimy water forcing the cats to step carefully. Beraal moved easily, darting down the broken stone steps towards the centre, turning to face Hulo.

"What rules?" sang Miao. "Will first blood do, or must the fur fly?"

"First blood," said Hulo quickly.

"No," said Beraal. "Let this be open throat."

There was a murmur among the cats, and Katar and Miao both cocked their ears in Beraal's direction. Open throat was serious business; the first cat to get a clear slash at its opponent's throat would win, but they could risk serious injury before that opportunity presented itself. Hulo had the advantage of weight and muscle over Beraal; the young queen was lethally fast, though, and both of them were known to be dangerous fighters.

Hulo twitched his whiskers in assent. Miao hesitated, and then took up her song again:

> *"The rules, then, for all cats to hear;*
> *   this fight will be blood-filled and chilling.*
> *But the rules of open throat are clear;*
> *There shall be no killing.*
> *First blood can be drawn, so can third;*
> *Bleed too much, and I may give word*
> *To stop the fight, however thrilling."*

From the dusty alleys near the shrine, from the rooftops of Nizamuddin, from the banks of the canal: in ones and twos, cats began to appear. Qawwali from the dargah, Abol, Tabol and the other canal cats, and a veritable clowder of the normally busy market cats arrived, attracted by the prospect of watching a rousing battle.

They slipped in silently, perching in small clusters on the stone steps, arranging themselves on the walls, a few watching from the branches and generous shade of a neem tree. Southpaw was the only kitten present, but the Nizamuddin cats were so used to him tagging along in their wake that they let him stay. Curled up between Abol and Tabol, the brown kitten's eyes were wide as he took in the baoli—this was the first brawl he'd witnessed.

Katar and Miao backed off a few paces, to allow the fighters sufficient room. They would stay close enough to intervene, if there was need, but far enough so that they didn't risk getting side-swiped.

The two cats circled each other, tails swishing. Hulo let out a long, low keening, raising it slowly to a high ululation, and Beraal could see the scars rippling on the big fighter's flanks and forehead. In response, she deepened her growls, allowing them to rise from the back of her throat and swell outwards until they filled the arena with menace. Her hackles were up, her whiskers taut; her tail flicked like a whip from side to side. They moved like dancers who knew the steps, following a rhythm audible only to the two of them.

Hulo slid into attack first, raising his voice to an ear-splitting shriek, gathering his haunches and launching himself into the air. He should have come down with his forepaws on Beraal's back, forcing her to either drop to the ground or risk her neck if she tried to bite him. But Beraal had seen the muscles in his neck bunch up, and she scrabbled out of reach just in time, moving fluidly to the right and turning sharply so that she was within striking distance of his flanks. She unsheathed her claws, raked his tail, and scored the tip of it cruelly.

Hulo howled and turned, faster than Beraal expected. He pushed himself upwards, arching his back, erecting his fur, and despite herself, Beraal flattened her belly to the ground at the menacing figure he made. Hulo screamed his anger into her whiskers, and circled to the right; Beraal skipped back and feinted to the left, moving her paws nimbly to avoid being cornered by him.

They moved in that fashion for a while, the big black tom and the sleek black-and-white queen, each looking for a weakness in the other's guard. Beraal changed it up, shifting from a growl to a menacing yell that made Hulo shake his grizzled head.

From the back of his throat, he growled, and before Beraal could react, he lunged to her left. She moved swiftly, but not fast enough. Hulo barrelled into her, his great head down as he knocked the smaller cat tail over whiskers.

Katar's tail twitched as he watched. "Well played," said Tabol beside him, the canal cat's ample flanks rolling as he shifted for a better view.

"First blood went to Beraal, but now Hulo knocks the little fighter flat," Miao called for the benefit of a few stragglers from the dargah, who had just entered the baoli.

On the ground, Beraal rolled to the side, narrowly avoiding Hulo as he turned to sink his teeth into her neck. He got a fold of skin from her flank, instead, and she turned, aiming at his face. The tip of one claw caught his ear and he shrieked, slashing back at her flank; she felt the blood flow freely.

The two fighters separated briefly, their sides heaving. Blood matted Beraal's fur now, and in the clean morning light, the blood on Hulo's fur seemed ominously thick. For a moment, they stared into each other's faces, and she smelled the acrid sweat coming off him.

Hulo's eyes were yellow and he was watching her carefully. He and Beraal got on well in the normal course of things, and she had known him since her kittenhood. He had often taken her side when she'd meeped defiance at her older brothers, insisting on climbing trees that were too high for her small paws to scale.

When she'd had her first season, he had lined up with the other toms, hoping to win her favours, but Katar had wanted so badly to mate with her that he had fought all of them with keen ferocity.

Despite his fondness for her, Beraal could tell that Hulo meant to win this fight, but even as his claws had ripped through her flanks, he had retracted them slightly; and when she had slashed at his face, she had used only the tips, not driving the punch home, not hooking her claw in to rip out more flesh. Neither of them wanted to inflict more damage than was necessary to win the fight, but both would push the limits as far as they could.

Beraal raised her voice again, cutting through the baoli,

issuing a second round of challenges. Before Hulo had gathered his thoughts, she pounced, in mid-yell, taking him off guard. She landed just before him, perfectly balanced on all four paws, reaching up with gleaming teeth towards his throat. The old fighter felt her breath on his face and knew he would have to move fast.

He swung his front paw like a massive gauntlet, batting Beraal's face so hard she heard her mandible click as she was knocked off her feet. She lay there on the ground, stunned, the breath knocked out of her. Hulo circled her warily, wondering whether the helplessness was faked. Once she had won a fight against a much larger tom by faking a limp so cleverly that the tom moved in for the kill, leaving himself unguarded. Hulo had been lounging against the walls of the bridge, watching the fur fly, and had marked her down as a cunning warrior, not just a skilled one. But though Beraal tried to get up, her paws scrabbled feebly and her breath came in short bursts—she was thoroughly winded. All Hulo had to do was get over his caution and sink his teeth into her throat, and the fight would be over.

If he won, Beraal knew Mara wouldn't stand a chance. It wouldn't just be the grizzled tomcat who'd go after the kitten— every able warrior in Nizamuddin would make it their business to kill the intruder, if the opportunity presented itself. Hulo began to inch nearer.

Katar and Miao circled the pair of cats. Up in the branches of the neem, Qawwali yawned and prepared to jump down. "Good fighting," he commented. "Plenty of fancy footwork, and enough blood spilled to make it an honourable loss." The cats watched to see what Hulo would do; he could, of course, go for the kill, but he was much more likely to let Beraal off with a warning nip and a scar.

Beraal closed her eyes. It wasn't that she was afraid to face Hulo's bite, or his claws. But she wished she could have given Mara a better chance. Before Beraal had left the Bigfeet's house, the kitten had eagerly shared her milk with the older queen, and rubbed heads, purring loudly and happily. She had padded around and waited for the Bigfeet to open the kitchen door, then bounded down the length of the rooms, guiding Beraal out when the Bigfeet were otherwise occupied. Just before Beraal left, Mara had reached up and head-butted her new friend, and let her small, stubby tail wrap itself around Beraal's magnificently plumed one.

"Come back, Beraal," she had said.

Beraal's whiskers trembled. It felt as though Mara had just said those words, instead of saying them that morning— what was that? *"I just woke up! It's dark here and very stuffy! Where am I? Where are the Bigfeet? Where's Beraal? No one's here! Woeisme!"*

The voice boomed in her head, making her wince, and Hulo, startled, shied sideways. He had padded up to Beraal and was about to sink his teeth into her throat to claim victory, when Mara's lamentations filled the air, and thrummed loudly in all of their minds. Hulo's teeth snapped shut on empty air, and he swore, turning to attack Beraal a second time.

The queen was on her feet, swaying slightly from side to side. She took a wobbly step forward and felt the blood from Hulo's earlier strike run down her face. Hulo sprang at her, and

Beraal hugged the ground, letting her belly go absolutely flat, folding her ears in, looking up at him as the leap brought him within range. Hulo's claws grazed her belly as she rose up to meet him, but Beraal pushed the pain away.

She yowled once, a feverish battle cry, and closed with her opponent. Hulo's weight sent them both falling to the ground, the tomcat pinning her down. But he was off-balance, too, scrabbling for leverage with his back legs. On her back, Beraal raked her claws lightly over his forelegs. And then she stretched her head up, pinned down though she was. Hulo's throat lay exposed in front of her. Beraal bit, taking care to break the skin, but staying far away from the veins.

Miao and Katar unleashed miaows of victory: "A good fight, and both cats may gloat/ As Beraal wins this round of open throat." The blood ran down Beraal's flanks, and ruefully, Hulo examined his neck, noting how cleanly his skin had been punctured. The queen and the tom disentangled themselves, Beraal shaking herself back into shape, washing first each paw and then the wounds on her belly and flanks. Hulo sat down, too, grooming his fur back into place, licking at the blood so that the saliva would start healing the wounds. They would both hurt from this fight for a few days.

Beraal reached out and gave him a quick head-rub. "Well fought," she said. "I remember you teaching me how to go for the throat."

"I wish I'd taken my own lessons more seriously," said Hulo wryly, responding with a head-butt of his own. "So you win, but how do you plan to stop that infernal kitten from yowling the place down?"

"*Free! Free at last!*" said Mara's happy voice, booming out again over the airwaves. "*Thank you, O Bigfeet, thank you for releasing me from the fell captivity of the fearsome sock drawer! See—I have killed a sock for you!*"

Beraal sighed. "I think it'll take a lot of lessons, Hulo," she said, "but I have an idea that it can be done."

"I hope you're right, Beraal," said Hulo. "Look around you." Beraal's whiskers twitched interrogatively. "What do you mean?"

Hulo indicated the restless knots of cats, some leaving the baoli, some lounging on the walls and the trees, all of them with their hackles ever so slightly up.

"You might persuade me and Miao and Katar to leave your noisy young protégé alone," he said. "And I promise you I won't harm her—so long as she doesn't come out too far into my territory. But how will you persuade *them*?"

Beraal tuned into the whispers. "Demoniacal!" Qawwali was saying. "It shouldn't be allowed." Abol yawned and washed his plump flanks. "You can never trust an inside cat, everyone says so," he agreed. Qawwali pushed past both of them, his ears pinned back. "Can't get a decent night's sleep these days," he snapped. "Don't know what the neighbourhood's coming to."

"All I'm saying, Beraal," said Hulo, "is that your young friend had better stay inside, even if she does manage to turn the volume down." Katar and Miao came up to offer Beraal their congratulations, but as she turned away to rub noses with them, and Hulo limped off, Beraal was troubled.

"*Freeeeeeeeeeedommmmmm!!!*" said the voice of a happy kitten in all of their heads.

Lessons had better begin at once, thought Beraal.

CHAPTER FIVE

The Sender's First Walk

The sleeping kitten added a touch of colour to the steel
sculptures decorating the table near the kitchen window.
From time to time, her snores made her fur ripple.

Beraal adjusted her rump sharply on the ledge, and made an
exasperated blowing noise. "I wish she would wake up!" the
black-and-white hunter said to the world at large. "I've been
mewing at her for ages!"

There was a flutter of wings and a cross chirp from the
ashoka tree nearby. "We know," said a shrill voice. "Probably
everyone in the neighbourhood for miles and miles around does.
How my fledglings are ever going to get any sleep, I don't know."

"Shut up, Tuntuni," said Beraal. Mara's refusal to wake up
had tried her temper sorely. "Or I'll put your damned twitter-
ing nestlings to sleep between my jaws."

A whirring in the hedge below indicated that Tuntuni's
indignation had spread.

"Well I never . . ." said Sa.

"In all my years . . ." said Re.

"Thought I'd have to . . ." said Ga.

"Remind a Nizamuddin . . ." said Ma.

"Cat what it owed . . ." said Pa.

"To its own sense of dignity . . ." said Dha.

"Carrying on like an unschooled . . ." said Ni.

"Kitten, the very idea!" finished Sa.

As the oldest of the grey-plumaged flock known collectively as the 'seven sisters' to their friends and 'those blasted babblers' to their critics, Sa always took it upon herself to start and finish sentences.

Beraal, stung by the criticism, all the more because it was justified—she'd been mewing at the sleeping Mara for ages now, just like a mannerless kitten might—snarled. "You could help, you know," she hissed at the ruffled birds. "Flutter by and caw or something."

The babblers fluffed up their feathers, and Beraal sighed. She was in for it now. Typically, Sa led the way.

Sa: "Caw!"

Re: "Like a common crow!"

Ga: "We have never—"

Ma: "Well, hardly ever . . ."

Pa: "Been so offended"

Dha: "(Our feelings rended)"

Ni: "We form a Babble,"

Sa: "Not like those rabble."

Sa, Re, Ga, Ma, Pa, Dha and Ni in chorus: "Cats more gracious and more wise

Would think it time to apologize
Say sorry now
And we'll forget—somehow
But only if
You interrupt this riff
To say you're very very sorry
You're truly very sorry
You couldn't be more sorry . . ."

And Sa, her voice soaring to an impossible pitch, sang: "Nnnnnnowwwwwwwwwww!"

First came a tinkling sound, and then the high ping and clatter of crystal glasses breaking into a thousand tiny little pieces from inside the house. The kitten shot off the table in an orange blur, skimmed lightly over the floor and came to earth under the pantry cupboards.

"Now look what you've done!" said Beraal crossly. She caught the look in Sa's eyes and fluffed the fur on her neck in irritation—while the Seven Sisters might qualify as legitimate prey under certain circumstances, there was an unspoken agreement between the cats and the birds to share territories as best as they could for the most part. "All right, all right, I'm sorry," Beraal said ungraciously.

"Don't mention it, I'm sure," said Sa, and Re, and Ga, and Ma, and Pa, and Dha and Ni, politely but with an undercurrent of triumph. Beraal gave in. "Well, without your penetrating singing, I would never have woken Mara up." The babblers looked pleased, and Sa clacked her beak happily.

AN HOUR LATER, Beraal was huffing, stropping her claws irritably on the side of the staircase. Mara just didn't seem to be getting the hang of long-distance linking today, and it was frustrating trying to teach a kitten who wandered off into the rooms of the house whenever she got bored.

And Mara had so much to learn. The kitten's powers grew as rapidly as her whiskers and fur. Unfortunately, her control didn't match her abilities.

Neither Katar nor Miao had been especially amused when images of a small kitten twitching and dreaming that some Bigfoot had removed her favourite marrow bones began to invade their personal dreams. Miao, combing out her ruffled whiskers, told Katar that it was a pity Mara was an orphan. "Tigris's mother trained her from the time her eyes lost their blue," Miao said. "In all the fables about Senders, none of them has the smallest mew to share about what to do with orphan Senders!"

And even Beraal had been distinctly ruffled when the *"WAOWW!"* of a kitten in distress had apparently emanated from her right ear, waking her out of a much-needed afternoon nap. ("Sorry, Beraal," Mara had said contritely. "I was just experimenting with volume control.")

Qawwali and the dargah cats grumbled to Beraal after Mara accidentally interrupted one of the biggest and most avidly anticipated brawls of the season with a range of vocal exercises.

No self-respecting tom or queen who'd progressed past their second set of scars could work up the same lust for battle after a kitten had projected its image right across the dusty open field where these battles were held and sung, oblivious to the magnificent war cries already in progress, *"Mrraow, mrraow,*

mrraow-ow-ow, miao-miao-mi-mi-mi." The really frustrating part was that Mara had the force of an adult Sender, but the short attention span of most kittens. The grumbling of the cats bored her, and she often left the link if she was playing with her Bigfeet, so none of the feline reprimands and curses sent her way were effective.

". . . and that's why estimating the range of your signals is so important," finished Beraal, only to discover that her chief audience was a buzzing bluebottle. Mara was chasing her tail up and down and over and under and around the furniture. Beraal, her temper sliding out of control, switched from mew to whisker, administering a rebuke so stinging that she could practically feel the invisible wires between her and Mara crackle.

Mara fell with a thump onto a cushion, bounced once, and scrambled hastily to her side of the wire screen. Her whiskers radiated meekness, for a change. "If we're quite ready, Mara? Here's what I want you to do—ignore me, or any of the other Nizamuddin cats, you've got that?"

"Yes, Beraal," said Mara, quite subdued now.

"Just reach outward, as far as you can go—within your levels of comfort, of course. If you meet any other cats, send them a formal greeting, but move on. When you're tired, just end the sending. Got that? Any questions?"

"Well," said Mara, "I was wondering . . . how will you know how far I've got?"

"I'll be linking as well," said Beraal. "Remember, you'll be using the general bandwidth, so anyone who's interested can link—without disturbing you, of course. We'll be able to tell how far you're moving away from Nizamuddin, though we may not be able to see as much as you do—it depends on how strongly you can send while you're exploring the limits of your territory."

BERAAL SETTLED DOWN against the kitchen door, on the outside of the stairs; the kitten curled up on the inside. Beraal's head sank down onto her chest. The hunter appeared to be drowsing, though her eyes were shut in concentration and all of her senses were on alert. Her whiskers stayed up, ready to warn her if any Bigfeet or predators came too close. She focused on the link.

The kitten had slumped into a furry heap. She was concentrating so hard on sending she had tuned out everything happening around her. The incessant cheep-cheep of Tuntuni's brood demanding their evening meal was lost on her, as was the clatter from the drawing room, where the Bigfeet were wondering how their crystal had shattered behind the locked doors of the cabinet.

Her long whiskers rose, vibrating slightly. The whiskers above her eyes tilted forward. Mara let them extend, the way Beraal's whiskers or Miao's whiskers would extend when they wanted to link.

Beraal felt the prickle in her own whiskers so strongly that she almost flinched. The hunter opened one eye to stare at the kitten: so much force from such a tiny creature!

Mara let her mind float, prepared for the way her stomach lurched when the sending began. She had to knead her paws to bring her tummy back to normal. Then it was like stepping into the sky, and feeling herself soar across distances, able to move in any direction she wanted. But her whiskers could also sense currents eddying back and forth, and invisible channels that she could follow or not as she became more proficient.

Eyes half-closed, the kitten let out a long purr as she felt her way through. There, like a broad band of silver, was the cat network, gleaming and blinking with flurries of cat activity. Winding through this was a pulsing ribbon that indicated the Nizamuddin link. Mara reached her whiskers out, soaring between the two. "It's the way the pariah cheels fly," she had told Beraal when she was trying to explain sending to her teacher. "They don't see the empty sky we do. They see roads and pathways and intricate webs that tell them where to go, and how far away they are over the tops of the trees, and when to swoop and when to hitch a passing current."

Beraal felt her own stomach churn as she—and, the hunter sensed, some of the other Nizamuddin cats—followed Mara into territory that for them was new and uncharted. The whisker link was an extension of their scent trails, leading as far as they could smell and see. But Mara went further, travelling rather than linking, as though her whiskers could reach all the way across the colony to the other side, like a slender, vibrating bridge to the sky.

Slowly, meditatively, the kitten washed her paws, one after another. She found that sending became easier if she was washing herself, so she let her tongue rasp a steady rhythm, allowing her to concentrate on where she was going and what she could see.

Chasing after a bright-red rubber ball in the park, a Dalmatian, two Labradors and a couple of frisky mongrel pups faltered for a moment and looked at one another. Then a passing Dachschund nudged the ball back to the bunch, and the game began again.

"That's strange," the Dalmatian said to the older Labrador as they trotted off to the far end of the park, "I could've sworn an orange kitten brushed by my flank just now, but I didn't see a thing." The Lab sniffed the air. "I had the same feeling," he admitted, "but it would have left a scent, and the only cat scents here are ages old." The rubber ball came bounding their way, and in the scuffle to reach it, the two forgot the incident.

An ambling cow in the small marketplace paused in the process of abstracting a cabbage leaf from the vegetable seller's stall and ruminated briefly. She was sure a little kitten had leapt lightly onto her back, then trotted off down the road, but there wasn't a hint of the creature anywhere that she could see. She turned back to the stall, but the seller had tucked the cabbage smartly out of her reach. Philosophically, she sniffed at a discarded garland of marigolds instead. She tended to take life pretty much as she found it, kittens or no kittens.

The squabbling of the sparrows tucked away in a nest high up on the crest of Humayun's tomb ceased abruptly. The hen and the cock ducked instinctively, positive that they had just seen an orange kitten move swiftly along the dark crumbling roofs of the tombs. But there were no signs of predators, and after a minute or two, they relaxed their vigilance. "Sunte Ho, I told you to build a little bit higher," said the hen to her mate. Sunte Ho sulked.

"Higher, still higher, what you want, that we should sit out there and tell the cheels to come and get us?" And soon they were bickering amiably again.

STRETCHED OUT NEAR THE KITCHEN STAIRS, Mara appeared to be half-asleep. She barely noticed the cats who were linking in droves—from the dargah, the market, the rooftops and the alleys of Nizamuddin. The kitten skipped over entire colonies as though they were no more than puddles in her path, and she registered a larger world opening up in sudden sharp glimpses full of glorious, confusing colours, sounds and smells. Her sendings were smoothening out. The greetings to the astonished cats who felt or saw her as she went by were becoming easier, more automatic.

She felt cats receiving her hurried twitch of greeting in Nizamuddin, at Humayun's Tomb, in Jangpura, in far-flung Delhi colonies whose names she had never heard of. *Calico cats, tortoiseshell cats, pedigreed cats, strays; neighbourhoods where cats roamed on vast manicured lawns; areas where their territory was a twisting mass of bylanes brimming over with filth and abundant life; old scarred fighters' faces, blinking kitten faces, furry maternal faces; she could hear them all as a distant, humming noise in the background.* Despite the effort, Mara was having fun, on what was the longest and the most fascinating walk of her life this far.

The fur on her flanks stirred, and then Mara felt her whiskers rise, tingling so hard that it was almost unpleasant. There was a crackle in the air. Her paw pads gleamed with sweat, and her claws came out reflexively. The kitten's pink tongue hung out and she grimaced and shivered all over.

Somewhere out there, a family of cats was responding to her sendings. She felt them tug on the line, insistently, with more strength than seemed possible. The air had thickened with the slow rumble of their linkings, though Mara couldn't see them yet. The kitten's tail switched back and forth, the hairs on its tip fluffing in alarm. It was as though her fur had been brushed hard, and she felt the presence of the strange cats as surely as though they had entered the room.

Something had gone wrong, she thought. The cats were slowly coming into focus, their faces gleamed into sharp-edged clarity, but the images were too large. The air around her felt hot, and the kitten's whiskers trembled from the sudden strain.

On the other side of the door, Beraal sat up, her tail rising uneasily. "Mara?" she said.

The kitten's paws curled under her flank. Mara's tiny nostrils flared at the scent that seemed to fill the air: fire and musk. The scent padded through her head, and her fur stood up as though a predator had walked silently through the kitchen, its hot breath burning her ears and the back of her neck. She heard Beraal mew, but the hunter's voice seemed very remote.

Mara opened her eyes briefly, but there was nothing in the park outside her home, just the high friendly chirps of the babblers. Her Bigfeet had moved to another room; she heard their voices far away. It seemed as though black and gold flames danced before her eyes and the air in the kitchen was now heavy with the carrion stink of meat and blood, underlaid by a whisper of dust and grass. Mara's head throbbed; it felt to the kitten that the unseen predator was padding closer and closer.

A low, menacing rumble ripped through the house; Mara felt her stomach turn over in cold fear, her claws shoot out in instinctive terror. The rumble seemed to go on forever, as though the kitten had called the thunder itself down from the skies.

When the kitten opened her eyes again, she was staring at a

great, red, open mouth with pointed yellow fangs, each one the size of her own face, and great white whiskers that sent out rolling waves of anger. Slowly, she looked up into a pair of huge golden eyes, the pupils tiny glowing orbs of black, ringed by fur striped in all the colours of fire. When its whiskers rose, Mara felt her own tiny whiskers tighten and tingle in fear, but she couldn't stop sending. "Hello," she whispered. "Who are you?"

There was silence. Mara's fur began to unruffle itself, and her tail stopped twitching. She felt Beraal outside begin to relax, too. *Just a glitch, Beraal,* she sent, *perhaps we're seeing a close-up—pulling back now.*

If Beraal had a response, neither cat heard it. Mara yelped and scrabbled with her paws as her whiskers went painfully taut and adrenaline jolted through her body. The great cat was standing up, and Mara watched in shock, her head tilting upwards as the golden and black fur rippled out endlessly, the tiger growing and broadening until it towered monstrously above her, its eyes never leaving her face.

Another furious rumble shook the line. Mara felt the vibrations deep in her flanks and her belly—it felt as though she had been picked up by the scruff of her neck and was being shaken from side to side.

"*I am Ozymandias, king of kings. Who in hell's name are you and what are you doing in my head?*"

"I'm just me," Mara stammered back, "just a Mara." Instinct overrode the system of greetings Beraal had dinned into her head, and she reverted to the patterns of her earliest sendings. *Sorry, just me, just small orange kitten, don't mean any harm at all, Mara terrified, Mara shivering! Sorry, big cat.* Waves of disbelief radiated back along the connection, and Mara heard the deep-throated growl as clearly as though its perpetrator was right in front of her.

"You're a kitten? Not even a cub, a common KITTEN? And you dare consort with tigers, Justamara? You're either very brave. Or very foolish. Or . . . very, very insolent."

Mara was frozen with fear, too terrified to attempt to break the sending. The enormous red mouth equipped with long, curving, deadly teeth, opened in a deafening roar. *"I want my mommy!"* cried Mara. *"I want Beraal! Don't like this Ozymandiwhatever . . . I want to go home."*

If she'd been listening to the Nizamuddin link, Mara would have realized that she was merely echoing popular sentiment. As the tiger shimmered in the air of Nizamuddin, his great form stalking the minds of the cats, the scramble to clear the link was unseemly but swift. Beraal's nerve broke when she saw that deadly mouth. Flattening her ears, she shot down the stairs into the park. Hulo, who'd linked furtively, unwilling to admit that he was impressed by Mara's progress, was so taken aback that he almost fell out of his tree. Back in the dargah, Bigfeet watched in surprise as Qawwali and the two other cats who were on the link sat up sharply, yowled and then fled. Southpaw, who'd linked in his sleep, woke from what appeared to be the worst nightmare he'd had in his life.

So there was no one to witness what happened next.

IT HAD BEEN A TRYING TIME for Ozymandias. The Royal Bengal tiger liked to do his pacing in peace, and ever since the zoo had acquired another couple of great cats, space had been at a premium. The grass in his enclosure had long since dried out; in summer, the tigers stirred up clouds of dust as they walked, and Ozymandias hated the way it tickled his whiskers.

He disapproved strongly of the new feeding policy, which required all the animals in the zoo to fast once a week. Worst of all, his litterbox had been dragged out into the open, which meant he had to do his business in front of a gaggle of gawking Bigfeet—any self-respecting tiger, he felt, would have objections to this sort of thing.

So when his nap was disturbed by, of all things, an orange kitten that materialized out of thin air, levitating directly in front of his eyes (Mara hadn't yet quite got the hang of positioning herself while sending), Ozymandias felt justified in snarling at her.

He put out a gigantic pad, unsheathed his claws magisterially and swatted at the kitten.

Mama! it howled, but infuriatingly, it remained exactly where it was.

Ozymandias furtively checked his claws just to be sure, but they appeared to be in perfect working order. He swatted at the air again. *Go away! You're mean and evil and I don't like you one bit!* sniffled the kitten; but it stubbornly refused to dematerialize.

"Ozzy, stop that at once," commanded a velvety voice firmly. "You're frightening the poor thing." Ozymandias mutinously swung at the kitten again, and received a sharp smack on his ear. "Hunh!" he growled in surprise. "You didn't have to do that, Rani."

Scared as she was, Mara couldn't help noticing that the white tiger who'd smacked "Ozzy" into submission was one of the most beautiful creatures she'd ever seen. Then Rani peered closely at her. "You are a common little thing, aren't you?" she commented, and then rounded on the Royal Bengal again. "It's just a cat, Ozzy, there's no reason to throw a fit. I wonder what it's doing here, though."

From under Rani's belly, a small, almost Mara-sized head popped out. "It said it was a Justamara, Ma," piped a small, almost big cat-sized voice. "Hello, Justamara. What're you doing in our cage? And why're you in the air?"

Mara's ears began to rise ever so slightly. She still wasn't very sure about Rani and Ozymandias, but this was more in her league. "Hello," she ventured uncertainly, and then Beraal's training paid off as she recalled her manners. "I'm so sorry to . . . to bother you like this, I was doing a sending . . . uh, a range exercise. I never meant to disturb you, Ozymandias . . . uh, Ozzy Sir . . . I don't know what to call you . . ."

This was a bit much for Ozymandias to take. *"Call me? Call me nothing! Tigers do not talk to kittens,"* he snorted, turning his back on Mara and stalking to the other side of the cage.

"Pay no attention to him," said the small tiger cub. "He's always like this in the evenings, especially if his nap hasn't gone off that well." Rani licked the cub affectionately and peered at Mara again. "I suppose you two had better introduce yourselves," she said.

The bars rattled. Ozymandias growled and stalked back. *"No cub of mine is going to consort with a mere cat, Rani, and that's fine . . . ouch! Aargh! Let go!"* What Rani said to him next was slightly muffled, because she had his tail in her mouth, but the gist of it was that the small tiger cub had had no one to talk to in months from his own species. Ever since the leopards had been shifted to another set of cages, their cub's only company had been a bunch of monkeys. And while she was glad he and the silver-furred langur monkey Tantara got on so well, she didn't know why Ozzy was being such a stick-in-the-mud about cats, considering that he was one himself, if of a superior species. Besides, this young kitten appeared to have far better manners than the leopard cubs who were so terribly undisciplined, if Ozzy only cared to remember. It seemed odd to Rani that the kitten appeared to be levitating in mid-air, but she was sure an explanation would be offered in the fullness of time.

While the big cats bickered, the small tiger cub and Mara eyed each other—one from behind the bars of his cage, the other from her insubstantial post in thin air. "He's called Ozzy because it's short for Ozeem, which is short for Ozymandias," said the tiger cub. "It's a nice . . . it's an impressive name," said Mara. "And what's your name?"

The tiger cub looked important; his whiskers sprang to attention. "I am—" he took a deep breath, "Rudra TheGreat-AndPowerful, SonOfOzymandias TheKingOfKings, Look-OnOur TeethYeMightyAndDespair . . . but you can call me Rudra for short."

"I'd like that," said Mara, and she whiffled happily at him. Outside Rudra's cage, cameras whirred as Bigfeet took pictures of the cub standing so close to the bars, and in the kitchen back in Nizamuddin, the Bigfeet looked down at Mara, and smiled to see her twitching and cycling her paws in her sleep.

CHAPTER SIX

The Shuttered House

From the point of view of the cheels who sailed the skies above Nizamuddin, the neat residential colonies offered slender pickings. The tidy borders of the handkerchief-sized lawns, the carefully trimmed stubble of foliage and the rows of cars offered little in the way of hiding space for the small animals the birds preyed upon. Of far more interest was the last stretch of road that connected the canal and the dargah, where the houses sat in straggling lines, some almost as broken down as the ruins of the nearby baoli. Here, and on the garbage-strewn banks of the canal, good hunting was to be found, especially for those with sharp eyes, patience and strong talons.

Tooth unfurled his wings like feathery sails and hitchhiked a passing current, circling his territory like a spy satellite, taking mental snapshots of all the changes that had happened groundside since he last patrolled. The ditch contained a new traffic victim—the second mongoose to run afoul of the road in recent days, its body too decomposed to be of interest, even to him. His predator's brain registered a rat skittering into a drain, and dismissed it almost immediately. Tooth's stomach was full of pigeon, and pigeon eggs—rat wasn't a tempting enough second course to warrant the effort that a SD&K—stoop, dive and kill—would take. He noticed that the sparrows who had nested in a rusting automobile had been evicted; a small, feathered corpse lay on the pavement, and he could see the thin yellow splatter patterns that the eggs had made. Tooth dipped his wing-tips briefly—he had no objection to eating sparrow, despite the profusion of small bones, but he and the other cheels had conferred on the falling numbers of the birds.

"Bad, very bad," his mate, Claw, had said, quoting the old saw. "The sparrow may be small/ But when it leaves/ So will we all."

A flashing line of movement triggered his predator's brain, and he automatically flexed his wings in preparation for a possible SD&K. "Target: kitten," his mind registered. "Terrain: open, but riddled with boltholes. Prey mindset: young, inexperienced, unaware. Obstacles: cars, ledges, brickpile, foliage. Kill probability: 46 percent."

Southpaw felt rather than saw the approach of the cheel—a momentary coolness on his fur as the shadow overhead blotted out the afternoon sun—and reacted instantaneously.

"To the hedges!" he thought, sprinting, his short paws covering the distance at surprising speed. There was more than enough time, and he risked an upward look.

The cheel was coming down fast, and even at this distance, Southpaw shivered when he saw how large its talons seemed, curved like grappling hooks. The predator was terrifying, but also mesmerizing.

He didn't realize he'd taken his eyes off the ground entirely until he slammed into an abandoned plastic bucket. Southpaw miaowed in distress as its green edge caught him hard across the stomach, knocking the wind out of him, and then he scrambled to stand up again. The hedge that had seemed just a paw's length away loomed up in the distance, the thorny roots of the lantana grim and forbidding. The kitten tried to run but could only limp along. Fear knotted his small stomach when he realized how close the dark and rapidly growing dot spiralling out of the sky was to him. He felt the fur on the vulnerable back of his neck stand up, and he urged his paws to move faster, but they were still shaking from the collision.

"Kill probability: 87 pe cent . . . 89 percent . . . 91 percent," Tooth was in the last arc of his dive and sure of his kill now. He refined his aim, flexing his talons as he prepared to sink them into the spot on the kitten's neck so helpfully defined by a band of white fur. If he got it right, the neck would break in an instant and he would take off with a limp body instead of having to cope with a wriggler on the line.

The bushes rustled; a streak of muscle and fur erupted forth and rolled Southpaw over and away. Katar was on his feet before the kitten knew what had happened; with a swipe of his sheathed paw, the tom batted the brown kitten off the ground and into a pile of dried, dusty leaves near the lantana hedge.

"Kill probability: 71 percent . . . 24 percent . . . 9 percent . . . PULL OUT!" signalled Tooth's brain as he attempted to pull up, rise and avoid Katar's scything paws simultaneously. From his vantage point, Southpaw had a brief but unforgettable view of a glaring yellow eye, a confused impression of gleaming, rushing brown-and-gold wings and polished beak; Tooth executed a neat three-point-turn in mid-air and within seconds, the predator had soared back up into the sky, a shrinking dot in the distance.

Katar stared up at the sky until he was sure that the cheel wouldn't return. Then he nudged Southpaw roughly with his head, checking to see that the kitten hadn't broken or bruised anything serious. When Southpaw sat up, his whiskers vibrating an abject apology, Katar cuffed him, but with his claws retracted to show that this was just a token reprimand. This was the fourth time that week he'd had to smack the kitten; Southpaw and trouble had a natural affinity.

"If you're old enough to go exploring on your own, Southpaw, you're old enough to know that you never look up at predators," Katar said, watching the kitten dust bits of leaves and ants out of his light brown fur, which had chocolate stripes running through it. "Where were you off to anyway? Shouldn't you have been learning paw-washing and whisker-cleaning with Miao today?"

"Miao was busy," said Southpaw, reflecting that this was the truth. The Siamese had been very busy looking all over the park for him after he'd run away from the day's lessons—it wasn't his fault, whisker-cleaning was for the little four-weekers, not for a nearly adult kitten at the ripe old age of two months. "And I wanted to see the Shuttered House. Ow! Katar, that hurts! Ow! Ow! Stoppit! Put me down!"

Katar was growling slightly as he shook the kitten back and forth, holding Southpaw by the loose folds of skin around his neck. "The Shuttered House! Haven't we told you it's forbidden? Didn't Miao and I tell you time and time again not to go there? And if you were fool enough to explore forbidden territory, why were you heading off on your own?"

"Because," said the kitten, "you said it was forbidden, so I didn't think it was safe to take any of the other kittens with me."

Katar's tail was lashing back and forth, but hearing this, he dropped the kitten back onto the ground. "You were on your own because you didn't think it was safe to take any of the other kittens with you," he said slowly.

"Yes, Katar," said Southpaw meekly.

"It didn't occur to you that if it was unsafe to take any of the other kittens with you, it might be unsafe for you to go to the Shuttered House because—you're still a kitten yourself, you fluff-brained idiot!"

"Yes, Katar," said Southpaw. "Um—no, Katar. Um—yes, Katar. Anything you say, Katar."

Katar stared at the young cat suspiciously. "I mean that, Southpaw. The Shuttered House is out of bounds for very, very good reason."

"Yes, Katar," said Southpaw. "Umm . . . what are the reasons?"

Katar exhaled—a short, exasperated sound not unlike a dog's wuff, at the other end of the spectrum from the cat snuffle used to indicate pleasure. "It's a fair question, Katar," said a voice from behind his ear. "I told you he'd be the first in this year's batch to start getting curious."

"Well, maybe you'd like to explain, Miao," said Katar. He'd never gotten used to the venerable Siamese cat's ability to sneak up silently behind him, and harboured an uneasy suspicion that she did it just to keep him from getting too big for his paws. Miao left almost no scent trails behind her, unlike the other cats—it was a gift of her Siamese blood.

Miao's eyes looked deep into Southpaw's. "Perhaps we should show rather than tell," said the Siamese, curling her tail out gracefully. "Follow me, Southpaw, and if Katar and I tell you to do something, do it, don't argue with us, is that understood? Have you got all the ants out of your fur? Are your paws back to normal or are they still stinging? Can you move fast? Have you done a whisker check for dogs, or other predators? Right, then, come along."

Southpaw's head was buzzing with the barrage of instructions. "Where are we going?" he said, confused.

"To the Shuttered House," said Miao. Katar and she touched muzzles, and then the cream-coloured Siamese and the tom led the way through the lantana bushes, as the kitten scrambled behind them as fast as he could.

THE ROOTS OF THE BANYAN TREE had grown in thick tangles, and getting through them was a fight, even for the cats. Southpaw watched in admiration as Miao flattened herself, seeming to flow past the thick creepers; Katar hacked his way through, using his shoulders to push, his tail flicking back and forth in unease.

It seemed to the kitten that they had left Nizamuddin behind. The banyan towered above this abandoned plot of land. The ground was dark, cool and clammy under his paws. He felt his claws come out involuntarily, and had to retract them so that they wouldn't catch on stray roots. He followed Miao's example, staying flat to the ground, but he almost mewed in terror when a spider dropped down onto his ear, scurrying off rapidly when he twitched it loose. Southpaw could feel thick cobwebs on his fur, and as they moved further into the grounds, he had to duck and weave past the banyan roots.

He was so intent on keeping up with the two elder cats that it took a while before the kitten realized what had been bothering him ever since they crossed over the broken stone wall into the grounds of the Shuttered House. The sounds of Nizamuddin, the cacophony of the Bigfeet's cars and their voices, the barking of dogs, the clutter and bustle of a busy neighbourhood—all of these were muffled by the under-growth, and by the banyan tree whose offshoots shrouded the place.

Instead, the quiet clicking of beetles built up in his mind, making his whiskers twitch with their steady, unbearably regu-lar beat. Every now and then, the clicking would stop, and Southpaw found his fur tingling as he waited for it to start again.

They were advancing through a tangle of undergrowth and scrub now, Miao cautiously scanning the ground for predators. "Watch out for snakes," she linked quietly, using her whiskers to transmit rather than risking a mew. Southpaw felt his paws freeze in place. He had seen a cobra take a crow's eggs once, and had watched its black hood with mixed fear and bloodlust, unsure whether he wanted to kill it, or run until his paws would carry him no further.

Katar turned his head. "We can go back if you're afraid," the tom signalled. Southpaw twitched his whiskers in the negative, hoping neither cat would sense just how scared he was. The kitten had prowled along the perimeter of the Shuttered House before, unable to stay away, but being inside its grounds, with the sound of the beetles and the dread that rose up in his small stomach, was different.

They were still in the thick of the scrub, manouevring carefully through the prickly acacia bushes, when Southpaw smelled it. His teeth bared and his lips drew back

"That dry scent, like the heart of a rotting tree branch, is woodworm," said Katar. It was a dusty, insidious stink that made Southpaw's nostrils curl, but far worse was what was beyond it: a sour stench, heavy as a cloud. "This is a Bigfoot smell, Southpaw," said Miao's gentle voice. "Mark it well: it's the smell of age, and decay, and sadness."

By now the kitten's teeth were fully bared, his hackles up. He growled, a low, warning sound, as they approached the crumbling, ramshackle house.

Behind the festering woodworm and sadness, Southpaw could smell something else, and he flinched as they crept closer, hunter-fashion, bellies to the ground. There were tendrils of damp unfurling from the Shuttered House, and they carried in their wake a combined, rotting smell of unkempt cat fur, sickness, stale food, and dried blood many, many moons old. The kitten shivered as the breeze changed direction, amplifying the sweet stink of madness coming from the house. It felt like being swatted by a gangrenous paw.

Katar pressed his flank to the kitten's shivering sides, and Southpaw felt the warmth of the tom, and took heart. The rasping of the beetles was much louder now, but behind that, he heard something else. It was indistinct, and it took a while for him to place it: the faint clicking of claws across the floor.

Miao watched him with curiosity, the Siamese's smoky tail twitching at the tip. The pilgrimage to the Shuttered House was a rite of passage for the Nizamuddin cats, who learned its dark history in their first year, but Southpaw was the youngest kitten in her memory to make the trip. "I think he's old enough for this," she said quietly to Katar, knowing that Southpaw wouldn't catch the whisker transmission easily— he had just started his linking lessons, and wasn't very good at receiving yet.

"Better he come with us than stray in here on his own," Katar responded.

The clatter of Bigfeet rose up from the lane at the back of the House. The tom used his whiskers to signal to the other two that they should take cover, and by the time the Bigfoot—a clumsy, shambling fellow—rounded the corner, the three cats were shadows in the undergrowth, Southpaw to the right near the Shuttered House, the other two further to the left. The Bigfeet usually avoided the area, though they would have been hard pressed to explain what kept them away—something in the atmosphere made most of them take an instinctive detour around it. Though birds nested in the tangled hedges and made their homes in the trees, they were quieter here. The bulbul songbirds and sparrows called out occasionally, but the stillness was unbroken by the raucous squabbles of the babblers or the endless chatter of the mynahs.

This Bigfoot seemed in a hurry, and was probably taking a

shortcut. He passed within a foot of Southpaw, who looked up at his white pajamas, marvelling for the umpteenth time at the remarkable obliviousness of Bigfeet. The kitten thought it must be the lack of whiskers, or perhaps they just couldn't smell very well.

Miao made them wait until she was certain that the Bigfoot wouldn't return. She and Katar rested, cat-fashion, the tom letting his whiskers stay outstretched and alert, but allowing his eyes to close and his chin to drop as he drowsed for a few moments.

The kitten, at a slight distance from the two adults, was restless, far too excited to catnap, and from under her eyelids, Miao watched him, pleased that he managed to stay still. His pink nose twitched every few seconds, trying to make sense of the tangle of smells coming his way from the Shuttered House.

Far above their heads, a cheel shrieked, its cry breaking the silence. Southpaw looked up, wondering whether it was the same bird that had attacked him. The sound had made them all jump; but that was followed by another sound, an ominous rustling in the bushes on the other side of the house.

The attack came so swiftly it took them all by surprise. Miao's whiskers crackled a warning: "Watch out! Dog!" and then the Siamese was springing up a tree, hissing as a massive black dog barked at her heels. Katar saw that the kitten was frozen in position, and began to run towards him; but the tomcat had to swerve when the dog abandoned Miao's tree and bounded in his direction, growling and baring its teeth.

To Southpaw, the dog seemed as large as a cow—he had never seen one of the beasts at such close quarters, and as it snapped at Katar's tail, the kitten closed his eyes and shivered. But he had to look, and to his relief, Katar was in control.

The tom streaked away at a fast clip, but when the dog followed, Katar braked at the edge of a clump of acacia, turned, arched his back and hissed. Alarmed, the dog fell back, barking; the tomcat had fluffed his fur to twice his size, and Miao was joining in from her high perch, issuing blood-curdling screeches into the air.

The dog laid its ears flat, looking from one cat to another. Katar continued hissing, though Southpaw could see that the tomcat had an escape route in mind: at need, he could do a quick about-turn and climb up into the friendly branches of a large magnolia tree. It seemed as though they would be safe after all. The dog turned. It ignored Katar's hisses and Miao's fighting yowls, and Southpaw found himself looking into its menacing red eyes, at the flecks of foam on its glossy black jowls.

The dog lolloped towards him.

"Run, Southpaw!" he heard Katar say from what seemed like a great distance away. "Towards the trees—at the back, Southpaw!" Miao said. The kitten was unable to move his paws. He watched in horror as the dog came steadily closer and closer. Its teeth were bared, and Southpaw could imagine what it would feel like when those large fangs tore through his skin.

And then, from deep inside the Shuttered House, the kitten heard a mocking voice whisper, as though its owner was sitting right beside him, "Stupid, foolish piece of meat. You'll be dead soon if you don't get your paws moving, not that it's any of my business." It was an insidious, cold voice, with not a touch of warmth in it, but for some reason it helped Southpaw break through his terror.

The dog was inches away from the kitten now. Southpaw let out his best high-pitched warrior's yell, put his ears back, turned and ran for it.

Behind him, he heard the dog bark. From the tree, Miao's voice said frantically, "Southpaw! Not there! You'll be trapped!" He could sense Katar coming down from the tree, streaking across the grounds to battle the dog. And he could tell that as fast as he was running, the dog would catch up soon. Its stink was in his nostrils, the smell of damp fur, adrenaline and a predator's sweat. Southpaw's ears were flat to the side of his head; two predators in one day was a bit much for a kitten who hadn't even been on his first hunt yet.

Katar's urgent warnings were now so sharp that they made his whiskers crackle: "You have no room to turn, get away from the veranda: look up, Southpaw." Too late—the kitten was heading straight towards the Shuttered House, and with the dog so close behind, he had no time to try and streak down the side. But though the verandah was a dusty place that radiated forlorn abandonment, the kitten's heart beat faster when he saw the two or three bits of broken furniture that sat on the porch.

Miao was still howling defiance at the dog, trying to attract its attention, and Southpaw sensed that the old Siamese had come down from her tree. But the dog was barking, joyously, bounding up the stone stairs of the veranda behind him, its muzzle dangerously close.

Southpaw knew exactly where he was headed, though, and feinting to the right, he shot sharply to the left instead, leaving the dog skidding behind him, its paws clacking on the slippery stone. On the veranda, pressed up against the peeling front door of the Shuttered House, was a low cane bed, and the kitten had just enough space to squeeze himself under it. His whiskers crackled, and he knew Miao was calling in all other cats in the area to help with this emergency.

"Good thinking," Katar said, "Hang on in there until we can lure the dog away—just stay under the bed no matter what happens, Southpaw."

The dog barked again, and through the cane slats, Southpaw could see its black eyes, keen, hungry for a kill, frustrated. There was a scrabbling above his head, and the kitten scrabbled backwards as a large, heavy paw slammed through the cane. Splinters and dust rained down on Southpaw's head, making him sneeze. The cane was rotten, worn through by years and years of monsoons, warped by the heat of many summers. It would yield soon enough. The paw slammed down again, perilously close to his nose, and the kitten whimpered. He was trapped.

Katar growled, trying to get the dog to turn, but the beast swivelled once, snarled in warning at the tomcat and barked defiance at him. "My kill!" said the dog in Junglee, the language of the hedges; all animals knew it, even though most could communicate only the most basic warnings and requests in that tongue.

In response, the tomcat bit his tail; the dog whirled, howling in anger, shaking the cat off with such force that Katar was thrown a considerable distance. Dazed, he lay on the grass, and Miao slipped over to his side, standing guard so that the dog wouldn't attack him while he was down.

Intent on its original target, the dog nosed the dry wood where it had cracked, then jerked its head up, splintering the cane further. Southpaw backed away as far as he could, trembling.

From behind the door, a cold whisper reached him. "Poor helpless kitty," said the voice. "Look at the way the beast crunches the cane. It has such powerful, strong jaws, doesn't it? Look at its teeth: they're such sharp, yellow teeth, aren't they? It'll hurt a lot when those reach you, meat, but it won't hurt for very long, will it?" There was a rusty, prickling tug at his whiskers that sounded like dark laughter, and the kitten shuddered.

The dog slammed its paw into the cane, and the bed sighed and broke. Southpaw yelped as the cane dropped in front of his face, grazing his whiskers; now he was caught firmly like a rat in a trap. The kitten scrambled backwards, feeling the door behind him, and then he heard a ripping sound, and felt one of the old, sodden planks of the door begin to give way.

At the edge of the veranda, Miao had crept up, and she slashed twice, viciously, at the dog's leg. It howled as her claws raked its side, but when it spun around, Miao had melted away into the shadows. The dog padded a few paces away from the bed, head cocked as it tried to scent the Siamese. Then it lost interest, and turned back to the kitten.

It shoved a paw right through the part of the cane that was over Southpaw's head, and the kitten cringed, looking up into air, his gaze locking with the dog's victorious eyes. The next blow, or the one after that, would get him, and he saw the gleam of saliva on the dog's teeth as the animal contemplated its next move.

Miao had climbed up to the roof of the veranda, and now she dropped down, landing on the dog's back. She sank her teeth into its flank, screaming a battle cry at the big beast. It whirled, growling ferociously, and for a time it looked as though the cat was riding a bucking horse rather than a dog. "Get off or you'll be killed!" Katar called, getting unsteadily to his feet. The Siamese narrowed her eyes, preparing to leap clear. Cats rarely attacked dogs, and when they did, the best chance of a clean attack was to make a fast, dirty assault and then a quick getaway.

"Move one: she'll lose her balance, fall off, but land on her feet," said the cold voice in Southpaw's ear. "Move two: she's a fast runner, so she'll get away before the dog realizes she's off its back. Move three: back to where we started. You're dead meat. It's a sad little story, but it's just not your lucky day."

The Siamese was shaken so hard that it looked as though she was flying off the dog's back. She hit the ground running, and the beast's massive jaws snapped shut on empty air. The dog howled its anger and defiance, but Miao, moving so fast she'd looked as though she was floating across the grass, was already halfway up a tree. The dog wasted no further time on her; it was back at the veranda in two paces, and it was in a killing mood.

"Or," said the cold, bored voice, "you could take your chances with us. We'll kill you as well, but at least we're your own kind. I'll give you a sporting chance, how about that?" From inside the house, a paw flicked at the rotten planks, creating a hole in the door.

Southpaw stared at the dog. The animal was poised above

him; its tongue was hanging out, and in a few seconds, its paw would slam down, perhaps for the last time.

From where he was, standing but wobbly in the under-growth, Katar guessed the kitten's thoughts. "Not the Shuttered House, Southpaw! It's too dangerous!"

The stench of the Shuttered House was strong in the kitten's nostrils, the scent of death, decay, blood and madness. The house held the promise of death, but perhaps, thought Southpaw, he might escape from whatever was in there. But there was no escape from the dog, who was leaning in for the killing bite.

"Oh, do come in, meat," said the insidious voice. "It"ll be so much fun."

The dog's paw came crashing down just as Southpaw threw himself backwards, breaking through the soft wood of the plank, tumbling into the Shuttered House as Miao and Katar watched helplessly.

"For us, that is," added the chilly voice, as Southpaw disappeared from view.

CHAPTER SEVEN

Datura's Domain

The fall was longer than Southpaw had expected; the floor of the house was sunken, lower than the verandah, and the kitten twisted in the air, trying to make sure that he would land on his paws and not his back.

He was ready to fight for his life, spitting for all that he was worth. But he landed into silence and a deep, pervasive gloom. Outside, the dog barked and hurled itself against the door, but the rotten panel aside, the frame and the wood were solid and they held fast.

The kitten could smell cats, though he could see none. The odour was sharp, and close, as though the space had only been recently vacated, and he felt the fur on his face, the whiskers on his forehead, stand up as he sensed the presence of others. Southpaw kept his back to the splintered door, and tried to make sense of his surroundings. The only light in the room came from a single grimy, dim lightbulb; it was like looking through a winter fog. The kitten's nose and his whiskers gave him a better feel of the place.

The Shuttered House was quiet, but besides the clicking of the beetles—much louder in his ears than he would have liked—Southpaw could hear the rustles and scurries of many animals. Overhead, a set of claws clicked across the floor; and then another, and then more. To his right, the darkness yielded to give him a glimpse of a long room, and to his disgust, the kitten realized that the ground beneath his paws was filthy, the floor matted with a thick film of what appeared to be old newspapers and long-rotted food. At the far end of the hallway he stood in were lines and lines of bowls, the smell of stale food rising sour and thick into the air.

The curtains were drawn and tattered, and where they had fallen into shreds, the glass of the windows was thickly layered with grime. Dead flies clustered on the sills. The kitten knew without being told that the doors and windows hadn't been opened for a long, long while. The rank vapours of unclean litter from the back of the room offended his nostrils. It added to the soaring, unpleasantly high scent he had smelled from outside. Southpaw had a sudden flash of intuition. "This is a place," he said to himself, "where cats have forgotten what it is to feel the sunlight on their whiskers."

"Impressive," said the cold voice, from a distance. "Our little visitor here thinks we miss the sunlight? He thinks we have no games of our own, yes? Shall we show him how we play? Aconite? Ratsbane?"

Southpaw growled, twitching his whiskers to see if he could locate the owner of the voice. But the darkness was still too thick; his eyes hadn't yet fully adjusted, and moving further inside was far too risky. He could still smell the dog outside, and hear its growls, but he hoped it would go away before it was too late, and he could use that bolthole.

"Where are my manners?" said the voice. "I'm Datura, little piece of meat. Forgive me for not making introductions: we aren't used to visitors here." The voice was moving across the room, and Southpaw snarled, baring his tiny teeth.

This time, he could sense the laughter rippling out from several sets of whiskers, all around the room. Upstairs, the sounds of scurrying became louder. Southpaw tried to remember what Katar had told him about using his whiskers to sense predators, but though he could raise his black whiskers up just as the tomcat had, he felt nothing in the air. He hadn't learned the finer points of sensing, and the kitten hoped his unseen enemies wouldn't be able to guess how vulnerable he was.

"Fresh meat," another voice whispered, making Southpaw bristle in alarm. This one sounded as though it was at the far end of the room. "Hold, Aconite," said Datura's voice, his mew sharper than normal. "But it's been so long since we had visitors." There was something oily about the second cat's voice, and Southpaw felt his fur crawl, as though he had sat in a nest of ants. "Two seasons since the roofboards rotted and that stray tomcat fell in. It was summer, do you remember?"

"I remember," said Datura. There was a sigh among the unseen cats in the room, and Southpaw felt his whiskers rise along with theirs. It was an unpleasant feeling, as though someone had tugged on his whiskers without his permission. The air felt prickly, claustrophobic, and though Datura had stopped talking, Southpaw felt himself included in the silent images that the cats of the Shuttered House were sharing among themselves.

The stray cat had fallen in at the height of summer, when the cats were restless from the heat, picking fights with each other, vying for the coolest spots in the shade. The roof had parted, rotten from the previous monsoon, and Aconite had jumped back in alarm as the cat came yowling down in a shower of plaster. It was a young tomcat, and it had screamed in pain as it hit the ground, unable to turn its paws in time.

"How he cried!" said Aconite's voice, remembering. "His poor paw was broken, wasn't that so? He could barely stand up; his paw was swelling, and he had to drag himself upright, drag himself away from us. Such a pity that he didn't get very far."

"Where did he go?" asked Southpaw, feeling sorry for the unknown tomcat, empathizing, as all cats instinctively did when they heard of another's mishaps.

Aconite laughed, a rusty sound, as though her whiskers were unused to laughter. "Go?" she said. "No one ever leaves the Shuttered House."

The kitten's ears flattened slightly. There was a sound from the staircase on the right, and he peered into the gloom, which seemed a little less impenetrable, now that he had been here for a while. He thought he could see a shape on the stairs, a blur of white, but he couldn't be sure.

"It would have been better sport if he had been able to run," said Datura, his voice regretful. "But you can't have everything, can you?" "How he mewled!" said Aconite, with relish. Southpaw felt that tug on his whiskers again, the sound of rusty laughter. "The funniest part was when he asked for refuge. What was it he spoke about, Datura? The law of cats? Sanctuary for the wounded? Some such rubbish."

Southpaw's head spun, and the kitten froze in horror as the story began to make a terrible sense to him.

"You refused an injured cat sanctuary? But what about the laws of hospitality?"

The laws were the first thing Miao had instructed him about, when he was a young three-weeker with his eyes still the blue of all newborn kittens. The laws were the first thing all cats learned when they were old enough to leave their mother's side, and like all wildings, Southpaw had the words running through his mind:

> *Help, water, shelter and feed*
> *To any of the clan in dire need;*
> *No one shall refuse a stranger*
> *Sanctuary, should he be in danger;*
> *Hear these laws, and hold to them fast*
> *As have all wildings from the days of Bast.*

Datura's amused growl broke into the kitten's thoughts. "Funny, that's what he said, too, just before we tore out his stinking throat. It must be one of your strange outside cat ways. But we've spent enough time on pleasantries, meat. Will you stand, or will you run?"

"Oh, run, do," pleaded Aconite's oily voice. "It's been so long since I chased anything larger than a rat."

"You lie, Aconite," said a third, bored voice that made

Southpaw jump, because it was so close to the door. "You chased those kittens around from Hemlock's last litter."

"They looked like tiny rats," said Aconite. "Like blind mice. They would never have lived anyway, Ratsbane."

"Three blind mice," said Ratsbane softly to himself. "See how they run. And how fast can *you* run, kitten?"

Southpaw screamed, his mew high and helpless, as a massive black cat with blazing green eyes sprang out of an alcove towards him.

"Flushed from his lair," said Datura as the kitten shot away from the door, into the middle of the room. "Good opening move, Ratsbane. Now perhaps we'll see some sport."

"Wait!" said Southpaw, trembling in fear but holding his ground. "I'm sorry I had to rush into your home, but you heard and smelled the dog, and all cats may seek sanctuary from predators. We don't know each other, Datura, Aconite, Ratsbane, but I mean you no harm. Can't we—?"

Aconite's rusty laughter rose to the roof. "Wonderful!" she said. "Datura, where did you find this one? He means us no harm, did you hear?" Southpaw felt the presence of many other cats, and swinging around, he stared up at the stairs. Now he could see Datura more clearly. The cat was a perfect white, his fur clean and shining despite the filth in the house. He had curious eyes; one was a mottled blue, the other a glaring yellow. The tip of his tail was ringed with black. He looked at Southpaw with an idle curiosity, and the kitten's small gut constricted as he recognized the look: it was the same one he'd seen on Miao's face many times when the queen went hunting. The look said: hello, prey.

Around the kitten, creeping out from under ancient wooden wardrobes, dropping down silently from crumbling pelmets where thick velvet curtains hung, the ring of feral cats was growing. Southpaw took his eyes off Datura and circled, turning to face his predators one by one. His heart plummeted: Ratsbane lounged against the door, covering his one hope of escape, and there were far more cats than he'd expected, at least a dozen, possibly a score.

Upstairs, a slow thumping noise made Datura look up. The white cat's tail flicked from side to side in annoyance, and he signalled to the others to stay where they were. Southpaw stayed crouched to the floor, trying to ignore the squelch of what felt like mouldy newspapers pressed against the fur of his belly. The stench made him feel sick to his stomach.

He considered surrendering—most toms and queens would not fight a kitten who rolled over on its back and offered its throat in abject submission—but for a small kitten, he had a full-grown cat's worth of pride. Southpaw looked up at Ratsbane, with his great yellow teeth bared, and then at Datura, and some instinct told him, pride apart, that if he bared his throat to these two ferals, they would tear the soft flesh into shreds as though he were a mouse.

"The meat isn't scared enough, Datura," said Aconite's sinister voice, right behind Southpaw. "Shall I play with him, then?" And before the kitten could run, a paw cuffed him hard across his back, the blow heavy, the cat's claws raking his back paw painfully.

Southpaw miaowed and turned to slash back at Aconite. But the cat—a skinny grey with malevolent golden eyes—was circling the kitten lazily, padding around just out of reach. It seemed to the kitten then that time slowed down, and he could almost hear Miao's injunctions, out in the park, to the older kittens: "Never leave your back unguarded! Let your whiskers and the fur on your tail tell you what walks your way, wherever you are!" He flattened himself to the ground and rolled, just in time to escape Ratsbane's chattering teeth. The black cat had moved away from the door, drawn by the prospect of sport, and would have bitten the kitten's paws or tail right through if he hadn't shifted in time.

The circle of cats was tightening around Southpaw. Fear made the kitten's heart hammer. He stared into Aconite's eyes. His blood hummed with a sudden understanding: this was not just play, nor was it the often savage defence of territory that many cats would consider a reasonable response to intruders. The kitten slashed at Aconite's nose swiftly, watching the blood flow and exulting in his small victory as the cat howled and backed off. Southpaw whirled and slashed, blindly, driving three would-be predators back; his size gave him an advantage—he was so small that he made a difficult target for the ferals.

He knew now that these cats would kill him as soon as they had finished playing with him. Then, oddly, an unbidden thought came to him. Looking in Datura's direction, but speaking to the room at large, he said, "I feel sorry for you." The whiskers stilled, and then they crackled all around him in outrage.

"He feels *sorry* for us?" said Aconite, the grey's voice incredulous.

"Let me rend him limb from limb," said Ratsbane. "Let me break each of his paws, slowly, so that he cries the way that stray did, and then let us tear out his whiskers and his tongue, Datura. I want to feel his bones snap between my teeth."

The white cat barely flickered an ear, but the room fell silent, and even Ratsbane didn't venture further towards Southpaw.

"You interest me, meat," said Datura. "You smell of blood and fear, and you will soon stink of pain and regret, before we take pity on you and end your foolish life. You are alone, and we are many; your friends have deserted you. And yet you feel sorry for us? In the few seconds left to you before you join the rats and the mice whose bodies litter the floor, as you can see, you choose to feel *sorry* for us? Explain yourself."

The white cat's purr was mild, even reasonable, but Southpaw's ears were sharp enough to catch the undercurrent of rage, and to sense the anger that Datura held tightly contained in his whiskers.

"The crows peck at strangers as you do; the rats round on the young and helpless as you do, Datura; but no true cat would behave as you and your kind do," said the kitten.

Datura turned on the stairs and Southpaw saw the white cat's whiskers start to extend. No doubt, this would be the order to Ratsbane, Aconite and the others to finish the game.

"I haven't finished speaking," the kitten said, letting his own voice rise sharply and fill the room, a skill he had learned from watching Katar conduct the colony's sometimes uproarious meetings on the link between the older cats.

A murmur of incredulity rippled through air, but the kitten cut through the rising storm. "Miao and Katar always told me that even cats of a different scent should be heard when they ask for shelter, unless they are a threat to the clan," said Southpaw.

"I came here to escape the dog, because you said I could come in, Datura. But you don't behave like the cats I know."

Datura began descending the stairs, his yellow eye blazing in fury, his blue eye opaque and inscrutable.

"What fine entertainment we have today!" he said, his fur radiating contempt. But he did not stop Southpaw, or order his kill.

The kitten's heart was beating so fast that he wondered if all the ferals in the room could hear it.

"When was the last time you went outside, Datura?" he asked. Aconite hissed. "Let me kill him now! The impertinence!"

The ring tightened around the kitten, and he sensed that there were more ferals coming around the back. He was surrounded.

The white cat was on the bottom-most stair, his tail flicking steadily back-and-forth.

"Why should Datura go outside?" asked Ratsbane, his teeth bared in a growl. "Why should any of us go outside? Here, we have everything we need, you stupid piece of meat. This is our kingdom, our domain; we feast on rats and the few pigeons who flutter through the windows, we live by our own laws, not your foolish, weak rules, and we are disturbed by nobody."

Southpaw drew on all of his reserves of anger, allowing it to well up inside his small chest and bury the sharp fear he felt as the ferals of the Shuttered House crept closer.

"I'm asking Datura," he said, "not you." The white cat snarled, his ears back, and now the kitten could see the madness in his eyes. Datura began padding towards the kitten, his claws clicking on the floor. Southpaw's fur was taut from tension, his sparse eyebrows and black whiskers crackling.

"Were you born here?" he asked desperately. Datura stopped, his tail waving from side to side.

"I was," he said. "What of it? What difference does it make where I was born?"

Southpaw felt his terror slip away from him. His black whiskers rose slightly as he tried to imagine what it would be like to exchange the vast expanse of Nizamuddin—the canal roads, the Bigfeet's lawns and rooftops, the narrow alleys and old ruins—for this confined, reeking space. He now understood where the thought that had briefly interrupted his impending demise had come from. "You were the first, weren't you?" he said to Datura.

"The first what?" said Ratsbane. "Datura, just raise a paw, and I'll tear the little scum's whiskers out by the roots."

Suddenly, Southpaw realized he was no longer afraid. He ignored Ratsbane, backing further until he could feel the broad comforting expanse of a wooden wardrobe behind him.

"The first to be born in the Shuttered House," said Southpaw. "Isn't that true, Datura? You grew up seeing the outside, feeling the wind from the skies on your whiskers once in a while, through the windows, out on the roof, but you've never really been outside, have you? The rest of the cats came here later, didn't they? Most came here when they were still very young kittens, some were born here, but you were the first of them."

"What of it?" said Aconite. The grey cat was staring at the kitten, but there was open space between her and him, and she would have to launch a direct assault if she wanted to go on the attack. "You speak of things we all know, or even if we didn't, these are matters of no importance."

There were twitches of assent all around the room, but Southpaw noted that only some were strong; a slight, almost imperceptible uncertainty also travelled along the whiskers, and he thought he could sense hesitation in the air. The kitten found his paws sweating; whatever he had picked up from those powerful but scattered images in their brief sharing added up to little more than a feeling. But his only chance was to hold the attention of the cats, to keep talking until—and here his mind shut down, refusing to accept that there was no escape.

"You say these are matters of no importance, Aconite?" the kitten said, letting his whiskers relax. "But why haven't you been outdoors to see what it's like? Why are all of you shut up here like mice, like rats, like a band of scuttling, scurrying roaches, living off stale food and stinking milk, when the hedges outside teem with fresh, fat prey?"

"I'll pull your whiskers out myself!" hissed Datura, and came sideways at him. Southpaw bared his small teeth and growled. The white cat stopped just a foot short, arching his back and hissing hideously, but careful not to get too close. The kitten's claws were tiny, but sharp, as he had demonstrated to Aconite.

"I'm not done," said Southpaw. Out of the corner of his eye, he was judging the distance to the velvet drapes, wondering whether they would bear his weight if he had to make a run for it. A low hum was rising up from the ferals.

"You're done," growled Ratsbane.

"Look at yourself, Ratsbane!" Southpaw called, as loudly as he could, startling the large black tom.

"You're so proud of your strength, of your muscles, of your killing abilities, aren't you? And yet, why have you never used these outside? Never battled the crows for the right to your kill, never brawled gloriously with another tom, never fought a dog? Look at your kills—a cat with a broken paw, a kitten with its whiskers not even white yet. Are you proud of yourself, Ratsbane? You, Aconite?"

The snarling that greeted him made the kitten back up and shiver, but he could not let them see how scared he was. Pushing himself up to his greatest height, which placed him a long way under Ratsbane's massive shoulder, he fluffed his fur out and hissed.

"The only reason you haven't gone out is because your leader never went out. Datura shut you all up in the Shuttered House because he had never been out as a kitten! And you followed his example blindly! You call yourself cats?"

Southpaw saw a flash of doubt in Aconite's golden eyes, and felt triumphant when Ratsbane sat back on his haunches, washing a paw to hide his obvious perturbation.

Datura moved so fast that the kitten didn't see him coming, until a cruelly sharp set of claws slammed his tail against the rotting wood of the wardrobe, holding him pinned. The pain shot through his body like a lance of fire.

"That was very clever, meat, and very entertaining," said Datura. His yellow eye stared down at Southpaw, pinning him just as mercilessly to the ground with its fury as his claws held the kitten's tail to the wood. "But the only law that matters is the law of the Shuttered House. And that law is absolute: when we find meat, we kill it." There was a gleam in his dissonant eyes. "Slowly," he added, and then Datura pulled lazily at one of Southpaw's whiskers, using his teeth delicately, almost gently.

The words the kitten was about to say, the grand defiance he had thought his whiskers would carry to the sea of cats around him, all of it died in the face of the pain that went through his small body. His face felt as though it was on fire, and he wriggled only once; the pain doubled, and Southpaw realized that any movement would hurt him even more. Datura's face was so close to his own that he could see right into the cat's strange blue eye. Far off, he heard an animal screaming in pain, and as blood gushed out of the hole where his whisker had been, he realized the screams were coming from his own throat. He tried to stop, but what came out were choked mews. Somewhere at the back of his head, he thought he could hear a loud thumping from upstairs, but the kitten was in too much pain to try to make sense of anything.

"First blood," said Aconite, her voice greedy.

"If you ask nicely, Aconite, I'll let you do his tail," said Datura. The white cat was still holding Southpaw down with a heavy paw, examining the kitten dispassionately. It seemed to the kitten that Datura relished each one of his involuntary mews of pain and fear, and once again, he tried to stop himself from crying out.

"What about me?" said Ratsbane.

"I said we'd do him slowly," said Datura. "You'll have plenty of time to play." Southpaw's shock grew. He could hear Miao's voice in his head, telling the older kittens as they went out for their first hunt: "The best hunters make a clean kill, and will make it fast. Play with your prey to tire it out, if it's injured and dangerous. But in all other circumstances, remember that the best kills are clean, fast and painless."

Then Datura's claw stabbed through the very tip of his ear, shredding it, and Southpaw screamed again. He felt rather than heard the Nizamuddin cats respond, and realized that he had finally linked to them, probably propelled by the pain and distress, though he had no idea how.

Datura shifted position, sinking his teeth into the scruff of Southpaw's neck. He lifted the kitten, who felt the tender skin on the back of his neck tear, felt the blood start to trickle down his throat. He slammed the kitten down on the ground. Southpaw tried to roll, but Datura was too quick for him. The white cat's massive paws held him pinned, and he heard Aconite come up behind him. Her eyes were feverish, filled with bloodlust, and the kitten—pinned and helpless on the ground—decided he would try and provoke her to kill him fast.

His face throbbed; he couldn't stand much more pain. A slow tapping noise from the stairs became audible, and a part of his exhausted mind feared that it might be more ferals, coming down to join in Datura's game.

"Shall we begin?" said Datura. And Southpaw shuddered, closing his eyes. He thought of Miao and the way she often washed him to sleep, the comfort of her rough tongue on his fur; he thought of the times he had followed Katar around Nizamuddin, learning how to be a tomcat from the bravest, kindest tomcat of them all. He tried to think of how the sunlight felt on his whiskers, of the taste of fresh, juicy mouse, of the fun of chasing squirrels in the branches of the trees, of all the things he loved about his world. As Datura's teeth filled his vision, Southpaw tried to think of anything but where he was. "There you are, pussycat!" said a quavering voice from the stairs. Southpaw felt his fur rise in alarm; Datura's whiskers trembled and the white cat jerked away, though he held the kitten pinned. The kitten couldn't see anything, but he smelled a Bigfoot. His nose told him this was what he had smelled earlier: the smell of old age and the unmistakeable stench of illness.

"Naughty kitty," the voice continued. "I called and called, but you didn't come, Fluffy. Why weren't you listening to your Papa? Bad, bad Fluffy!"

"Fluffy?" Southpaw thought, despite his pain. The expression on Datura's face, hunted and truculent, was priceless.

"What's that you've caught? Is it a nasty mouse, then? Or— Fluffy! It"s a kitten! Get away from it right this minute, you bad kitty!"

Southpaw found himself staring into the wrinkled face of the oldest Bigfoot he'd ever seen. He leaned on a walking stick, and looked down at Datura—Fluffy. Southpaw was once again struck by the blindness of Bigfeet, he had never seen a less Fluffy-like cat in his life. Datura's paws came off his chest as the old Bigfoot picked up the white cat, and Southpaw realized that the circle of ferals was quietly dispersing. Ratsbane and Aconite had slunk off under the stairs, and the rest were creeping back into the corridors and the large hall.

He tried to stand up, but now that the fear was subsiding, the pain hit him in waves. The kitten refused to mew, though, and struggled to his feet. The Bigfoot had scooped up Datura and now held him in his arms. The cat's blue and yellow eyes bulged in anger, but he lay limp as the Bigfoot crooned endearments to him.

Southpaw eyed the door, which seemed very far away. "Let me look at you," the Bigfoot said. "Where did you come from, then, little one?" He placed the white cat on a nearby sideboard, Datura's paws stirring up the dust and making a line of black beetles scatter back into the rotting wood. Southpaw cringed when the Bigfoot bent down, but he couldn't run. He yowled when he was picked up, unused to any kind of contact with Bigfeet. His heart was hammering so hard he could feel his ribs contract. The old Bigfoot held him gently, though, cupped between his papery, soft hands; his eyes were kind and inquiring.

"They've had a go at you, have they, little fellow?" he said. Gently, he stroked the kitten's fur, his hands trembling with fever. Southpaw didn't always understand what the Bigfeet were saying, but like all cats, he could sense their intentions. This Bigfoot meant him no harm, and his touch was soothing, though he smelled very sick. He looked around at Aconite and Datura, and then his gaze travelled to Ratsbane, who sat sullenly on a windowsill, his eyes blazing.

"We can't keep you," he said to Southpaw. "I think they would kill you, even my darling Fluffy."

Stiffly, with some difficulty, he walked over to the window near the door, and opened the shutters. They creaked as the rust came off the bolts, and the glorious, rich scents of the outside world reached the kitten's twitching nose. He drank them in gratefully and mewed.

"Go, little one," the Bigfoot said, placing Southpaw on the windowsill. The kitten hesitated, but the grounds appeared to be clear. The dog had gone; he couldn't see Miao, Katar or the other cats, but he knew he would be able to link now that he was out of the Shuttered House. He took a tentative step, and then gingerly nudged the Bigfeet's hand, to say thank you.

The Bigfoot limped back into the house, and picked up Datura. "Fluffy's been a wicked, bad cat," he heard him say. And then Datura's voice came across the distance that separated them, silent and cold as the white cat's whiskers twitched.

"This isn't over, meat," said Datura, his voice rasping. "He won't last. You smelled the sickness. And when he goes, we might want to make you run, and pull out the rest of those impertinent whiskers."

"I'm not afraid of you," said Southpaw, and it was, surprisingly, true.

"But you will be," said Datura.

"You will be," said Ratsbane.

"When we start playing with you and the rest of your miserable lot, you will be," said Aconite. The stink of the Shuttered House stayed in Southpaw's nose for a long time, even though his paws unfurled with gratitude at the fine, clean earth beneath them. Overhead, a cheel circled and called out, his hunting voice sharp and clear, but it didn't come down to disturb the kitten's glad return to freedom.

IT WAS LATE AT NIGHT by the time Miao and Katar had finished dealing with Southpaw's wounds. For Miao, the wait had been terrible. The dog had held them at bay for a long while until it finally scented other prey and bounded off.

Just as Hulo and some of the other cats joined Miao and Katar, all of them had to lie low as a marriage procession went by outside the Shuttered House. The raucous cries of the Bigfeet didn't worry the Nizamuddin cats, nor did the fireworks they set off. They found these unpleasant, but it was part and parcel of living in the Bigfeet's world. The problem was the number of Bigfeet who strayed, every so often, into the usually silent grounds of the Shuttered House. There was no opportunity for the cats to plan a counter-attack; and the crowds had only started to clear when they received Southpaw's anguished linkings.

Katar had been agitated, but Miao was calmer. She had lost enough litters of kittens to know how difficult life was for the young ones. "It's up to Southpaw," she told Katar. "We can only wait, and hope." Going into the Shuttered House was out of the question, she reminded them. It was not their territory; even Hulo didn't leave his scent on its walls and porches. It smelled unmistakeably of ferals, and while Southpaw had entered in extremis and was entitled to sanctuary, the cats of the Shuttered House would tear other intruders to bits. "As would we, if outsiders invaded our territory, claimed our rooftops," Miao said. And yet, Katar almost broke the unspoken but ancient pact between the ferals of the Shuttered House and the wildings of Nizamuddin. Hulo held him back. "No," he said. "If anything happens to the young fellow, it's our fault for not teaching him to hunt, but we can't intrude. Would you save him from every dog that snapped at his paws? Will you be there when some cruel Bigfoot brands his tail, or breaks his paws? If you go into their territory, you could start a war between our clan and the ferals. You can't take that risk, Katar."

It was Miao who caught Southpaw's scent first, and it was the old Siamese who came out first from the ramshackle pipes at the side of the Shuttered House. She and Katar had taken up their vigil there, hoping against hope that the kitten might have survived whatever was happening inside.

And now Southpaw curled into her warm, furry belly, happy to be safe and home with his own kind, despite the pain from his various wounds. Katar had licked and licked steadily at the hole left by the missing whisker, until it felt cooler and the ache lessened to a dull sting. Miao had washed his torn ear and gently used her teeth to nibble and suck at his throat until the puncture marks were clean of all dirt and of Datura's saliva. Southpaw lay between the two cats, looking up at the stars in the night sky, remembering the grim, dusty, cobwebbed ceiling of the Shuttered House.

The cats rested, drowsing in the cool, calm night. Katar disappeared for a brief while and returned with fresh kill—a large bandicoot, enough for all three of them—and they ate well, the two older cats nudging Southpaw towards the best and tastiest morsels.

Fed, warm and safe, Southpaw slept against Miao's comfortable flank, too tired to join Katar and the others in the night's activities, even though a first-class prowl had been planned for the evening.

He slept only briefly, and the moon was still high in the night sky when he woke. It was a murky moon, the light from it a mottled orange and yellow, and it gave the kitten bad dreams, so that his paws cycled in his sleep and he yelped once or twice. Miao washed his head and his ears gently, knowing that Southpaw's nightmares would continue for a while.

"Miao," said Southpaw when he was properly awake, "will the Shuttered House ever be opened?"

The Siamese looked up, and then over in the direction of the strange house that the ferals called home.

"Don't let it give you bad dreams," she said.

"But will it be?" Southpaw persisted. "Datura said the old Bigfoot wouldn't be there, and then they would come out—but they've never come out before. So why would they come out at all? Why wouldn't they just stay there?"

Miao snuggled closer to the kitten, and decided that after everything he had witnessed and survived that day, he could be told the truth—even if it was a harsh truth.

"You've never known ferals, have you, Southpaw?" she said. "They're different from us wildings. We have our brawls and our territories, but, mostly, we live in peace with each other. Ferals are always strange creatures, Southpaw. Can you imagine what it would be like to grow up in the Shuttered House, without the thumping of the Bigfeet world, or the feel of the rain and the wind in your fur, or parks and gardens to roam in, trees to climb, roofs to defend and claim?"

Southpaw's eyes went opaque as he recalled the thought that had come to him in his moment of danger, how it had given him that tiny reprieve that had undoubtedly kept him alive. He refocused on what Miao was saying. "They think food comes from Bigfeet, and they only ever hunt old, lame rats or diseased beetles, Southpaw," said Miao. "And living inside, shut up all the time, something warps in them. Their minds scurry in circles, like the grubs you've seen living under tree bark—here and there, here and there, never going anywhere. So if their Bigfoot dies, because that's what Datura was talking about, they won't have any food left after a while. And perhaps other Bigfeet won't let them stay inside the Shuttered House, Southpaw."

"Then what will they do?" asked the kitten, trembling just a little as he thought of Datura, and Aconite, and Ratsbane, and the hatred in their whiskers as they made their final threats.

Miao stared out across the park, her eyes not quite seeing what was ahead of them.

"Then they'll either break out and try to kill us, or turn on each other in a killing frenzy," she said. What the Siamese didn't tell the kitten was that neither outcome would be good for the Nizamuddin cats. Anything that drew the attention of the Bigfeet to their small colony of wildings would be bad for them.

She realized that Southpaw's trembling had intensified, and she laid her muzzle against his small face.

"Never worry, Southpaw," she said, "until you have to. Besides, we're not helpless."

"We aren't?" said the kitten, wanting to believe Miao but remembering all too clearly the terror that the ferals of the Shuttered House had raised in his mind.

"Not at all," said Miao. "Katar has led us through many rains and summers, and we have warriors like Beraal and Hulo. It seems we also have a Sender on our side, though she is still very young."

"As young as me?" said Southpaw, curious. There were no other kittens of his age in Nizamuddin—the rest were a whole season older or a season younger, and sometimes the kitten wished he had litter mates.

"Yes," said Miao. "Beraal tells me she's very small, so perhaps she's even younger than you. Imagine that, you're bigger than the Sender!"

"I thought the Sender would be big," said Southpaw, disappointed. "I thought she would be bigger than Datura—as big as the tigers!" He shuddered, remembering the day when he'd woken up to see Ozzy's massive, wickedly curved teeth, that gigantic black-and-gold striped face.

Miao's whiskers and eyebrows shook in silent laughter. "No, she's just a kitten," she said. "But all Senders have amazing powers. Tigris, for instance, could speak to the cheels and share their soaring flights." And washing his whiskers, gentling his fur, telling him stories until he was soothed, the old Siamese managed to lull Southpaw into a deep, healing sleep. He shifted and muttered as his paws kneaded her flank, but he didn't open his eyes, and Miao felt the tension go out of his small body after a while. Soon, he was dreaming: of happier things, she hoped.

The Siamese remained awake for much of the night, watching the wood owls make their sorties overhead, and listening to the chorus of the bats who lived near the baoli. She stiffened when a mongoose darted out from behind a clump of queen of the night creepers, but it barely glanced at her and Southpaw. Its sleek brown head pointed in the other direction, and Miao wondered whether it was hunting cobras or harmless rat snakes and lizards. She blinked away a buzzing mosquito, and when she opened her eyes again, the predator had melted away into the undergrowth.

Southpaw hooked a paw into her stomach, nuzzling up to the cream-coloured cat like the tiniest of kittens. Miao washed the top of his head until he was purring in his dreams. She drank in the pre-dawn peace of Nizamuddin, the quiet hours before the Bigfeet stirred, and hoped that Datura and his pack would never want to leave the Shuttered House.

CHAPTER EIGHT

Southpaw Makes a Friend

The weeks passed without incident, until Southpaw landed in trouble yet again, this time with Hulo. The kitten's complaints were so loud that they reached the ears of even the passing mynahs and cheels. "You're nipping me! Miao is much gentler."

"You're an ungrateful brat," said Hulo, who was using his rough tongue to clean dried leaves and the remains of a termite's nest out of Southpaw's wounds, which were healing quite nicely. "Hold still, there's a good kitten."

"Groof!" said Southpaw. "Hulo, that's my eye!"

"Quit wriggling," said the tomcat. "If Miao or Katar hear you were climbing trees with those wounds not yet healed, and that too the fig tree, which you were told not to climb . . ."

". . . because it had snakes in the branches, but it didn't have any, Hulo," said Southpaw, trying not to mind the rasping of Hulo's tongue. "I checked very carefully and there were only some mynah birds and those babblers, making a racket as usual. They make such a noise, how would any snakes live there? They'd be frightened away, wouldn't they?"

"But suppose there had been snakes," Hulo said sternly.

"I would have been so scared!" said Southpaw. "But there weren't, you know. Just birds. Besides, how was I to know if there were snakes or not without going to see for myself? No one seemed to know for sure, Hulo."

Hulo left off washing Southpaw and thought, not for the first time, that he didn't envy Miao and Katar. Southpaw wasn't the first orphan kitten to be found in Nizamuddin, but he was much more of a handful than most. The tomcat refused to parent Southpaw in any official way, but he kept his whiskers out for news of the kitten, which tended to arrive at distressingly regular intervals.

There was his brush with the pariah cheel, the Shuttered House episode, and then he'd sneaked off to steal fish from one of the Bigfeet houses while he was supposed to be resting, and now there was the fig tree expedition. If Hulo were Katar, he'd have smacked Southpaw's bottom so hard that the kitten would be sitting on a smooth behind. Hulo had been the one who'd found Southpaw, stumbling down the canal road with sore paws, mewling and still almost blind—the kitten's eyes had just about opened. When the tomcat sniffed at him, Southpaw had reared back and tried to fight Hulo, his tiny paws flailing. For some reason, this had amused and touched the tom, who had a weakness for a good brawl. Hulo had picked him up in his jaws and carried him to the other cats, unsure why his instincts told him not to kill the foundling.

Southpaw was holding still now, and Hulo sensed that the kitten was suppressing a whimper as the gash where his whisker had been pulled out was cleaned. The wound had scabbed over, but had to be kept clear of dirt and pus; the cats took turns to wash the kitten. The kitten's remaining whiskers shot up as a series of mews rang out above their heads, apparently coming from the rooftops.

"But why do you not rejoice, Bigfeet? I have found a game we can both play—see how carefully I push these nasty figurines and doodads off the shelf, just to give you the pleasure of picking them up yourself? We can play for hours—noooooo! Put me down, you beast! How dare you smack my bottom!"

Southpaw started in surprise; it seemed to him that an orange kitten wriggled upside down in the air, suspended from an unseen hand. Her paws swiped at the breeze, and her eyes crossed as she displayed her indignation. *"Waaooooowww!"* she said to the top of Southpaw's head, and then she was gone.

"What was that?" he said, astonished. His whiskers extended as far as they could—he'd been practising—but there was no kitten-scent in the air, nothing except for the faint, distant hint of rain.

The tomcat's black scruffy tail was lashing back and forth, and his eyes had gone a vivid green. "That," he replied, his ears stiff, "is Beraal's appallingly noisy little pupil."

Southpaw's nose wrinkled in disappointment. That was the Sender? A scruffy orange kitten with her paws flailing in mid-air, at the mercy of her Bigfeet? He had thought she would be mysterious and solemn, like a miniature version of Miao.

"So what's so special about her?" Southpaw asked.

"You'd have to ask Beraal," the tomcat said. "I don't know what everyone's making such a fuss about—aside from interrupting our daily business, she doesn't seem to do much. And besides, she's an inside cat. You can't trust them an inch."

Southpaw's tail wavered and went all the way down.

"She's like Datura?" he said in a small voice, his whiskers trembling ever so faintly. Somehow he didn't like the idea of the Sender, whom everybody talked about with their whiskers raised in grudging respect, being like Datura and his friends.

"Like Datura—no, no," said Hulo, "though you have to wonder why she brought the tigers into Nizamuddin, that didn't seem friendly at all. It's just that inside cats are different from you and me, Southpaw. What kind of cat would rather live with Bigfeet than have all this?"

"So the house she lives in isn't like the Shuttered House?" Southpaw said, thinking of the stinking floors and the old, shuffling Bigfoot.

"Not at all!" said Hulo, seeing what was going through the kitten's mind. "Didn't you come with me when we did the kitchen raid—"

The tom glanced at Southpaw and saw the kitten's ears rise in sharpened interest. "Never mind the kitchen expedition," he said, not wanting to encourage Southpaw to plunge into more trouble. "Most Bigfeet houses are like large, clean cages, and though everyone knows the Bigfeet are mad, building hutch after hutch for themselves like rabbits, some of them seem to like our kind. It's just that—come on, youngling, let me show you what I mean."

The tom stretched and, checking for cars and Bigfeet, padded away from the fig tree, back towards the row of houses near the canal. Southpaw followed in his wake, trying hard to imitate Hulo's swagger, but conscious that what he could manage with his shorter paws was closer to a waddle than a walk.

The tomcat took a shortcut up a massive Bengal quince tree, ducking the large globes of fruit that hung from its branches, waiting for the kitten to make his way through. The two cats made their way through the branches, Hulo sending a quick twitch of his whiskers to clear the way, and also to let the tree's inhabitants know that they weren't on the hunt. Southpaw loved walking through the green, papery leaves, high above the world, the bark massaging his paw pads. The winds were picking up now, and he could smell the sharp change in the air: a storm was on its way, making the walk through the tree that much more exhilarating. He was almost sorry when the tom dropped down from the Bengal quince onto a gatepost, moving easily from there to a window ledge.

Hulo made room for Southpaw and they settled down behind a row of flowerpots, the kitten batting aside the dahlias so that he could see better. They were looking directly into a courtyard attached to one of the Bigfeet houses, and an Alsatian pup looked up sharply when he heard the leaves in the Bengal quince tree rustle, but the cats had moved fast, and all he saw were the squirrels running along the branches. His black-tipped ears, creamy on the inside, stayed cocked for a while, but then the dog relaxed and settled down again.

A young Bigfoot woman came out with a large red plastic bowl of food. Though he was perched so far up, Southpaw could smell the meat and his whiskers rose in greed. The dog jumped up, barking happily, and rubbed his head against the Bigfoot's hands. She settled down, petting him. Up on the parapet, the two cats watched as the dog ate his food in great gulps. Southpaw's stomach emitted a hopeful gurgle, but Hulo glared at him, and the kitten flattened his stomach against the ledge, hoping it would shut up.

"Now watch!" Hulo signalled.

The Bigfoot picked up the empty bowl and left. The dog whined and stared at her, clearly willing her to come back with more food. The screen door that led back into the house shut with a click.

The Alsatian pup stared at the place where his food had been set down. Then he stared at the door, and Southpaw could tell he was willing it to open again.

It stayed shut.

The Alsatian began barking. When no one came out, his barks grew louder and louder, until, losing patience, he lunged towards the door and was brought up short by his leash. He growled and then, his tail held expectantly still, he resumed barking.

The door swung open, and a different Bigfoot came out. Southpaw wished he could tell the pup to shut up. Something about the way the Bigfoot was standing, arms folded across his chest, spelled trouble. "If he'd had a tail, it would be twitching," Southpaw thought, and Hulo's whiskers twitched, acknowledging the truth of this.

The Bigfoot was staring down at the pup, who was barking hysterically now, tugging at his leash.

The Bigfoot smacked the pup hard across his nose. Southpaw ducked back behind the dahlias and rested his whiskery chin on the flower's soft petals. He didn't like dogs, but it was hard to hear the pup's sorrowful little whines without feeling sorry for the creature. Hulo was impassive, but his fur stood up just enough for Southpaw to think that perhaps the tom felt it too.

THE DAY WAS ALMOST AT A CLOSE when they came back to the park in the centre of Nizamuddin, crossing over the rooftops, taking the stairs and the long route through the gardens and the lantana hedges. Southpaw loved coming over the roofs, especially those that were festooned with clotheslines: there was something about the scent of clean Bigfeet clothes that made him want to rub his face against them, and he was happy to dry his wet fur on some of the larger bedsheets and tablecloths. Sometimes, the Bigfeet could be surprisingly thoughtful.

The kitten's stomach rumbled again. He'd been so busy climbing the fig tree and then going on the excursion with Hulo that he hadn't been able to forage in the garbage dump for a meal. It had been raining steadily for a while, and it seemed to him that it would go on all night. The stars were coming out, and with the rain pelting down like this, Southpaw knew it was unlikely that they would be able to hunt.

Hulo stopped at his favourite spot, a corrugated tin roof that lay like a crooked hat over an abandoned garage. There was enough crawl space under its overlapping tin sheets to provide cover for the two cats after their long, wet trek. It was close enough to the houses and the park for him to keep an eye on the movements of the Bigfeet and other animals, and isolated enough to be a comfortable resting place.

They listened to the fierce rat-a-tat of the rain on the roof, so loud now that it drowned out all the other sounds of the park at night. The headlights from the Bigfeet's passing cars lit up the road every so often, and Southpaw shivered when he saw how the water ran off the streets in small rivers. He wondered if the pup had been taken into the house for shelter; he hoped so.

"Do you remember the smell from that dog's food bowl?" Hulo said suddenly.

Southpaw couldn't stop his stomach from letting out a gargantuan rumble. The small whisker twitch that meant "yes" was entirely superfluous.

"What did it smell like to you?" the tom asked. His matted fur hung over his eyes, and he had picked up what looked like a tree's worth of dead leaves and filth as they came back through the storm, but he radiated alertness to Southpaw. If Hulo was as hungry as the kitten, he hadn't let it show.

Southpaw moistened his pink mouth and his whiskers began quivering on their own. "It smelled like marrowbones and rich meat stew," he said. "It smelled even better than fresh rat, and it smelled warm and good."

Hulo's green eyes were almost opaque; Southpaw couldn't tell what the tom was thinking.

"Every meal that pup eats is like that," he said. "Rich and warm, and savoury. Filling, on a day like this, when you can feel the first cold fingers of winter running through your fur and bones. He doesn't have to do anything for his meals. No hunting, no digging through the garbage and fighting the rats for every scrap. No going out in the heat of summer to find food that isn't spoiled, no expeditions in the rain when your fur soaks right through to your skin."

The tom stared out across the park. They were comfortable enough, but drifts of rain blew into their corner every so often, and Southpaw shivered from time to time from the cold.

"Some Bigfeet will do that for cats as well," he said. "Feed you milk and fish—you've tasted fish, haven't you, Southpaw?— three times a day, give you a warm bed. Wouldn't you like that?"

The kitten's eyes were huge, considering the lovely pictures that had begun dancing in his mind as Hulo shared his thoughts.

"Yes," he said, but his whiskers were uncertain. The tom said nothing. "Would the Bigfeet tie me up?" the kitten asked after a while. "No," said the tomcat. "They never tie up cats, perhaps because we would bite through any leashes. But they might lock you up, in their hutches."

"Would the Bigfeet beat me?" the kitten asked.

The tip of Hulo's tail moved back and forth as he considered the question.

"Perhaps," he said.

"Would they let me stay in the park and climb the roofs?" the kitten asked after considering the matter. He could still almost smell and taste that bowl of meat stew, and imagine how good it would feel to clean what little remained off his whiskers. His belly would be warm and bulging, instead of empty and slack.

"Probably not," said the tom. "Some cats around the dargah visit Bigfeet houses for the food and come away, but it's an uncertain life. If you want your meals three times a day, then you have to become an inside cat. And as I've said earlier, it isn't a bad life at all, if you don't end up in a place like the Shuttered House."

Southpaw washed his paws several times over to try and sort out his thoughts.

"Is the house the Sender lives in nice?" he said.

"Yes," said Hulo.

"But she never comes out of the house?" the kitten asked, unable to imagine what that would be like. His thoughts went back briefly to the gloom and stench of the Shuttered House. He blinked the nightmarish image away and thought that even if he were to live in a comfortable Bigfeet house, the idea of being unable to see the sky would be unbearable. In summer, a few days after his eyes had opened, he had wandered into a cardboard crate and been unable to find his way out. His heart began to hammer as he remembered how closed in and suffocated he'd felt, before Katar heard his mews and clawed a path through the cardboard.

Hulo said, "Only up to the stairs."

"How horrible it would be to live in a box!" Southpaw said. "Why does anyone want to be an inside cat?"

The tomcat said, "How does your belly feel?"

"Empty and sad," said the kitten.

"If you found the right Bigfeet family," said Hulo, "you would never have to be hungry again."

Southpaw lay back, confused again, and tried to grab his tail with his paws to get his mind out of the dilemma. He could see what Hulo meant, and with his stomach reminding him that it didn't like being empty, he began to understand why the life of an inside cat might have some appeal. But his mind refused to go beyond the sense of claustrophobia. He played with his tail, fluffing it up with his claws, smoothing it back down, and then he thought of the pup and the way it had whined, wanting more food, dependent on its Bigfoot. "I'd rather be an outside cat," he said at last. And he felt Hulo's smile radiating through the other cat's fur and whiskers as clearly as if it had been light and he'd been able to see the tom's face.

"It's a choice every cat has to make at some point," said Hulo.

"Did you ever want to be an inside cat?" Southpaw asked, thinking that he couldn't imagine Hulo anywhere near the Bigfeet.

The tom was licking his tangled fur clean, but at this he stopped, and his fur rippled with laughter. He turned his battered fighter's face with the scars and the broad ugly features to Southpaw.

"What kind of Bigfoot would invite me with a face like this?" he said. "They usually greet me with their brooms!"

Southpaw wriggled, enjoying the joke, and was about to curl into Hulo's bulk for warmth when the tomcat stiffened, cocking his ragged ears. "Rats!" he said. "Look at them, swarming out into the street! The drainpipe must have flooded their homes out—all right, Southpaw, I'm off to hunt. Stay here!"

The kitten scrambled to his feet, his nose twitching in excitement. "I'm coming too, Hulo!"

The tom cuffed him gently, rolling the kitten over and back into safety.

"No, you're not," he said. "You haven't been on your first hunt yet and there's too many of them—you might get bitten."

The black creatures were disappearing down the alley on the left, and the tom was already at the edge of the roof as he talked. "Don't leave the park, Southpaw, stay right here. I'll be back with fresh kill for you." His bristly bottlebrush of a tail stayed waggling in the air for a second as he braced his paws on the broken drainpipe, and then Hulo was gone, his teeth already chattering in anticipation of the hunt.

Southpaw's tail dropped all the way down as he watched Hulo go. It's not fair, the kitten thought. Hadn't he watched Katar, Miao, Beraal and Hulo hunt from the time the blue had left his own eyes and he could see? But Hulo had been very clear: he was not to leave. Southpaw often got in trouble, but he never disobeyed the older cats when they gave him a direct order. He scratched at a discarded paper bag, feeling better when he'd torn it up into small, grease-stained shreds. "That's what I'd do to a rat!" he said to himself. "Right paw! Left paw! Teeth at the ready for the killing bite! I'm a great ferocious hunter, look at me!"

The storm seemed to be blowing itself out, and the rain dropped from its clatter to a low, steady, pleasant thrumming. Southpaw killed the paper bag again, but the second time around wasn't as much fun. He chased his tail. He cleaned his whiskers. He stropped his tiny, emerging claws on a piece of cardboard.

Across the park, the lights went on in the house Hulo had said the Sender lived in. Southpaw wondered what it was like, living in a house. Would it be exactly like living in a box, dark and stifling? Or would it be different? Idly, he skewered some strands of tinsel that were flapping in the breeze and killed them until he was sure they were dead. It must be different, because otherwise there would be no inside cats at all, even if Hulo and everyone else was right and inside cats were crazy.

The rain had died down to the lightest patter. Southpaw looked across at the Sender's house, at the well-lit staircase, the open kitchen door. Perhaps he could go and take a look, just a quick peek, he thought. There was no sign of Hulo, perhaps he had met another cat, or decided to do his night rounds.

The kitten sat up on his hind paws and sniffed the air carefully, his whiskers taut and listening for any sign of the tomcat. He stared at the Sender's house again—it was such a short distance away, just a hop, skip and climb really. What Hulo had actually said was, "Don't leave the park." The kitten's paws padded off more or less of their own volition, and Southpaw bounced down the roof and bounded across the wet grass. He would be inside the park, he told himself. Inside a house inside a park, but that was the merest quibble.

Southpaw crept up the steps, flattening his belly the way he'd seen Beraal go up the stairs, keeping his nose alert for the scent of any passing Bigfeet. But the rain must have corralled them indoors, for he saw and smelled none. "Just a peek," he told himself as he approached the kitchen door, which had been left ajar for the Sender's convenience, he assumed.

And then the smell hit him. The kitten let out a mew as he stuck his head cautiously over the sill, before he could tell himself to shut up. If the aroma from the pup's bowl of food had been rich, meaty and filled with doggy wonders, this was an elixir carefully blended to perfection for cats. It smelled of fish-heads and fish broth, and fresh, caught-this-minute fish, better than the freshest of fresh rats, and Southpaw's nose quivered with such intensity he thought it was going to fall off. The kitten stuck his whiskers out to check for Bigfeet: it was a hasty check, but they seemed to be elsewhere. Then he was across the floor and his head was in the bowl. As he gobbled he purred like a steam engine.

He was almost through when he heard the loud clump-clump shuffle of a Bigfoot, and the kitten found himself painfully torn. "Quick, get out of here—you'll reach the door in two shakes of your tail," said part of his mind. "Please, just one more mouthful, there's a bit here that tastes of shrimp," begged the other part of his mind. Unfortunately, it was the louder part, and Southpaw stuck his nose back into the bowl, practically inhaling its contents.

The Bigfoot was at the entrance to the kitchen. Southpaw leaped back from the bowl and stared up at it—such a long way up. But it wasn't looking at him, and the kitten, terrified, squeezed himself under the kitchen table, his paws propelling him to the nearest hiding place. Slam! The doors shut, and staring from under the table, Southpaw saw the dark, rain-spattered sky narrow and disappear. He could see the Bigfoot's shoes, now, and he shook like a leaf under the table, expecting to be discovered at any moment.

The Bigfoot turned around and left, its shoes booming back along the corridor, the footsteps fading away into the house. "The thing to do," the frightened kitten said to himself, "is to stay right here and wait until—until they open the door or something."

But slowly, as the hand on the kitchen clock ticked over the minutes, Southpaw's terror began to ebb. Inside the house, it was warm and quiet. There was no sign of the Sender, and the Bigfeet seemed to be on the other side of the house, their voices echoing in the distance. The kitten crawled out from under the table. He padded up to the kitchen door and pushed it with his nose, but it stayed firmly shut. He eyed the open doorway that led back into the house with cautious interest. "I should stay right here," he told himself. "They'll open the door in the morning so that the Sender can sit on the stairs. It's always open when we're coming back from night prowls. I wonder how far away the morning is?"

Restless, Southpaw padded around the kitchen, investigating the many different smells, patting at a runaway potato, stropping his claws on the wooden leg of a stool. He stopped once more at the doorway that led to the rest of the house. From here, he could smell the Sender; the most recent scent trail was an exciting one, and indicated that she had tried to climb up to the curtain pelmets. It also indicated that there were points at which she'd been less than successful. He raised his whiskers gingerly, but there was no whiff of the Bigfeet.

"It wouldn't do any harm to poke my nose in, just for a second," he thought. "Would it?"

Southpaw padded in slowly, and kept going.

MARA'S DAY HAD BEGUN wonderfully well, with the Great Pelmet Expedition occupying most of the morning. This had gone better than the most recent expedition, the Garbage Can Trawl, which had led to sharp words from both the Bigfeet and a smacking of her bottom. This was deeply injurious to her dignity, and the kitten had heaved out of her Bigfeet's hands, marching off with her tail, ears and whiskers up to let them know what she thought of the situation. Given that it was a First-class March, with a Flounce thrown in, it was unkind of them to laugh—and by now, she knew exactly when the Bigfeet were laughing at her.

She had scaled one pelmet after another, revelling in the discovery of dust bunnies and other unexpected surprises—half a bangle, a candle stub that was great fun to roll around on the carpet, a dead beetle that she had eaten and wished she hadn't. It tickled her stomach and made everything from her morning bowl of milk onwards taste distinctly beetleish. By afternoon, she was curled up on the back-door staircase, purring and ready for Beraal's company.

Then the skies opened up unexpectedly. She shot in off the stairs after sticking her paws cautiously out into the rain— Beraal tended to go on about the beauty of the monsoons, but the salient feature of rain was its wetness. Mara disapproved, strongly.

She sat for a long while at the kitchen door, waiting for the rain to stop and Beraal to come. Neither wish was fulfilled and gradually, Mara's ears and whiskers began to droop. Her Bigfeet were out, as they often were in the afternoon, and as she padded restlessly around the house, its emptiness gnawed at her. The kitten pounced listlessly at the lizard who sat on the door-frame, but he ran up into the corner and said "Girgit!" to her accusingly.

She played with her ball, but her heart wasn't in it. The Bigfeet came back to find the kitten slumped in a corner, and she made no protest when they picked her up with exclamations, cuddled her and finally tucked her into her blankets, thinking that she must be ill.

Mara listened to the rain, wondering when Beraal would come and see her next. If the rains continued like this, would the cat stay away for days? She tucked herself deeper into her blankets, thinking of Beraal and the many cats her mentor had mentioned—Miao and Hulo, Katar and Southpaw.

Mara's only memories of her own clan were confused. She remembered squirming bodies, the pleasure of drinking warm milk, the rasp of a loving tongue over her still-closed eyes. It was so different from the Nizamuddin cats—except for Beraal, their wariness and their dislike of her bristled across the link. She could smell the unease and ever since she'd become aware of it, the kitten had linked less and less to the cats, preferring to watch the squirrels and the mynah birds.

Mara washed herself and tried to go to sleep, but her mind wandered restlessly. She found the crash of thunder and the flare of lightning terrifying, yet another reminder that the world outside her house was a dark place, filled with unknown perils. The kitten wondered what it would be like to have a friend who said more than "Girgit!" and who didn't come here just because she was the Sender. She thought she'd like to have a friend she could actually cuddle up to—a friend who was a kitten like her.

The plastic bucket of toys in the corner of the room made a thundering, clattering sound as it overturned. Mara opened her eyes and stared at the striped brown kitten who had cannoned straight into the bucket.

Then she closed her eyes again. Beraal had said that the problem with being a Sender was learning to control one's imagination as well as one's talents. It was clear to Mara that she'd been thinking so hard about having a friend that she'd conjured up an imaginary one.

"Sorry!" mewed the imaginary kitten. "I didn't mean to knock things over—um, will your Bigfeet hear that and come running in and beat me up or something? I was about to leave anyway, I just didn't know where to leave from. Um. Or to. I've never been in a house like this before."

Mara stared at the imaginary kitten, who looked far more solid than one might expect from a creature who existed only in her mind.

He had the most bedraggled coat she had seen, and his brown fur was streaked with dirt, while showers of bark and rain fell in a very unimaginary way on her carpet.

"I can see that," she said with a sharp lift to her whiskers, getting up and arching her back in some menace. "You must be an outside cat. How did you get here?"

Southpaw ducked the question, intent on explaining himself fully. "Also, I ate the food in the bowl at the back. Sorry. I was starving. I'll—er, kill you a rat and bring it in tomorrow." He could see the Sender's stiffly curved back, and hoped he wouldn't have to fight her—or worse, surrender. As the intruder, every instinct told him to be polite, but the thought of rolling over and exposing his throat to this tiny orange puffball was more than a little humiliating.

Mara hopped down from the bed and walked up to him, her gait stiff-legged.

Southpaw kept his head down, watching her out of the corner of his eyes. He hoped she wouldn't start spitting and screaming—he found out-and-out brawls a much happier way of settling the intruder issue.

Mara extended a claw and poinked him delicately on his left flank. "Mrrraaawwwwppp!" he howled, forgetting the Bigfeet.

"You're definitely real," she said.

"You didn't have to do that—yes, of course I'm real, what did you think I was? What are you doing? Gerroff!"

Mara was sniffing him all over with immense curiosity. Since he'd intruded into her territory, she didn't have to be polite, and she found the smells rising off his wet fur fascinating. Southpaw wriggled around, protesting, as Mara started to walk up his flank, her nose buried in his fur.

"Is this some kind of surrender ritual?" he mewed, his whiskers and ears twitching uneasily. "Because Katar and Miao said that if you go into another cat's territory, you have to surrender, but they didn't say it would be this ticklish."

Standing on his flank as Southpaw lay on the ground, doing his best to lie still and surrender properly, Mara sniffed at the top of his head one last time, and then she jumped off and stretched her paws, her eyes slightly distant.

"You were with another cat—a bigger fellow, a really big tom, in the rain, and before that you were in the trees (and you didn't wash the bark and mealy bugs off, either) and you went to see a dog together," she said. "Something like that? And you were in a tree where you weren't supposed to be, and just thinking of all the places you've been to outside in a single day makes my head spin. Don't you ever sit still and think?"

"Yes, I do—no, actually I don't, it's really boring sitting still, besides there's so much to explore, even if Katar can be really horrid if I explore the bits that he says I shouldn't—wait a minute." Southpaw raised his head and stared at her, his ears alert. This kitten with the fascinating monsoon green eyes might be smaller than him, but she was full of surprises.

"How did you know all that just from smelling my fur?"

"It's all there," said Mara, digging her claws into his neck as she tried to balance on his spine. "First there's the smells, and then they separate into pictures."

"Really?" said Southpaw, forgetting that he had surrendered. He scrambled to his paws, and Mara slid down his back, landing with a small thump on the ground. Southpaw sniffed at her with interest, and drew back his nose in disappointment.

"I can't smell where you've been today," he said. "But you do smell really—clean. Oh well, I guess that counts as an introduction: I'm Southpaw, and you must be the Sender."

"Just call me Mara," said the kitten. Her natural exuberance was washing over her again, brought back by the surprise visitor. "You're the first cat who's ever come to visit, except Beraal, but she came to kill me, so that doesn't count. How clever of you to find me, was it very hard?"

"Not at all," said Southpaw. He saw the adoration in Mara's eyes dim. His ears drooped. He thought fast, wanting to see those lovely green eyes light up again. "I mean, yes! I've been wanting to come here for many, many moons, but Katar and Miao said the house was off limits—I mean, they vilely prevented me from coming here, and it was only after many battles and skirmishes that I made my way to you, battling this fearsome storm." He wondered whether he'd overdone it, but Mara's eyes shone with admiration and a small but distinct purr rumbled up from her stomach.

"How brave of you," she said, her whiskers oozing adoration. "I had the tigers to play with, but it's been so lonely not having friends of my own. You wouldn't understand, though, you have so many cats to play with outside."

"Play with?" said Southpaw uncertainly. He thought about Hulo and their excursions, of the sorties and raids he'd made stealthily in imitation of Katar and Miao, of their affectionate lessons and scoldings. Mara was purring and rubbing up against his stomach.

Southpaw felt a surprising surge of protectiveness towards this odd cat who preferred being locked up to exploring the outside, and whose unusual talents hadn't helped her find any friends in Nizamuddin. He rubbed heads with her, and brushed whiskers gently, and then he sprawled on the floor, curling himself around the kitten. Her fur was so soft that he felt like staying there forever.

"I have many teachers outside, Mara," he said, "but I have no littermates and no friends the same size as me. So I guess you're not the only one who's lonely. Tell me about your Bigfeet, then, and tell me what you do all day."

The two kittens conversed for a long time, Mara asking questions about what it was like to be outside (and shuddering sometimes at the answers), Southpaw curious about the life of an inside cat. They played a wonderful game of chase, and when the Bigfeet clumped in to the room to check on Mara, Southpaw played hide and seek so well that neither of the Bigfeet saw him.

("Poor things," said Mara. "They can't smell very well, or see very clearly in the dark. You have to be very patient with Bigfeet.") But though Mara was delighted, and happy to share her bed with Southpaw, the brown kitten woke up restless and uneasy just before dawn. The warmth and softness of the blankets was unbelievably luxurious—he hadn't been this comfortable since he'd been a very tiny kitten, cradled in the warmth of his mother's fur. And Mara was a pleasant sleeping companion, giving him enough space to wriggle in his sleep and fight rats in his dreams.

But it was being inside a house that made him uncomfortable. Without the orientation of the sky above, he had lost his bearings and felt as though he had fallen into a pit. The distant chirpings of the birds in the trees made him realize that he'd missed an entire night's hunting, and the air inside was too still, too tamely scented.

"I have to go," he told Mara after she'd coaxed her Bigfeet into bringing her a second helping of breakfast. "The other cats will wonder where I've been, and I should let them know I'm safe."

"No problem," she said, cleaning fish off her whiskers with a dainty paw. "I'll tell Beraal through the link, shall I? Then you can spend the day with me, and perhaps the Bigfeet won't mind if you stay. They're very nice to me, so I don't think they'd mind one more cat."

Southpaw, who'd been doing a perfunctory lick-and-promise instead of a proper toilette, stopped washing his ears and thought very hard.

"Mara," he said, going over to the orange kitten and giving her an affectionate face-wash, "that's such a sweet offer."

Mara ducked out from under his paw. Her whiskers were stiffening. "I hear a 'but' coming," she said.

Southpaw's brown eyes were thoughtful and a little sad. "I'm an outside cat," he said. "The way you feel about coming outside is the way I feel about being inside all the time. So I can't stay."

The kitten said nothing, but he could tell from her tail and whiskers that she didn't want to hear this. He went over and touched his face to her little orange one, watching the golden flecks in her ravishing green eyes.

"I'll come back this afternoon, before I go on the evening sorties with the other cats," he said. "And if you'll let me, I'll come and see you as often as I can, Mara. Deal?"

The Sender's whiskers sprang back to life, and she head-butted him with such vigour that he almost fell over.

"I don't know what it is that you like about being outside," she said, "it seems smelly and scary to me. But come back when you can. I've never had a friend like you before."

Southpaw heard the kitchen door open, and listened for the Bigfeet to leave so that he could make his exit.

"Neither have I, Mara," he said. "Keep your whiskers up, little one. I'll be back soon."

He didn't know that the Sender watched him from her windowsill as he bounded down the wrought iron staircase, and ran madly through the park in search of Hulo and the rest. She watched him until all she could see was a brown smudge disappearing into the green hedges, their leaves washed and gleaming from the night's rain.

CHAPTER NINE

Mara's Kingdom

Sitting on top of the bookcase, Mara surveyed her kingdom with a strong sense of triumph. It had taken her three attempts to scale the bookshelves. The first had been summarily interrupted by her Bigfeet, who had plucked her off the last but one shelf from the top, restored the books she had knocked down in her mountaineering efforts and grumbled at her good-naturedly.

The second was rendered unsuccessful when she decided to try to scale the bookcase from the back. She soon found herself suspended in mid-air from a shelf, holding on with her front paws and cycling furiously with her hind legs to try to get her bottom back on the shelf after the encyclopaedias fell forwards, depriving Mara of a foothold. On her third try, the kitten considered the books on the shelves carefully before charting a path over the paperbacks and the leather-bound volumes of Tagore, giving the loose-leaf manuscripts a wide berth. She made it up to the top and stared at the room, enchanted by the way it all looked so different from her new perch.

One of her Bigfeet walked by, and Mara had to restrain herself from jumping onto his shoulder. She thought she could make it if she used her claws to find purchase, but previous leaping-on-Bigfeet exercises had been met with a certain lack of enthusiasm. Besides, it felt good being up on top of the bookcase. It made the kitten feel like the queen of explorers, and her Bigfeet would find it hard to reach her, unless she wanted them to.

After swatting at a fly, and eating a cobweb, and surveying her kingdom yet again, Mara silently admitted the truth: she was bored. Her morning was spent with the Bigfeet, who were slow learners and resisted most of her efforts to train them. Beraal usually came by in the late evening for training exercises—it had taken them several tries until Mara could go for her walks without sending the Nizamuddin cats into a tizzy, but she'd finally got the hang of it. This left the whole afternoon, and there were only so many catnaps she could take. And Southpaw hadn't reappeared, and she didn't know where to find him.

As she pondered her options, her whiskers rose thoughtfully. There was one place she could go, she thought. She would like to see Rudra The Great And Many Striped or whatever his name was, but would the other cats make a fuss if his father roared at them again? They probably would; but what if she tried her hand at sending without linking to the general band of cats?

Mara chased her tail, almost catching it several times, and

stirring the dust on top of the bookshelves, while she thought about this. Beraal had managed to teach her not to broadcast her status updates on an hourly basis to the entire cat community. It was something to do with whisker and nostril control, and Mara wasn't quite sure how she did it, but when she twitched her whiskers a little to the left and screwed up her nose a little to the right, she seemed to be able to control her linking better. Sending and not linking, though, would probably require whisker, nose and ear control at the same time—something she and Beraal had practised separately, but never put together. No time like the present to try, she decided, and shut her eyes.

She sped out of the park, feeling light and happy inside. Mara hovered over the trees for a bit, watching the squirrels play, and it was only when a baby squirrel chittered in dismay at seeing a cat so far up that she hastily moved on. Over the Golf Course, she had to adjust the height: she was moving far too high, and she startled several crows and an indignant pair of bulbuls before she managed to come down to a relatively more sedate level.

She seemed to be moving faster, and Mara gave her whiskers free rein, inadvertently moving onto the bandwidth of the Supreme Court cats for several moments before she could readjust. The colony of stately cats at the Court was unpleasantly surprised when she whizzed by. "Did you see an orange cat go past, by any chance? At a very fast and, if I might say so, unseemly clip?" Affit, a plump black cat with a neat white ring of fur around his neck, asked his colleague.

Davit considered the question. "The problem," he said, "is that your question ignores the salient facts. The aforementioned cat is a kitten, and it appeared to be moving at speed through the air. As your learned self will agree, since it is unlikely that a cat qua cat (or a kitten qua kitten) would sail through the air, my learned self concludes that the kitten qua kitten is a hypothetical kitten."

Affit raised a paw. "We are agreed. Unless we see sufficient proof, to be submitted in triplicate at the office of the Bigfeet Registrar before tea time today, our conclusion will be that there is no such cat or kitten thereof."

"Quite," said Davit, resuming his slow, magisterial stroll around the lawns of the Supreme Court. "Though it made my ears twitch when it brushed by—too damn close, even for a hypothetical kitten, Affit, too damn close."

Mara was grappling with other dilemmas as she hovered over the zoo. Instead of going blindly in, as she had the first time, she wanted a better feel of this new territory. She entered cautiously and was immediately overwhelmed by a cacophony of sounds and smells.

The kitten shimmered in confusion. Back in her home, Mara had to catch herself before she fell off the bookshelves, and relocated herself more securely at the back of the top shelf. The zoo was almost too rich in scents and life, the images and odours swirling in her tiny head, making her feel dizzy.

The zebras whispered in her ear, singing long poems about the hills and plains of Africa. The bears rumbled as they thought of the fruits they missed so much, the apricots and peaches of the Himalayas. The orangutans scratched their bellies and tails and dreamed of their homes high in the trees of the jungles of Borneo.

And in the middle of all of this, the roars, the chitterings and chatterings, the miaows and the bird-calls, Mara heard a small, clear voice. "I know you have a tail, Tantara, and so do I, but I've tried and I've tried and I just can't hang upside down from the bars the way you do."

Mara took a deep breath and shot past the cages, past the birds, past the sambar deer, past the sinister snakes who were sunning themselves on the rocks in their enclosure, past the eland antelope and the scaly anteater, past the leopards, who were glaring at a family of Bigfeet who were making loud comments and offering them popcorn.

She almost skidded into the tiger enclosure, but at the very last moment, the memory of Ozymandias's massive face and gigantic whiskers (and large, sharp teeth) came back to her. She slowed and cautiously peered into the enclosure.

Rani and Ozzy were nowhere to be seen, but from the scent markings they had left, which stood out in Mara's head like flashing lights, she guessed the two big cats were sleeping in the small cave towards the back of the enclosure. The grass was green only in patches, and near the artificial river that flowed through the middle of the tigers' domain, Rudra sat on the grass, talking to thin air.

Up on the bookcase, Mara cycled her paws in the air, mewing happily. "Hello, RudraTheGreatAndPowerful—I'm so sorry, I've forgotten the rest. How're you? Why are you talking to yourself?"

The tiger cub raised his tail and roared cheerfully. "It's Justamara, isn't it? I wondered where you'd disappeared. Would you like to meet— Tantara, stop that at once!"

The langur had sneaked around silently behind the kitten and was glaring at Mara from the branches of the large silk cotton tree. The kitten had her back to the monkey, and what Rudra saw was Tantara's tail whipping out to curl around the kitten's neck.

"Gotcha!" said Tantara, ignoring Rudra and tightening her tail into a noose. The young langur didn't like the idea of an intruder, and was hoping that the kitten would be so scared that she would leave. But to Tantara's surprise, her tail slid harmlessly *through* the kitten's shoulders. Mara didn't seem to have noticed.

"Who's Tantara?" asked Mara.

"What manner of beast is this?" asked Tantara, who was trying to smack the kitten over the head with her tail and finding it very disconcerting when the tail simply slid to the ground each time.

"Tantara, I said 'stop that'!" said Rudra, baring his small fangs in a growl. "This is my friend, Justamara. She's a kitten, and she came to visit me the other day. Justamara, this is Tantara. She's my best friend in the zoo."

The kitten turned and watched in surprise as Tantara was caught in the middle of trying to pat her own orange tail. The langur was chittering to herself as her paw went through Mara's tail, and it didn't sound as though she was very happy about it.

"Could you stop doing that, please," said Mara politely, following Rudra's example and switching to Junglee when she spoke to the langur. "I can't feel your paws, but it makes my whiskers go wobbly when you do that." She got a good look at Tantara, who had a beautiful black face crowned by soft, almost-white fur, and blinked. "How pretty and silvery your fur is!" she said. "And how beautifully long your tail is! And what a lovely plume it has at the end of it—mine is so short, I wish it would grow, but it hasn't. And how perfect your paws are! I've never met a langur before, but I expect you meet cats all the time over here. Please, call me Mara. That's my real name."

Tantara scratched her head, more than a little dazed. She peered at the orange kitten and realized that in addition to being apparently permeable, Mara was hovering a few feet off the ground. The langur didn't know what to make of this—but Mara's flattery, however, was very welcome. She preened and twirled her tail round and round.

"It is a lovely tail, isn't it?" she said.

Rudra let out a long, tigerish sigh. "You've got her started," the cub said wearily. "Now we've had it."

Tantara ignored him, happy to show off in front of a new audience. "I've been trying to teach Rudra how to do the ballet," she said, "but he refuses to try. He insists you cats can't use your tails properly, the way they were meant to be used."

Mara's eyes were worshipful as she looked up at the langur. "But how are tails meant to be used?" she said. "I use mine all the time, for balance, for curling up to sleep in, to listen to the way the wind is blowing and who's coming my way."

"Oho!" said the langur. "But can you do this?"

And she hooked her tail onto a branch, and swung upside down from it. "See?" she called. "Look, Mara, no hands!"

Rudra settled down morosely. "Now she'll never stop," he said to Mara.

"But it's wonderful watching her!" said the kitten.

The langur was swinging from branch to branch. She used her long elegant hands to do dazzling aerial loop-the-loops while her tail acted as a balance; she went all the way to the tops of the trees, and trapezed from one to another; then she used her tail to help her rappel back down the massive trunk of the silk cotton tree.

"Wow!" said Mara.

"Thank you, thank you," said Tantara, grooming herself modestly. "I've been working on that trapeze act for some time. Any old monkey can use their hands to swing around, but it takes a langur to use your tail with real grace."

Before Rudra could grumble some more, Mara looked at her two new friends and said, "Do you think we could play a game of Hide-and-Seek? You're so fast on the ground, Rudra, and Tantara is so quick in the branches, and I'm sort of in between. It might be fun."

Passing by the tiger's cage, the zookeepers were surprised to see what looked like a langur and a tiger cub playing a complex game. It seemed almost as though they had a third companion, but of course there was no other animal inside the cage. The oldest keeper watched for a while and then shrugged. In the jungle, langurs always called to warn other creatures of the per-ambulations of tigers, and tigers sometimes killed the beautiful grey monkeys. But being in the cages changed animal behav-iour, and he wasn't surprised to see the unusual friendship. Stranger pairings had happened in the zoo, and he personally remembered a time when a very young nilgai antelope had imprinted on the rhinos, and spent a year walking around thinking it was three times its size.

The youngest keeper watched for a while, entranced. It was the oddest thing, but as the white tiger cub and the silvery-grey langur played together, he could almost swear he saw a small orange kitten flash in between the two of them from time to time. The muggy heat of the monsoon made one see the most peculiar visions, he reflected, before he moved on to see how the great Indian bustards were doing.

That visit marked the first of many, and over time, Mara became quite a fixture in Rudra's enclosure. Tantara often joined them, and the three became close friends, as Ozzy and Rani watched the younger generation contentedly. The only problem was caused, inadvertently, by Mara's Bigfeet: if they picked her up or cuddled her or moved her from one spot to another while she was sending, the connection broke. It was often hard for Mara to come back, if the Bigfeet wanted to play with her (or more ominously, to brush her fur or clean her ears or feed her cod liver oil pills), but the tiger cub and the langur got used to her sudden departures.

One evening, as they lay sprawled out under the cool shade of the banyan tree, Rani watched her mate's tail twitch back and forth, back and forth, and said, "Out with it, Ozzy. What's gnawing at your mind?"

The tiger brought his tail to a halt, and rubbed his giant head fondly against his mate's shoulder. "Is it that obvious, Rani? I'm just concerned about where this friendship will lead, that's all."

Rani indicated the happy pile of striped fur, where the langur and the tiger were rolling around in the mud while Mara's red fur shimmered above their heads.

"It seems to be going well, Ozzy," she said. "They're all good friends, and while it may be unusual to be friends with a kitten who's not really here, Rudra seems so much happier, much less lonely."

"What about Mara?" said Ozzy. "She's coming here to play with a tiger cub and a langur—shouldn't she be prowling her own territory, hunting and playfighting with other kittens? And besides, Rudra's growing up."

The tiger turned his great head, and his amber eyes looked deeply into Rani's questioning face. "Do you remember how long it took the two of us to fight back the urge to eat Tantara?"

Rani began washing her long whiskers. "We were jungle-raised, Ozzy," she said. "Rudra came here when he was so young—he barely remembers the forests."

Ozymandias rose to his feet and padded around their part of the enclosure, trying to explain what had been going through his mind. "You and I carry the jungle with us in a way Rudra doesn't, that's true," he said.

"Rudra knows only the zoo," Rani said. "Here, we become friends depending on who's in the next cage—so the snakes have to get on with the turtles, and the hyenas talk to the jackals, even though they would be at each other's throats outside the bars. So perhaps Rudra will always see Tantara as a friend—never as a langur, really, never as prey."

Ozzy shook his great head in dissent, and the stripes on his fur rippled.

"Rudra's not a tiny cub any more," he said quietly. "His instincts will begin to kick in one of these days. And then we had better be prepared to handle that. For Tantara's sake, not for our little cub's sake, Rani."

Though he was aware that it was against his nature, Ozzy had become surprisingly fond of both the kitten and the langur. The kitten reminded him of a cub he and Rani had lost many years ago. And Tantara made him laugh. In the days when Ozzy had prowled the jungles, ruling the night, ruling the ravines, king of the gullies and thickets of Ranthambore National Park, he had enjoyed the company of the langurs and often secretly watched them, marvelling at their quick intelligence and liking their loyalty to members of their troupe. He might sometimes growl at Tantara when the monkey's antics went too far, but he would never harm her. But Ozzy remembered how his own blood had leaped and tingled at the prospect of a kill—any kill—when he had begun to learn the ways of a hunter, and he wondered how Rudra would respond when he grew up.

There was no easy way out that the tiger could see. He agreed with Rani that their cub had been much happier since his two companions had lightened his time in the cage, but Ozzy had a deep respect for the silent songs of instinct, the calls that ran in the blood. He worried about the future of this friendship between his son and the langur, but for the moment, he let them enjoy this season of play and untroubled contentment.

AND THEN, JUST A WEEK LATER, the tigers received a surprise. The large grille door of their enclosure opened with a clanking, whirring sound that made Mara, Tantara and Rudra look up from their exhilarating game of chase-the-dried-leaves. The keepers usually opened the smaller grille, and while they kept a cautious eye on Ozzy and Rani, they didn't often go through the full drill.

Ozzy growled, an ominous "hoooom" that throbbed through the enclosure, when the keepers moved towards Rani and him. He guessed from the nets and tranquilizer guns they carried that they meant business, and while he was normally a very co-operative, easy-going tiger, he growled and growled until one of the keepers realized what was bothering him.

"HALOOM!" Ozzy roared. "HALOOOOOM! HALOO-OOOM!" "Quick," the keeper said to his colleagues, "bring the cub back to him. The father's worried that we might take the cub away." Tantara bounded up into the branches, emitting alarm calls, when the keepers moved in their direc-tion, and Rudra, imitating his father, growled menacingly too.

"Haloom!" he said, growling as loudly as he could.

Mara listened to the keepers' chatter and the kitten's whis-kers came down in relief. "It's all right, Rudra," she said. "All they want is for you to go and join your parents. They're bring-ing something in, not taking any of you out, so I guess it should be fine."

The keepers watched in puzzlement and surprise as the small tiger cub suddenly seemed to listen very hard, his big ears cocked, and then padded over to his parents. They stared even more when the cub rubbed up against Ozzy and Rani, offering a few halooms, and when all three of the tigers turned and stalked into their artificial cave.

"Well, that was easy!" said the head keeper in some surprise. He made sure they had the grille leading to the cave securely locked, though. He had no idea why the tiger clan was being so co-operative but he wasn't about to take any chances. "Bring her in!" he called.

Mara stared as a small, covered cage on wheels was trundled in. As the scent from the cage reached the tigers in the cave, they all heard a slow, enraged rumble from Rudra, much louder than his "haloom" had been. Rani growled, low in her throat. Mara could see the beautiful white tiger pacing up and down the length of the cave, her eyes blazing. Ozzy was up on his feet, too, his paws slamming against the walls as he roared.

Across the rest of the zoo, the roars and growls of the tigers rippled outwards, setting off a chain reaction. The bears woke up and slouched out of their cages. The hoolock gibbons howled and gibbered, racing each other to the very tops of their cages. The sambar deer barked; the nilgai antelope shivered and pawed the ground, seeking shelter in the cool, dark bushes at the backs of their enclosure. "Heee heee heee *heee* heee!" called the hyenas, their laughter rising in manic waves.

The keepers were opening the cage doors cautiously, using long, wooden poles. The cover was lifted off and the keepers backed away en masse. Mara blinked as a small, golden-and-black striped cub with glittering green eyes walked sedately down the ramp.

She paused at the foot, taking in her new surroundings, and stepped out daintily, ignoring Mara and moving straight to the pool that served as tiger wallow and water bowl. The cub washed her face and her whiskers with perfect serenity, as if she couldn't hear Ozzy's bellows or Rudra's snarls.

One of the keepers took a cloth out of the cage and Mara smelled the new cub's scent on it. He shoved it into the tigers' cave at the end of a pole. There was a murderous roar from Ozzy and the steel grille shook as the tiger charged at it, but the grille held, and then there was silence, as the tigers took turns sniffing the cloth.

Tantara reappeared in the trees, watching cautiously as the new cub stretched and walked around the enclosure, checking out the food bowls, stepping around the mud wallows. The keepers backed out of the enclosure, taking up positions just outside the walls with their tranquilizer guns at the ready, Mara noted. The langur and the kitten stared at the intruder, who seemed stunningly pretty by tiger standards, and very poised.

Mara felt a tug on her line and sighed. Her Bigfeet were back. "I have to go," she told Tantara. "I'll be back as soon as I can."

"Hurry back," said the langur, whose black face and liquid golden eyes seemed uneasy. "I don't know what to make of this, Mara. Come back as soon as you can."

But the kitten had a difficult time getting away from her home in Nizamuddin West. The Bigfeet had brought her catnip mice and her favourite feathery toys from the market, and they wanted to play. Mara wrestled with her instincts, which were urging her to comply, and her conscience, which was suggesting she should go back to the zoo, pronto. Her instincts won, and the kitten spent a guiltily happy hour playing Kill-The-Fearsome-Feather with her Bigfeet. Then it was time to eat, and she was so tired after the morning at the zoo, and an afternoon of rough-and-tumble, that she went to sleep in a small, untidy heap on a pile of cushions. Her naps were always deeper, and longer, after she had spent time at the zoo—sendings were fun but tiring, and her Bigfeet sometimes murmured among themselves about the kitten's extraordinary ability to sleep through all the friendly clamour and bustle of the neighbourhood.

Mara meant to go back the next day, but the Bigfeet had an unexpected visitor, and between trying to steal the new Bigfoot's shaving brush and socks and finding time for Beraal's lessons, a week went by before the kitten could get to the zoo.

When she did, she popped up near Tantara, who was rocking moodily on a high branch. "Sorry, my Bigfeet kept me really busy," the kitten said. "Where's Rudra?"

"With his new friend," said Tantara, wrapping her tail around herself and rocking harder. There was a rough patch on her tail that Mara hadn't seen before, an abrasion with an ugly scab like knotted wood.

Down on the ground, the two tiger cubs were exploring a brand-new sandpit.

"Shall we join them?" said Mara.

"Oh, I'm not welcome," said Tantara. "Her royal highness doesn't think tigers should consort with common langurs, and after the last play session with Rudra—never mind that. You go join them if you want to."

The kitten shimmered in confusion. "But I thought he spat at her when she came into the enclosure?"

Tantara looked sad. "Not for long. Rani smelled the scent of the cub on that piece of cloth, and when they let her out an hour later, she went over and made friends. Rudra followed, and he spat at the cub the first four times she tried to talk to him. So she went off on her own with Rani, and soon enough, he began to follow them around. Now they're the best of friends, as you can see."

"So maybe we can all play together—one more cub means that we can play different games, can't we?" said Mara.

The langur groomed her long paws, looking down at the kitten, who was hovering in mid-air just under a branch.

"Mara," she said gently, "I know we've had a lot of fun together, but something that cub said some days back made me think hard. One of the reasons why I come over here so often is that I don't have other langur friends. There were no other langur babies when I was born in the zoo, and the orangutans and chimps are just—different, that's all. I can't talk to the other monkeys; they can't help their instincts, the macaques run away from our kind. Rudra's like me. He was brought here when he was really little, and though there were always the leopards and the lynxes, there were no other tiger cubs. And I sometimes wonder whether you shouldn't be making friends with cats back home, wherever your home is."

"But we're friends," said Mara. "What's wrong with being friends?"

The langur shook her head sadly. "Nothing's wrong with being friends, Mara," she said. "It's just that it's—well, as young Tawny said, who ever heard of a tiger being friends with a langur and a kitten?" Mara looked from the langur's lonely figure in the branches back to the two tiger cubs. "But she doesn't understand, Tantara, she only just got here. I'm going to go over and introduce myself. I'm sure it'll be fine once I've explained the situation."

"Mara—," Tantara began, but the kitten had already left.

The langur watched her thoughtfully. And near the tiger cave, Ozzy watched, too. The tiger's grave eyes met the langur's golden ones, and both silently acknowledged a mutual sadness.

"—we never did that in the jungle, of course, but I suppose you have different rules here," the golden-and-black tiger cub was saying. "Hey, Rudra! Sorry I couldn't come over earlier. What are you playing? Can Tantara and me join in?" Mara brought herself down to hover closer to Rudra's face.

The new cub let out a surprised growl. "What on earth is *that?*" she demanded.

To Mara's astonishment, Rudra seemed embarrassed. "This is a friend—well, a visitor. Mara comes by from time to time to see me, though she lives quite far away. Mara, this is Mulligatawny, but she prefers to be called Tawny."

"Hello," Mara began to say, but the tiger cub interrupted, her tail lashing slowly to-and-fro.

"You poor, poor fellow," she said sweetly to Rudra. "I can see how difficult it's been for you, having no friends."

"But he does have friends," said Mara indignantly, bobbing into Tawny's space so that the tiger cub had to acknowledge her presence. "Tantara and I are here every day. We'd love to get to know you, too, of course."

She stopped when the lovely tiger cub's whiskers began to tremble with laughter. "She's a scream, Rudra!" said Tawny. "No wonder you allowed her to entertain you." The tiger turned to face the kitten. "It must have been so tiring for you, Mara, coming all the way from—wherever. You don't have to do that any more now that I'm here. But you're welcome to drop in once in a while."

The kitten's hackles rose. "Rudra, you're not going to let her talk to us that way, are you?" she demanded.

Tawny stretched, and Mara saw how beautifully her muscles rippled, taut under her striped skin. "Us?" she said. "Kitten, I don't know what world you live in, but me, I live in the real world and it truly is a jungle out there. There's no room in the jungle for a cat who—" swiftly, she unsheathed her claws and swatted lazily at Mara, her paws passing right through the image of the kitten—"doesn't even actually exist in this cage. And as for a tiger making friends with a langur, oh please. Ask Miss Golden-Eyes there whether she enjoyed their last little wrestling match. Go find your own kind, kitten. No hard feelings, but it's like calls to like in this world."

Mara's tail and whiskers had gone all the way down. The orange kitten stared from one cub to the other. When she looked back at the tree, Tantara made a wry, I-told-you-so gesture with her expressive paws.

"So that's it?" she said slowly. "Rudra, you don't want to be friends with us because Tantara's a different species, and because I'm not really here? That's what you feel?"

"Yes," said Tawny. "That's what he feels."

The white tiger cub was standing there, looking from Mara to Tawny, his tail switching uncertainly. He turned to his mother, but Rani was impassive, and didn't come forward. Ozzy's great head was turned away. The two adult tigers sat motionless and silent by the watering hole.

"Tawny," said Rudra, "would you go away for a moment, please, and leave me alone with my friends?"

Tawny's green eyes narrowed and then flashed with anger.

"If you insist," she said, padding away with her bristly chin up and her back held very, very stiffly. She settled herself under a tree, with her back to Rudra and his friends.

"Come down here," said Rudra to Mara. The kitten hovered stubbornly above his head. "Please? The three of us need to talk."

The cub padded over to Tantara's tree, and after some hesitation, the langur came down to the lower branches.

"I'm sorry about the way Tawny spoke," the cub said. "She isn't used to our kind of friendships—she's grown up in the jungles, and there the rules are different."

Mara's tail began to rise every so slightly. "So we can still be friends?"

Tantara and Rudra exchanged glances. "You know, Mara," said the langur, "perhaps this is a good time for all of us to step back a bit, take some time out. I've been thinking that I never hang out with the lemurs, even though they've often tried to make friends. And Rudra and Tawny need time to get to know each other."

The kitten couldn't believe what she was hearing. "Why can't all four of us be friends? We never cared before about being different species, did we?"

Rudra sighed. "It didn't matter before, Mara, because in a way we were all cubs, or kittens, or younglings—we were just babies playing together. But Tantara's right, and while Tawny may be harsh, both of them are saying the same thing. We need some time to find our own friends."

Mara flicked her ears stubbornly. "I don't see why the differences matter," she said.

The tiger cub caught his mother's gaze, and for a long time, he and Rani seemed to be engaged in a quiet, private exchange.

"All right," he said. "I hate doing this, but maybe you should see this for yourself."

And with that, he opened his mouth and roared.

It was not a small haloom this time. His voice had broken, and this was a full-throated, slow growl that deepened into the menacing roar of an adult tiger. Rudra's fur rippled and as he roared, his chest expanded. Mara mewed and mewed in instinctive fear at the metamorphosis of her friend. Tantara had shinnied back up, all the way to the top of the branches, and she gibbered and chattered, sending out deep warning cries.

It was only by a whisker that Mara managed to hold on to her control, and it took all of her efforts not to break down and broadcast her terror across the general cat link. But Beraal's lessons held, and when the kitten finally opened her eyes, Rudra had stopped roaring and was watching her with compassion.

"I'm growing up, Mara," he said quietly. "For the last month, it's been harder playing games with the two of you and keeping it gentle. It's the hunting instinct. I can't help it. I—no, you should ask Tantara to tell you the rest."

Tantara, who had slid back down the branches, rejoining them but staying several lengths away from Rudra, felt a pang go through her at the sight of Mara's miserable face. "Mara," she said gently. "Look at my face. Look at my tail." The Sender's whiskers went taut as she saw the claw marks on the langur's face, understood the meaning of the healing scar on her tail; familiar scars, left by a paw so much like her own.

"You mustn't blame Rudra," Tantara went on. "We were

playing a game of chase-and-catch the other day, while Tawny was napping. It was an accident, at first. His claw scratched at my tail—just a scratch, nothing more. But we both smelled the blood. He's not a cub any more, Mara. He's a young tiger, a hunter. He couldn't stop himself from attacking me."

"If Rani hadn't bounded up and stopped me, I don't know what would have happened," Rudra said. His voice was low and sad, but when he raised his head, he held Mara's gaze with steady eyes. "Tawny doesn't understand the friendship the three of us had, but she's my kind," he said. "I can play-wrestle with her without worrying that she'll be hurt, or worse. But Tantara can't join in any more."

"It's true, Mara," said Tantara. "I could never play with Tawny at all, or even come as close to her as I can even now to Rudra, because her hunter's instincts are fully developed. And just as he needs to be around his own kind right now, at least when he's growing up and learning to be an adult, so do I. Our scents are changing, Mara. Our blood is changing."

Mara's face had become very small. "Does this mean I can't visit, ever again?"

"But of course you can visit, Mara," said another, richer voice. Ozzy had padded silently over to the group. The great tiger had been listening to the exchange for a while and he felt sorry for the kitten.

"You'd be welcome any time, and you're not at risk, because you're not really here," he continued. "None of us can harm you, not even Tawny."

Mara sent Ozzy a warm hug through her whiskers, grateful beyond words to the big cat.

"Tawny thinks I'm a freak," said the kitten.

"You know, Mara," said Ozzy, "you're not a freak. I've seen some freaks in my time—a tiger cub with two heads, a pair of deer joined at the hip—and you're not part of that company. But you are a very unusual kitten. And you may not realize this now, but as time passes, you may not want to come back so often, though I hope you will always visit us. Think of it, though. If Tantara's making friends with the gibbons and Rudra has a tiger friend, shouldn't you be making a few kitten friends yourself? What about that Southpaw chap you've mentioned—doesn't he drop in?"

Southpaw did drop in, intermittently, and Mara enjoyed playing with him. But Southpaw was always urging her to come outside and that was something Mara didn't want to do—not yet at any rate. She preferred being safely at the zoo, visiting her friends but not having to actually step out of the comfort of her Bigfeet house. As she took a deep breath to say just this, something in Ozzy's wise, concerned eyes took the words from her whiskers.

The langur and the cub watched the kitten as she shimmered uneasily in and out of view. Then Mara got a grip on herself and her outlines solidified.

"Thank you for explaining, Ozzy," she said. "I'll come back often to visit all of you."

She gave Rudra a wordless head-rub, and twined her tail briefly with Tantara's long, grey one. "See you," said the kitten awkwardly.

"See you, Mara," said Rudra. "Take care of yourself, and come back, don't forget us when you've made new friends."

The kitten left before they could see how sadly her whiskers were drooping. Rani guessed just how lonely and sad Mara felt, and the tigress's heart went out to the kitten. "I hope she grows really close to someone of her own kind soon, Ozzy," she said to her mate later that night.

"She will, Rani," said Ozzy reassuringly. "If that kitten can make friends with tigers, she can make friends with the whole world. Just give her time."

BACK HOME, SITTING MISERABLY on the steps, Mara made a pathetic heap in the twilight. Beraal watched the small, sad figure, linking via whisker for a while and listening to the kitten's sorrows. When Mara had finished, Beraal was beside her.

"If you please," said Mara, "no lessons today?"

"No, Mara," Beraal said. "No lessons today." She touched her whiskers to the kitten, and she washed Mara's ears until the kitten felt comforted.

As night fell, Beraal said to Mara, "They're right, you know, the tigers and your friend the langur. You need to come out of the house, Mara. Southpaw and I would be glad to take you around, introduce you to the other cats—we could spend some time getting used to the park, if you like."

Mara withdrew her whiskers. "I like it inside," she said. "The outside is scary unless I'm sending and travelling by link. I don't want to come out of the house, Beraal." And nothing the black-and-white cat could say would change the kitten's mind.

Beraal gave up finally, and after making sure that Mara was all right, she went off to do some mousing down at the dargah.

She would have asked Miao for advice, but the Siamese had stationed herself at the Shuttered House these past few days. Before she had taken up her watch, she had said to Beraal, her fur radiating menace: "That place has been on my mind and my whiskers ever since Southpaw brought back news of Datura and the ferals. The air in that house is changing, and if their Bigfoot is sick, we may have to prepare for dark days."

Beraal had not entirely understood—to her, as to the rest of the Nizamuddin cats, the Shuttered House was a sinister, brooding place in the heart of their colony, but one to be avoided and padded around. Miao had watched the queen's puzzlement, and said only, "I'll need to spend a few days near the Shuttered House, to scent the ferals better. And if they are indeed going to come out, then we may need allies. Help Katar look after the clan, Beraal, I'll be back soon."

AFTER BERAAL LEFT, the kitten stayed out on the stairs longer than usual, watching the mynah birds squabble and the squirrels play games of tag. The cheels circled overhead in companionable pairs. The grey musk shrews took turns digging up their mounds of earth, far down below at the bottom of the neem tree. It seemed to Mara that every creature in Nizamuddin had friends and companions, except for her.

Southpaw's visits were unpredictable, and she thought miserably about how sometimes when her Bigfeet were out and she was alone, she would wander around the empty house, her tail down and dragging on the floor. If she couldn't visit the tigers as often as she used to, there would be a lot of empty hours for Mara to fill.

The Bigfeet found her crying softly to herself on the stairs, and when they picked her up, she was grateful for the cuddle. They fed her a rich meat stew and cooed to her, and let her sleep on their bed, and gradually, the kitten began to feel better. But the sore, empty space in her heart didn't go away, and Mara was often aware of it over the next few days, even when she and Beraal were busy with their lessons, even as she played cheerful games with the Bigfeet.

When the clouds began to gather a few days later and the skies rumbled with thunder, Mara sat by the window and watched the first monsoon of her young life come down, the grey of the outside mirroring the way the little kitten felt inside. The high winds brought in tantalizing whispers of the rain-spattered trees and bushes, the rooftop universe of the wildings. But Mara didn't think she would ever be at home in that vast, wide world where the skies yawned endlessly and the whiskers of the other cats bristled when they talked of the Sender.

CHAPTER TEN

First Blood

"Yes, Katar," said Southpaw. "No, Katar." This felt lamentably familiar to him, and his bottom was still hurting from where it had been soundly smacked by the tom.

The tomcat glared at the kitten. "First you go bouncing into the Shuttered House, then you sneak into a Bigfoot house, and now the Cobra's Tree! What in the name of my whiskers and paws were you—" Miao emerged silently in their midst. It was as though she had materialized from out of the roots of the ancient flame tree, where Katar had taken Southpaw. She sat with her paws neatly folded, as if she'd been there all along. Her steady gaze rested on Southpaw for what felt, to the striped kitten, like an eternity. Then she moved forward. Southpaw felt the creamy fur on her face, soft and silky, brush his own fur with extreme gentleness; the Siamese's whiskers rose, quivered, and wrapped around his smaller, more bristly whiskers. He didn't dare move. They stayed like that for a few moments, his frightened brown eyes locking with her faraway but sharp blue ones, and then she sighed and moved back, stretching prettily.

"I agree with Katar that wandering into Bigfoot houses is a very bad idea but you may go to the Sender's house, so long as you stay out of the way of her Bigfeet," said Miao. "It might not be a bad thing for either of you to be friends—it may even be necessary. And as for your inability to keep your whiskers out of trouble, I'll see you at twilight on the wall of the cow shelter. Don't be late."

She turned to go, her beautiful, black-tipped tail tilted for better balance.

"Miao," said Southpaw, his own stubby tail waving uncertainly, "what are we going to do?"

The Siamese's blue eyes met his again.

"If you're old enough to climb the Cobra's Tree, and to get into the Sender's house without permission, you're old enough to hunt."

Katar's ears flicked in protest.

"But he's not even six months old yet!" he said. "His whiskers are still black, he doesn't have even one white whisker in the lot!" A kitten had to have at least three white whiskers before being allowed to hunt.

The Siamese's tail flicked once, sharply.

"At the rate he's going," she said, "he won't have even one white whisker before he gets himself killed. If he's canny enough to survive Datura's poisonous lot, he has what it takes to be a real predator. At twilight, Southpaw, remember."

THE NOISE OF THE BIGFEET'S CARS had dwindled, and lights twinkled in their houses, making them look to Southpaw's eye even more like rat warrens. He had spent the afternoon at the Sender's house, creeping in when her Bigfeet weren't looking. But he'd reached the wall before the sky began to darken, even though he'd had to weave through the legs of Bigfeet on their way to a wedding. Southpaw took a detour to avoid the gaudy ceremonial tent, and though his nose twitched greedily at the smell of meat cooking, he resisted the temptation to carry out a one-kitten raid.

The pearly light of the evening slowly shaded into indigo; the kitten waited, motionless on the wall of the cow shelter. Night fell, and there was a touch of cold in the air. Southpaw listened to the chatter of the birds, their high-pitched evening quarrels, but he stayed where he was, foregoing the pleasures of chasing squirrels and beetles along the wall.

The moon had sailed high up into the deep indigo sky, and the chattering birds had long since gone to sleep by the time Miao arrived. The Siamese wasn't there one moment, and then the kitten felt the fur on his back rise. He turned his head, and there she was, perched on the wall as though she had never been anywhere else.

He made no reference to the time he'd spent waiting, nor did the Siamese, but as she indicated with her whiskers that he should follow her, the kitten received the impression that he had passed some sort of unspoken test.

The night was humid, the air scented with queen of the night and jasmine blossoms. There was a half-moon, partly obscured by clouds. As they slipped down the wall into the undergrowth, Southpaw felt his fur quiver with excitement. "Miao, where are we——?"

The older cat turned and cuffed him, her claws out just enough to leave a thin red line on his neck. "The first rule," she said. "No mewing. No whisker linking unless I say so, because your prey is small enough to pick up the vibrations if they're close enough to us. And smart enough to make a run for it." She cuffed him again, this time slamming his head to the right and holding it down so that he could see a frightened grey musk shrew scutter away into the safety of the lantana bushes.

Southpaw's flanks were heaving from the pain, but more than that, the kitten was in shock. Miao had washed him every day from as far back as he could remember, her tongue gentle as she teased out the tangles in his fur.

She had brought him his first piece of mouse, which tasted heavenly, and fed it to him herself. She had let him play with her tail and pounce on it, only lifting him gently away when he nipped too hard. The older cat had never rolled him on the ground, as Hulo did when he exasperated the tom, or smacked his belly, as Katar often did, or so much as nipped his neck in warning—but she had just cuffed him much harder than either of the other cats would have.

For a while he followed her in miserable silence, his head still ringing from the blows. The earth was cool under his paws, and when they crossed the stone path, he followed Miao's example, retracting his claws.

Gradually, his mind cleared and he began to watch Miao more closely. She appeared to glide swiftly over the ground, and he realized that she set her paws down as lightly as she could, often switching pace in mid-stride in order to avoid stepping on leaves, twigs, slippery mud, paper bags or anything that might make a sound. Twice, she froze in mid-glide, once to allow a stray dog to trot past—luckily, he didn't even see them—and once for no reason that Southpaw could tell. She listened, the second time, with her head to one side, her whiskers stretched tight, and whatever she heard appeared to satisfy her, for they continued along the hedge, following its curved path all the way to the empty lot that stood behind the Bigfeet's houses.

Southpaw's tail, which had been dragging sadly on the ground, began to rise ever so slightly. The empty lot was on the edge of the wide stretch of scrubland that lay between Nizamuddin and the next set of buildings. It was a kind of no-cat's-land, as wild as the grounds of the Shuttered House but much less threatening. The real badlands lay just beyond, where lantana and acacia had grown into a bristling tangle, and where the whippy branches of untamed queen of the night wound their way around the frame of a Bigfeet building.

The kitten had only been here once, briefly, when he had followed Katar furtively as he prowled the long grass in search of prey. This was at the outer limit of the territory of the Nizamuddin cats—beyond this, and they ceded ground to the canal pigs.

They were moving into clumps of tall sarkanda grass, its purple plumes transformed by the dimness of the light into nodding shadows waving far above Southpaw's head. Miao suddenly stopped, taking cover behind a pile of wood chips, paper and plastic bags and other Bigfeet detritus. She signalled to Southpaw that he should listen, and he could see from the way the fine, tiny hairs in the inside of her ears rippled and stood up again that she was excited about what she could hear.

He concentrated, but the sounds that came to him were the ordinary sounds of the night. The far-off clamour of car horns from the road, the cheerful chirruping chorus of locusts, the occasional rustle in the dry grass. From above, owls called at random intervals, their soft solemn cries breaking the silence and rippling into the night. Miao had gone taut, the muscles of her flanks standing out as she pointed, her whiskers quivering at something in the long grass. Just as suddenly as she had signalled, she relaxed; a second later, a lizard came scurrying out of the grass, reflexively avoiding both cats. Southpaw tensed to pounce on its tail, but one sharp twitch from Miao's whiskers stopped him.

They waited in this fashion, and slowly, Southpaw felt himself calming and felt his senses spread as they took in his surroundings. He wanted to ask Miao a heap of questions, but though they could have communicated by whisker, he had already been warned not to.

Miao radiated a deep quietness as she settled in to wait. She was almost invisible against the long grass; a moth settled on the top of her head, fluttering away in alarm when the older cat twitched a whisker.

A rough map of the place began to form in Southpaw's head. There were many rats here, or had been: he could sense their runways, and was startled at how orderly and widespread their lanes seemed to be. Many of the trails led to the very back of the lot, and when he closed his eyes and inhaled, it seemed to the kitten that he could smell the odour of old droppings. He could see holes, but they smelled different and were away from the rat runways, with a more oily set of rubmarks.

The scent was tantalizingly familiar and yet alien: it took a few seconds before the kitten placed it, allowing his night vision to expand enough to let him see the holes more clearly. They were almost snout-shaped, and the odour was—he'd got it! Bandicoot rats lived here. And there was something else that the kitten couldn't place: a dark scent, powerful but not evil, sending warning drumbeats out into the air.

Miao sent out a tiny sniff of warning, and then the older cat was crouching, her belly flat on the ground, hindquarters waggling, claws out and ears pricked. Southpaw found his teeth chattering like hers in excitement, and dropped to the ground himself—just in time to see a bush rat shoot across the path, its tiny black eyes panicked. Miao's paw moved so fast that Southpaw didn't see the action. Nor did the luckless rat, its body flying up and landing with a small thump on their right. Southpaw forgot his manners and bounded towards the rat's body, driven by an urgent need to get his teeth into its flesh. There was a hiss, and then Miao swatted him, right across his tender nose.

"Never do that!" she said. "Always check that your prey is dead, not just stunned." Moving warily forward, she watched the rat for a few seconds. Then her paw shot out and she flipped her prey through the air. It came down on Southpaw's flank.

Miao held back. When Southpaw looked at her for direction, she said nothing, and her eyes were opaque. "Your kill," he said politely. "Owwwwwwww!"

The rat had sunk its yellow teeth into his rump, and it was trying to scurry away.

"It's nobody's kill until it's dead, Southpaw," Miao said.

He looked at the rat, and the rat looked back at him. Its eyes held terror and anger in equal measure, and the kitten hesitated. His instincts urged him to kill, and he could feel the saliva at the edge of his mouth at the thought of tasting its blood and its flesh. But the rat was bigger than he'd imagined, and its teeth were sharp; the blood he could smell in the air was not just the rat's.

Southpaw put his whiskers out and almost lost one more as the rat ran towards him instead of away, against all expectation. Its eyes were glazing from the loss of blood, but it nipped as hard as it could at his face, and skittered past his left flank. The kitten wheeled; the rat wheeled too, staying near Southpaw's back paw. The kitten twitched his tail out of the way just in time to prevent himself from being bitten again.

The pads of his paws were sweating. He could no longer see Miao, and he was not aware of the path, the runways, the rat holes, the lantana bushes or the grass. All he could see was the rat, its body tensed as it prepared to circle around, behind him—and he swung around, catching the rat by surprise, his paw connecting with its body, his claws out.

The rat flew through the air again, but this time, the body was limp and still. Southpaw wasn't taking any chances. He batted the corpse twice, thrice, before he was sure it was dead, and then, though his mouth was salivating in anticipation, he exerted a great effort and turned to Miao.

"Your kill," he said.

Miao came up and examined the body. She patted it twice, too, to make sure it was dead. Then she carefully tore out the throat, considered a delicacy. Southpaw looked away; only young kittens would drool, he told himself, trying very hard not to drool at the prospect of a tender, fresh-killed rat dinner.

"Yours, I think," said Miao. She dropped the morsel of flesh from the throat in front of him, and when Southpaw did nothing, she pushed the kitten's mouth gently downwards. He needed no further bidding, and they ate companionably, Miao feeding from the rich stomach, Southpaw relishing the back and the tail.

"It was a good kill, for the first time," said Miao when they were done. "Room for improvement, could've been better, but not bad, young Southpaw."

Southpaw rubbed his face against hers gratefully, purring his thanks. Miao allowed him to take the next two kills—a mouse and a shrew, both easy once he'd got the hang of swatting with claws extended. Each time, the kitten was scared: even the smallest prey could cause damage, especially when it knew it would be fighting for its life. But Miao watched him face down his insecurities, and she thought to herself, this one would make a good warrior. In her experience, it was never the bulk of the cat that counted or even the speed of the paw, the sharpness of the claw, as much as it was the ability to conquer one's fear.

As they moved through the long grass and noted the rat tunnels, explored a rotting set of branches and followed scent trails in the mud, Southpaw began to see that there was much more to hunting than just killing. He stalked a few more mice, just for practice, but Miao stopped him when he would have killed. "Never kill for fun," she said. "Only for food. When you have a full belly, you may not kill, unless it's in self-defence or defence of other cats."

Both Katar and she had told him this before, and he had remembered their words when Datura cornered him in the Shuttered House. But this was the first time the kitten could see how it worked in practice.

Southpaw let the trembling mouse under his paw go.

"Why does Datura kill for fun?" he asked.

Miao's tail lashed from side to side, and her eyes narrowed slightly. "He and his foul clowder of cats break almost all the laws. Their food dishes are unclean. The air of their house is blood-soaked. They kill kittens and young nestlings just because they can."

She glanced down at Southpaw, who was listening intently.

"Some animals, Southpaw, are rogues. We don't know why that happens, but it's a bad thing when it does. Cats go feral and peculiar, horses go mad, and creatures like Datura were born with something wrong, something broken, inside them. If you ever link with their minds, you'll smell it: madness and evil have their own stench, like rotting flesh, and it's best to stay away from the stink."

They began to stroll back home; the moon was passing behind clouds and its light was touched with purple and yellow, like an old bruise. They had almost reached the safe, comfortable row of Bigfeet houses and the road that led back to the park, when Southpaw felt all his fur stand up at once, Miao whirled, and the air filled with the thick aroma of damp fur and cedar. Behind that was the powerful warning scent Southpaw had smelled before, drumming through his head.

He turned, not wanting to see what was there. Miao had hunched her shoulders up, her face was down, her teeth bared, and she was growling in a low, deep voice. But Miao was to his left and a little behind him, and the scent came from his right side. Whatever it was that had spooked Miao, he would face it first. Slowly, the kitten turned, his eyes wide, his paws trembling.

The first thing the kitten noticed was the creature's eyes: inquiring, intelligent, assessing. Its face was neat, the fur beautifully combed in bristles of brown and silver, the whiskers black and questioning. The ears were round and made it look almost cute; but the creature was nearly their size, it rippled with muscles, and Southpaw gulped as he noticed the claws. They were thin, like curved stilettos, and he sensed they would be razor sharp.

"Don't even think about touching the kitten," Miao said, moving up to stand beside him. "Whoever you are, you'll have to get past me." The creature cocked its head to one side and considered her with some amusement.

"I could rip both your throats out, cat," it said, speaking in Junglee.

"But I have made my kills for the night and the bloodlust has dimmed. As it has for your kitten, I see. One kill or two, boy?"

"Three! And it's my first hunt!" said Southpaw, forgetting for a second to be afraid.

The creature's eyes crinkled. It turned to Miao.

"It is good to be young and out on your first kill," it said. "I'm Kirri, of the Clan Mungusi. Perhaps we can find a way to end this evening that does not involve bloodletting, perhaps we can't. What do you say, O Cat?"

Miao had stopped growling, though her fur was still spiky in warning.

"Hail, Mongoose," she said pleasantly enough. "I am Miao, and it has been many years since I met one of your kind. Are the snakes back in Nizamuddin, then?"

Kirri gave her a long considering look.

"Not here," she said. "But over there, where the Bigfeet are building yet another of their warrens, I met an old Nagini—old in years, not too old to fight—and how we danced! She had me pinned, but I wriggled free; I had my teeth at her throat, but she threw me off balance with her tail. It was a dance such as I haven't danced in months. She is dead and I have dipped my muzzle in her blood, but she was a worthy warrior."

"I have no doubt," said Miao, "that you have killed many snakes, and been a mighty warrior yourself."

It was just common politeness, but the mongoose looked pleased.

"So I have, Miao. You may not be of Clan Mungusi, but you are indisputably a huntress yourself, a member of Clan Scar. You and the kitten may pass unmolested this night, and because I have killed well and so has this young warrior, he may ask me a question."

Miao turned, and nodded at Southpaw. From the way her fur stood up slightly, he picked up her anxiety: the mongoose, so relaxed now, might be quick to anger, and the kitten knew without being told that he must get the question right. Should he ask Kirri about how one killed a snake? Should he ask her for advice, what the best killing moves were?

To his horror, Southpaw found himself asking none of these questions. Instead, he said: "If you please, Madame Mongoose, might I look at your mind?"

The mongoose's eyes went black. She stretched and stood up on her hind paws, letting the scimitars of her claws show.

"You ask to link with my mind? A kitten asks this? Of me?"

Barely twitching her whiskers, so quietly that Southpaw was almost sure Kirri hadn't heard, Miao said: "If she attacks, run. I'll take care of her. Run the moment you see her move, don't wait." Every muscle in her body was tense, and looking down, Southpaw saw the ground near her paws go dark from the sweat.

The kitten took in the mongoose. Everything about the creature terrified him; the patches of blood on Kirri's fur near her mouth, the wicked claws, the body that was all muscle, no fat. But he straightened his whiskers and said: "You had one kill today, Madame Mongoose. I had three, and one of them was my first. I beg pardon if what I said was wrong, but I just wanted to know what a true hunter's mind looked like."

The mongoose stood down, and said: "So you want to know what a hunter's mind is like, kitten? Come. Come inside, little one." She fixed her stare on the kitten, and Southpaw found himself looking back into her intense black eyes.

The first impression was of hardness and sharpness, like standing in the middle of an obsidian plain; the mind of the mongoose was smooth and opaque, like black glass, and the kitten felt as though hidden claws combed his fur very, very lightly, as the mongoose let him link.

Kirri's memories were carefully organized. The kitten found himself looking at receding images of snakes, and rats, and smaller prey—first, images of the living, caught in mid-battle, then of the dead, often bloodied and snarling. Another set of memories filed away battle plans: how to twist in mid-air, how to stalk one's prey from behind, how to dance with a cobra.

"Southpaw, that's enough."

He ignored Miao's voice, and moved a step forwards, fascinated. There was something in the centre of the plain that the kitten was being drawn towards.

"Come," said a voice softly in his head, and the kitten looked deeper into Kirri's black eyes. "Come closer, little one. See what you want to see."

"Get back, Southpaw!"

Southpaw sensed the predator's arrowhead mind, the single-minded focus on making a clean, good kill. The link between them was strong; he wanted to move closer, to see more.

The image began to flicker into shape, its outlines coming together now. It blurred, then sharpened. Southpaw was looking at his own face, the black whiskers trembling, the brown eyes large and filling with terror as he began to understand.

A sharp pain in his flank made him howl. He leapt backwards, and felt the mongoose's teeth—so close, too damn close!—snap shut on his ear. Southpaw yelped and backed away. A paw slashed at his neck, but the curved claws just missed him; and then Miao was there, calmly smacking at the mongoose's belly. For a second, there was a blur of brown fur and white fur—and then there was nothing.

Miao blinked. Southpaw blinked. Kirri had vanished, melting away into the whispering grasses.

"That was close," said Miao. "And now you know never to trust a predator. Sorry about nipping you, but you were leaning right into her mouth like a wet-behind-the-ears kitten who knows nothing whatsoever about hunting."

Southpaw was abashed, even as he tried to ignore the stinging pain where Kirri had ripped his ear. "It's just that—," he said weakly, "she was so fascinating."

"Most mongooses are," said Miao. "You want to be careful of the fascinating ones, young Southpaw, they're dangerous. And now home. It's time for you to rest."

Over their heads, an owl circled and hooted. It was wondering whether they would make good prey, but while the small kitten was a possible target, the larger cat was forbidding, and it didn't want to risk any of its plumage.

The rats and mice in the empty lot sniffed at the remnants of blood and fur that indicated the loss of three of their number, and the message spread along the runways to be more cautious: Nizamuddin had a new, young, eager hunter. And then the long, soft, purple grasses settled back into silence, disturbed only by small scurryings. If Kirri was there, she made no further kills, and nothing else disturbed the peace of Nizamuddin for the rest of the night.

"CAN'T YOU TURN DOWN the volume or something?" begged Southpaw. Mara sniffed. On his last two visits, she had connected much better with him. They had had a lot of fun playing pat-the-ball and chase-your-tail but on this visit, he seemed to have regressed and was acting like a Great Big Bossy Bully.

"Mara, that hurt!" said Southpaw. He had folded his ears flat across his skull and was huffing crossly at her. "And besides, I'm not a bully. I'm only trying to teach you how to hunt."

"I don't want to hunt! I *hate* hunting! Southpaw go away."

"Yowwrr!"

"Sorry!"

By mutual consent, the kittens took a washing break. Southpaw washed his flanks and the tip of his tail, wondering what to do with Mara. His playmate was being stubborn today, and he had no idea why she was sending so fiercely—it was painful being at the receiving end, like being spanked inside his head.

Mara washed her whiskers three times over as she tried to focus on keeping her thoughts private. She didn't really think Southpaw was a bully, well not lately anyway—he had been very patient when she chased his tail by mistake instead of hers, for instance—but she just didn't get why he was so excited about this hunting business he'd been on the other night.

And every time her thoughts spilled out of her head into the public cat domain, she got crosser and crosser. It wasn't as though she was doing it on purpose, it's just that she had to work very hard to keep her thoughts in the private zone, and when she got upset, that became even harder, like trying to prevent spilled water from spreading. *And why would I want to*

learn to kill a mouse anyway when everyone knows that food comes
to you in pretty pink plastic bowls . . .

"Mara, you're doing it again! Please stop, it makes my head
hurt!"

"Sorry!!!"

The kittens stared at each other. Mara's whiskers were
drooping. "I'm sorry, Southpaw," she said. "I just don't get this
hunting business, and it seems to be really hard today to switch
off my thoughts. But I don't understand why you're so excited
about it—what's the big deal?"

Southpaw huffed with impatience, but Mara was looking up
at him with so much genuine curiosity that he stopped, thought
about it and made an attempt to explain.

". . . and then the mouse went to the right, but I'd already
blocked its exit, and Miao had the left flank covered, so it was
easy," said Southpaw.

Mara patted her bundle of threads back and forth across the
floor. She was trying to pull out just one, but every time she
tugged at it, another would come out alongside.

". . ."

Perhaps if she got her claw under the thread while holding
the other threads down with her paw?

". . ."

Ah. The other threads were now firmly stuck to her left
paw, so she had to use her right paw to pick them off—and
curses, the single thread went back into the bunch.

". . . MARA!"

She leapt in the air, startled; the air crackled with the annoyance Southpaw's whiskers were transmitting.

"I'm so sorry, Southpaw," she said.

"You weren't listening to a word I said, were you?"

Mara rubbed her flanks along Southpaw's, but the older kitten turned away. She head-butted him, but he refused to butt back. And when she nipped him, he laid his ears flat, hunched his shoulders menacingly, and growled at her until she took a step back.

Mara sighed. She didn't quite understand it, but something about playing with the threads had turned down the volume of her thoughts, and she didn't have to work as hard to separate the private and public ones. But she was bored, and she wanted to play with Southpaw; she didn't want to know about this "hunting" business.

Southpaw was genuinely upset. The events of the previous night were still fresh in his brain, but when he'd told Mara about his kills—three! On a first hunt!—she'd just yawned and played with the end of her tail.

Mara was watching him, her eyes big and slightly dreamy.

"I see," she said. "I'm really sorry, Southpaw, I didn't realize this meant so much to you."

Southpaw glared at her. "Mara," he said. "Could you please stop reading my thoughts? It's really rude, especially since I can't read yours."

"The thing is," Mara said, "I don't have to hunt, because I'm never going to that nasty place you call outside. I like it in here; all my things are here, my threads and my ball and the toy mice. My Bigfeet give me as much food as I want, so why should I learn to hunt? It sounds awful to me. You've got yourself a bunch of scars, you can't lie down where Katar smacked you, and what about the mouse?" Southpaw blinked. Sometimes, he wondered whether Mara was a cat at all. She looked like one, and she smelled like one, but she didn't think like one.

"The mouse?" he said. "What *about* the mouse?"

"Do you think the poor things like being hunted? Don't you think it scares them? How would you like it if you were going about your business and some cat pounced on you?"

Southpaw had to wash his fur three times before he could trust his whiskers not to quiver with indignation.

"Mara," he said, "we are hunted, all cats are—only by dogs and Bigfeet, not mice. And we hunt mice because that's the way things are—mice are prey, we're predators, and how else do you expect us to eat?"

"What's wrong with cat food?" asked Mara sulkily.

Southpaw had had enough. He stood up, his tail twitching, his flanks heaving, his ears flat to his scalp. "You are such a spoiled brat, Mara," he said. "Your mother was probably one of us, you know. I'll bet she killed her fair share of rats and mice to feed you, and she probably lived out in the park with dead leaves for a pillow, the hedge for a home, and she loved it, just as we all do. She wouldn't have traded her freedom to be a precious inside cat, living off Bigfeet—no self-respecting cat would!"

"You just don't like Bigfeet! You can't admit that they can be nice to cats! And maybe not all cats like being outside. Maybe some of us prefer being in houses."

"The only ones who want to be in houses and never go outside become weird, Mara. You want to become like the monsters in the Shuttered House?"

"That's so unfair!" Mara mewed indignantly, her tiny tail

swishing back and forth as she bristled at Southpaw. "I would never pull out your whiskers or be horrid to strangers!"

"No, you wouldn't. But they went peculiar after being locked up for years, Mara. And if all you want to do is live inside, why be a cat at all? If this is what you want to do—bat around stupid toys, pretend that you have no normal instincts, refuse to step out of this Bigfeet trap and meet all of us—then what kind of cat are you?"

Mara was so upset that she was scratching the upholstery on the chair to bits. *I Hate You Southpaw Go Away I Hate You!*

"Stop doing that! I'm leaving anyway, you don't have to yell at me, you green-eyed freak!"

"You're the one who's yelling, I bet they can hear your mews three doors away! Leave, then, go off and hunt some poor mouse who never asked to be killed and see if that makes you feel better! You're the one who's a freak, a savage, murderous, horrid furry freak! And if we were all meant to have hunting instincts, how come I don't want to kill anything, ever?"

It was at that moment that a large Atlas moth fluttered in through the window, a striking target with its red wings and white triangular pennant markings.

There was a swift rush of movement, and before Southpaw could do more than raise a paw, the moth had been plucked out of the air by a leaping orange kitten, its wings hanging heavily down from either side of her mouth.

For a moment the two kittens stared at each other. Mara's face was ferocious, and when she dropped the moth and Southpaw moved towards it, she issued a small but definite mew of warning.

"Congratulations," said Southpaw. "Your very first kill. Well done, young Mara."

Mara looked down at the moth. Frantically, she patted it, careful to pull her claws in, but the moth stayed there on the ground, its wings slack, lifeless.

"I didn't mean to kill it," she said. "I really didn't, I don't know what came over me."

Southpaw head-butted her affectionately.

"It was a great kill, Mara," he said. "Just brilliant for a first-timer. That leap! That grip! I'll bet it didn't feel anything, it was a really clean kill, you know."

Mara's tail drooped and her ears and whiskers went down.

"But it did, Southpaw," she whispered. "It said, oh please don't, and I killed it anyway."

Southpaw looked into her eyes and saw that she was telling the truth. He didn't know what to say, what message his whiskers should carry.

"Mara," he said. "The thing is, we don't talk to our prey. Or at any rate, we don't listen to our prey. It's just not done. And we follow instincts. We're cats; hunting is in our bones and claws, little one."

Mara put her head down on the floor and mewed sadly. She nudged the moth once with her mouth, willing it to come back to life. *"I'm a bad kitten. I didn't mean to kill you, I'm so sorry,"* she sent forlornly.

And that was all Southpaw could get out of her for the rest of the evening. Her Bigfeet had gone out, so there was nothing to distract Mara, unfortunately. In the end, he calmed her down by washing her from the top of her small head to the tip of her tail until she fell asleep, her whiskers still on the down-droop. He stayed so late that he had to run the gauntlet of the neighbour's dogs. The Dalmatian and the Labrador were just coming back from their evening walk, but he managed to nip deftly out of their way, running down the banisters and swinging just in time into the branches of the laburnum tree outside.

As he headed home, he thought about Mara; he had never met a cat as odd and as difficult as her.

"But the speed at which she made her kill," he said to himself. "That was something to see, that really was." Perhaps there was hope for Nizamuddin's most unusual kitten yet, thought Southpaw.

CHAPTER ELEVEN

The Tiger's Tale

"What if you don't want to kill anything, ever?" asked Mara. She had been able to talk about nothing but the killing of the moth with Beraal, when the queen came by her house.

"But you do," said Beraal firmly. "Don't worry about it. It's just your instincts at work, and that will happen whenever you meet prey."

The kitten struggled to explain what she meant. "I didn't like killing the moth," she said. "It spoke to me, and it didn't want to be killed at all."

Beraal stretched her paws out and let her claws shoot out, sharp, curved, potentially lethal. "See these, Mara?" she said. "Run your tongue over your teeth. Look at your claws. We're meant to be killers; it's what we do. You don't have to hunt more than once in a blue moon, because your Bigfeet feed you. But it's useful to know how—just in case you find yourself outside, or if you're attacked by a bigger cat, or an owl, or a cheel." She was as puzzled as Southpaw had been by Mara's attitude. Most cats wanted to know the how of killing, not the why; and the how was complicated enough. The world was divided into predators, prey and Bigfeet, and what made it hard was that all three could change places at any time.

"But the moth said—," Mara began.

Beraal yawned and stretched, cutting Mara off. "The point of being a predator is that you're not supposed to listen," said the older cat. "If I listened to every plea for mercy, I'd never eat again in my life, or I'd become one of those wretched creatures you see who survive by picking through the Bigfeet garbage heaps. That's a rat's life, not a cat's life. Now shall we practise sending to the cats on the Nizamuddin link? We've done enough work on moderating the volume of your sendings, but we haven't broadcasted directly to the clan for a while, have we?"

The kitten huffed, her tail curved around her paws. "I don't want to," she said.

Beraal held her ground. "You know, you'll have to talk to the rest of us one of these days, Mara. You may live inside with the Bigfeet, but you're the Sender, and—"

The kitten was meeping, quietly at first and then in rising wails. "I don't want to link!" she said. "The Nizamuddin cats don't like me, except for Southpaw, and even he thinks I'm strange, I can hear his thoughts sometimes! The only reason you come to see me is because I'm the Sender, and I don't know what I'm supposed to do with my sendings, and I don't want to talk to any of you at all!"

Beraal stropped her claws in confusion, at the side of the staircase, staring at the kitten.

"The moth spoke!" Mara wailed. "And I didn't want to kill it but I did, —and I don't want to be the Sender and I really like living with Bigfeet—and—and—!"

The orange kitten fled up the staircase and back into the house. From inside her bedroom, eventually, Beraal heard the soft, muffled sounds of a kitten crying into a pile of blankets. She sat outside for a while, as a watery sun did its best to warm the afternoon, and she tried to link to Mara, but the kitten stayed determinedly out of reach. The queen drowsed for some time, and then she padded down the stairs and left to explore the park. She understood some of Mara's confusion about being the Sender, but now was not the right time to try and console the kitten.

It took some time, but Mara cheered up when the Bigfeet brought her a ball of wool. Patting it and chasing it around the floor was calming. She waited for Southpaw, but there was no sign of him, and Mara assumed that he was off with Miao or Katar, or one of the other cats. When her Bigfeet left, the kitten hesitated, wondering whether she should have another catnap. But she was well rested. Mara sat on the carpet, unfringing its knots absently, and then she stretched. "Time to visit the tigers," she said to herself. She had put it off for almost a full moon, and perhaps going to the zoo would undroop her whiskers.

She climbed a stepladder going all the way up to the top of the kitchen cupboards. Once up there, she settled in behind a jumbled heap of baskets and abandoned cardboard cartons.

Mara didn't want her Bigfeet scooping her up, even for a cuddle, while she was out at the zoo.

WHEN OZZY SAW A TINY ORANGE BLOB shimmer into the shape of a kitten over the small artificial pond in their enclosure, all of his great white whiskers stood up in glad greeting. It was only when he saw Mara that he realized how much he had missed the kitten; she made him laugh, and on her visits, he could briefly forget the bars that kept him penned.

Drowsing at the mouth of their cave, Rani opened her beautiful blue-green eyes a trifle as she watched her mate. Ozzy had been moody and difficult to handle all through the rains. The monsoon reminded him of the way summer yielded to better weather in dusty Ranthambore, and he had been pacing the length of the cage since the last full moon, restless, growling at the keepers and gawking visitors. As Mara hovered over the water, Rani sensed happiness ripple through her mate's mane and was relieved.

"Brat!" Ozzy roared, letting his voice rumble through the air and rattle the branches of the leopards' cages next door. "What took you so long? Forgot all about your old friends, did you?"

The kitten was so pleased to see Ozzy that she almost cannoned into his stripy muzzle, stopping herself in mid-tumble. She wouldn't have been hurt, but Mara knew from experience that other animals found it disconcerting to have a kitten, however virtual, shimmer through their bodies.

"I missed you!" said the kitten, surprised to discover how true this was.

Then Ozzy did something very unusual, by his standards. He leaned over, and gently brushed Mara's virtual whiskers with his muzzle. Mara felt a jolt run through their link, and for a second, the air around her ears bristled as she picked up on the immense, carefully contained power and strength that ran through the great tiger's frame. Ozzy's great golden eyes widened, too, and his whiskers trembled; it seemed to him that the Sender's strength was greater than the kitten knew, and for the first time, the tiger wondered how far Mara's powers extended.

"Thank you, Ozzy," she said, still tingling from the exchange. "Hey, Rani, how've you been? Where's Rudra, is he sleeping?"

Ozzy's whiskers went flat again, and the tiger's eyes went opaque. His massive head turned away from Mara, and he growled deep in his throat.

The white tigress kept her voice impassive, but Mara could hear the sadness in the low tones. "Rudra and Tawny have been shifted into another cage, on the other side of the zoo," she said. "They're old enough to breed. It's not that bad; we link and chat every day, and Rudra's a big boy now."

The growl from Ozzy was so menacing that it made the ground shake, and the few visitors who had been lounging against the bars of the enclosure, on the other side of the moat, were so startled that they leapt back.

His golden eyes were furious as he spoke to Rani and Mara. "They took our cub away, Rani! Our cub! Without asking me or you, or him!"

"Ozzy," said Rani patiently. "At least he's still here; he's in the zoo and you and I know he's safe. They could have sent him to another zoo, the way they did with the baby leopards—at least he's not halfway across the world."

"They had no right!" roared Ozzy. His roars were making Mara shiver, but though the kitten flattened her ears and dropped to the ground, she didn't leave either the zoo or the link. "If we'd been in Ranthambore, he would have left to start his family, but do you think we wouldn't have met? We would have explored the dark, cool dens together, Rani! You would have taught his cubs how to hunt and how to study the ravines and the plateaus, what prey to chase through the gorges, what prey to leave to the sand and the sun. They took my boy away without asking me!"

"Ozzy," said Rani quietly.

"How could they?" roared the tiger. "He's MY boy! I should have killed them all! I should have torn them limb from limb."

"He couldn't do that," Rani said in an aside to Mara, "because they tranquilized him. It's been eating him up for days."

The great tiger was pacing up and down, and his roars were echoing across the length and breadth of the zoo now. The hyenas woke up and added their insane, laughing barks to the sound; the monkeys gibbered and far away, the elephants began trumpeting.

"We have to stop him," said Rani, getting to her feet. "Or the Bigfeet will come in and give him the sleeping medicine again. He hates that."

"Ozzy?" said Mara, timidly following the great cat as he marched up and down, his orange and black flanks rippling.

"THEY TOOK MY SON AWAY FROM ME!" the tiger roared. "Yes, and that can't feel good at all," agreed the kitten.

"VENGEANCE! BLOOD! DEATH TO THE CUB-STEALERS!" Mara's ears flickered; she saw the keepers standing outside the cage, in urgent Bigfeet discussion. There were four of them, and two more joined the group as she watched. Ozzy would have to stop roaring, or else it would go badly for him.

"I'm so sorry, Ozzy," she said. "It must be terrible not to have Rudra right here. But are you sure he's feeling as bad? I mean, he must miss the two of you, but he was born in the zoo, wasn't he? And he's seen other cubs being shifted away from their parents, so perhaps it isn't as hard for him as for you."

"RIP THEIR INTESTINES INTO TINY . . . what?" Ozzy said, his last roar tailing off.

The kitten was looking at him, her head to one side, and as he paced up and down, Ozzy found his anger disappearing when he considered Mara's question.

"BLOOD! REVENGE!" he said stubbornly, but his heart wasn't in it.

"You must miss him a lot," said Mara. "Your fur has the scent of sadness. But you know he's safe and happy, so isn't it really the jungle that you're missing?"

Ozzy opened his red-tongued mouth to roar, but what came out was a confused, "Grrmmmmphhh."

The keepers were watching him closely, one leaning on the bars.

"My head hurts with all this thinking, Rani," the tiger said crossly. He glared at Mara. "I was doing fine until you came along and confused me, you—you—miniature furbag!"

Rani eyed her mate, and Mara could see the beginnings of a smile on the white tigress's face as her whiskers twitched upwards.

"Go for a swim, Ozzy," she said, her low growl so soothing that Mara felt her own fur settle back into calmness.

The Bigfeet keepers relaxed as the tiger plunged into his pool. "Aaroo!" he said happily, splashing around. Swimming always made his head feel cooler. Ozzy did a grand rolling dive and splashed and splashed until he felt much better. Reassured by his action, the Bigfeet keepers dispersed.

Later, as he lay on the rocks, letting his skin and fur dry in the afternoon sun, Ozzy eyed the kitten's curled-up shape with grudging respect.

"In the jungles," he said presently, "there are no bars and no boundaries."

"That seems scary to me," said Mara. "I don't like the outside at all."

"Why not?" said Ozzy.

Neither Beraal nor Southpaw had asked her this question, and Mara washed her paws slowly, first the left, then the right, trying to explain why being outside in person, without the safety of the link, felt so terrifying.

"It's because there's so much of it," she said at last, "and it confuses my whiskers—there are too many scents to follow, too many cats and other animals thinking at the same time, and it all seems so difficult! You have no shelter when it rains, and the food isn't already dead—you have to kill it, and it talks to you . . ." The kitten bent her head and washed her back paws with fierce concentration.

Ozzy didn't contradict her. Instead, he let his whiskers stretch out in Mara's direction, questioning, open, friendly.

"So you've killed, little one?" he asked gently. She had grown up since that first surprising sending, he thought. A season and more had gone by since the kitten had tumbled into their lives; she would soon be a full-grown cat.

Mara meeped, very softly.

Ozzy raised his immense white whiskers, each one of which could have circled the kitten twice over, and his eyes met Mara's. The two looked unblinking at each other, tiger and cat. It was Ozzy who blinked and looked away, after a few moments.

In the distance, a baby elephant trumpeted, the shrill call followed by the rough bark of a cheetah. The cats, the big one and the small one, ignored the sounds from the zoo, and the attempts of the Bigfeet visitors to get them to come closer to the bars. Some of the Bigfeet were throwing plastic packets into the enclosure. Usually Ozzy would have warned them off with a growl, but he ignored them this time round.

"Thank you for letting me share your memories, little one," said the tiger. His flaming flanks rippled as he shifted, and once again, Mara was reminded of how much power lay dormant in his massive body. The kitten was curled up in a small heap near Ozzy; Rani had padded back to the cave, knowing that it was best to leave the two alone.

Ozzy let the silence grow and deepen, allowing Mara to consider the endearment he had used: from the time he and the orange kitten had met, the bond between them had grown, in a way that the tiger could not explain. She reminded him of his first child, the feisty tiger cub he had lost so many years ago—the two had shared the same spirit, even though they came from different species.

"I was just a young cub when my mother came back to our den one day, her jaws bloody, an ugly wound raking her hind leg, and told us that my father was dead," said Ozzy. His voice was low as he roamed the forests again in his mind. "There had been a fight with a pair of wild boars; my mother won her battle, my father lost his. My sisters left soon, to make their claims to their territory; I was too young to leave my mother, but I was old enough to learn how to hunt."

The artificial river, the dusty grass, the bars of the cage: all of these seemed to disappear as Ozzy shared his life in the ravines and the forests, the territory that he and his mother would roam for nights in a row without scenting another tiger's scat or seeing unfamiliar pugmarks.

"The first deer I hunted spoke to me," he said. Mara sat up, her tail flicking back and forth in interest. From what Southpaw and Beraal had said, she had gathered that most cats didn't hear their prey, or didn't listen to the voice of the kill.

"What did it say?" she said, her ears upright and alert.

"It caught my scent first, and it begged silently for its life," said Ozzy. "As I drew closer and it sensed how eager I was for the kill, as I lay crouched in readiness, it shared with me the joy it felt when it drank water from a stream that had not dried in summer, when it raced its friends and mates to see who was the fastest; it spoke of the babies it hoped to have, the mate with whom it hoped to raise a family in the shelter of Ranthambore's jungles."

"And so you spared it," said Mara, thinking of the moth, wishing she had been less impulsive.

"I broke its neck in two with my first bite," said Ozzy, "and when the hot blood ran out, I was sorry only for a moment before I began to feed."

The tiger shifted and let his giant paw shoot out, resting on the ground right near Mara. The claws extended, and the kitten could see how wickedly sharp and curved they were; massive, deadly versions of her own.

"Killing is in my bones and blood, Mara," the tiger said, "as it is in yours. I felt sorry for the deer, but I showed it mercy."

"You killed it," said Mara. "How was that any kind of mercy?"

Ozzy yawned, and she saw his long, curved teeth exposed, the fangs larger than her furry head.

"I killed it fast," he said. "That is no small mercy, Mara. You're running away from being a Sender, because it sets you apart from the other cats; but you can't run away from being a cat. When your prey speaks next, listen to it for as long as you choose, and then kill it as swiftly as you can. That is the only mercy, little one."

Mara blinked, and then she gazed again into his golden eyes, and saw that what he was saying was true. She set it aside neatly in a corner of her mind to think about later, but the way in which the tiger had said it made the kitten feel better. Ozzy understood. And if a cat as large and powerful as him could listen to prey, perhaps she wasn't as much of a freak, after all.

"Tell me about the jungles and the ravines," she said. "Why did you love them so much?"

"Where shall I start?" said Ozzy, his eyes flashing into life.

When Rani came to the mouth of the cave a while later, what she saw made her growl softly in relief. Her mate was resting on the rocks, his whiskers and ears radiating enthusiasm, and he seemed to be telling Mara one story after another. Rani's beautiful eyes softened as she watched the kitten, but the white tigress's tail stayed low to the ground. She sorely missed the play and chatter of her cub, and the kitten's tiny presence made her ache with sadness. It was not the right age for Rudra to have left her side; another turn of the earth, another season, a few more moons, and the white tigress would have pushed him away herself. He had left so bravely, walking with a cub's swagger into the cages the Bigfeet keepers brought. His courage made Rani see again how very small he was to face a separation.

It could have been worse, she told Ozzy often. If they had been in the jungles, Rudra would have faced poachers, and predators; the fires from the nearby villages often took the lives of cubs, who couldn't breathe in the thick smoke, and Rani remembered the hyaenas who had wounded her first cub so grievously.

But their enclosure had seemed lonely and empty after Rudra left, and the white tigress felt his absence more grievously than she would ever let her mate know. As she watched Ozzy and Mara, her belly warmed at the pleasure her mate was taking in the conversation, and Rani felt some of the emptiness in her heart ease.

Mara spent much of the day with the tigers. She wondered whether she should go and visit Rudra, but when she noticed the sad downwards curve of Rani's whiskers, she decided to see her friend on another day, rather than risk making the two adults sad at the thought that they couldn't go with her to see their cub. Instead, she drew Ozzy out, letting him share all of his memories, and for a pleasurable afternoon the jungle invaded the cage, and the bars and the zoo faded from the tiger's mind.

"Perhaps you should come for a walk with me one of these days," the kitten said to Ozzy in jest when she left, as the rain started to pour down again.

The tiger rose to his great height, the orange-and-black stripes rippling, his bulk silhouetted majestically against the sunset.

"If I did, what do you think the Bigfeet would say?" he asked.

Mara imagined a tiger strolling through Nizamuddin, scattering the babblers and the mynah birds left and right. Then she tried to imagine Ozzy pacing menacingly through her house.

"Ozzy," she said seriously, "I don't think you'd fit in their kitchen."

Ozzy thought that was very funny. The tiger's enormous chuffs filled the air, a happy, explosive sound that the animals in the zoo heard with relief. It had been a long time since Ozzy had done anything except sulk or roar.

CHAPTER TWELVE

A Shift in the Wind

K atar felt the first questioning touch of rain on his fur
and lingered, liking the way the drops felt as they
soaked through to his skin. He was unusual among
the Nizamuddin cats in his love for the rain; while the rest of
them shivered and sought shelter, the tom would stay out in
anything short of a heavy downpour, spreading his paw pads
in pleasure as the rain washed his whiskers and fur clean.

Beraal had once watched from the shelter of a park bench,
astonished, as he chased water insects through puddles. She
agreed with Miao, who had narrowed her eyes one monsoon
and pronounced that Katar must have been descended from
the river cats of the North, or perhaps from even further away
in Bengal, that was famous for its swimming cats of the
Sunderbans forest.

It was only when the sound of the rain deepened, from a
light percussive rumble to a heavy, steady drumming and his

fur stood in danger of waterlogging that Katar reluctantly leapt down from the roof, taking the road to the Bigfoot fakir's shelter through the inner lanes. The tom took one look at Nizamuddin before he left: the maze of rooftops that announced the dargah to one side, the dark sprawl of the Shuttered House like a sullen blot near the part where Nizamuddin proper began in serried rows of neat, often green rooftops. To his left ran the great, muddy sludge-filled waters of the canal, which the rains had transformed into a fat, silver snake.

Miao and Beraal were crouched under the spreading branches of a ficus, lapping at bowls of warm milk that the fakir had thoughtfully placed outside for them. Katar bounded in, stopping to shake the water off his fur. He lapped greedily at the milk, looking up once to see Qawwali slumbering inside the shrine, drowsing by the fakir's side as the evening prayers started.

The three cats lay curled up afterwards, letting their combined warmth combat the sudden chill and damp of the rains. Katar stretched out luxuriously, burying his paws under Beraal's belly to keep them warm. He barely flinched when a few Bigfeet hurried by. "You're getting more comfortable around the Bigfeet these days," said Miao.

"Only when the fakir's here," said Katar sleepily. "He understands us. Perhaps it's his whiskers." The fakir had a fine beard and moustache, and it was Katar's private belief that if the Bigfoot tried hard enough, he might be able to communicate like cats some day, but this had never been tested. "But other Bigfeet are treacherous. All Two-Feet are dangerous."

There was an edge to his mew. Katar's father had gone hunting in a Bigfeet home and never come back again; his mother had met her end on the roads. The tomcat had little love of the Bigfeet, staying away from their houses even if he loved exploring the rooftops.

Beraal watched as visitors to the shrine petted Qawwali. "But not all Bigfeet are bad, are they?" she asked. "Mara seems to love her own Bigfeet—she treats them as though they were fellow cats." She thought of the way the Bigfeet carried the kitten around in their arms, the bowls of food that were so carefully replenished, their patience with her pounces and leaps.

Katar whiffled contemptuously. "Your Mara is hardly a cat, is she? We've seen her sendings, but she hasn't stepped out of her Bigfeet cave. Except for Southpaw and you, we don't know the scent of her fur, and our whiskers haven't touched, for all that she's our Sender," he said.

"Perhaps it's a Sender thing," said Beraal, her nose questing as she turned to Miao.

The Siamese lay on her side, half-asleep. Her blue eyes opened at Beraal's question. "Tigris was born in the hedge behind the Shuttered House and grew up playing on the canal road," she said. "She was an outside kitten through-and-through, part of a large litter."

"Perhaps your Mara's just weird," said Katar. The tomcat's tail rapped lightly on the ground. He had accepted the result of the battle between Hulo and Beraal as all the other cats had—whiskers didn't turn backwards, as the ancient saying went. But as time went by and the Sender remained indoors, the tom's view that inside cats were strange creatures was only reinforced.

Miao stirred before Beraal could reply. "I knew Tigris well," she said. "She grew up like every other wilding in Nizamuddin, learning to dodge the Bigfeet and stay out of their way. Mara had no mother or litter-mates to teach her the freedom of the canal road, or help her make her first kill in the wild. All she's known from the time her eyes opened is the four walls of her Bigfeet's home. And besides—"

The Siamese's sleek ears went up, the black patches of fur on her face standing up too as a muffled thud sounded in the distance. At the entrance of the shrine, the fakir looked around, puzzled, but turned back when he saw that there was no immediate cause for concern.

"That sounded as though it came from the Shuttered House," said Katar, his nostrils flaring as he scanned the rain and the wind for further information. The cats were alert, their ears swivelling around in the direction of the Shuttered House, but there was silence, and after a few moments, Miao and Katar let their hackles down.

"—Tigris learned that she was a Sender when she was much older than Mara," continued Miao. Beraal's nose whiffled in interest. "It was only after she had seen her first summers and monsoons that her whiskers grew longer, and even then, her first sendings were pallid, faint glimpses, weak affairs compared to what your young pupil can do. It took Tigris three seasons to learn what Mara's shown us in three moons. And in that time, Tigris changed." The blue of Miao's eyes deepened as she recollected the past.

"Was Tigris still the Sender when I was born?" asked Katar. The tom's tail was twitching in uncertainty. He didn't remember

Tigris at all, and felt that he should have remembered meeting the Sender, even if he'd been a youngling at the time.

"By the time you were born, the Sender had retreated from the rest of us wildings," said Miao, sadness lightly touching her whiskers. "After Tigris learned to send, she spent most of her time in the courtyard of a Bigfeet house—one of the old mansions on the canal road, it's empty now. She wasn't unfriendly, but she spent more and more time in her own world, and she had less and less time for us. Besides, you were born after the neighbourhood had quietened down."

"Quietened down?" said Beraal. Her mew was surprised: Nizamuddin bustled with the constant clamour of the Bigfeet, the cheerful chatter of the babblers and the predatory sorties of the cheels, besides regular upheavals among the canal pigs who were always fighting interporcine wars.

Miao let her whiskers ripple in the rain and the wind. "Stretch your whiskers out," she said. "Tell me what you feel."

The three cats raised their whiskers, and Katar felt his eyebrows tingle as they linked simultaneously. The link was calm, unruffled by turbulence or disaster; none of the cats they checked with had much to report. On the canal roads, Tabol had found shelter under a parked car and was trading stories with some of the older kittens. The market cats had retreated under blue tarpaulins, or curled up in the dry spaces behind stalls. Qawwali, who also didn't mind the rain, was waiting patiently at the butcher's shop in the dargah for a few scraps; the other dargah cats were curled up at the back of the fragrance seller's stall, soothed by the vetiver and rose that scented the breeze.

Katar's tail rose questioningly as they left the link.

"It's all so normal," said Miao. "But there was a time when there were only a handful of wildings in Nizamuddin—two or three families, not the many we have now. We lived in fear of the dogs, and the Bigfeet in those days were not friendly: we had to be prepared for them to hunt us out of our hiding places, or to pick cats up in their trucks and shift them elsewhere, entire families made to move away from the scents of their childhood years."

Beraal's green eyes flashed with understanding. "That was when you needed the Sender," she said. "The Sender could scent further than any of you, and understood the Bigfeet better—was that it?"

"Yes, and more," said Miao. "Tigris could smell danger long before it came to us, though it took time before the wildings learned to trust her nose."

Katar turned, yawning. "There is no danger in Nizamuddin now," he said. "All we have to do is stay away from the Bigfeet, and every kitten learns to be careful—even rascals like Southpaw. No offence to you, Beraal, but the time you're spending with Mara, training her as though she were from your own litter—what do we need a Sender for?"

The fakir came out with a few scraps for the cats. Katar retreated cautiously behind the trunk of a graceful flame tree, though Miao and Beraal rubbed their heads happily against the fakir's ankles, purring as they weaved through his legs so that he could accept their thanks. When he went back to the shrine, the three cats ate, Miao generously letting Katar have an equal share from her saucer.

The Siamese was turning over Katar's question, but it was only when they were done, and washing their whiskers, that she responded. "When you two linked, did you feel anything else in the air?" she asked.

Beraal thought about it, her ears angled. "No," she said. "Or wait—there was something rising in the air, but it was no more than a ripple. A hint of change to come, perhaps, but that happens with every season, Miao."

The Siamese was still, and her eyes hooded. "There was change in the air, *and* something darker," she said. "I am no Sender, but my paws have been prickling ever since we went to the Shuttered House. We have had seven good seasons, Katar; you were born in the first of them."

Katar licked the last of the meal off his whiskers. "Seven mild winters, seven fat summers," he said, thinking of the mice and rats, the abundant game that allowed most of the wildings of Nizamuddin to live well without needing to raid the Bigfeet's garbage dumps.

"Perhaps we will have seven more, but my bones tell me the winds are changing," said Miao quietly. "It is just as well that we have hunters like Beraal and Hulo; perhaps we will need them. And as I reminded you once, the old saying about Senders, here and everywhere else I've travelled, is that they appear when the need is strong."

Katar caught Beraal's unblinking eyes. He knew what the other cat was thinking, and though he raised his whiskers instinctively to test the air, neither of them understood why Miao was worried. They had full bellies, and so did most of the wildings; there was peace between the clans, a reasonable state of truce between the stray dogs and the cats, and the Bigfeet by and large left them alone.

"But you wanted Mara dead," said Beraal. Now that she'd spent time with the kitten, it was hard for her to imagine that she had once stalked and hunted Mara.

"If she had been an adult with an outsider's scent, I would have ripped her throat open myself," said Miao calmly. "But a kitten with a possible claim on us is a different matter—we have to wait and see. Though I will give you fair warning: if Mara brings harm down on the wildings in the future, one of us will kill her. No clan can let a rogue Sender stay alive."

The Siamese saw the flash in Beraal's eyes and curled her paws outwards, to show that her claws were held in. "It's like culling kittens," she added more gently. "Sometimes it has to be done, and as her teacher, you'll see the warning signs before any of us. It's more likely that her powers will help us some day, Beraal."

Katar poked his head up, pausing as he cleaned between his paw pads. "Some help she's likely to be," he said, "that Mara of yours doesn't know whether she's a Bigfoot with four paws or a cat with a Bigfoot brain."

Beraal's eyes glittered emerald, always a warning sign with the young queen. "The tigers accept her," she said, her whiskers reaching out to Miao as much as Katar. "She became friends with their cub—just think how unusual that is. Could she make friends with the dogs? The cheels, who speak only to Miao? The pigs from the canals? Would she try to? And if she did, what would it mean for us? What about the Bigfeet—can she understand their endless chatter?"

Katar had roamed the lanes and rooftops of Nizamuddin long enough to understand what this might mean. A complex web of alliances, temporary truces and occasional invasions and wars allowed the creatures who lived here to get on with each other, and it was understood that they all lived at the mercy of the Bigfeet's often inexplicable whims. A Sender with Mara's powers, and her apparent ability to make friends with other species was a rarity.

"Why doesn't she come out?" said Katar truculently. "How can she be our Sender when we don't know her scent?"

Beraal's whiskers fell. She didn't expect Katar to share her feelings for the kitten; Mara had filled the place either a mate or a litter of her own would have taken this year.

"She smells our suspicion," she said. "And she's lonely, despite Southpaw's visits. The last time I went over, she was trying to make friends with a house lizard."

Miao's ears pricked up in curiosity. "How did that go?" she asked.

"Not very well. All it had to say was 'girgit, girgit.' She said it was hard to carry on a conversation," Beraal said, her eyes half-closed. Katar's whiskers twitched, and then the whiskers over his eyes twitched, and then his entire belly began to shake as he contemplated the frustration of Nizamuddin's most talented Sender attempting to chat with a lizard. Beraal and Miao found their whiskers rising as they saw the funny side of it. The three cats curled into each other, glad for the warmth and the company, and slept as the rain pattered down, ignoring the murmuring of the Bigfeet who went back and forth from the shrine.

A little further away from where they slept, the rain beat down hard on the staircase outside the Shuttered House, rapping sharply on the metal rungs. The muffled thumping Katar had heard earlier started up again, but there was no one to hear it, except for a small brown mouse.

The mouse wasn't bothered by the stench from the Shuttered House—the stink of cat litter, mildewed walls and dry rot was like a signpost indicating that he would find food here. He had often raided the house for crumbs, keeping a cautious, beady eye out for the ferals, but tonight the atmosphere was different.

When the mouse risked a peek through the door, the ground floor of the house seemed carpeted with cats. They crept around on the floor, fighting for scraps of food. Several sat on the stairs, hissing and yowling.

He sniffed the air, and his sensitive nose recoiled at the odour of sickness. It was sharp enough to cut through the clean scents of the wind and the rain; it told the mouse that the Bigfoot who lived in the Shuttered House was seriously ill. When he saw a white cat with peculiar eyes pad down the stairs, the mouse trembled and skittered away. The cat had once almost trapped him under a broken chair when he'd been on a raid, and the mouse had never forgotten the malevolence in the yellow eye.

As he scurried off, the mouse heard a terrible wailing break out, and he shivered even more in the cold. He didn't turn to look back at the rain-darkened, windswept bulk of the Shuttered House—rich though the pickings there might be, he didn't think he would visit the place for a while.

CHAPTER THIRTEEN

Unshuttered

The time of night Katar loved most were the hours just before dawn. To the tomcat, these were the hours of freedom. Except for the Bigfoot night guard, who did his rounds thumping his wooden staff slowly on the ground as he walked, the Bigfeet were mostly asleep. Sometimes their noisy cars went racing by, but cats could hear the racket they made a mile off, and it was much easier to avoid them at night than during the day, when few cats except for the most intrepid veterans would risk crossing the road.

The few predators other than Bigfeet that Katar feared were asleep at this hour; even the most alert watchdogs had stopped their barking and were at rest, the canal pigs, who could be of uncertain temper, were wallowing in the stinking mud, and the cheels were slumbering on their high perches. Nizamuddin was his kingdom, then, and the tomcat enjoyed his dawn rounds.

As usual he paid little heed to the rain, but when he got to a dry patch, he was glad for the chance to shake his coat dry. The branches of the great neem and the intertwined magnolia trees blocked out a lot of the rain, and the ground under the cat's paws was damp, but not wet, except for a few patches here and there that were easy to avoid. He felt his spirits lift.

He stopped at the magnolia tree, leaned back against the base and scratched his tail and flanks luxuriously on its bark. Then he turned around and scratched his tummy up and down. Then he stretched his front paws and his back paws and his tummy and his tail until all of the worry over bringing up Southpaw and the tiredness from his night of hunting bandicoot rats had been stretched away.

A frog hopped down the path, and checking to make sure he wasn't being observed, Katar gave in to the kittenish urge to hop after it. Hop, went the frog; hop, went Katar, all the way down the rough path that bisected the clearing. He was glad no other cats were there to see him. The tom was very conscious of his dignity, but sometimes he missed the fun of his kittenhood.

It was only when the frog went "plop" instead of hop, into a fresh new puddle, that Katar realized he had moved out of the dargah and was almost at the grounds of the Shuttered House.

He hesitated; after Southpaw's experience, he and the other cats had given the place a wide berth. The tom was happiest when negotiating the maze-like networks of the roofs and balconies, endlessly curious about the very different lives of the creatures who lived in the empty lot and elsewhere, beyond the confines of the park. But something about the house made him uneasy, and set his fur to prickling at the best of times; and as he sniffed the air, his nose wrinkled. Drowning out the scent of rain was something dank and ugly—he smelled the restlessness of the cats inside and whiffled his nose at the high stink of Bigfeet illness.

Now, sounds cut through the silence of the night: in the Shuttered House, an animal was moaning, calling out in low, guttural cries. "Waooww!" it said, and then other voices joined in. "Aaaoooww!" they called. The timbre sent cold shivers down Katar's backbone—shivering, high-pitched, evocative of deep distress. The ferals were calling in lamentation, though the tomcat didn't understand why.

High in a tree behind the Shuttered House, a sleepy barbet raised an alarm. "Plink-plink!" it called into the night, and a startled mynah picked up the refrain: "Keek-keek-keek! Keek-keek!"

Katar began to back away from the house. He was about to link to ask Hulo or any of the other cats in the area to join him and see what was going on, when a musky, furry scent hit his nostrils. The tom swung around, and placed his paw in the path of a mouse that was scurrying away towards the hedges.

The cat turned and their gazes locked, predator and prey. But the mouse had its short, bristly fur up, and was agitated in a way that had nothing to do with being caught by Katar. "It smells wrong," said the mouse. "Smells terrible wrong."

The tomcat was about to respond when the night air erupted into sound. From behind the door of the Shuttered House, the cats began to moan again, the low keening sound rasping along the tomcat's nerves. He twitched, and the mouse used the opportunity to make a successful dash into the broad leaves of the cannas.

The wails of the cats were making the birds restless, and Katar crouched near the cannas, his tail flicking wildly back and forth now. He sent a quick, all-cats alert to the link, letting them know that something was wrong at the Shuttered House, and then he froze as Bigfeet came running through the grounds. The cat pressed himself into the safe embrace of a clump of lilies, watching as the lights went on in the house, unable to get the high-pitched keening of the ferals out of his mind.

More knots of Bigfeet were coming up the path. The Bigfeet found the path difficult going in the rain—it was disused, weed strewn and dangerously slippery—and Katar had to curl himself even deeper into the foliage when one of the Bigfeet slipped and almost fell into the lilies.

There was the creaking of rusted hinges, and Katar's whiskers went rigid as he watched the door of the Shuttered House, closed and barred for as long as he could remember, swinging open. For a terrifying moment, the tomcat wondered whether a flood of cats would come pouring out of the stinking depths of the house, but instead, the Bigfeet went in and out. Unbidden, his whiskers brought him a brief, fleeting image of many cats sullenly shrinking back into the corners and crevices of the house, as the Bigfeet swarmed in.

There was a hiatus, and he could hear the Bigfeet chattering and exclaiming from inside the house. They seemed to be distressed, and there were now many of them stamping up and down the path. Katar wondered whether he could escape from the back, but there were so many Bigfeet milling around that it seemed more sensible to stay where he was.

At his feet, the earth stirred a fraction, and a tiny, brown, whiskered head popped up.

"This is a terrible business," said the mouse. "For me, for you and all of us."

Katar was unsure of the etiquette of talking to prey—he had seldom done it in the past—but the mouse spoke in Junglee, and had addressed him directly. Besides, if he pounced on the mouse, he risked drawing Bigfeet attention to himself. The cat considered his options, and then his natural curiosity kicked in. "What's a terrible business, mouse?" he said.

"The ruckus at the Shuttered House," said the mouse, eyeing the cat shrewdly and keeping a judicious distance between the two of them. "I could tell you, if you were willing to consider a truce, O Cat."

"Let there be a truce," said Katar grandly. "Why are the Bigfeet getting their tails in a twist, mouse?"

"Himself is dead, isn't he?" said the mouse.

"Himself?" said Katar, wondering whether this was a cat or a mouse. "Himself," said the mouse. "The Bigfoot who lived there with the cats. Can't you smell it? He was ill and he's dead, and now there isn't anyone to keep those cats inside."

Katar could smell it now, the unmistakeable odour of death riding down to them on the back of the rain.

"Perhaps the cats will stay where they are," he said. "They've never left the Shuttered House in all of their lives, mouse. What makes you think they'll leave?"

The mouse sighed; it came out in a small squeak.

"I was born there myself," it said. "The pickings were rich, for us mice and rats, but the cats had kittens, and more cats came, and over the years, the cats turned sour."

Katar knew what the mouse meant; he was listening intently. "So you left?" he asked.

"I left, though many of us made sorties there for food from time to time," said the mouse. "The ferals had nothing to do inside except play games. You might say they learned some very nasty games, O Cat."

Katar glanced at the house. The wails had deepened into a chorus. His fur was standing up, and it had nothing to do with the cold and the rain—every time the ferals inside the house keened, he could feel a shiver in his bones. The door of the house opened again, and a sour stench gusted out. The mouse was telling the truth; the old Bigfoot who lived in the house was dead.

"I'm Katar," he said. "Forgive me, but I don't know your name, mouse. Tell me why you think they won't stay inside the house. They've never wanted to come outside before."

The brown mouse considered him intently, its short whiskers questioning.

"They call me Jethro," he said. "I have never exchanged names with a cat before. I will remember your courtesy, Katar. The cats won't stay because there'll be no one to feed them, and because the Bigfeet will open up the Shuttered House—look, the door is already open."

"I don't understand," said Katar. "Even if the house is opened up, it would still be their territory, wouldn't it? Why wouldn't they hunt in these grounds—excuse my bluntness—and continue to live there?"

The mouse's ears rose. "Because once Datura comes out and sees what the outside is like," said Jethro, "he'll want to come out to play."

The Bigfeet were leaving the house now, carrying something huddled on a stretcher. A few Bigfeet remained. The door shut; the wailings abruptly stopped, cutting off in mid-dirge. Katar found that more unsettling than if they had continued.

There was silence again, and except for the lights, the Shuttered House seemed the same as always. The tomcat wondered if the mouse hadn't been too scared, too timid—he was only a mouse, after all, and they weren't known for their courage. The house looked its usual shuttered, closed self. Perhaps the Bigfeet would take Datura and the other cats away, or perhaps some other Bigfoot would move in. But his tail continued to flick back and forth, and as he padded away, intending to discuss this with Miao and Hulo, he was uneasy.

He had got less than a few paw's lengths away when the wailing started up again, and this time, there was an edge to it, a menace that made his hackles rise. Katar turned, unwillingly, and stared at the Shuttered House. If the ferals did come out, would they stay in the grounds and keep to themselves? Would Datura be willing to behave the way the Nizamuddin cats did—would he keep the peace between the clans? The image of Southpaw shivering as Katar and Hulo cleaned the wound where his whisker had been pulled out came back to the tom's mind, and the cat flinched.

The wind changed direction, driving the stench from the Shuttered House into the cat's nostrils. It filled Katar with dread.

The keening rose again, and from the trees, the barbet sounded its alarm once more. From near his front paws, Jethro spoke. "Datura took my siblings and my mother, and his friends took my first four litters," he said. "I don't think you and your cats would like the games he plays at all—no, Katar, I don't think you'd like it one little bit." The brown head melted away into the shadows. Behind Katar, as he padded steadily away from the Shuttered House, the wails rose to a crescendo.

CHAPTER FOURTEEN

Miao and the Cheels

Perched next to the stone gargoyle that decorated the rusting wrought iron railings on the roof, Tooth looked a bit like a gargoyle himself: a wet, feathery, angry gargoyle.

The great pariah cheel could feel his fleas digging deeper under the pinions of his feathers, searching for a warmth and dryness that eluded both parasite and host.

Tooth loosened his grip on the body of the rat that he'd killed the previous day; the carrion flesh was too sodden with rain to be appetizing. Miserably, he ruffled his feathers, trying to shake off at least the worst of the wet. He closed his eyes and thought of a warm nest of twigs and bones, high on the very end of a friendly telegraph pole, a nest where the air would eddy and swirl around his feathers in breaking waves, each different gust carrying news and scents and warmth with it. Then he huddled closer to the stone gargoyle—it was only cold stone, but it was something to lean against.

He closed his eyes, tightened his claws around the railing and was almost asleep when he heard a mew. Instinctively, Tooth stabbed, his claws with their wicked talons slashing upwards.

But the cat—an elderly Siamese with a quizzical look on her face—had stayed well back. Tooth's talons and beak closed on thin air. The cheel overbalanced and plummeted off the railing, doing a hasty three-point turn just in time to avoid falling into the potted plants on the balcony below.

"What the bleeding fleas and ticks?" he spluttered. "Back off, you flearidden old—Miao? What's up?"

"If you're awake now, Tooth, may we speak? On truce terms, all right? It's important," said the Siamese.

Tooth was suddenly wide awake. He had known—and hunted—Miao from the time she'd been the fastest six-weeker in her litter, and over time, he'd grown . . . well, he wasn't sure. Pariah cheels didn't make friends with cats. Everyone knew that. But he and Miao had seen a lot of monsoons come and go in Nizamuddin, and they'd developed a silent truce; he rarely stooped or hunted her these days. For one, he knew that she might have trouble with her left hip, but she still had a wickedly fast paw. And then, if he was honest, he'd have to admit it had been fun watching her grow up. Still, they'd spoken face-to-face perhaps thrice in the last fifteen years.

"Come up, Miao," he said. "Rules of truce: in this circle, for this time, may the winds hear my rhyme; all the laws of host and guest shall hold fast and be blessed. Safe from talon, safe from claw; I'll harm neither whisker nor paw. Enter then and have your say; you are my honoured guest today."

On the stairs, Miao let her whiskers relax. She had hoped for this response, but predator birds were often of uncertain temper, and she hadn't been confident of Tooth. The rhythm of the age-old words brought her comfort.

The roof was wet, but she sat down near the gargoyle, looking up at Tooth. "It's about the Shuttered House . . ." she began. And then she told him everything she knew, starting from the history of the house, to Katar's news from the previous night.

". . . so that's the situation," she finished. "We need the Alliance, Tooth, and I'm asking you to mobilize the pariah cheels."

The hunter hooded his eyes. "This is cat business, Miao. I understand your concern, but I don't see what it has to do with us. Different species. Not our fight."

Miao flickered her ears in gentle disagreement. "See it differently, Tooth," she said. "Whatever those creatures in the Shuttered House may have been when they first went in, they aren't cats any more. You know what happens when a dog goes rabid, or a cat goes feral, or a cheel goes rogue. Now imagine that happening over two generations.

"Imagine kittens who have never known what it is to be kittens, who have never known anything but this twisted, unnatural life. Imagine a pack of cats—Tooth, a pack, like a pack of wild dogs or hyaenas—trained to hate all the other creatures who live in Nizamuddin. They'll start fights; not individual fights but carefully targeted attacks. Not just on the cats, Tooth, but on dogs. On the sparrows, the crows, on the Bigfeet's pets. On you and on your mate Claw's hatchlings, whenever she has her next batch. What we're facing is not a bunch of strays coming out of a Bigfeet house and fighting for space; we may be facing a feral invasion. And we need you. Without you, the rest of the birds will do nothing."

Tooth preened his feathers, thinking. Then the hunter turned towards Miao. "They're still cats, Miao. This is your fight. We have the skies to go to, the winds will take us sailing wherever we please. The birds are not earth-held, and we don't fight the earthbound. It seems like a classic stray versus stray territorial bust-up to me. But even if I thought there was some danger from these ferals, what do we of the high winds have to do with this? The truce holds if you like, Miao; I'll get Claw to lay off attacking the cats for as long as you want, but we're not getting our talons in a tangle."

The old Siamese flicked the rain off her paws, washing them absently. There was no defeat in her posture, though her eyes had filmed over with a mist that was more than age; she was looking back in time, looking back through memory.

Tooth wished she would go. It made him uncomfortable to say no to Miao but he really didn't see how this was any of his business. The winds were whipping up again, and a grey drizzle had begun to fall. The air smelled of storm and gale, and he wanted to be out surfing the thunder.

"Do you remember your mother, Tooth?" Miao said. The cheel turned, startled.

"Stoop was a good friend of mine," the cat continued. "I didn't get on that well with her mate, Conquer; he didn't have much time for cats. But many's the time Stoop and I sat up here and talked. You remind me a lot of her."

"I do?" said Tooth. He shuffled uncomfortably, his talons gripping the balcony a little tighter. His mother had been a legendary flier and fighter, the warrior queen of the air waves. He had spent the first part of his life as a fierce fledgling trying to be her, and the second part of his life as a stellar Wing Commander who understood that he would always fall short of Stoop's standards, but tried to do his best anyway.

"Yes, you do," said Miao gently. "You have her sense of justice, but perhaps not the recklessness."

Tooth chirred in warning and involuntarily, his feathers ruffled. "My mother wasn't reckless," the cheel said.

Miao laughed quietly to herself. She had seen the warning flare at the back of Tooth's eyes, the red ring around his pupils lighting up just for an instant.

"Stoop was fearless," she said. "She was the best fighter of her batch—the one with the most kills, the one who flew out of the sun straight at her enemies, the one who never refused a fight. And she had a large and generous heart, she looked after her fledglings very well indeed, and she knew the last tail feather of every member of her squadron."

Miao stopped to wash the very tip of her tail.

"But she was reckless, Tooth. Do you know how she died?"

The pariah cheel said nothing, though pain flickered for a second in his eyes.

CONQUER HAD COME BACK HOME *one night with a gash in his wing, his talons in shreds. He had watched Tooth come jerkily out of a fast dive, saying nothing. Then he'd said, "You'll have to do better than that if you lead the squadron, son. Your mother trained them all herself, down to the last raptor, and they'll be watching you for mistakes when you join as Flight Lieutenant—no, that's too junior, better make it Group Captain. Be ready to take over as Wingco in three months."*

The young Tooth had asked, "I'm joining the squad? I thought there wasn't a vacancy until next monsoon?"

Conquer had been licking his wounds, trying to seal the ends of the torn feathers in his wing. There was no expression in the grey hawk's eyes as he looked at his son.

"There is now," he said. "Stoop died this afternoon."

Tooth had never known how it happened. He asked his father about it once, and was cuffed so soundly that he flew with a slight downwards dip for a while, from the rip that Conquer's talons had left in his right wing. He did not inquire again.

Now, his own feathers greying ever so slightly at the tips, he faced the cat who had been such a good friend to his mother. "Will you tell me the story, Miao?" he said.

The cat's smoky eyes looked deep into his golden ones. "Are you sure you want to know?" she said.

Tooth stared up at the grey skies, letting his feathers rise and fall as he thought it over. "Yes," he said finally. "It's time I knew what happened."

Miao settled down, a judicious distance from Tooth, her gaze drifting out over the rooftops."Do you remember Tigris?" she said.

"Your Sender?" said Tooth. "Yes, my father spoke often of her when he told us stories of his fledgling years. She was a Far-Seer of the old school, wasn't she? I haven't met too many like her, among the cheels or the cats."

"It was Tigris's first year as a Sender," said Miao. "Her

mother had discovered her abilities that winter, when she realized that Tigris's whiskers let her reach further than any other
kitten in the litter—further even than any of the adult cats."

The hunter listened intently, his eyes hooded, his talons
relaxed, as the Siamese spun her tale.

CHAPTER FIFTEEN

The Summer of the Crows

All through that winter, Tigris saw dark visions. She dreamed of black clouds coming down from the sky until they became shrouds for the wildings. She was anxious—first she asked the wildings to consider leaving Nizamuddin, and then she grew more insistent. But who would make a clan shift because of the dreams of a young cat just over a year old? Even her mother, Neferkitty, who was the clan's most fierce queen, refused to take Tigris's demands seriously.

In spring, the dreams that haunted Tigris grew more vivid, but it was one of the most beautiful springs we had seen. One of those rare ones, where the nights were jasmine-drenched, the prey thick on the ground, and the Bigfeet left us alone for a change.

If it was a perfect spring, the following season was anything but, for that summer was the summer of the crows.

First there was just one flock, and then two, and then more and more, settling raucously in the hedges and trees of Nizamuddin. We wildings were indifferent—crows had always been part of the colony—and then, as more and more of them came in, wary. You know what crows are like, Tooth: loud and bustling and given to throwing parties every evening with brawls between the younger lot. And they can be mean, and some of them are very clever thieves—they'll wait for a cat or a cheel to make the kill, and then sneak in and swipe the lot.

But they're also fun: look at Blackwing and Brightbeak and their brood, and the way they keep watch for all of us here. These crows, though, were different. They came in like the gathering monsoon clouds, masses of them, shrouding the trees in black and grey, filling the skies with their relentless cawing and squabbling. And then the clan remembered Tigris' visions, and in our hearts and whiskers, we were afraid.

At first, Stoop paid them no mind. She went on her daily patrols as always and stayed far away, on the highest gables, roosting in the trees in the wild, unclaimed lot. Conquer wasn't happy when she issued an order that all cheels were to leave Nizamuddin and make their homes as far away from the crows as possible, in Humayun's Tomb and across the canal in Jangpura, but he obeyed her, coming back himself for flying visits.

I was puzzled too, it wasn't like Stoop to cede territory—she was always one for a good fight, your mother. But she told me one day when our paths crossed, "I don't understand this, Miao, there's something behind the crows' behaviour. It's not your normal invasion—they've run away, they don't have real leaders or tribes and that makes them dangerous. I need to think about how to get them out of here."

She tried to speak to their leaders, but Bitterbite and Bakbuk flapped out of their nests at her and cawed their threats furiously, refusing to answer questions. Stoop parried their darts at her easily, rising into the feathery embrace of the nimbus clouds, and didn't try to engage them again.

We missed the cheels. Your family sometimes preys on kittens, or old cats, or ones that are sick, but mostly they leave our kind alone—and we raid their nests when we can find one on lower ground, we've killed fledglings too. There's no real enmity between us, though, and the tradition you grew up in, Tooth, where we leave part of the kill for you and you for us in lean hunting weather—it goes back to the first cats and cheels who settled in the old alleys of Nizamuddin.

I sometimes looked up at the sky, and I'd see a tiny, faraway speck against the sun—Stoop, gliding above us, looking down at Nizamuddin, quartering her turf. I often wondered what she saw, and when her shadow floated over me, darkening the ground for a fleeting second, I missed her.

The crows were becoming bolder. They stole from us, attacked our kittens until we had to keep all of them, nine-weekers and younger, carefully corralled in the tiny park at the back, with the toms guarding them, and even so we lost quite a few. They harried the lizards and the mice, the rats and the bandicoots, and then they began to attack the Bigfeet's homes and their pets—and this was dangerous for all of us, Tooth.

Six of the crows got into one of the homes, opened up the cage of these guinea pigs who were kept as pets, and killed them all. Poor things. They were silly little creatures with no conversation at all: "I gots food! I not gots food! I gots more food than you gots!" was about as much as they could manage. But they didn't deserve that ending, and there was no need for it—the crows who did it weren't even looking for food. They were just bored.

After a pair of hutch rabbits went the same way, and the crows attacked a Bigfoot child, we saw that the Bigfeet were getting restless, and angry. And we were fearful, because we didn't know what they would do, but we were sure it wouldn't be anything good.

I would have gone to Stoop then, but she had disappeared. Oh, her patrol was there all right, but they flew further and further away, only circling Nizamuddin once during the day, and Stoop was nowhere to be seen.

I had too many troubles of my own to worry about Stoop for long, anyway. Nizamuddin has always been rich in hunting, and the Bigfeet leave wonderful things out for all of us in their garbage heaps, but there were too many crows, and more crowding in every day. Bitterbite and Bakbuk led several murders of crows out foraging most days and they were becoming more vicious, stalking us cats and stealing our kills whenever they could. One murder of crows left suddenly, led by Breakbone, and we heard they'd settled in the Jangpura market, across the canal.

Then one day Stoop flew back with worrying news. "The Bigfeet are setting out poison," she said. She tried to tell Breakbone, because she believed it was her duty to warn all other creatures, even the hostiles.

"Get away with you, you bag of bones," was what Breakbone said, "you're just trying to keep us away from good feeding so that you and your flea-ridden friends can hunt without competition." So Stoop said no more, but a week later, she came back to tell us that all the garbage heaps in the market were covered with black feathers. Breakbone and his gang had fallen victim to the poison.

After that, not a single crow tried to leave Nizamuddin, even though more and more crows came flooding in by the day. Living became a desperate struggle; we kept our eyes on the sky, never knowing when their sharp beaks would attack again. "We have to do something," I told Neferkitty one evening. That morning, I had seen the squirrels keening in a sad huddle, mourning the loss of yet another of their family.

Neferkitty had a gaunt look to her, by then. She'd been a handsome, well-muscled queen but the last few months had taken it out on her—she'd melted down to bone and muscle. It was only later that I discovered she'd been feeding the kittens and nursing mothers from her kills, barely eating enough herself to keep tail and whiskers together. But her mind was as sharp as ever.

"I have a plan," she said. "It's desperate, but it'll have to do." She told me the details and I agreed; it was desperate, but what other choice did we have? We would give Bitterbite and Bakbuk one chance—ask them to get half the crows to leave, perhaps to find homes a little further off, at Humayun's Tomb with the peacocks and the bulbul songbirds. Or perhaps they could go even further out, to the golf course with its spacious, green grounds. If they refused, we'd attack that night itself.

The dogs were with us. They had suffered equally from the invasion of the crows, and when we approached them to ask for a truce, their leader Tommy went further and said they'd stand by us and fight if need be. But there were only a few strays, and ours was still a woefully thin force.

"It would help if we had the pariah cheels on our side, Miao," she said. "Any news of Stoop?"

There was none; and when I spoke to Conquer that night, your father was civil but distant. "Not our fight, Miao," he said, "The cheels have moved on. Besides, I haven't seen Stoop myself in many moons. She's all right—my pinions would fluff and tell me if she was in serious danger—but that's all I know." I pleaded with him until his tail feathers began to ruffle in annoyance, and then I had to back off.

It would have made a difference to have Conquer and his squadrons on our side. Without the cheels, the other birds refused to get involved.

"Look at us," said Spackle Sparrow and Grackle Sparrow. "We're too small, Miao, the crows would make mincemeat of us in no time." The pigeons had long since fled; Bismillah, the bulbul, said he'd do what he could, but he couldn't put his brood in further danger. And Petuk and Potla, the vultures, had left for a long holiday, preferring the Yamuna river with all its pollution to overcrowded Nizamuddin.

Neferkitty and I went to meet Bitterbite and Bakbuk. It was an unpleasant task; they were squabbling over one of their kills, though we couldn't tell what animal it was. Just as well; sometimes it was best not to know. Bakbuk lifted his head; his beak was bloody, his eye angry.

"You dare interrupt my meal, cats?"

"Mine!" cawed Bitterbite furiously. "Mineminemine! I found it first, so I did."

Bakbuk stabbed at her, tearing a feather slightly. Then he turned back to us. "Well?"

Neferkitty's feathery tail twitched warily as she laid out our terms. All were welcome in Nizamuddin, but he would agree there were too many crows. Food for all—the crows as well as the other animals—was running short; the Bigfeet were getting restless and would soon take steps, as they had with the garbage heaps in the market. We didn't want a fight, and there were many other parks and neighbourhoods; if half the crows would agree to leave, we could continue to live in peace. Would Bakbuk agree?

Before Bakbuk could say anything, before I could do anything, Bitterbite flew at Neferkitty, slashing fiercely at her face. Neferkitty screamed as the crow's sharp talons shredded her ear. "Trucebreaker!" I cried in shock, leaping out of Bakbuk's way. "We came here under truce terms!"

Neferkitty, despite her bleeding ear, was now swatting at Bitterbite, but I could see the rest of the murder swarming into formation. "Neferkitty, follow me!" I howled, and we both fought our way out of there. If the dogs hadn't helped us, we wouldn't have made it.

Bakbuk's hoarse, mocking caws followed us: "Come to us next time and we'll tear you to shreds, you furbags! Nothing will make us leave, you hear? Our trees. Our park. Our kills. Ours!" The sky was black with crows, cawing and shrieking their defiance.

We rejoined our clan in the small park at the back. None of us had much to say; we didn't need to link to know that we were all apprehensive of the night to come. Instead of even considering the situation or offering some sort of solution, the crows were now on guard, and there were so many of them.

"Neferkitty," I said after a while. "Should we attack as planned, or is there no hope?"

"I've been thinking the same thing," said Neferkitty, her black fur gaping here and there with red where the blood still streamed from her cuts. "It seems desperate, doesn't it? Perhaps it's us who should leave."

I'd thought about that too, but the idea of leaving Nizamuddin, turning our backs on the neem trees and the familiar alleys, abandoning the rooftops we'd played our stalking games on as kittens . . . it was too much, and how would we shift all the cats?

The crows could take flight, map neighbourhoods, find trees; it would take one cat scout many moons to locate a suitable territory. Where would we find a place that had enough scavenging for so many of us, that was free of other cat clowders, that didn't have too many predators, that was close enough to Nizamuddin?

And even if we did . . . in the vast shared memory of Delhi's cat clans, I could see not even the faintest pawmark that indicated a successful migration. Cats were not birds; we grew up and lived in the same territories as our mothers and fathers, and that was that. I said as much to Neferkitty.

"It sounds crazy, I know," she said. "But Miao, we can't go on much longer. With the crows here, we'll starve this winter; we're all weakening, and who knows if we'll be able to protect the next litter of kittens? We have to think of the unthinkable."

We would have talked further, but there was a great beat of wings, and then we heard the high, pitiful screaming of one of the young stray pups, and the sound of the caws rose until we were nearly deafened. Nizamuddin was under attack.

YOU HAVE TO IMAGINE it for yourself. All of us, cats and dogs, squirrels and mice, hedge pigeons, mynahs . . . scattered in disarray, while great black clouds of crows poured out like smoke descending from the trees. The noise! The rustling of their wings, the crescendo of caws—it was deafening and confusing, some of the smaller animals could do nothing but run up and down, making targets of themselves, the poor things. The squirrels ran back and forth along the branches, getting picked off two at a time; the mice scurried in desperate circles on the ground. It was terrible.

That first hour was dire. Neferkitty got out there, of course, and did the best she could, along with the fighting toms. The dogs helped, but soon we were bombarded by clusters of crows. The only thing that saved us was that the crows weren't proper fighters. They were from different families, unused to fighting in formation, and I suppose they hadn't really expected much resistance. They made a fearsome racket, but they weren't attacking in order—any old group would take off any time it felt like it, and they banged into each other, in the air and on the ground. They squabbled too, and stabbed each other when they grew cross, and that saved many of us. Bakbuk got so annoyed with his best fighters for diving before he did that he snapped at three of them, wounding them so badly they had to retreat.

Even so, they had the advantage of numbers—however badly they fought, each injured crow was replaced immediately by another ten, and they covered the grass with the black of their wings. Neferkitty kept her head. She had crept into the trees, and she moved fast from branch to branch, from neem to the flame tree to the laburnum, attacking the crows from behind, attacking their leaders just as they were poised for take-off, ducking back into the leaves if they tried to turn on her. The pups stood with us, the Nizamuddin strays, barking their heads off, bounding into the thick of the press, not letting the crows land.

Neferkitty was bleeding heavily—some of the wounds of the morning had opened up again. But the owls had woken up and rallied around her. Hootem and Hutom made darts from the safety of their hole in the ancient laburnum tree, getting in some good shots and buying Neferkitty a little breathing space. But the beat of the black wings never stopped; it seemed the trees were spewing out crows nonstop, one after another.

Bitterbite was in between us and Neferkitty, with a proper murder of crows, six of them who had clearly seen fighting before. I measured the distance between us and shuddered—the thought of trying to get to her, or her trying to get to us, through a thicket of sharp beaks and blood-hungry claws, was not pretty.

There was a hard thud and I felt something bounce off my back. I whipped around, my whiskers quivering, and found myself staring at a tiny, terrified, chittering squirrel, who was tugging its furry tail around itself in fear. "If you please," it said through chattering teeth, "a friend sent me. My name is Aaaaooooo ooww owww." I was too shocked to even take a swipe at it, but before I got my brains in order, there was a second shock.

Flying so low that her plumage skimmed the ground, Stoop shot over us, braking in mid-air to hover, hummingbird-fashion. "Miao, meet Ao; this is Jao," she said, depositing another small heap of tumbled fur on the ground. "Friends of mine; keep them safe for me, you hear? No time to explain. We'll touch talons later." And then she had pulled out of her brief hover and shot away, a lethally fast, soaring streak aimed like an arrow at Bitterbite.

The crow never saw what hit her, Tooth, your mother was that fast. There was a ripping sound, a desperate squawk—that was all, and then we saw a bundle of black feathers falling out of the sky. Bitterbite was gone, and before the crows in her murder could react, Stoop had done a three-point roll and come back at them with her talons extended. Two more plunged down to the ground. A third screeched in pain and flapped slowly over to a nearby branch to rest; the fourth tried to engage Stoop in battle and had his wing torn off; Bakbuk flapped his wings in fear and fled. Bakbuk was the kind of crow whose caws were louder than his courage—he didn't like getting his feathers bloody.

But as Stoop rose above the black mass, their caws now deafening, we could all see that something was wrong. She flew at an angle, dipping her right wing slightly, and seemed to be in pain. The crows saw it too. The birds that had ducked and weaved out of her way started to gather again, massing behind her even as she tried to gain some height. It's odd—they didn't attack her in a group, but every so often, one of them would dart out from its murder and fly at her, staying just out of range of her talons.

TOOTH LOOKED INTO MIAO'S EYES and then away. "Counting coup," he said, his eyes yellow and sad. "It's a classic crow manouevre when they're faced with a predator bird on its own. Cornered, a cheel can take on a murder—even injured, we're— well, let me demonstrate."

Tooth's talons slashed viciously at Miao's face. She felt the rush of air on her whiskers, felt the claw miss her nose by a millimetre—and then the cheel was offering her a wet leaf, impaled on one of his deadly, curving nails. "It was stuck on your cheek," he said, "kind of annoying to look at."

Miao had too much self-control to mew, but she quickly washed a paw. "I see what you mean about speed," she said.

"Crows are cowards," Tooth continued. "They don't like getting hurt. So instead, they take turns coming up close to the predator, close enough to disturb our flight patterns and paths, but pulling back before they get hurt. If they come in one after another, weaving and ducking around a predator, especially a wounded one, they'll tire the predator out, cause confusion, get the raptor to use up all its energy in useless attacks. And then, once the predator's weakened, that's when the whole murder will attack . . ." He turned away and ruffled the ends of his feathers. "So that's how Stoop died."

Miao hesitated, and then gingerly, not knowing if Tooth would be angered, she put her head up and very quickly, brushed it against the hawk's feathery face. Tooth jerked his head back, his eyes flaring bright red for a second, and then stilled.

"No, Tooth," she said gently. "That wasn't how your mother died."

STOOP'S WINGS DROOPED, continued Miao. She appeared to be losing height, but awkward as she was, she kept ahead of the crows, using her right talon to fend off attackers.

"Don't worry, Miao-ji," said a squeaky voice near my paw. "Stoop knows what she's doing."

Does she? I said sharply—I wasn't used to talking to squirrels. Flying by the side of your foes when you're badly injured doesn't seem like much of a plan to me, squirrel.

Ao kept her squinty eyes on me. "Been watching Stoop for many days, Jao and I have. Stoop often flew near us but never hurt us, never even threatened us. It was different with the crows. First, the crows went after my mum. Then the crows went after my dad. Then there were just the two of us. We didn't know what to do. We sat at the top of the trees, scared to come down to the ground and feed, scared to look for shelter. Every time we came down the tree trunk, the crows attacked. Then one evening, there was Stoop, resting on the high branch above our heads."

The squirrel took a deep breath, her fluffy tail quivering nervously. "Jao took his courage in both paws and said, cheel, cheel, may we speak? She whipped around, her red eyes glaring

226

at us, but in curiosity, not challenge. I was scared. But Jao said, cheel, maybe you'll kill us, maybe you won't, but those crows, they're going to kill us anyway. That's the truth. So we're asking for help. Cheel, you're a predator, one of the big ones. We're just squirrels, us little ones. But perhaps, sometimes, the big ones look out for the little ones?"

Jao pulled his head out of his bushy tail and nodded in confirmation. Ao touched her tail to his, gently, and went on. "Stoop stared at us for a long, long time. She said nothing, just took us in with her tired red eyes. So I spoke up next, seeing that Jao had been so brave. I told her about our mum, our dad, what the crows did to so many of the little ones. And as I was speaking, suddenly, Stoop put her beak out and picked me up by the middle. She brought me close to her great sharp talons, and I thought, this is it: a cheel will get me instead of the crows. I hoped she would kill me fast. But instead, she just looked me over, closely. And then she put me down, and said, almost to herself, this has gone on too long. It was the next day that she flew in, landing on our branch, and told us: get on my back."

Jao nodded, holding his paws together as he took up the tale. "We were scared, my teeth chattered and I could hear Ao squeaking in fright, but we got on and we stayed on, holding hard to Stoop's feathers. She took us first to the roof—over there, that house, can you see it?—and then she told us what she planned to do. You know the rest; she's brought us to you, and now she's off putting her plan into action. Stoop knows exactly what she's doing. It's all under control."

I looked up at the sky. The crows were close to the perimeter of Nizamuddin, now, near the saint's shrine, and three of them were tagging the small black dot that was Stoop's form in the sky. It seemed as though she was towing a flotilla of crows behind her; the trees down in our park were bare and empty. They had to duck every so often to avoid the thick tangle of electric lines, and the brightly coloured kites the Bigfeet kids were flying from the roofs. As we watched, the trio slashed at Stoop, in arrow formation; she wheeled sideways, and stabbed back at them, but again, she was dropping, and then the trio closed in on her, and she went into a steep dive, the crows cawing in celebration as they followed.

Jao squeaked. "Over there," he said. "Do you see?"

Stoop did a triple roll and shot, unbelievably, upwards, slicing through the black wave of crows like a claw going through butter. There was no sign of a damaged wing now, no sign of distress as she arced towards the sky.

Too late, the crows saw the still dots hovering motionless at the corners of the park. Cheels from the next colony, dozens of them, scattered at intervals across the horizon in tight knots of ten or so; others rose up now from the surrounding buildings, from the edges of the roofs and the crowns of the telephone poles and trees that were scattered through the dargah. Led by Conquer, they formed a kind of net around the confused cloud of crows, hemming them in, almost herding them, the way dogs will sometimes herd their pups. And now, the crows could see that Stoop had led them into a trap—straight towards the tangle of power lines that criss-crossed the perimeter of the dargah.

Without Bitterbite and Bakbuk to guide them, the crows were in disarray. Some flew into the powerlines, and with more and more birds colliding into each other, they were soon in a tremendous tangle—and then there was a spark and a horrible smell, and first one and then another of the powerlines went up in flames, taking more crows with them. Three of the best crow fighters tried to take on Conquer himself, but the feathers flew as the massive cheel fought back, and soon he rose triumphant, if somewhat worse for wear, above the vanquished crows. A few murders veered to the right and the left, but the cheels closed formation on them and the air was thick with their torn wings and hoarse cries. Some crows—a small cluster towards the back of the murder—managed to get away, screeching their dismay and surrender as they plunged for the safety of the trees, clearly on the run. We never saw them again.

It was over in a matter of minutes, and I saw Neferkitty and some of the toms slump to the ground, grateful for the rest. Jao and Ao chittered behind us in celebration. "Incredible," wuffed Tommy—he and the stray dogs had watched the crows retreat in wonder. I knew what he meant; it had all happened so fast, and now the cheel squadrons were reforming into a large, neat arrowhead. It was a stately, soaring group of cheels that came to roost in the rooftops of Nizamuddin—this very roof, Tooth.

Stoop arced overhead as Conquer watched her proudly. "Little ones," she called, streaking down so low between the trees that she almost brushed our heads, "I kept my promise, little ones! What a day, Miao! Did you like the show?"

And then she was off again, soaring, rolling and diving, a beautiful black streak across the sky, hitchhiking the winds and gliding along. Up on the roof, I saw her Wing Commander,

Slash, spread his feathers out in sudden alarm. He gave a loud startled call. "Stoop! Watch out!"

She was doing her aerobatics between the edges of the roofs of the dargah and the long black power cables, and she was, not for the first time, too close, far too close. She heard Slash's alarm call, flicked her tail feathers into a closed fan and dived smoothly downwards, easily avoiding the ominous dark line of the cables, streaking far above its deadly width, towards us. I saw Slash shift his claws back on his perch, riffing his feathers back into shape in relief.

She looked so beautiful in that moment, Tooth. Your mother had a knack of cutting through the air cleanly, her wings held back just an inch more than the other cheels. The sun glinted off the brown feathers on her back, turning them gold. And then: "Slash! Have you ever seen an upwards triple roll?" she called as she plummeted all the way back down, hovering in the air like a hummingbird rather than a cheel, near a first-floor parapet. Slash tensed: "Stoop! No, it's too dangerous!" he said, and his voice shrilled with alarm. "Come back!" called Ao. "Come down!" squeaked Jao.

But she had already risen into the air, spinning like a golden top, doing a perfect roll upwards into the clear blue sky, then a second, skating higher on a sudden tug from a sharp breeze, and then the third, spectacular, looping roll. There she was, a golden-brown streak of light, and we saw her rise higher, higher, upside down now. And then Slash called out again, his hoarse voice urgent and harsh, as a smoking power cable, damaged from the battle, erupted in a shower of sparks.

We couldn't tell her golden feathers from the flames.

FOR A LONG WHILE, there was no conversation—only silence and the rain. Miao said nothing, just sat next to the cheel, both of them gazing out and down into the park, and if they saw a slim, graceful golden-brown phantom skimming the trees and the rooftops, neither of them said so.

Finally, Tooth turned back to Miao. "I'll have to speak to Conquer and to Claw, but this is what we can offer. We won't start your fight for you, Miao. We won't attack first. We won't take orders from any cat but you or Katar. But when you need our help, we'll be there."

Miao let her whiskers relax, wanting to give Tooth another head-rub, but knowing from the stiffness in his maxillary feathers and the way his talons tightly gripped the edge of the roof that the cheel wouldn't welcome a touch at this moment. "Thank you, Tooth," she said and began to make her descent. As she went down the stairs in brief hops, Tooth called out to her. "Miao?" he said.

"Yes, Tooth?"

"Just tell the little ones in Nizamuddin, the mice and the shrews and the sparrows . . . tell the little ones it'll be all right." And then the raptor turned his head back to the rain, which was falling in a steady torrent.

CHAPTER SIXTEEN

A Feral Hunger

Crouched behind the tattered velvet curtains, Datura silently observed the Bigfeet who tramped through the house. "Hide!" he had growled to the others. "Spread out in groups, stay away from the line of feeding bowls, don't attack the Bigfeet. Yet."

But as the night and day wore on, the flood of Bigfeet had only grown. The night watchmen had raised the alarm, peering into the Shuttered House when the cats began to yowl their great lament, as was custom. Datura had started the dirge for the dead, and had cuffed or bitten the throats of the few who hadn't joined in. The white cat retreated when the police came in, watching from the stairs, sure that other Bigfeet would follow. He felt no sadness as they carried the body of the old Bigfoot out; instead, he sniffed the air, smelling the vans and cars drawing up outside, tasting what came in through the windows.

"We could stay here," Ratsbane had said defiantly. "We could hide from the Bigfeet and live in the back, couldn't we?"

Datura didn't think so. One look at the Bigfeet who came stumbling in, wincing at the darkness of the house, calling out to one another in horror at its squalor, was enough to tell the white cat that they had lost their privacy and their home. The air rushed in from the window and doorway, polluting the close, comfortable stench that spoke to him of family and home. When Ratsbane growled at a Bigfoot who was distastefully pushing the filthy food bowls around with an old Malacca cane, Datura didn't stop the black cat, but he didn't join in either, and he held the other cats back from attacking the Bigfoot with a single flick of his whiskers. Two of the Bigfeet stamped their feet menacingly at Ratsbane, and though the black tom hissed again, he had to fall back.

"But this is our house! Datura, we must fight them for it!" growled Ratsbane.

"This *was* our house," said Datura. "Now it's theirs."

"And where will we go?" asked Aconite, sidling up to them. "Outside," said Datura. "Leave me, Aconite."

He would answer no further questions, and when Ratsbane tried to ask what his plans were, Datura spun around from behind the velvet curtains, his claws unsheathed, raking a bloody line across the black cat's nose. "I said, leave me!"

Ratsbane went yelping away. Aconite watched Datura for a while, her golden eyes narrowed, and then she went off to find a hiding place away from the Bigfeet. They unsettled her. She had never paid attention to the few she saw from the windows, and didn't know their harsh, guttural language. But as more of them marched through the rooms, opening the windows, pushing back the tattered drapes, letting the light and air in, she felt the invasion keenly.

Behind the velvet curtains, Datura let his mind drift outwards. The outside smelled rich to him, much to his surprise. He had hated the sky since he had tumbled out on to the roof as a kitten and looked up—it was such a long way away that it made him dizzy. Datura preferred close spaces where he knew exactly where each predator or prey was to be found; the sky made him uncomfortably aware that the outside was too vast for him to patrol on his own.

But when the windows were first thrown open after the death of the Bigfoot, the rusted catches squealing, the dead flies that hung off the cobwebs that encrusted the panes falling to the floor in thick clusters, Datura had been intensely fascinated. It was dark, and the rain blanketed the night so that he couldn't see the sky. Without that high, arcing blue emptiness, the outside didn't seem so menacing, and the hedges carried the rich scent of prey to his whiskers. From his spot behind the curtains the white cat stared out at the grounds. Both his eyes gleamed, the sane blue one and the mad yellow one, as he inhaled sharply. Datura tallied the bounty; the fat mice in the hedgerows, the juicy bandicoots bustling about in their tunnels, the grubs and beetles, the sleeping birds. It was a world of prey begging to be hunted.

A smoky, thin dawn had broken the morning. The rain had become a sulky drizzle. The cat shook out his ears and stretched his paws; absently, he listened to the screeching pleas of some poor unfortunate who had crossed Aconite's path. She was clearly in a temper, he thought, though both cats subsided into silence when two Bigfeet came thumping down the stairs, talking loudly.

"Aconite," he called. "Come here and tell me what you smell."

The grey cat stopped what she was doing—smacking some of the smaller ferals, in an attempt to work off her irritation at the Bigfeet invasion—and joined Datura. "Stretch your whiskers out," he said. "What does the outside feel like to you?"

Aconite fluffed her fur along with her whiskers, trying to make sense of the dizzying world revealed outside their windows and doors. "It stinks of Bigfeet," she said, "but they walk like ants, up and down, up and down, never exploring the gardens. Beyond that—" The cat extended her whiskers, and Datura saw her eyes open wide in delight.

"Meat," she whispered. "Fresh meat, in the grass, in the trees, sleeping in the hedges." Aconite's whiskers were trembling in surprise. Like Datura, she had smelled only the sour whiff of bird droppings and old litter in the courtyard, while the front veranda reeked of dry woodworm. No one had opened the windows of the Shuttered House in years, and as she sniffed at the clean air, the winds and the rain brought to her a great longing to feel the earth under her paws, the brush of grass against her belly.

"Where are the cats?" Aconite asked Datura, looking puzzled. Her nose had the sharpness of a true hunter's nose, but the winds carried only the scent of trails, not the strong, unmistakeable odour of clan markings. The air whispered to her that the wildings sometimes walked here; but none of them had claimed the territory or left scent markings around its perimeters. If the grounds were not claimed by the wildings, they weren't claimed by the Bigfeet either. "The strongest trails are from the rats and mice," Datura said. "And the birds weave skeins through the bushes. But this belongs to no one."

Datura watched Aconite, his blue eye calm. It was clear that she had no fear of the outside; his whiskers told him that more of the ferals were beginning to come out, groups of them sitting close to the windows and doors, drinking in the fresh air. Despite the Bigfeet, there was a crackle of excitement running through their ranks. Even Ratsbane sat quietly, watching and mapping what he could see of the rat holes and the clumps of earth left by the moles. Sooner or later, perhaps even as soon as tomorrow, the ferals would want to explore.

The scents of Nizamuddin wafted in his head, forming a map of the colony. The Bigfeet were everywhere, but like the canal pigs, they were to be treated as obstacles to be avoided, and their trash cans and unguarded kitchens would be of great use. Prey was everywhere, too; Datura couldn't understand why the Nizamuddin cats seemed to hunt only for food, given the abundance of prey in the trees, the gardens, the wild, empty lots. They hadn't even broken the necks of birds like the babblers, who were so easy to catch, judging by the silly way in which they hopped along the ground.

He cleaned his claws, sharpening the points by stropping them on his teeth. He thought of his few excursions into the closed concrete veranda at the back of the Shuttered House, a dead space littered with dried leaves and the husks of locusts. He thought of the barren roofs where the bats made their homes and the spiders wove thick webs, inhospitable even for birds.

Then he raised his head again and sniffed the air, so rich with prey and the tantalizing scents of green grass, trees, Bigfoot homes. The white cat's chest fluffed out as he growled. In Datura's mind, an immense anger was beginning to form and grow, though he could put neither words nor whiskers to it. The outside he had stayed away from all his life was inviting and filled with promise—for all the cats of Nizamuddin except for the ferals of the Shuttered House, he thought. It would not have occurred to Datura to blame himself for not venturing outside earlier. Instead the rage built within him at what he thought had been unfairly denied to him.

Aconite's contention that the grounds of the Shuttered House were free of cats was correct, he knew, the scent trails he had followed through his whiskers told him that a large colony of cats lived just beyond the grounds. Another skein of scents led to a dargah, the smell of meat from the butcher's shops and the restaurants making his whiskers ripple. He could scent no battle lines or hostility between the dargah cats and the colony cats—both sides had young hunting queens and warrior toms, from what he could tell, and yet they seemed to live on peaceful terms.

A bird flew low across the horizon, and next to him, Aconite chattered her teeth in the classic hunter's reflex. The longing on her face was unmistakeable, her neck stretched up as she pointed towards the bird. The ferals of the Shuttered House would soon start going out, thought Datura. The question was whether to treat the wildings who lived just outside the grounds as a threat or to ignore them. What did he know of the wildings that might be useful? How should he approach them?

A shiny green beetle trundled up near his front paws, its antennae twitching in excitement as it scented the outdoors. It hesitated, then moved forward. The white cat watched it climb the dusty wooden sill with some effort; it fell down twice, but kept going back. The third time, it managed to heave its fat bulk onto the sill. It twitched its antennae again, cautiously testing the breeze.

The outside was brimming with prey, ripe for the plucking. The more he looked at the open grounds, the more he let his nose travel the rooftops and explore the rich possibilities of the Bigfeet houses, the more Datura's eyes gleamed with avarice. If the Shuttered House had been left alone, he would have known none of this. But his home had been flung open to the winds and the rain and the scent of prey from the outside—the white cat would make it his home, then.

His blue eye watched the beetle idly, as it began to move out towards the wall and the faint rays of the sun, his thoughts veering back to the wildings. What were they really like? He didn't think they would be good predators; too soft, too kind. They were the kind who would offer—his mouth drew back in an unconscious snarl—to 'share' their world, the kind of weak clan who would try to talk to those of a different scent instead of killing them straightaway. He thought of the brown kitten who had wandered into the Shuttered House and how it had escaped their claws and teeth. The kitten and those like him had been free all this time to roam the lands and roads outside, while he and his feral family had been shut up indoors . . .

The beetle was moving faster, now, clicking its antennae eagerly as it scented wet mud.

Not predators, then, the white cat thought. So what did that make the wildings of Nizamuddin? His mad eye blazed up at the sky, and looked back at the beetle, which was almost over the lip of the wall. Its glossy back waggled back and forth as it tried to make a smooth descent. Casually, Datura stretched a paw out, and back; then his paw moved so fast that it was a blur as it smacked hard into the beetle's shell. The creature, smashed across its centre, landed on the ground, half-buried in the earth. Its antennae twitched once, feebly, as it lay on its back, and then it was still.

"Prey," said Datura aloud, his mew slow and sharp. It made the white cat feel much better. He knew how to deal with prey.

CHAPTER SEVENTEEN

Fear in the Dark

Though it was well past midnight and dawn would be lightening the heavy, clouded night skies soon, the old stone baoli was filled with cats. Some sat in the trees, glad for the shelter their wide leaves offered from the rain. But most were gathered on the ancient quartzite steps that ran in great tiers around the dull green waters of the stepwell.

"They must all come," Miao had told Katar, Hulo and Beraal, before sending out an urgent message on the link. The dargah cats had arrived, their tails waving like banners. Abol, Tabol and many of the canal cats were missing, though. The Bigfeet had put up a gaily coloured tent just across the bridge to celebrate a minor religious festival and two large groups of canal and market wildings were camped near the awning, feasting on leftovers.

Now the Siamese stayed motionless on the highest step, listening to the uproar that had burst out among the cats after she had shared Katar's news. Her delicate black nose was hard at work, trying to scent the way the decisions would go.

Katar's tail swished back and forth as he confronted Qawwali.

"Surely this is a matter for the colony cats?" Qawwali was saying. "I sympathize—a plague of ferals is a very dangerous thing—but what does this have to do with the dargah cats? The Shuttered House is not in our territory."

"Do you think the ferals will respect our boundary lines?" asked Katar. His mew was sharper than usual. None of the various clans of cats in the area were used to gathering as a group, except for the odd brawl; Miao was the only one present who could even remember a time when all of the cats had been summoned for a clan council. They did most of their business over the link, and it made Katar nervous to be in the company of so many different felines, to feel that his back was always being watched.

"But who is to say that the ferals will attack us at all?" asked one of the few market cats present. Katar felt the murmur of assent ripple along everyone's whiskers. Above him, Miao stiffened as the scent of the gathering changed.

Hulo bared his teeth, his rough hair slicked down and sodden by the storm. He was standing in the thick of the rain, and he didn't seem to care.

"Of course they won't attack us," he said, his whiskers raised belligerently, and the feline assembly murmured its assent. Hulo glared at them, his ears flicking the heavier drops of rain away. "No, they'll be good little ferals and ask if they might have a few drops of milk, if we don't mind sharing. Use your whiskers, fools! If they're losing their home, if they're not used to foraging for their own food, if they have no sense of boundaries, what do you think will happen? This is war, you understand?"

The rain carried the gathering's uncertainty to Miao's flared nostrils, but the Siamese showed no emotion in her eyes.

"I ask again," said Qawwali patiently, the old cat's gentle twitch on the link silencing the murmurs, "how this is a matter for the cats of the dargah? Katar and I are old friends, and I have every respect for Miao; but aside from volunteering a warrior or two from our ranks, should you need help, how does this affect us?"

Hulo growled in disgust, but before he could speak, Beraal dropped down from the branches of the tree where she had been listening to the conclave. Like him, she ignored the rain, letting her fur stick to her sides.

"From what we know of the ferals," she said, "they do not respect boundaries or scent markings, or territory lines. Most of them have grown up in the Shuttered House; they do not follow our rules. What we fear, Qawwali, is that there are so many of them—they will need a lot of space. And recall that the house is on the edge of your territory. It's closer to the dargah than it is to the Nizamuddin park where the Sender lives."

"Perhaps we can offer them settling grounds, then," Qawwali said. "Some could come to the dargah, some could stay in the colony. There's enough space for a few strays."

Hulo's back arched and the tom spat. Qawwali stared at him and then narrowed his eyes, growling in unmistakeable challenge.

Katar moved forward to stand next to Hulo. "No offence, friend," he said, his whiskers signalling them both to stand down. "What Hulo means is that it may not be possible to negotiate with the Shuttered House ferals. They are not like us, or indeed, like normal cats, though I think we should try to talk to Datura."

Qawwali glanced up at Miao, who sat impassively, like a statue of a cat. The Siamese didn't seem to have noticed the rain, and when a thunderclap startled them all, she stayed still, her deep eyes looking out into the distance.

"For years, we too have avoided the Shuttered House," said Qawwali. "None of the dargah cats will go there—the smell is more foul than the middens the Bigfeet pilgrims leave behind after their festivals, and we eat well enough in our lanes. But my memory goes back a long way, as must yours, Miao. Attacking strangers whose fur does not share our smell is one thing. But the ferals are not strangers, are they? Do we not owe them hospitality?"

Miao stirred, but instead of answering Qawwali directly, she washed a splash of mud off her paw. "Who here has been an inside cat?" she asked the wildings.

The clan stirred uneasily, but then one or two mewed softly. A marmalade cat had joined Qawwali's crew after his Bigfeet had moved out of Nizamuddin. Another, a smudged tortoiseshell queen, had been found by the market cats wandering disconsolately near the traffic, trying to hunt cars that looked as though they belonged to the Bigfeet who had moved house without her.

"I once spent time as an inside cat, when my mother was expecting a second litter and we were sheltered by Bigfeet," Miao said. "When they left, kind as they had been, they put us out at the edge of the dargah. We had been fed for so long that we had forgotten how to hunt. It was your mother, Ghazal, who found us and gave us shelter, Qawwali. So you are right; we might fear the Shuttered House ferals, but we owe them hospitality."

Qawwali's tail rose in relief. "My mother used to tell me how ancient and unbroken the tradition of hospitality was in Nizamuddin," he said. "My whiskers are glad that we will not have to break it."

Katar turned to the Siamese. "So you believe they will settle among us, Miao? Then why call this council at all?"

The Siamese met his eyes gravely. "I do not believe they will settle peacefully," she said. "You and I have seen the house. Hulo is right when he says this might be war."

Hulo relaxed his arched back a trifle. "My nose tells me that it will come to war," he said, his truculence yielding to worry. "Beraal thinks so too, and she has a fine nose for trouble."

The Siamese stretched her whiskers out, turning to Qawwali as she did so. "My friend," she said gently. "We meet most often at the fakir's shrine, and on the canal road. Will you walk down towards the Shuttered House and tell us what your nose tells you? Beraal will take you there."

The young queen and the old dargah cat left the baoli, Beraal leading the way over the slippery stones and through the slush. They made faint shadows in the dark, and soon they disappeared from sight.

Sitting behind Hulo, Southpaw watched the wildings with fascination. Except for brawls and the occasional gathering of cats when the Bigfeet had a large feast, he had never seen so many members of the various clans of Nizamuddin wildings in one place. From the restlessness on their whiskers, the way their ears were flicking back and forth uneasily, he picked up on the tension in the atmosphere.

The kitten was too scared to offer his mews in front of the rest of the wildings, but when he thought of Datura, Aconite and Ratsbane, it was hard for him to imagine the ferals settling down quietly, like old tabbies in the sun. The darkness seemed to press down on all of them. In the silence that had followed Qawwali's departure, they could hear the low wails from the Shuttered House, the warning cries of nightjars and barbets.

"Hulo," said Southpaw, patting the tom's large black paw to get his attention, "what will a war be like? Will Katar or you have to fight Datura and will we have to watch?"

The black tom's whiskers were unusually grim, and his worry came through in his low mew. "It won't be like a brawl in the baoli," he said. "If we have to fight the ferals, it'll be every wilding dragged in, Southpaw."

He saw the kitten's puzzled eyes, and tried to explain. "When you were in the Shuttered House, did only one or two of the ferals attack you, or did they all draw around?"

Southpaw shivered as he remembered the ring of menacing, bristling whiskers. "All of them were ready to attack," he said, his mew tiny and scared. Involuntarily, his tongue went to the sore spot where his whisker had been pulled out. It had healed, and the black bristle of a new whisker was beginning to come out, but he remembered the pain of it all too well.

"When we go hunting, we go on our own, or in pairs," said Hulo. "The ferals hunt in packs, because their territory is so much more cramped—and being inside cats for so long twists them, Southpaw. So if there's a war, we'll have to fight together."

Southpaw tried to imagine a war and failed. Except for the time Miao and Katar had tried to fight the dog who had chased him, he'd never seen wildings fighting side by side.

Miao sat up, her sharp ears alert. They heard the sound of cat's paws padding fast, back to the baoli.

Qawwali came in with heaving mud-splattered flanks, his whiskers exuding distress. He went straight up to Hulo, and touched his scruffy nose in apology.

"I hadn't realized," he said, turning to Miao and Katar. "The link tells one only so much. The ferals—they stink of blood and madness! I tried to send a greeting asking if we might approach, and Datura sent such a harsh message back that my whiskers are still tingling."

The rain fell softly on the wildings, washing the stone steps clean. The last of the night breezes stirred their fur. Dawn would soon be here, and the Bigfeet would be stirring.

"What did Datura say?" asked Miao softly, and it was Beraal who answered.

"Come closer, meat, and I'll kill you," she said, mimicking Datura's cold mews perfectly.

Miao turned to Hulo and Katar.

"We may not attack first," she said. "Much as you might want to, tell me what your paws think of going into their territory and setting about them with tooth and claw."

Reluctantly, Hulo acknowledged the truth of this. He had thought often of killing Datura, wanting to get his claws into the feral's throat ever since Southpaw came back with his tiny face bleeding. But they had skirted the house of the ferals for many summers and winters and it would be hard to break that convention.

"No," he said, his tail flicking to one side. "We cannot invade, but perhaps we must be ready for an invasion. Qawwali, where do you and the dargah cats stand?"

The old tom was staring at the path, his clouded eyes still gazing back at the Shuttered House, though he couldn't see anything in the darkness.

"With you," he said. "Call on us at need, and we'll be there."

Miao let her breath out silently. With the wildings of the dargah pledging their paws in battle, with the talons of Tooth and the cheels on their side, perhaps they had a fighting chance.

"Katar," she called to the grey tom, "how shall we prepare?"

Qawwali looked up at the sky, where the first fingers of dawn were lightening its indigo ink. "I will stay with one or two warriors to lend our whiskers to your battle plans, but may the rest of the dargah cats go? Dawn breaks, and once the Bigfeet open their homes and their shops, it will be difficult for such a large clowder of us wildings to go back without being noticed."

When the dargah cats had left, there were about a dozen of the wildings on the baoli steps, including Miao, Katar, Hulo, Beraal, Qawwali and Southpaw. There were also a handful of the market cats, but none of them were fighters.

"How much time do you think we have?" Miao asked Beraal.

The young queen hesitated. It was difficult to guess whether the ferals would come out one by one or in a pack, or whether they would only leave the Shuttered House once the Bigfeet stopped feeding them. But her sensitive nose hadn't smelled the unmistakeable signals cat colonies emitted when hunger had overtaken them, and she said as much to the group.

"The Bigfeet are still clumping around," said Hulo. "The ferals aren't likely to come out while they're there."

The sky rumbled, and in the breaking dawn, the rain came down in hard bursts. The intertwined branches of the trees that grew wild over the baoli protected the wildings from the worst of the storm, and they watched idly as the path disappeared under water.

Katar paced along the stone steps, his grey tail flicking the raindrops off his fur. "We may not have much time," he said, his fur standing up against the cold. "The Bigfeet will be there for a while, and Datura didn't seem to be the kind of cat who would tolerate their presence for long. Miao, we should call Abol and Tabol back as soon as possible—I think Datura and his ferals will come out in a few days, no more than that."

Qawwali's rheumy eyes looked into the distance, and his tail slumped to the ground. "Should we even try talking to Datura?"

"Yes," said Katar. Miao's ears flicked once in agreement. "It may not help," said the Siamese, "but we have to give the ferals the chance to live like us, perhaps some of them want peace even if Datura doesn't."

"We should go when the rain stops," said Katar. "Qawwali, will you join Miao and me?"

"And if they refuse?" said Hulo. "What then?"

"Then we fight," said Katar. "Our best chance is to keep them pinned inside the grounds of the Shuttered House—once they get out, we'll lose the battle."

Qawwali's ears went back at what seemed like unnecessary caution from Katar. "Even if a few ferals get out, what of it?" he said. "They can join our clans if they want, can't they?"

Hulo jumped down from his step to the ground, leaning over a puddle to lap water. "If the ferals start sneaking into Bigfeet houses, or attacking Bigfeet pets, you think the Bigfeet will see the difference between them and us? Katar's right, we have to keep them pinned here. To start with we should organize regular patrols. Abol can take the side nearest the Bigfeet houses when he comes back, and if your gang at the dargah can handle the baoli side, that would work well. We'll always have a pair of whiskers trained in this direction, so at the first sign of—"

In the distance, rising high above the drumming of the rain, they heard the scream of a bandicoot. It was a terrible sound, panicked and fearful, and then it cut off abruptly.

"That came from the Shuttered House," said Miao.

"I'll go and see what that was," said Hulo, padding towards the muddy lane.

"Wait," said Katar. "Don't go alone—I'll come with you."

The two toms had only just stepped into the lane when the birds began screaming. First the mynahs called out, their intelligent voices filled with fear. "Danger! Danger! Keek-keek!" they called. Then the barbets started up, hammering out a rising alarm, and next the crows began cawing in terrible shrieks. "Beware! Take to the skies! Every bird for himself!" The wildings watched as the morning sky filled with great clouds of birds, flocks of sparrows and bulbuls taking to the air in desperation, their feathers still ruffled with sleep.

"Get behind me, Southpaw," said Hulo, padding back to the steps before the kitten could run away. "Stay with me and Katar no matter what happens."

The rain was falling heavily, and the wind changed direction, blowing in great gusts from the side of the Shuttered House towards the baoli. Every one of the wildings caught the scent, but it was Katar who said it, his hackles slowly rising. "Blood," he mewed. "From fresh kills. The ferals are out, Miao."

CHAPTER EIGHTEEN

Into Battle

Someone was suffocating Mara, smothering her. She struggled frantically, spitting in her sleep, feeling her claws rip through something that made a silky tearing noise. The kitten sat up, her fur ruffled, and saw that she was locked in mortal combat with a torn quilt. "No more than that," Mara said to herself, but when she padded out for her morning bowl of fish, the unease from the dream stayed with her. She cuddled closer to her Bigfeet than usual, demanding that they pet her and soothe her, but even as they smoothed her fur down again and again, it stood up in spikes.

It was the rain, Mara thought, eyeing the greyness of the day from the window near the kitchen sink. It was something in the air, stirred up by the storm, brought here by the winds that were gusting against the kitchen door. Her fur remained fluffed, no matter how much she washed it with her rough pink tongue. Her Bigfoot ruffled the top of her head affectionately and opened the window.

The Sender's growl started at the back of her throat and deepened into a warning. "What's wrong," she heard her Bigfoot say. "What do you see?"

It wasn't what she could see—the birds seeking shelter, the rain beating down on the flame tree, darkening its vivid green leaves. The kitten's fur was standing on end and her nostrils were flared, her teeth chattering as she stared at the window. The rain drummed heavily, changing direction, and Mara growled again at the scent it brought to her: the unmistakeable stink of blood, and behind it, the darker scent of fear.

She leapt towards the window, just as her Bigfoot closed it. "No!" she said, trying to explain as her Bigfoot picked her up, making soothing noises, attempting to calm her down. Mara struggled as she was borne away in the Bigfoot's arms. "Let me go! Danger! Death! Woe!" But when she caught the puzzled look in her Bigfoot's eyes, the kitten stopped squirming and allowed herself to be carried off. She had no way of explaining to her Bigfoot that something was terribly wrong, that the messages carried by the rain and the wind had raised her hackles with a fear she couldn't name.

Mara meekly suffered the indignity of being fed a cod liver oil pill, and accepted a catnip mouse as a palliative. She even played with it, willing her Bigfeet to leave; they watched her with concern, but after she had batted the toy around for a few minutes, they seemed to think she was all right.

The moment they were out of the room, Mara abandoned her toy. She leapt up to the windowsill, and closing her green eyes, she dropped her head to her paws. The rain still whispered songs of blood and horror into her ears, but she shut down her fears. "Beraal?" she sent hesitantly, but though she waited for a long time, there was no response.

Mara washed a fat paw, and thought of Southpaw. The brown kitten's face shimmered in her mind. She thought of the times they had played chase in the drawing room. She thought of the way he bullied her but also cleaned the dustballs out of her fur when she'd spent too much time exploring under the bed. Now all of her instincts told her there was something badly wrong, that he and Beraal were in trouble.

The kitten spread her whiskers out, wondering whether Beraal would respond. Beraal had often tried to get her to stay in touch after their lessons had ended; it was Mara who had refused, because she hadn't wanted to risk hearing the exasperation in the mews of the other wildings when they spoke of the Sender.

The rain and the thunder rumbled ominously. The skies boiled over with dark clouds, and every time the wind drove against the windows of the Sender's house, they brought the stink of blood and death with them. Mara had never wondered much about Beraal's life outside, but some of the things Southpaw had told her about predators and Bigfeet came back to her. The blood on the rain spoke to her eloquently of the risks that all the outside cats took—including Beraal.

The kitten unfurled her whiskers and sniffed at the air. Perhaps she should go into Nizamuddin, she thought, and the idea took her by surprise. Hesitantly, Mara let her whiskers rise. Sending came so easily to her now; her green eyes blinked and closed as she focused, stepping out into the park, feeling the familiar shift in her small gut as she hovered over the rain-darkened branches of the trees. The thunder rumbled close by, and Mara watched the squirrels shiver and run for cover. But neither the thunder nor the rain worried her.

Her whiskers radiated uncertainty. There was the familiar, well-known route to the zoo; the other way was a clear path between the rooftops that would probably lead her to the wildings. The Sender wished Beraal was here to tell her what to do. The rain beat down on the trees in the park as Mara tried to make up her mind. Out in the open, the smell of blood was even stronger, but it came in gusts as the wind eddied back and forth. Perhaps she should go and see if Beraal was all right, Mara thought. But what if she was, and the blood on the rain was just some sort of residue from one of the outside cat's endless hunts? What if she met Southpaw and he laughed at her, or thought she was even more of a freak, once he saw her hovering in mid-air?

The kitten's concentration broke as, back in her house, the Bigfeet picked her up off the bed, one of them holding her close and offering a new catnip mouse. Mara made her decision; she broke the sending, curling up into her Bigfeet's arms for comfort. From time to time, her nose twitched as the wind rapped at the window, but the outside was too big for her, the clan of wildings too intimidating. Mara stayed indoors.

"GO," GROWLED HULO. "Get out of here and don't let me see you back in the grounds again!"

Southpaw quailed in fright as the black tom slashed at him, so surprised at Hulo's attack that he didn't realize the tom's claws were carefully drawn in so as not to cause any hurt. "But Hulo, I'll stay in the baoli—" he said, his mew almost piteous.

The tom glared at the kitten. His black fur had matted with the rain and the mud, and when Hulo fluffed it up menacingly, he looked truly terrifying.

"For once in your life, Southpaw, do as you're told!" he snarled. "Don't make me cuff you! There's a road running along the perimeter of the garden, the one lined with wild-rose hedges—that's not the one you take, you hear me? Go through the back roads, over the rooftops if you can, to the market. Shelter there or in the park. I don't want you anywhere near the Shuttered House! Now run along!"

He smacked Southpaw sharply across his striped backside to give the kitten the best start possible. Then the great black tom frowned and bounded down the muddy path, flying through the puddles of water without so much as shaking his paws out, in order to catch up with the other wildings. Miao and Katar had led the group, Beraal and Qawwali pausing only long enough to send urgent calls to the canal and dargah cats—they were to come to the Shuttered House as soon as they could. Hulo had his doubts that the canal cats would get there any time before sunset—the other side of the canal was a long way off, and too many Bigfeet used the bridge to make the crossing safe for cats during the day

Qawwali was worried, too; his group of wildings had spent the night awake and would be tired. The Bigfeet were beginning to emerge from their homes, and the dargah cats would have to creep along the alleys and rooftops to avoid them on their way to the Shuttered House. He didn't think they would be here any time soon, and when he caught Hulo's worried eyes, he understood what the great tom's fears were.

"The birds are not used to the ferals roaming the grounds," he said to Hulo as they splashed through the puddles, both toms ignoring the rain on their fur. Neither liked being wet, but both were used to the perils of a life outside. "Perhaps it was only an alarm."

"More than that," grunted Hulo. "I've never seen Katar move so fast or with such urgency. And the smell of blood in the air makes me uneasy."

"Yes, they must have killed a few of the wild rats and mice," said Qawwali. "Unsporting to do it at daybreak, but the ferals wouldn't know any better."

Hulo grimaced, thinking of how bewildered the prey must have felt, to be caught sleeping. All prey, napping or not, was fair game from twilight to past midnight, but once the inky blackness of the night started lifting, most animals obeyed the silent but deep call to sleep. Few predators would kill at dawn or in the first hours of the morning, unless they were driven by gnawing hunger or were too old to make their kills fairly, when prey was at its most alert. "Ugly to think about it, but I suppose a few ferals couldn't control themselves, like mannerless kittens on their first hunt."

"It would happen to ferals who'd been indoors for a long while," said Qawwali. "But they can't have done much damage—their leader would have curbed their claws and teeth before long."

The toms slowed down as they approached the Shuttered House, reaching out cautiously with their whiskers to see where the other wildings were. In the thick undergrowth, with the morning light a weak grey in the rain, scent was a better marker than visibility.

"It reeks of blood," said Hulo uneasily.

"They must have killed something large," said Qawwali warily, wondering if the ferals could possibly have brought down a dog or even a mongoose. But they had heard no barks, none of the typical mongoose alarm calls.

The two cats moved through the lantana bushes, using their forepaws to push back the branches. Hulo thought he could smell Beraal and Katar ahead, but wondered why the other cats were so silent—perhaps they didn't want to alert the ferals.

"It smells as though the hedges are drenched in blood," said Qawwali. The old cat was not easily scared, but his mew was hoarse, his whiskers trembling in disgust. The two toms turned the corner, into a clearing. Hulo blinked, his eyes adjusting to the light, and then he saw what the ferals had done.

THE RAIN SLOWED, turning from downpour to gentle shower in the abrupt fashion typical of Delhi weather. Mara's Bigfeet opened the windows, letting the breeze cool the house. The kitten stirred uneasily. The whiskers over her eyes tingled painfully each time she smelled the iron stink of blood, and she heard the squirrels and the babblers asking each other if they knew what was going on.

She considered getting onto the Nizamuddin Link, but if she didn't find Beraal, she'd have to talk to the other wildings. Mara cringed at the thought, and Southpaw's words came back to her: "You're such a freak!" he had said. Southpaw knew her; they had played together, slept paw-to-tummy and eaten from the same bowl. If he thought she was a freak, what would the other wildings think?

She missed Southpaw. With Rudra and Tantara, she had never been able to play hunt-the-paw or chase-your-whiskers, and though she wished Southpaw was better at his grooming, she loved digging her nose under his belly, making him yelp when she gently bit his tail.

She found his stories of the rooftops and the excursions with Hulo fascinating, even if she secretly thought the way he swaggered sometimes in imitation of the older toms was very funny—instead of the menacing swagger Southpaw aimed for, he often ended with an undignified waddle, though Mara would never tell him that. She could almost smell his wet fur, imagine that the scrabbling outside was him balancing on the parapet as he came through the window.

And then, there he was. Southpaw jumped down from the sill, his brown eyes filled with terror. "I missed you so much!" mewed Mara delightedly, forgetting all about their quarrel. She rushed up, her tail raised in happiness, eagerly rubbing her whiskers along his furry face, feeling the rain and the mud and the quiver of fear that ran through his small body. Southpaw was trembling so hard that Mara could feel him shaking before she touched him.

"What's wrong?" she said. "Is Beraal all right? Why does the rain smell of blood today?"

The brown kitten allowed himself to be gently nudged onto a cushion, and made no demur when Mara started to wash him, using her rough pink tongue as a sponge.

"Beraal's all right, I think," he said. "Though I don't know how long she and the others will be safe—oh, Mara, it's terrible out there. The ferals—"

Instead of telling his friend what had happened, Southpaw reverted to early kittenhood, wrapping his black whiskers tight around Mara's white ones. He shivered as he let her retrace his travels.

AFTER HULO HAD ROUNDED ON HIM, Southpaw meant to go back to the park by the market route, except that the road that led away from the Shuttered House, across the clusters of homes that stood back-to-back, was waterlogged. The kitten stared at the road in dismay, wondering how he could possibly cross. In the shrubbery nearby, a family of beetles traipsed wearily away from the muddy water that threatened to drown them.

The sun was behind a rack of grey clouds, but it was high in the sky, as by now it was well into mid-morning. When he trotted left, trying to see if he could go through the hedges instead of across the waterlogged road, the rain dripped insistently onto his neck from the lantana leaves, and tiny spiky thorns pushed into his stomach and back.

There was nothing in front of him except for a stink-beetle clicking its mandibles inquisitively. Southpaw had the distinctly unpleasant sense that the ground under his flattened belly was turning to mud and slush. He wriggled forwards, only to be brought up short by another line of ants, marching in the opposite direction.

"Do.not.step.across.this.line," droned the ants in a quiet monotone that drilled through the kitten's head. "Do.not. attempt.to.pass. We.have. spray.in.four.strengths: pepper.chilli. jalapeno.bhutjolokia and.we.are.not.afraid.to.use.it." Southpaw froze, but the ants kept marching and as they came closer, the kitten had to wriggle ignominiously out of the hedge, his striped brown backside picking up quantities of mud.

Southpaw couldn't stay in the baoli—if Hulo found him afterwards, the tom would tan his bottom until the stripes fell off his fur, as he had once memorably threatened. Gingerly, staying close to the perimeter, the kitten began to crawl through the acacia and the grass, hoping that Hulo wouldn't see him if he stuck to the perimeter of the Shuttered House. The kitten had padded more than halfway up the perimeter, pushing through the tangled bushes, making his stubby legs stretch to clamber over the old fat tree roots, when he heard the screams break out. He couldn't see what was screaming, but it sounded horribly like very young prey—baby mice, fledglings—and then more screams joined in.

He had stopped, almost paralyzed with fear, his paws sweating. It seemed to him that the rain dripped with blood.

Mara curled around Southpaw as he told this part of the tale, and he was grateful for her steady, comforting purr. And then the kitten felt his blood chill again, as a familiar scent came like an arrowhead towards him—the thick aroma of damp fur and cedar, a powerful, warning smell. The bistendu leaves rustled, and Kirri stepped into Southpaw's path.

"Your paws sweat with fear, little hunter," said the mongoose. Tiny droplets of rain trembled on her silver fur, giving her an eerie, almost ghostly aura. "Is it your clan that bloodies the morning? I had not thought to see the day when wildings hunted their prey across the border of sleep."

Southpaw stared into Kirri's red eyes, wishing Miao or Hulo were there with him. There was an angry glint in her eyes that he had not seen at their first meeting.

Far away, a mew he recognized all too well called out to some unseen victim: "Run, meat, run if you can—no? Very well, then. Ratsbane, kill him where he stands." And Southpaw suddenly understood.

"My kind, but not my clan, Madame Mongoose," he said, trying to keep his fear out of his voice, and wishing his whiskers wouldn't tremble so hard. "The Shuttered House opened up after the Bigfoot who lives there died, and the ferals came out this morning."

The mongoose raised her dainty paws with their deadly claws, standing up as she sniffed the air. "So that was the stink, behind the pall of blood," she said. "I had wondered. And your teacher? The Siamese? Is she not riding into battle? Will your clan not dance with the ferals today?"

For some reason, Kirri's words made the kitten feel better, until he thought of how small their numbers were. "I think, Madame Mongoose, that they will. But they are outnumbered: there are only a scant handful of wildings today, against the ranks and ranks of ferals whom Datura leads. The rest of the clan is across the canal, though some may come from the dargah."

The mongoose's red eyes flared, and she looked longingly towards the Shuttered House. But then she dropped back onto the ground. "This is between your clans," Kirri said, "between the ferals and the wildings. And besides, I have hunted the night through. Perhaps I will come back once I have rested."

They heard another set of screams rise, and Southpaw shuddered. "Perhaps I will come back very soon," said Kirri, the anger dancing like flames in her eyes. "And you, little hunter?" She sized him up, her sleek head reaching out to sniff at him.

"No," she said. "Old enough for first hunt is not old enough for first battle. But if I were you, I would bring the other cats. The stink tells me that the ferals surround your clan like flies around a broken honeycomb. A handful of wildings cannot do much—well, no, there is one thing they can do. But in your place, boy, I would run for help."

Southpaw watched as the mongoose trotted away, not sure whether to be relieved that she had left him unharmed or sorry that she would not stay to fight.

"Madame?" he called. "What is the one thing you mentioned that my clan could do?"

The mongoose turned, and her red eyes bore into his hopeful brown ones.

"They could die well," she said softly, and then her silver shape disappeared into the bougainvillea bushes.

Except for the sound of the rain beating against the walls outside and Mara's comforting, tiny purr, the room was silent when Southpaw finished. She washed his neck and flanks, soothing him as best as she could, sensing his distress and fear for his clan.

"That's why I came here," he said, his mew muffled because he had pressed his whiskers into Mara's belly as he told the last of his story. "You'll be safe here," she said gently. "And my Bigfeet will feed you—if you don't want to see them, I'll mew once I've finished eating and they'll fill my bowl again."

Southpaw squirmed his head out from under her belly. "I didn't come for your food, Mara," he said. "I came because everyone says the Sender helps the clan in times of trouble."

Mara's eyes narrowed and her short tail waved uncertainly. "Help the clan?" she said. "But what can I do, Southpaw? I can't fight like Beraal and Hulo! I've never even been outside, except for being under the canal bridge, and that's not much help, is it?"

"You can send," he said. "The other cats all say you have more powers than them, so can't you do something? You don't know how scary Datura is, and that house was crawling with ferals! There were so many of them, Mara, like cockroaches coming out from everywhere, from behind the sofas, and the cupboards, and that filthy courtyard. Miao and Beraal and all can't possibly fight them."

Mara was stropping her claws in agitation on the bedspread, poking small holes in the cloth.

"That's your clan, not mine," she said, her green eyes sulky. "They don't even like me. They think I'm a freak."

The wind changed again, and as it picked up, Southpaw and Mara both smelled it—fresh blood, fresh fear.

"Mara, this isn't the time to argue about whether it's your clan or not," said Southpaw, almost growling. "Those are my friends who might—Kirri was right, they might die out there!

And they only think you're a freak because you've never come out and met us. And what about Beraal?"

"Beraal came in to hunt me first!" said Mara, her small nose wrinkling at the memory. "And she only teaches me because I'm the Sender."

"Beraal fought Hulo so that you would stay alive," said Southpaw, his whiskers rising fiercely. "And when she won, the rest of the cats left you alone, the way you wanted to be! None of them hunted you! And Beraal spends her time with you when she could be out eating juicy rats or lazing at the fakir's shrine and now Datura could kill her and you don't care!"

Mara stared at Southpaw, thinking of the times Beraal had been so patient with her, of the times the older queen had come in for the night even though she hadn't liked being inside.

"I didn't know Beraal had fought for my life," she said, her mew quiet. "But what can I do, Southpaw? I'm not a fighter. All I can do is send, and Datura isn't going to be frightened off by me showing up in the middle of his battle."

Despite his worry, Southpaw's whiskers rose in a grin as he thought of how the white cat would react to a small orange kitten bobbing around as he went through his vicious rituals of slaughter. Then his whiskers slumped, as he thought of the wildings who had brought him up from the time he was a tiny kitten. Miao, Katar and Hulo were the closest he'd ever got to having a family, aside from Mara. And what could she do? It seemed unfair that the Sender, the famous Sender that he had heard the other cats talking so much about, had no special powers.

"You're right," he said, collapsing into a sad heap of fur near her paws. "Sending isn't going to help much. I wish you had other powers. Like being able to grow seven times your size, or have claws as wickedly curved as Kirri's, or be able to change yourself into something that would really scare Datura."

"What would scare Datura?" asked Mara, not convinced that the white feral would be scared by much.

"A giant Bigfoot!" said Southpaw, imagining a massive Bigfoot striding towards Datura, picking up the white cat by his scruff. "Or a very large cat."

"A large growly cat," said Mara, growling helpfully as she cuddled up to Southpaw. "Datura would be very scared if a cat six times his size went growling at him, wouldn't he?"

"I wish we could find a cat six times his size," said Southpaw sadly.

Mara sat up, her ears suddenly alert. "You know what, Southpaw?" she said. "Perhaps we can."

CHAPTER NINETEEN

Blood Rain

Though the mouse had a clear view, he turned away, unwilling to watch the carnage.

It had been a mellow night. Jethro had discovered an almost-full plate of chicken biryani in a gutter near one of the Bigfeet houses. He spent a glorious couple of hours tunnelling through his dinner, unmolested by rats for a change. In the hour before dawn, he watched the last of the night bats make swooping sorties over his head as it returned to the ancient stone eaves that overhung the baoli.

When the thunder rumbled and the raindrops grew fatter, the mouse found shelter in the tangle of scrub and silk cotton trees near the Shuttered House. At the other end of the grounds, where a neat row of houses indicated the colony of Nizamuddin proper, he could see a large, well-fledged pariah cheel shaking out his feathers—even at this distance, he could tell that they were well and truly soaked. Jethro shivered in sympathy. He hated his own short brown fur getting wet, and was glad for the shelter of the tree.

The tree's wide green leaves spread out like graceful hands above the mouse, offering protection from the worst of the rain. Curling up between the gnarled roots, the mouse let the sounds of the morning seep into his dreams without disturbing his sleep. The Bigfeet began to stir, clumping up and down the canal road by the side of the Shuttered House; he ignored them, as he ignored the sleepy chirps of the squirrels, chasing each other through the branches.

He woke with his fur standing on end in premonition, but Jethro didn't know why. His minuscule paws curled around the bark. In the hedges, a bandicoot sat up, twitching its grey nose, its eyes wide and startled. The rodents made eye contact, but neither could tell what had woken them. The mouse felt his fur tingle unpleasantly, and he looked nervously at the Shuttered House.

The quiet trill of cycle bells and the sounds of Bigfeet hawkers pushing their handcarts down the canal road restored some sense of normalcy. The rain had let up a little, and the steady patter of the drops on the leaves calmed the mouse down. Up on the roof where the mouse had first seen him, the cheel seemed to be testing his pinions, fluttering his feathers like large sails that furled and unfurled in the wind.

Jethro never saw the cats come out, they moved so fast and so silently. It was only when the bandicoot shrieked that the mouse peered in its direction. He squeaked in horror as the bandicoot—a young one, just a baby—twisted in the air, its rump held fast in the jaws of a white cat, its back legs scrabbling to get free. Then a black cat snapped at its neck, and the poor creature's cry turned into a gurgle as the blood spilled. "The black should deliver the killing bite," thought the mouse. "His kill, since he's closer than the white."

But to Jethro's shock, neither cat made any attempt to kill the bandicoot cleanly. Instead, the animal continued to shriek and gurgle as the two cats played with it. "Oh, don't!" said the mouse. He froze when the white cat turned. Datura's yellow eye blazed at him, the pupil narrow, black and vindictive. "The meat speaks," said the cat. "All the meat speaks here, Ratsbane."

"They'll shut up when we bite their beaks and snouts off, Datura," said the black cat, toying with the bandicoot, which lay limply on the hedge between the two cats. "Shall I get the mouse?"

"Later," said Datura. "First the hedges, then the trees. Does everybody understand? If you find any cats, don't stop to talk. Kill them. Play with the rest."

The mouse felt his fur tingle again and raised his eyes from the awful sight of the bandicoot to see a sea of cats fan outwards from the Shuttered House. They were silent as they eddied out, a wave of ferals creeping into the hedges and the gardens: they carried malevolence on their whiskers.

The mouse hesitated, weighing the risks. This was not his battle, and he was too small to take on the ferals. But then he looked again at the limp corpse of the bandicoot, and at the baby squirrels that were poking their alarmed heads out of a hole in the tree, and the mouse made his decision. He stretched his shoelace of a tail around him, his black eyes wary as he called in the loudest squeak he could manage: "The ferals are out! Run for your lives! Defend yourselves! The Shuttered House is open! The ferals are out!" At the very top of the tree, a cuckoo heard him, stared in disbelief at the ferals, and took up his call. The bulbuls picked up the cuckoo's alarm, and soon the mynah birds and the sparrows had joined in. Whatever advantage the ferals had hoped to gain by padding out from the Shuttered House in silence had been neutralized by the shrill chorus rising from the trees.

Datura climbed a tree, shaking the squirrels out of the branches to be slaughtered by the cats below. "You have no idea," he said to the mouse down below, "how good it feels to hunt little, soft, squealing things. It'll be your turn soon." The white cat watched Ratsbane go after a nest of screaming bulbuls.

The cats were moving in tight clusters of three or four, quartering the grounds, killing anything they found. The cries of the hedge creatures were piteous, and as if he had read Jethro's mind, Datura said, "It'll be even better once we've warmed up, meat." The cat's tongue hung out of his mouth, as he padded up and down, watching his troops.

The ferals were crazed with blood-fever. The mouse had seen this happen once before, with a clutch of white mice who had been kept as pets. A boy running through the crowded alleys of the dargah had sent their cage crashing down, and the mice had escaped into the maze of perfume shops and biryani sellers. Unused to hunting for their prey, once they had started, they hadn't been able to stop. They had marauded up and down until one bit the cheek of a Bigfoot baby, and then the Bigfeet had turned on the mice, trapping and slaughtering them. Blood always seemed to draw more blood towards itself.

Ratsbane and three cats had circled an old squirrel who stood his ground, trapped in the roots of a tree. He couldn't go back up, because a cat sat in the branches, watching him; he couldn't go forward, where the big black cat lay in wait. The mouse expected him to beg, but instead, the squirrel raised his tail over his head and waited for the cats, his striped face defiant.

Ratsbane was disappointed. He had expected the squirrel to run, or to chitter in fear. The cat closed in, his claws out. "Beg for your life, meat," he said conversationally.

"Cat," said the squirrel, "do you know something really astonishing? If you turn around—like that, yes—and look behind you—very good!—you can catch hold of your tail if you're really fast and kiss it goodbye. Because I'll get my teeth into that piece of string you call a tail with my dying breath, or my name isn't Jao."

Ratsbane slammed a claw into the side of the bark, right near Jao's nose. The squirrel didn't flinch, but then his mate ran out from his hiding place and began to chitter angrily at the cat. "Get back, Ao!" he called, holding his paws together anxiously. "I don't care what happens to me, but I can't stand it if they— no! Don't touch her!"

Ratsbane sprang, but before he could reach Ao, a black-and-white blur shot out from under the acacia tree and cann-oned into him. "Shall we even the odds a little?" said Beraal, breathing hard but rolling back onto her paws. "Shall we start by seeing how brave you are when you're facing something your size?" Before Ratsbane could react, Beraal spat a fierce battle yell at him, slammed her paw across his nose and bit savagely at his throat.

The black cat screamed and stumbled back, trying to get away from Beraal. The other two cats with him leapt at her, but the hunter queen was already whirling around. They saw her mouth widen into a deadly red yell, and then her jaws had crunched through one cat's leg. Before the other one could react, her paw swung out, raking five deep scratches across his face. She curled her claw, hooking it viciously into his pink nostril, lacerating it from the inside. The cat screamed and scrabbled to get away.

Beraal turned to the squirrels. "Ao, get Jao out of here! Up to the top of the trees with you. Get the rest of the little ones to safety—spread the word where you can."

Datura was loping across to help Ratsbane when the hackles on his back paws rose. He felt something watching him. The cat turned.

Standing on the road near the baoli was an old Siamese cat with stern blue eyes. Datura glanced at the line of roofs—if the Nizamuddin cats were ready for battle, it would be best if he and the ferals went over the roofs towards the Bigfeet. They would have to give up some slaughter here, but his eyes gleamed at the thought of the rich pickings they could find once they had spread out. They would have to move out of the Shuttered House's wild garden sooner than he had imagined, unless there was more than this one paltry Siamese and that fierce hunter to deal with, he thought.

Miao's eyes sharpened when she saw Katar and Hulo on the wall. Following her gaze, Datura assessed the two toms—the big black with the ramshackle swagger would be dangerous, but might also be a risk-taker, the other one was less obviously a warrior but had a keen air about him. A third tom came up behind them, more slowly; this one was old, judging by his rheumy eyes, and would be no threat. A cluster of wildings stood in a tight knot near the hedges, looking to Katar and Hulo for instructions. They were plump and well-muscled, but they looked too young to be good fighters.

Datura signalled to the ferals with his whiskers to tighten formation; they would have to wait to see how many more cats might join the fray.

The mouse was the first to realize that no more cats would join in, and his black eyes were worried. Beraal had dispatched three ferals with celerity and speed, but this small band of cats was no match for the dozens and dozens of blood-maddened ferals who had poured out of the Shuttered House.

Surveying the tangled garden from her position at the top of the path, the Siamese felt a shiver run through her fur that had nothing to do with the rain. It was horrific to see how many little ones the ferals had slaughtered in such a short time. She sensed Beraal's whiskers quiver in rage as the black-and-white saw the pathetic pile of dead birds under the hedges, and she felt Katar's anger and grief as he stared at the corpses of mice and rats scattered all across the gardens. And then Miao saw the bulbuls—the overturned nest, the motionless bodies of the young birds, the blood on the beak of the mother who had tried to defend them—and sadness welled up inside her.

When she saw Datura, she was reminded of a dog she had once known, a beast that had turned rabid. Miao had thought then that the problem with the dog was not the madness brought on by the rabies—but that he had always been a vicious killer, happiest when he could torment smaller creatures. Datura had not killed to eat, which Miao would have understood, and he had not killed out of simple bloodlust; he had killed because he could. She could not let him and the other cats fan out into the rest of Nizamuddin, no matter what happened.

The rooftops seemed all too close. "Head them back towards the Shuttered House," she linked as quietly as she could to Katar and Hulo.

"Is it just us, then?" Hulo linked back.

"Yes," linked Beraal. "Until the dargah wildings get here."

The tomcat's whiskers rose. His eyes flashed as he stared down at the tiny corpses, into the feverish eyes of the ferals. "For Nizamuddin, for Nizamuddin and the wildings!" he cried. Katar joined Hulo, the two toms never flinching as they leapt into battle.

The mouse watched, his whiskers trembling. He had never seen such an unequal battle. He could tell that the four cats were fine warriors, as Miao slashed neatly at the whiskers of the clowder that surrounded her, as Beraal whirled and growled and leapt, as Katar and Hulo waded into an army of cats. They were the best warriors he had ever seen, even if he included the mongoose clans and the fiercest of the rats and stray dogs.

But, he thought, as Miao went down under an onslaught of bodies, as Datura and eight other cats nipped savagely at Hulo's tail and back paws, as Beraal turned, trying to shake off the mass of cats tearing at her fur, even their ferocity, courage and skill were no match for the legions arrayed against them.

Katar called out to his tiny band, his mews urging the cats to hold fast and stay strong, and the mouse felt his whiskers rise in hope. From the branches of a silk cotton tree, more of the Shuttered House's ferals dropped down, joining the battle, slashing at Katar. The grey tom slashed back, but then he disappeared in the press of bodies, lost to the mouse's view.

CHAPTER TWENTY

The Wildings' Last Stand

J ust before he closed with the ferals, Katar thought sadly that no matter what the outcome of the battle was things would never be the same again. For years, the wildings had lived quietly, slipping in and out of the lives of the Bigfeet, not drawing attention to themselves. The ferals had changed that in just one bloody morning. There would be consequences, he thought with a shudder, and then his thoughts were swept aside as he heard Hulo cry "For Nizamuddin and the wildings!" He echoed the tom's call and made straight for the feral closest to him—a grey cat with golden eyes.

Startled, she lost her footing and dropped down from the wall. Then he had no time to think as he crouched on the wall, using his paws as gauntlets to bat away the advancing cats.

"Back to the ground!" called Hulo, and Katar saw what he meant. The wall was slippery with rain. The two toms were sliding around, and while they were more sure-footed than the ferals, sooner or later they would lose their footing on the mossy stones. Besides, silhouetted on the wall, they were targets for any enemy who wanted to creep up on them.

The tom caught the eye of one of the smaller wildings, an eager fellow from the market. "We're coming down," he called, "fight your way through to us, and we'll fight in a pack." Katar wished there'd been time for him and Hulo to discuss tactics; they were so unused to fighting side by side.

The two warriors landed on the ground at the same time; Katar had to roll hurriedly aside to avoid a wicked slash by the grey cat. "They're yours, Aconite," he heard Datura say. "Kill the grey first, he fancies himself as a leader."

Katar felt his hackles go up. He slammed his full body weight into Aconite, bringing her down on the ground. "Nice going," grunted Hulo, and then the black tom growled in pain as two ferals attacked him, one biting his paw and drawing blood. Katar's back jerked as he was tackled by Aconite and two others; he spat and rolled, throwing them off, and killed two with savage bites before he sprang up, backing off warily.

Katar risked a glance towards the baoli, hoping to see the dargah cats, but there was nothing. "Hold on," called Qawwali. "They'll be here soon." The old cat had sensibly stayed away from the thick of the fighting, but he was helping the young wildings from the market, calling encouragement to them as they battled. Katar growled in his chest as he fought another pair of ferals, even though deep down he knew they were up against hopeless odds—there were so many of them! How on earth was their small band of fighters going to contain them? It gave him a small sliver of hope to think that the ferals seemed to want only to attack and kill the wildings head on, and hadn't seemed to have given any thought to getting out of the grounds. Even as he thought this, he heard Aconite saying: "Datura? Should we try to get over the walls? There might be more prey that side, and we wouldn't have these annoying wildings attacking us if we went into more open terrain."

The white cat eyed the wall and Katar almost mewed out loud as he saw Datura carefully scan the perimeter of the wild garden. If Datura ordered the ferals to break out, the tom feared they wouldn't be able to hold them back.

"Let's kill them first, Aconite," said Datura. "Then we can take over their terrain in peace, and you can kill all the bulbuls you want to as slowly as you like, without any interruptions at all."

Katar turned on the ferals with renewed intensity. His target was Aconite, but the grey cat was very good at staying out of the way, sending waves of ferals at him instead of engaging in battle herself. "Katar, my friend," said Hulo from behind him, "I don't know how long I can keep this going."

Katar risked a look at Hulo, and his whiskers dropped. The black tom was bleeding badly; his flank had been ripped, and while it was a flesh wound, the blood was pouring out, weakening him. Katar grimly beat back another wave of ferals, then told the young wildings who fought by his side to hold the line for a moment. He crouched down beside Hulo, washing his wound as rapidly as he could with his red tongue. The saliva would stop the bleeding. Hulo stood stoically, but his yellow eyes showed the first tinge of fear as he stared at the advancing ferals.

"We had better hope the dargah cats get here soon," said Katar as he turned back to the fight.

Hulo grunted. "We had better hope for a miracle," he said. "There are too many of them, Katar. You cunning little rat, think I didn't see you coming at my left flank? I'll rip your ears into shreds! Yes, that's better, run away howling."

As he fought on, aware that the two of them and their small, brave band of wildings was being pushed back towards the wall, Katar wondered how Beraal and Miao were holding up. He hoped the two queens were safe.

THE PRESS OF PAWS on her chest hurt, but not as much as the sun in her eyes. It was a watery, weak light, but it made Miao blink and her eyes flicker. Lying on her back, pressed into the mud by her attackers, the Siamese cursed the slippery mud—once she had lost her footing, there was little she could do. She couldn't see her assailants any more—she was fighting by their scent. It seemed to her that one of them, a small orange kitten, brushed by her ear and said, "I'll be back with reinforcements" in what struck the Siamese as an oddly kind, familiar voice, but she hadn't time to dwell on the incident.

She heard Qawwali send an urgent message to all the wildings. "The dargah cats will be here soon—hold on! There's a Bigfoot festival on, so they have to come over the roofs of the dargah, not the alleys. Hang on, all of you!"

The Siamese used her claws to swat two ferals away from her throat. She dug her tail and back deeper into the mud, anchoring herself firmly. At least, she thought grimly, we've kept them here. They aren't out in the rest of Nizamuddin yet. There may be—her thoughts cut off abruptly as a fighting tom, striped about the face, yelled and launched himself at her.

Miao waited on her back until he was within reach, his mouth open, saliva dribbling out and falling on her fur. Then she used her left paw in a lazy hook, curving one claw into his mouth, puncturing the vulnerable inside of his gum and raking down until blood was gushing from his throat. He gurgled and died, flopping onto her stomach. The Siamese scrabbled with her back paws, trying to find the traction to rise from the mud, but her blue eyes narrowed when she saw three cats sneaking up from the side. There were too many attackers, she thought, despair beginning to rake its cold claws across her whiskers.

From behind the white glare of the sun, a black speck emerged, and then another, and a third. They moved in formation, growing bigger and bigger. Miao parried another two attacks easily, but cried out when a feral, cleverer than the rest, bit her lower paw. She couldn't reach him, but she kicked as best as she could manage, dislodging his jaws from her fur.

The three specks were growing larger. To Miao it seemed as though the pariah cheels fell out of the sky—they moved so fast! Tooth and his companions were black blurs in the rain. "Not her!" she heard Tooth call. "Not the Siamese, or the black-and-white, or those two and the small band around them! Kill the rest. The ones with the feral scent!"

The hunter was closing in on the cats now, and one or two of them had begun to look up, mewling in terror. "Kee-kee-kee-KILL! KILL! KILL!" cried Tooth. His beak dispatched the two cats who had been holding Miao's back paws down; the others fled, some turning to snarl and slash at the birds. But the cheels knew their ground well, and were experts at pulling back up into the safety of the skies. Within a few moments, four of the Shuttered House cats lay dead on the ground.

"Careful," called Miao. "They're warned now, and they're dangerous—Tooth! Behind you!"

She watched in alarm as Datura silently rose from the branch where he'd been watching the battle and slashed at the great bird's feathers. He connected, and Tooth went into a nosedive, spinning as he neared the ground. The cheel pulled out at the last moment, skimming the leaves, his feathers brushing the dead, still bodies of the mice. Then he had righted himself and was soaring into the air, his bright eyes furious. "Keek!" he called. "Kkkkk-urses!" But both Miao and Datura saw that he flew with a wobble, dipping his right wing down in pain.

The other two birds held themselves in flight, ready to attack. At a hissed command from Datura, though, the ferals pulled back—and there was ample shelter in the overgrown wilderness of the Shuttered House, few spaces where the pariah cheels could attack the cats with ease. But they continued to skirmish, ambushing those ferals who tried to cross from the jacarandas into the orange trees.

During the brief respite she was granted when the pariah cheels attacked, Miao was able to look around for her companions. But when she saw them, her heart sank. Beraal had been driven up a tree, from where she was spitting furiously at six ferals who were forcing her to back further and further up. She was out on a thin, slender branch that looked dangerously close to its breaking point, and a clowder of ferals sat around the roots of the tree, waiting for her to fall. The black-and-white was bleeding heavily from the mouth; her paws were stained red with blood, though Miao couldn't tell whether it was her own or from the cats she had fought.

In the overgrown flowerbeds filled with carrotweed and wild grasses, Katar, Hulo, and the young market wildings held another cluster of ferals at bay. Miao narrowed her eyes, even as she ducked another determined attack, sliding to the left away from her would-be assailant, using her tail to spin around and smack down a second one. The two toms and their tiny group had been pushed well back—they were too close to the crumbling wall that was the only division between the grounds of the Shuttered House, at that end, and Nizamuddin proper.

To Miao's dismay, more ferals appeared, keeping a wary eye on the skies, but slinking around the hedges—there had been an entire clowder hiding in the wild gardenias and the lawsonia shrubs. The garden seemed to writhe with cats, their sleek heads emerging from every hiding place. The Shuttered House had held at least six litters worth of ferals, by Miao's estimation, and here she counted more than thirty heads before she gave up. They seemed to respond to every twitch of Datura's whiskers. Miao looked over to where Katar and Hulo fought and saw with horror that four or five ferals were about to open a fresh front of attack from some shrubbery that concealed them from the embattled wildings. "Your back, Hulo!" she called—just in time. Miao darted towards them, her paws gathering speed, and as she ran, out of the corner of her eye the Siamese could see Datura's whiskers rise in unmistakeable pleasure. It was only when she cleared the lantana hedge and had to stop dead, her black tail waving from side to side, that she realized why. She had run into an ambush: beyond the hedge, she was caught in a part of the garden where the land dipped down. Ferals surrounded the Siamese, and as she turned, Ratsbane slipped into position, blocking her last exit.

Miao's blue eyes went blank. She wondered absently whether the dargah cats would arrive on time. She heard Beraal scream in pain from her tree. The bushes around her grew too thickly; the cheels would never make their way through the branches. Tooth yarked in frustration, soaring overhead, wobbling close to the tops of the branches, but he couldn't slide in—there was no gap, and even if there had been, it was too dangerous.

Ratsbane's eyes were febrile. Blood spotted his jaw. "I asked Datura if I could have you," he said, his mews a snarl. "I've always wanted to kill a Siamese." Miao stared at him, her eyes impassive. Her claws came out. She flung her head back and for the first time since the battle began, she let out a war cry, a yowl of implacable defiance. Around her, the ferals closed in.

Katar heard Miao and his whiskers sank in fear. With a massive effort, the tom swung out at the line of ferals in front of him, using his claws to rake deep slashes in their foreheads so that the blood would blind them. In the confusion that followed, he sprang up to the top of a stump.

"Datura!" he called. "Hold your troops! We have not spoken yet!"

"This is war, meat!" the white cat said, barely flicking his whiskers in Katar's direction. "I never talk to my prey."

Tooth dived towards the white cat, but had to pull back when his wing started to drag. The cheel flew instead towards

Katar, hovering over the tomcat protectively, buying him precious time as he spoke from the stump.

"This is my territory, Datura!" called Katar. "Perhaps there's some way in which we can welcome you to our lands and forget this skirmish. If the Shuttered House is no longer your home, what lands would you want? This and the baoli? Would you and your ferals wish to share our lives? Speak, Datura—do what is right for your clan!"

The white cat's eyes went opaque.

"You offer me a share of your territory? You have the temerity to make that offer, meat? Look around you: there are so few of you, against so many of us."

The garden was alive with the ferals, hiding from the cheels, their eyes glittering as they listened.

"What can you offer us, meat, that I couldn't take for myself?"

Hulo's voice rang out, hoarse and exhausted, but still filled with defiance.

"What kind of cat are you?" he demanded. "You attack the smallest and the weakest; you invade our territory, and when we offer you equal space under our skies, you spit on our whiskers? You attack in the daytime when the clan sleeps, like a dog or a Bigfoot? I spit on you. You and your kind make me sick!"

Datura's whiskers rippled in anger.

"Kill him," he hissed. "Kill the meat!" He stared at Katar. "You don't understand, do you? We had everything all these years—food, prey, shelter! We had everything except the outside, and now we have that. As for the rest of your clan, they'll soon be dead, just like you."

Katar heard Beraal call out, "The Nizamuddin wildings are almost here! They're in the lane, coming down from the baoli—back, damn you!—they'll be here soon." She growled in pain and he heard a branch snap, the snarls of many cats.

He couldn't see Miao, but Hulo's rough head emerged from what looked like a gigantic scrum of fur, baying defiance before the tomcat bobbed down again. Tooth and the cheels came diving in again, but with the hedges in the way, the best they could do was scare the ferals, picking off one or two who had strayed unwisely into more open terrain. Qawwali called out to the dargah wildings, his mew hoarse and urgent as he rapidly filled them in on the battle. They threw themselves into the fray, joyously—most of the dargah cats were fierce young toms and queens, hardened by their constant battles with the large and aggressive rats and bandicoots who lived in the alleys.

Katar snarled, baring his teeth, and hurled himself at the ferals advancing upon him. His ferocity drove them off, some howling. But the grey tom was tiring, and he could sense that Hulo and Beraal were hard-pressed. He couldn't see Miao; the Siamese was a tough fighter, but there had been too many ferals in that ambush.

"Miao?" he called, whipping his tail away from a marauding feral paw just in time.

"Lift your paw off her face," he heard Ratsbane say from the hedges, and Katar's blood went cold.

Miao screamed. Once, twice, and then the third time, the Siamese's voice abruptly cut off.

"No!" said Katar, mewing like a kitten. He could feel Datura's curious eyes on him, the white cat drinking in his grief and fear with avid interest. "Beraal!" he called, "Hulo! To Miao!"

"We can't," said Hulo in a low growl. "Or they'll be over the wall."

Katar had taken his eyes off the scrum, and the ferals noticed. Before the tom could collect himself, two cats slammed into him, pinning him to the ground.

Hulo went down under a sea of cats, and this time, the tomcat didn't come up again.

Beraal yowled, desperation in the sound. High above the Shuttered House, Tooth circled in frustration, calling out a war cry, hoping to draw the ferals out so that he could close in on them instead of having to chase shadows through the scrub.

Datura stirred on his branch, and dropped down to the ground.

"I hope the rest of the meat is like this," he said to Ratsbane. "It's so much more fun when they put up a fight. Shall we kill them all at once?"

Ratsbane's whiskers dropped in apology.

"Have you already killed yours?" said Datura, strolling over and looking down at Miao's limp body. "What a shame. Let's do the rest, shall we?"

A tiny brown shape darted out and flashed across his paw. The white cat felt a sudden sharp sting.

"What was that—mrraow!" His paw was under attack, and he hopped back in a hurry. The brown mouse who had sunk its teeth into Datura's paw was nowhere to be seen, but the tomcat had to move forward just as rapidly as he'd moved back—a nest of fire ants blocked the path.

"Do.not.pass.go." said their quiet voices.

Datura stared at them in distaste, wanting to smack his paw down on the line, but instinct told him that this would be a very bad idea. "The last warriors of Nizamuddin," he said, catching sight of the mouse's furious black eyes. His whiskers rose in laughter. Ratsbane joined him.

"So their bravest fighters are all three inches off the ground," said Ratsbane. "Ow! Meerrrowwwwww!" A mynah bird, squawking loudly into his ear, had smacked down her claws on his head. She rose up and flew just out of reach of the two cats.

Datura thought this was even funnier.

"Tomcat!" he called to Katar. "Behold your army—ants, mice and mynahs. What a glorious host you command!"

He paid little attention to the dargah wildings. They were strong warriors, but there were too few of them. With a flick of his ears, the white cat sent another battalion of ferals off to dispatch them. He was staring down at Miao, noting the bleeding muzzle, the whiskers she had lost to Ratsbane and his friends in her unequal battle. He felt he would have liked to know more about the Siamese—she had impressed him strangely. He placed a paw on her carcass—the cat was still warm—and then he turned away. It was time to move into the rest of Nizamuddin.

"Ratsbane," he called, and then his ears twitched, rising in inquiry.

It seemed to Datura that the air rumbled with something other than thunder. The fur on his paws rose. Then the fur on his back stood up, as though it had been touched by electricity. Instinctively, the white cat looked up, and the open sky made him vertiginous—he had to look away until the earth stopped whirling. In the distance, there was a slow, ominous rumble.

The ferals shifted uneasily.

"Enough!" said Datura, trying to ignore the way his whiskers were prickling. He glanced at the rooftops. Bigfeet were out on some of the verandah, pointing in their direction, clearly discussing the cats. "It's time for us to move into the colony— Ratsbane, first you—"

What he was about to say stayed on the tip of his whiskers. The ground seemed to tremble and split as a rumble shook the earth. Then it turned into a low, deep, unmistakeable roar, as though the largest cat in the world walked in their midst.

"Ignore that," shouted Datura, seeing that many of the ferals had their ears laid flat and were lying low to the ground. "It's just thunder, nothing more! Are you ferals, or are you scaredy-cats? Get up!"

The air in front of his whiskers shimmered and parted, like a heavy curtain. Datura's eyes widened. And then the white cat mewled in terror, foam flecking his jaws as he scrabbled to get out of the way.

Out of nowhere, a massive tiger had appeared. It strode down the path, roaring straight into Datura's face. Ozzy's black-and-orange stripes seemed to shimmer in the rain, lighting up the grey day, dazzling all the ferals and the Nizamuddin cats. Qawwali stopped dead, unable to believe his eyes. But when Ozzy roared again, every one of the cats felt the rumble in the depths of their hearts, and felt their whiskers go cold, their blood run thin.

Beraal was the first to recognize Mara, who was bobbing along next to the tiger's gigantic face. Few of the cats, wildings or ferals, had seen her tiny but jaunty figure, since she was so high up in the air—but Beraal had no trouble spotting her pupil.

"Hold your ground," she said to the Nizamuddin wildings, using the link so that the ferals wouldn't hear. "It's the Sender's work—the tiger is just a sending, it isn't real! There's nothing to fear—keep your whiskers unknotted. Well done, Mara!"

The ferals panicked. When Ozzy—who was enjoying his virtual stroll immensely—threw his head back for another immense roar, displaying his curved, wicked teeth, the ferals yelped and whimpered. In their fear, they scrambled out of their shelters—and the cheels saw their chance.

"Battle formation!" called Tooth, soaring out from behind the clouds. The other two cheels, Claw and Talon, rode the thermals with him, attacking the ferals savagely, clearing space for Hulo to struggle out from under a pack of the Shuttered House cats, for Katar to limp away from his own battles, staring in astonishment at the tiger. Beraal spat on her paws to stop the blood from flowing and got up unsteadily, as the ferals scattered away from the tree, flushed into open ground where the cheels continued to pick them off.

Qawwali watched the tiger nervously as it roared, its magnificent head thrown back, the great yellow eyes alive and brilliant. Then the dargah cat passed his greetings to the Sender over the link, and flicked his ears.

"For Nizamuddin and glory!" yowled Qawwali, raising his plumed tail as a battle standard, marshalling his troops to stand against the fleeing ferals. "For the clan! For the clan!" miaowed the Nizamuddin cats, who had joined Hulo and Katar on the ground.

Hulo chased Ratsbane through the bushes, until he had the other cat backed up against a tree. "Stand your ground and fight," said the tom. Ratsbane rolled in the mud, pleading for mercy, and despite what he had done to Miao, Hulo might have let him be. But when Hulo turned his back on the feral, Ratsbane leapt on the tom, trying to bite his spine. The black tom shook the cat off easily. His yowl was deadly and savage. His claws ripped through Ratsbane's throat, leaving the tree roots soaked in blood.

Aconite slunk along the grass, hoping to escape being noticed. The grey cat with gold eyes didn't intend to risk her own skin; she had a great aversion to the sight of her own blood, much as she liked shedding the blood of smaller creatures. She kept a wary eye out for Katar. The tom didn't look as fearsome as either Hulo or Datura, but he had dispatched a round dozen of the ferals, if she was any judge. As she reached the foot of the wall, the grey cat thought of the prey waiting for her on the other side—the fat mice, the lazy birds—and felt her mouth water. "Silly of them to have no one watching the wall," she said, her eyes on the wildings who were mopping up the fight near the Shuttered House and closer to the baoli.

There was no shadow; the sun was too weak for that, and the rain was coming down steadily. But Aconite felt the rushing beat of the pariah cheel's wings, and rose, too late, into a savage leap, hoping to rake the great bird's underside with her claws. She missed, and Tooth's talons fastened onto her neck. "I was watching," he said to the wriggling cat, before he twisted his talons sharply. He let Aconite's body fall back onto the grass. The kill had given him no pleasure, but it was necessary.

The ferals began to make a frantic retreat. Those who weren't killed outright were chased by a posse of dargah cats right up to the front line of Bigfeet houses that faced the road. Some braved the traffic, trying to cross to the other side; many more shuddered at the cars and looked for shelter at the mouth of the filthy canal, less scared of the pigs than of the dargah's fierce warriors.

Prowling around near the Shuttered House, Ozzy roared and roared—the only creatures that didn't seem to hear him at all were the Bigfeet. "Best walk of my life!" he said happily. "Haven't enjoyed myself so much since I was a cub chasing Bigfeet jeeps and sending them packing in Ranthambore! You're looking tired, Mara—is this too much for you?"

The tiger could sense that it took all of Mara's strength and energy to keep up the sending. The battle was almost over; most of the ferals were either dead or fleeing.

Ozzy roared again, and the Sender seemed to shimmer in the air. "Beraal," called Mara. "I can't hold on any longer. I'm taking Ozzy back home." The black-and-white cat watched her student leave, remembering the tiny kitten who had interrupted their sleep with her howls. And then she was fading, the Sender of Nizamuddin who had summoned a tiger to the grounds of their greatest, bloodiest battle. The kitten bobbed tiredly ahead of the tiger, who followed like an ocean liner in the wake of a tugboat. He roared one last time, just for the fun of it, and then the air shimmered around the unlikely pair, and they were gone.

Katar limped up to Beraal, and Hulo joined them. The earth stank of blood; fear still hung in the branches of the trees. Beraal's mind was on the Bigfeet. She could see their heads bobbing up and down on the roofs. They wouldn't have seen Ozzy and Mara—the Bigfeet appeared to be deaf where linking and sending were concerned—but they had certainly seen, and heard, the battle between the ferals and the wildings. They would not like this at all, and she hoped it wouldn't be the start of bad times for the Nizamuddin cats and other strays. Bigfeet were strange creatures, given to unpredictable bouts of fear.

In one of the neighbourhoods Beraal had lived in, she had watched an apparently insignificant incident as she lazed on her owner's balcony. The portly Bigfoot who lived downstairs was out on his morning walk, and he swung his cane at one of the local dogs, a pleasant enough fellow called Prince. Perhaps Prince was taken off guard, or perhaps he was just in a bad mood—whatever it was, he snarled at the Bigfoot and went for his ankles. He bit him gently, taking care not to harm, just giving the man a lesson.

But the man had shouted in his rough Bigfoot tongue and muttered darkly at the dog all day, kicking the few hapless animals he found in his way on the street. And the next day, a van had drawn up. The Bigfeet who went after the dogs had a bitter, hard-edged feel to them, and the stench of fear that rose from the van was awful for the other animals to feel, as they watched their old friends from the park being driven away. "Help!" cried Prince. "Help us, they're going to kill us!" cried the other dogs, including a sweet little golden-haired one who had been Beraal's friend. She could smell from the Bigfeet and from the van that this was true.

The memory of it could still make her shiver. Watching the way the Bigfeet moved around on the rooftops, Beraal wondered what the war between the ferals and the wildings would lead to.

Her companions were silent. After the tumult of battle, the silence seemed to echo in their ears. Except for a cheep from a badly injured bird, the quiet tap-tap of the rain and the normal bustle of traffic on the canal road, the gardens were hushed in the aftermath. It seemed to Beraal that there were corpses everywhere she turned—the tiny bodies of the mice, the feathered piles of birds, dead ferals and a few luckless wildings. A cold fear touched her spine at the same time that the thought reached all of them, but Katar said it first, turning his gaze from the carnage.

"Where is Miao?" he said. "We must find her. I don't see her anywhere." He had been sniffing frantically at the place where Ratsbane and the others had ambushed the Siamese. There was a deep, bloody indentation in the earth, and clumps of Miao's black and cream fur dotted the mud. But there was no sign of the old cat who had fought so bravely.

Then Beraal said hesitantly, her whiskers trembling from battle fatigue, "There's a trail here." Katar and the other cats followed her lead. Dark patches of drying blood led away from the site of the ambush. Hope rose briefly in the tom's heart; perhaps Miao had been able to drag herself away.

But the scents stopped abruptly at the foot of the wall; a forlorn clump of white fur stained with blood clung to a stone, and that was all. Beraal sniffed at the wall, climbing the old, slippery flagstones dexterously, ignoring her own injuries, but could pick up no scent. Katar felt his tail drop again.

Hulo raised his battered whiskers, the blood still streaming down his front paws from open wounds. "And where is Datura? I've found Ratsbane's body, but that white coward slipped away, did he?" The tomcat refused to think about Miao. That way lead to grief, and he preferred anger.

The four searched the garden, despite their own wounds and Beraal's fear that the Bigfeet would clump in to see what had happened, but there was no sign of either Miao or Datura. Both cats, the feral leader and the Siamese, had vanished.

CHAPTER TWENTY-ONE

Kirri's Dance

The mongoose woke with the scent of copper in her pointed nose. She sniffed the air, her beautiful eyes wide and entirely awake; Kirri always went from sleep to alertness without stopping at the frontier between the two.

In less than a second, she was pointing her nose in the direction of the Shuttered House. Her tail was up, her claws curved. The world smelled of death, as she had feared it might when she had spoken to Southpaw that morning. Kirri was on intimate terms with both scents, but the only time Nizamuddin had smelled so strongly of butchery was when the Bigfeet had laid down poison for the rats, many years ago.

The mongoose slid out of the gap in the pile of bricks where she had made a temporary shelter for the night, ignored the Bigfeet loitering around the lanes of the dargah, and pattered down the alleys towards the Shuttered House. Few saw her go by; Kirri was a brown-and-silver ghost who moved from shadow to shadow.

Long before she reached the battleground, Kirri knew the story. The winds told her of the massacre of the mice and birds; the rain spoke to the mongoose of the bloodshed by the wildings and the ferals; the trails left behind by the dargah cats whispered eloquently of the hurry with which they had rushed to the aid of the Nizamuddin cats. The mongoose knew everything before she slipped through the hedges into the grounds of the Shuttered House, and yet she was unprepared for the killing fields that lay before her eyes.

The dead creatures—the shrews, the bulbuls, the mice—didn't tempt Kirri, though she had woken hungry. The mongoose preferred to do her own killing, and would only eat from another's kill if she were starving. But as she surveyed the piles of tiny corpses, something in them stirred an unfamiliar shard of pity. The pity went as rapidly as it had come, but as she sniffed at the mice, and then the shrews, the sparrows, and then the bulbuls, a greater indignation began to swell in the mind of the predator. Kirri lived frugally, her love of fresh kills often making the gaps between meals longer than most animals would have been able to stand, and she couldn't abide waste.

The killer who had done this was profligate, careless in his slaughter. The mongoose sat up on her back paws, her tail curved to one side, and glared at the dead. The scent of blood seemed bitter and rank in her flared nostrils. And as Beraal had, she watched the Bigfeet stirring on their roofs. In her experience, Bigfeet tended to treat one animal like another. They might not draw distinctions between the combatants and the innocent.

Kirri chittered to herself in exasperation. At her feet, a diminutive brown head popped up. "He's gone, hasn't he?" said a brown mouse. "Are you speaking to me?" The mongoose was taken aback. She wondered whether to attack the mouse, but it didn't seem worth her while. She rarely killed something that small, unless she was famished. Jethro kept well out of range, making sure that he could duck behind the roots of the spiny bistendu bushes. "It seemed to me that you were looking for Datura, Madame Mongoose," he said. "Why else would you be here, sniffing through the corpses on this bloody morning? Forgive me if I spoke out of turn."

"Datura," said Kirri thoughtfully. "The kitten mentioned him too. That would be the leader of the ferals?"

"Yes," said the mouse. "He did this."

Kirri drew in her breath, looking around at the carnage. "All of this?" she said.

"All of this," said the mouse bitterly. "Except at the end, other cats had died. His precious friends from the Shuttered House had died. The Siamese—you wouldn't know her—had been unfairly set upon by his acolytes; how she fought, but there were too many for her. But he survived, didn't he? Sneaking off and hiding in the baoli the moment his side started to lose."

The mongoose was staring at the mouse. Her eyes were as red as burning coals.

The mouse grew uncomfortable, his nose twitching rapidly.

"Not that it's any of your concern," he said, preparing to dive back into his hole. "It was a terrible war, though."

"You interest me," said Kirri said. "Did you say the Siamese?

An elderly cat, but a fine hunter? With vivid blue eyes, creamy fur, a black tail, and a black patch on her face?"

"Yes," said Jethro, startled. "It was terrible, the way they set upon her. They gave her no room to defend herself. They fought the way dogs do, in a pack, not like cats. They fought the way the worst rats do."

The mongoose turned to go, her short brown and silver fur quivering, her red eyes alight with something the mouse didn't quite understand.

"What are you going to do?" asked the mouse.

"Dance," said the mongoose as she moved purposefully towards the baoli.

ON THE HIGH, slippery stone where Miao had stood just the night before, Datura lay with his paws spread out, liking the feeling of the wet quartzite on his fur. The white cat wasn't thinking of his companions—Ratsbane and Aconite, and the other ferals who had died or fled. Instead, he was thinking with some bitterness of the years he had spent in the Shuttered House, years he had thought of as rich and satisfying ones.

But what he'd had was nothing compared to this—a world with so much prey in it, and one that was full of small pleasures like walking on wet grass and letting it tickle one's paw pads. Nor had he known the pleasure of being able to kill animal after animal, instead of having to ration out one kill for months on end, waiting for the next unlucky creature to stray into the Shuttered House.

Datura had decided when he was just a kitten that the world had two kinds of creatures in it: the weak and the strong. He knew which kind he was. He had thought Ratsbane was strong, but Ratsbane was dead. The dead were, by definition, weak.

Datura had small doubt that he could continue to evade the cats of Nizamuddin. The tiger had terrified him, and the white cat had run until he reached the muddy path to the baoli. A glance at the panicked ferals told him that the tide had turned. He watched the ferals scatter, and then before the wildings could start hunting for him, Datura padded away down the road. The baoli was deserted; it seemed like a good retreat, and he settled in on the ancient steps, thinking about the wildings.

The only one he had feared a little had been the cat with the uncomfortably clear gaze—the Siamese whose blue eyes had looked so gravely at him that the feral felt she was staring into the depths of his mind. And she was dead, her blood staining the wild marigolds, killed by Ratsbane and his creatures. There was nothing else to fear.

Idly, he wondered if he should kill the other cats he'd seen. Datura had already marked Katar down as prey. The tom would put up a fight, but it would be a fair one. The white cat's yellow eye had a smirk in it: to him, the only kind of fight worth getting into was the kind you won.

If there had been so much prey in the small space of the Shuttered House's gardens, how much prey would there be in Nizamuddin? The white cat felt his muscles relaxing at the thought of the consternation the wildings would feel when one by one, their numbers were thinned by an unseen enemy. He would slip in and out of their ranks, until he slipped in and out of their nightmares.

Datura yawned and stretched, wondering if he should go back and snack on one of the dead mice, or if it might be fun to make a fresh set of kills while Nizamuddin was still swirling in fear. He was about to take a quick cat-nap before he decided, when something made his whiskers prickle.

Datura turned his head to the right. A neat creature, half his size, sat quietly on the stone tier just below, observing him openly. Her brown-and-silver head was freshly combed, and her claws were sheathed.

The cat's yellow eye gleamed, and he felt his whiskers tingle at the prospect of a good kill.

"Greetings to you, meat," he said, rising, his tail at a jaunty angle.

The creature made no response. Her eyes flashed red for a second, but otherwise she stayed where she was.

"Would you like to run, or shall we fight?" he asked.

There was still no reply, but now the mongoose began to dance, moving from one paw to another.

"You haven't asked my name," she said, as she weaved first slowly, then rapidly, back and forth.

The cat sneered, his whiskers radiating their disgust.

"I never ask the name of my meat," he said, stepping onto the stone where his intended prey danced. Datura meant to end this quickly and take his nap, after all.

Kirri moved so fast he didn't see the strike until her teeth had ripped across his right paw, his neck and his open throat.

"Kirri," she said. "They call me Kirri. You should always know the name of your killer, Datura."

Blood poured out of his wounds as the white cat growled in anger, but the anger was laced with fear. He had struck back, but Kirri had danced so deftly out of the way that his blow went wide. Datura licked rapidly at his neck, trying to staunch the blood, realizing that she had sliced a key vein.

"You can dance, meat," he said. "But can you fight?"

The cat lunged forward, his teeth ready to flay Kirri alive. But the mongoose waited till the last second and then flattened herself; Datura's throat was exposed to her sharp teeth and the cat screamed as she bit deep. He twisted around; with his hind legs, he raked at the mongoose, and had the satisfaction of seeing a light line of drops of blood bedew her tail.

Kirri didn't seem to notice. She slid out from under him, watching the blood drip down from his throat to pool and gather on the stone. Datura growled and leapt at her again.

"You can fight, Datura," she said. "But you can't dance."

The mongoose disappeared from his view, and when he turned his head to see where she'd gone, Datura found his eyes clouding over. He staggered a little and shook his head to clear it. Instinct told the white cat the mongoose had to be behind him. He whirled around. She wasn't there.

The pain in his left paw when Kirri crunched it into two was unbelievable. Datura howled even as he tried to slam into the mongoose, intending to wedge her between his body and the stone. But he slipped on the algae that covered the stone steps, and had to scrabble so as not to go over the edge.

"Try saying my name," said the mongoose as she sunk her teeth into his right paw. "Kirri. It's not so hard."

Datura howled.

The mongoose watched him, her red eyes aflame. She raised herself high on her back paws and danced to the right of the wounded cat, who was trying to limp up to the next stone.

"The right paw was for the mice," she said. "The left paw was for the birds."

"Stop," he said, his whiskers shivering with pain. "Stop it, meat. Wait till I get my teeth into your stinking hide."

His yellow eye flared, but his blue eye was watering with the hurt. Datura could barely see ahead of him; he didn't know it, but he was bleeding out from the deep puncture wounds the mongoose had left in his throat. He snarled, and tried for the last time to take a swing at the small predator. If he could only get closer, he could bite off her head. He could bite that snout in two, if he could only see her. Where had she gone?

When Kirri's teeth sank into his throat, Datura screamed and rolled onto his back. "That was for the Siamese," she said. "She was a better fighter than you, Datura. She fought for the little ones you slaughtered so rashly. And she gave me the honour of my name."

The cat would have scrabbled up again, but his front paws were useless, and the mongoose was sending unbearable pain shooting up his spine as she ruthlessly savaged his back paws. Datura mewed in fear—he was looking up at the sky, away from the baoli, away from the stone. It arced over him, endless and menacing. "Please," he cried to the mongoose. "Please, I'm afraid—the sky—take it away. Kirri—please."

The red died out of the mongoose's eyes, leaving them brown and a little sad. She moved up to the next stone, her eyes never leaving Datura's; she saw that the fear was genuine. Almost gently, she leaned over the white cat, her brown and silver fur tangling with his bloody white fur, and then she bit his throat out.

"That is more mercy," she said to her dead opponent, "than you showed any of them." Kirri dropped down onto all four paws, and slid out of the baoli, a brown-and-silver shadow. She didn't look back, nor did she clean the blood off her sleek muzzle. The rain would wash it off, in time.

CHAPTER TWENTY-TWO

The Cheel and the Cat

O nce, Miao had fallen into a river, and as she sank, all the familiar sounds of the world were cut off and reduced to faint, faraway murmurs as the blood rumbled in her long ears. As the Siamese dragged herself painfully towards the wall, that was how she felt. The sounds of the battle raging between the wildings and the ferals seemed to come from a long distance away, their cries much softer than the pounding in her ears.

Ratsbane and his friends had taken their time; as she lay there helpless against so many, she had been reminded of dogs worrying a mouse or a kitten. Then Miao had closed her mind to the pain and let her eyes wander elsewhere. She felt what they did to her, but she placed the pain into a small corner of her mind, the way Tooth's mother, Stoop, had taught her to do many years ago.

Stoop had been a young, proud cheel then; Miao had been a young, proud queen. "Fold up the pain until it's the size of a fledgling, and then the size of a fledgling's claw," Stoop had told her the day the cheel had misjudged a spectacular dive and ripped off one of her own talons. It was good advice, Miao found, until the pain rose beyond a certain point. The Siamese had lost consciousness, sinking so deep into stasis that Ratsbane had assumed she was dead.

It took her a long while to get across the dried leaves and twigs that littered the ground. The Siamese stopped only when she thought she might attract the attention of one of the ferals. But she was lucky; Ratsbane had chosen a spot a little further away from the battle to stage his ambush, and the way to the wall was clear. Miao drifted in and out of states of pain and weakness as she made her slow way up to the wall. Her back paws were damaged; one was broken, the other crushed. From the pain, the Siamese could tell that her spine had taken a beating. But she kept going.

She was at the wall when the Sender shimmered into view with the tiger, and exhausted though she was, Miao felt herself react with happiness—if she had still had whiskers, she would have raised them in salute. It seemed to her that the orange kitten turned and caught her eye, and when she saw Mara move away from the tiger, she knew that she was right.

"No," she whispered, hoping the Sender would hear it. "Stay with the tiger. The wildings need you more than I do, Mara— yes, I know your name, we all know who you are even though we've never met. Stay there. Do your job."

The Sender hesitated, and then Ozzy roared again. Mara stayed by his side, but when she could, she turned her serious little face towards Miao again. "Beraal told me all about you," she said directly to the Siamese, cutting out the other cats from the conversation. "I can't talk much—bringing and holding the tiger here drains all my energy—but can't I help you? Can't the other cats come to you, Miao?"

"No!" said the Siamese, "I'm dying, Mara, the wounds run too deep." She saw the kitten falter, and realized that Mara did not understand.

"When we're close to the other side, Mara, we prefer to die alone," said Miao. "It's—we're cats. That's what we prefer, quiet and silence. The other cats have their paws full with the battle. I'm safe here. You do what you must, Sender. But before you go—"

The Siamese stopped, and her old eyes glazed over with pain. Mara would have left the tiger and come to her, but the Siamese opened her eyes again and glared at the kitten, willing her to stay where she was.

"The Sender in my time ended her days as an inside cat, like you," said Miao. "She suffered for it, Mara. She had great powers, but because she stopped going outside, something inside her shrivelled up and died. What you're doing now is so brave—" the Siamese had to stop again, because her ribs were hurting her so much.

When she opened her eyes, the Sender and the tiger were watching the ferals flee.

"Mara," whispered Miao, and immediately, the kitten had turned to her, their eyes connecting across the battlefield. "Your courage—your strength and talents—are greater than any Sender who's come before you, even Tigris, who was Sender in my time. But you're not here. This is just a sending."

She had to stop. Blood had welled up in her mouth, and the cat bared her teeth, letting it spill onto the ground. It darkened the earth near her face. Mustering her fading strength, the Siamese continued.

"Nizamuddin is going to change, Mara," she said. "I can feel it, and so can Beraal. It's the battle, and more—I can't see it all—you might—" Her voice was fading into exhaustion.

"Promise me you'll step out of your house, at least a few times," said Miao.

The orange kitten's young green eyes widened. "But I hate being outside," she said. "You don't understand, Miao."

The Siamese would have smiled; Mara could see it in her blue eyes, though the light was fading from them rapidly.

"I do," she said. "I had a fear of heights when I was a young kitten. So I do know how it feels to tremble at the thought of something that seems so simple for other cats and is so hard for you. But Mara, you have to do it. The world is not a sending, little one. The world is real, and it is more than the four walls of your house. If you shut yourself in, away from the Nizamuddin wildings, something inside you will wither. I have no time left, Mara. Just promise that you'll try to come out. Promise me, by whisker and paw. Give me your word, by tail and by claw."

The words found their mark. Mara said, "I promise I'll try, Miao." And then her ears quivered, and the kitten's fur seemed to crumple from tiredness. "I have to go, Miao. If only we'd met before."

"We would have if you'd come out of your house before," said Miao, holding Mara's sad green eyes with her own calm blue ones. "Keep that promise for me."

When the kitten shimmered out of view, Miao let her head drop back to the ground, grateful for the soft pillow of the earth. The talking had been too much for her. The Siamese heard a babble of noise—the distant yelps of the ferals, the war cries of Qawwali and the dargah cats, the low conversation of Katar and Hulo, Beraal's clear tones. But she was too exhausted to listen to any of it. She lay at the foot of the wall, feeling a black tiredness seep into her mind, knowing that she was badly broken inside.

The wall brought her solace. It was a reminder that the ferals had stayed on this side of the crumbling boundary that divided the grounds of the Shuttered House from the colony the Nizamuddin cats roamed with such freedom. On the other side, the babblers went about their business, safe from Datura and his kind. The rats were free to roam their gutters, Blackwing, Brightbeak and their band of crows could call to one another across the trees in the park without fearing an unpleasant death.

Miao drifted between pain and the balm of her memories. She thought of Nizamuddin's Senders, and she thought of teaching Southpaw to hunt, and of the mongoose who had appeared so unexpectedly that night. Even as she lay slumped and mortally wounded on the earth her memories were happy.

She had taught Beraal how to hunt, watching as the tiny kitten tried to tackle rats three times her size—Beraal had been born without an ounce of fear in her whiskers, as the old saying went. A parade of kittens marched through Miao's mind, softening the pain in her blue eyes as she recalled each one's first hunt, how they had reacted at their first sight of prey. Some had shied away; some, like Katar, had been wide-eyed and determined not to let her down. A few, like Hulo, had been brawlers from the time their eyes lost their blue.

The Siamese flinched when she heard a mighty flapping of wings in the sky. She was vulnerable to any predator that came by, and many might arrive, attracted by the stench of blood. Perhaps it was better to be swiftly dispatched, thought Miao. It might be preferable to a long, slow, ending, or to the ignominy of being found by the Bigfeet.

The wings rustled close to her ears, and the Siamese forced herself to open her eyes; she wanted to see her predator, just as she had stared back into Ratsbane's face.

Tooth furled his wings. The pariah cheel seemed awkward on the grass, but he walked over to her, hobbling the way cheels did on land. Over his head, bulbuls and sparrows called, checking on each other in the aftermath of the battle.

"I saw you from the skies," he said. "Shall I call Beraal and the others to lick your wounds clean?" Then his great golden brown eyes took in the battered ribs, the damaged face, the broken legs. The bird raised his head, the curved beak conveying his sadness.

"I am sorry, Miao," he said. "Is it bad?"

She blinked her blue eyes in assent. "Don't need the others," said Miao with difficulty. "It's my time to go."

"But not here," said Tooth, taking in the grounds littered with bodies, sensing immediately that there were too many creatures, living and dead, in the gardens for Miao to be at peace. "Shall I move you somewhere quieter?"

It was a generous gesture, and Miao was touched to her heart. Her blue eyes said a quiet yes. The hunter flexed his chest feathers, rose high into the air, circled her twice, then swooped down and lifted the cat by her neck, just as though she was a kitten. Tooth was surprised at how light Miao was; the Siamese had such a presence that she had always seemed much larger than she actually turned out to be.

The flight was a short one; he took her to a part of the wild garden where the wall had broken, and deposited the cat in the quiet back lane that wound between the garden and another old house.

"Thank you, Tooth," said Miao, expecting the hunter to leave. He glanced down at her, but instead of rising into the skies again, he folded his wings.

"My debt is paid," he said to the Siamese, his eyes hooded as he saw how her ribs were heaving up and down, noting the thin line of blood trickling out from her mouth. "But only in part. We could not keep all the little ones safe, after all. I didn't think the ferals would kill so fast and so ruthlessly."

Miao managed to say, "Neither did I." The cheel took her in. She seemed so peaceful. Her black tail was as beautiful as ever, her blue eyes calm in the face of death, her creamy fur licked smooth, even though she hadn't been able to use her paws to comb out the twigs and the dust.

"Some of them fought back, you know," he said. "Ao and Jao, the squirrels, did a good job. And that mouse—Jethro Tail?—he bit Datura himself. Brave little creatures. I always wondered why you and I cared so much about the little ones. We hunt them often enough."

"Perhaps it's because we hunt them that we know them, Tooth," said Miao. Her voice was soft as a whisper. "Your mother—she knew all the little ones. Hunting is one thing, caring is another."

The pariah cheel flapped his wings involuntarily.

"Who will teach us these things when you're gone, Miao?" he cried.

"The new Sender will," said Miao. "Keep an eye out for her, Tooth. She's an inside cat, but one day she'll step outside, and then she'll need friends. Promise me you'll look after her."

Tooth was about to refuse—he was no cat babysitter!—but he saw the light dimming in Miao's eyes, and the hunter said, "Yes, Miao, I promise I will."

The tip of the Siamese's tail stirred, in acknowledgement, and then she closed her eyes. "Tell me a story, Tooth," said Miao. "Tell me what it's like to sail the skies." It was the first time in years she had asked for a story. She had often told them; even the most fierce hunter among the wildings loved a good story, and Miao was a good storyteller.

Now she listened, as the cheel drew pictures of the great empty space of the skies and how it was filled with the language of the winds, if only you cared to listen. He told her about their squadrons, and about vultures, about flying alongside the Bigfeet's gliders, about the way the birds risked injury to dance with the Bigfeet's painted paper kites. His voice was rough and hoarse, but Miao listened with happiness.

The hard stones of the back lane melted away as Tooth talked. The Siamese no longer felt the pain stab so sharply at her ribs; instead, the darkness seemed to gather around her, and the rain and the wind seemed to be growing colder and colder.

"Is it night yet?" she asked.

"No," said Tooth. "The noon sun is coming up."

"It must be dark, then, with the storm," said Miao.

Tooth's feathers fluffed out as he looked at the sun. The rain had stopped; the sun was out and the grey skies had given way to a bright monsoon blue.

"Yes, Miao," he said gently. "It is very dark indeed." And he went on with his stories, telling her one about the hunter who flew too close to the sun.

"Is it very cold now?" asked Miao after he had finished his story.

Tooth's voice shook. "Yes, it's getting colder," he said. "It must have been the rain this morning."

Miao was looking at him, and the cheel saw a smile in her eyes.

"I was thinking of all the kittens I knew, and how they grew up to be wonderful cats," said the Siamese. "You must have been a very special fledgling, Tooth. Your mother must have been very proud of you."

The hunter couldn't trust himself to speak. Instead, he gently touched the cat's fur with his beak.

"Shall I tell you another story?" he asked.

"Yes, please," said Miao. "Tell me the one about the cheel who flew to the edge of the world and back."

It was a beautiful story, and Tooth told it well, watching as the sun disappeared and the clouds moved slowly into the sky overhead. The rain started to drizzle as he came to the end of the tale.

". . . and so, the old hunter said, what you must do when you reach the edge of the world is very simple: keep your wings unfurled, and keep going."

He stopped and glanced at Miao. Her eyes were closed, and her face was calm and peaceful. But underneath, the concrete slab where he had set her down was soaked in blood.

"Miao?" he said uncertainly.

The rain came down in a torrent, washing away the blood from the Siamese cat's face. Miao made no movement at all, and Tooth understood that the finest, bravest warrior he had met in all of his life had gone to see for herself what the edge of the world was like.

Epilogue

J ust before she climbed the stair to the Sender's house, Beraal paused, listening to the chatter of the squirrels. Ao and Jao had shifted to the tree in the park, not wanting to be in the Shuttered House any more. The memories of the battle were harsh, and besides, the Bigfeet had overrun the wild garden.

The shock of the carnage had worn off, though, and the old squirrels were back to their squabbles. Ao insisted that the air tasted of winter. "Of course it's not winter weather yet, we're not even finished with the monsoons," said Jao crossly.

"Why is your tail shivering, then?" Ao demanded.

"Quivering!" said Jao. "It was quivering, not shivering."

"Nonsense!" said Ao. "I know what your tail does when it quivers. That was a shiver."

And they were off, bickering as they raced along the feathery branches of the ashoka tree. The babblers had generously composed a welcome home poem for them, which was only slightly ruined when Ga wandered off absent-mindedly, tempted by a worm, leaving Re and Ma to struggle with the missing rhyme.

Listening to the squirrels as she limped up the back stairs of the Sender's house, Beraal felt her spirits lifting slightly. The cats had grieved for Miao after Tooth flew back and told Katar about her death. They grieved hard, sharing stories and memories through a long night at the fakir's shrine, and then moved on to the urgent business of settling the young and the old into their winter quarters. A sharp chill had ridden into Nizamuddin on the back of the monsoon, and both Katar and Hulo felt in their whiskers that it would be a rough winter.

Though they didn't need to discuss it, all three cats felt Miao's absence every hour. Hunting, Beraal often imagined Miao's slim figure, saw the Siamese's blue eyes flash as she closed in on prey, imagined how her black tail would curl up to warm her paws.

Mara had slept for a day and a night after the battle, worn out by the effort of bringing the tiger into Nizamuddin. It was only their exceptional closeness that had allowed her to pull off the double sending: without his consent and his trust, the Sender would never have been able to carry Ozzy with her into Nizamuddin. Even with the tiger's co-operation, the effort of visualizing and bringing his image into the field of battle had taxed all of Mara's powers. Once the battle was over, the kitten realized how close she'd been to collapse. It was much harder to pull off a sending that included another creature than it was to simply send herself out into the world. It was like, she told Beraal when she finally woke up, hunting in two directions at the same time, or trying to fly like Tooth while simultaneously prowling like Hulo.

Beraal wondered how long their lessons would continue. Mara would always be a small cat—Southpaw had already grown bigger than her—but her powers were extraordinary, and Beraal didn't know whether she could keep pace. She had already taught Mara most of what she knew, and the young queen wished she had learned more from Miao. None of them had asked the right questions, because they had all thought they had many seasons with the Siamese. In cat-fashion, Beraal had asked only what was important for her to know when Mara was a tiny kitten. It wasn't just her; the black-and-white knew how much Katar missed Miao's wise counsel when he attended to the clan's everyday affairs.

Before Beraal could check for Bigfeet or go into the Sender's house, Southpaw jumped out of the window, almost landing on her. "Oof," he said, "Sorry about that, Beraal, wasn't thinking straight."

Beraal leaned forward to give him a gentle head rub. The brown kitten tumbled all over the place, and still got into trouble every second day or so. But Mara had told her how Southpaw had stayed steadfastly by her side when she had tried to summon the tiger. It was difficult, and the Sender had cried out in frustration when her first attempts misfired.

"Southpaw kept me going," she had told Beraal. "He never gave up, and he wouldn't let me give up either." Though he badly wanted to go back to the battle, though all of his instincts told him to give in to his curiosity and see how the wildings were doing, Southpaw curled up beside Mara, encouraging her, washing her paws and flanks when she almost collapsed from exhaustion. Beraal and the other cats were proud of him. "He'll make a fine tom when he's older," Katar had commented.

"Off you go, Southpaw," Beraal said now. "Hulo was looking for you. He's over there, across the park." The cat and the kitten turned to see Hulo hobble out on the tin roof, wanting to catch what little there was left of the winter sun. The tom moved slowly—he was still recovering from his injuries. As the brown kitten bounced happily down the stairs, a thought occurred to Beraal.

"Any luck?" she called out, her whiskers questioning.

"None," said Southpaw. His mew was resigned. He and Beraal had been trying to persuade Mara that she should come out and meet the wildings, but the Sender's fear of the outside only seemed to have grown since the battle. It made Beraal sigh. There was so much she could teach Mara, if only the kitten would step outside her Bigfeet's house.

When she walked cautiously through the house, it was to find Mara sitting bolt upright on the bed. Her tail was waving back and forth, and her eyes had gone a dark green.

"Southpaw left before we'd finished playing," she said crossly to Beraal. "He said he wanted to meet Hulo and go hunting, and I wanted him to stay here."

"He can't stay with you all the time," said Beraal reasonably, settling herself down on the flank that was less savagely injured. "He's an outside tomcat, you know, and he'd be very happy if you'd go out with him from time to time, just the way he comes here to visit you."

Mara's eyes had a tendency to cross when she was really

angry, and her tail whipped stiffly from side to side. "I don't have to go outside," she said, her mew sulky. "I summoned Ozzy without having to put one paw out of my house, remember?"

"Not everything can be unknotted by sending, little one," said Beraal patiently. "Aren't you curious about the other wildings, Mara? You remember what Miao told you—she hoped you would go outside one day and meet the other cats."

The kitten surprised Beraal by going over and stretching up to rub her whiskers gently against the older queen's face.

"It's too early," she said quietly. "I'm still scared of the outside, Beraal. It seems so big and so unsafe. Give me time, please."

For just a second, as she looked into Mara's solemn green eyes, Beraal thought of the small orange kitten who had gone tumbling down the stairs, and who had stared out at the world with such frightened fascination. Her mew was gentle in return, and instead of starting with lessons, she asked the Sender to tell her exactly what it had felt like when she had gone for a walk and come back with a tiger in tow. Mara's furry face brightened. "I didn't think I'd be able to pull it off—and neither did Ozzy until we got the hang of it," she began, and Beraal settled down contentedly to listen to Mara's tale, one wary ear cocked for the Bigfeet.

On the moss-overgrown wall that girdled the Shuttered House, a grey tom limped slowly along the perimeter, watching the activity with keen eyes. The day after the battle, some of the Bigfeet had arrived and exclaimed at the carnage in the wilderness, just as he, Beraal and the others had feared they would. The next day, there were even more of them, pointing at the bodies of the mice and birds and chattering about them in their big booming voices, as they cleaned up the grounds.

Katar had watched with growing alarm, sitting quietly on the wall. The Bigfeet seemed to be sad about the small, pathetic corpses that littered the grounds, and the tomcat stirred uncomfortably when they pointed at him. He had jumped down from the wall and left quietly, but his whiskers tingled with an unpleasant thought: the Bigfeet couldn't smell the difference between the ferals and the wildings. To them, all cats were the same. He didn't like the idea that the Bigfeet might think the wildings had killed the little creatures, but he let it rest in his mind.

Since then, the grey tom had come back every day, curious about what the Bigfeet were going to do. Today, Bigfeet trucks took up all the path, but despite the thumping rumble of their machinery, and though they had cleaned out the fetid Shuttered House, Katar felt that the Bigfeet were still tense. There were fewer of them, though, and he approached the Shuttered House out of curiosity, wondering whether the ferals had left their evil shadows behind. But it smelled clean, of paint and soap, and Katar padded away from the place, relieved that it carried no memories of Datura.

He had almost got to the wall when he heard a Bigfeet shout go up. The grey tom turned, puzzled. A knot of Bigfeet approached him, and when his whiskers tasted the air, it smelled hostile. The cat stared at the Bigfeet, wondering why they had noticed him. Most of the Nizamuddin Bigfeet walked past the cats, only grumbling or cursing at them if they were underfoot.

One of the Bigfeet stooped to pick up a stone, and Katar tensed, his ears pricking all the way back. His instincts told him to run; he turned, and felt a sudden, dull pain on his flank. The Bigfoot had thrown the stone at him, he realized, his tail dropping all the way down. He put his ears back and fled for the safety of the wall. From its height, he stared at the Bigfeet, wondering why they had tried to hurt him. He could see the hostility on their faces, and it worried him.

He took his worries to Hulo later that evening. The black tom listened, his unkempt head alert. "It happened to me, too," he said when Katar had finished. "A Bigfoot ran yelling at me, flapping his hands like a cheel. They think we're part of Datura's bunch."

It was what Katar had wondered, but hearing Hulo say it made it real. The toms lay on the tin roof, watching the yelling, playing Bigfeet in the park. Katar felt a sharp pang go through him; Miao would have known what this meant, and what to do about it.

"Shall we tell the others?" he asked. Hulo turned the question over in his head. Raising an alarm without a strong, obvious cause might be the wrong thing to do, when the wildings were already nervous and battle-fatigued.

"No," he said. "Not now. Just tell the wildings to stay away from the Shuttered House for a while. I'll tell Southpaw myself, make sure that brown imp obeys this time. Did you know he tried to cross the canal bridge on his own yesterday? I dusted his backside for him until he squeaked like a mouse, but we'll have to find some other way to keep him out of trouble. He'll soon be too old to be spanked."

"Southpaw will never be too old to be spanked, as far as I'm concerned," said Katar firmly. As their whiskers rose in shared laughter, the two toms set aside their fears. For a brief moment, as the evening sun warmed them all in the park, as the squirrels chattered and the birds sang their evening melodies over the roof of the Sender's house, it seemed to the tom that all would be well. Whatever winter had in store for them, the wildings would see it through.

ACKNOWLEDGEMENTS

Cats: Mara, Tiglath, Pantha, Bathsheba; Torty, Rival, Patience Waddle, Tweeter, Woofer, Phash, Phoosh, the Sillies and all the strays whose lives were raided for this book.

Vets: Dr. Ramandeep Chaggar, Dr. Ms Chaggar and Dr. Rupali, who gave our cats a few of their nine lives back; the animal shelter team at Friendicoes, Delhi.

Humans: My parents, Tarun and Sunanda Roy, Tara, JT, Neel, Mia and family, especially Rudra, Antara and Arun; Tini, Baba, Peter Griffin, always; Kamini, Malavika and Hironmay Karlekar for the love and for Mara; Yusuf Merchant, Raj Mathur, Kriti, Keshav, Arjun Nath and the gang.

Samit and Sayoni Basu, Ruchir Joshi, Jeet Thayil, Mitali Saran, Anita Roy, Namita Devidayal, Rajni George and Manjula Padmanabhan for telling me to get on with it. Arshia Sattar and DW Gibson, for the priceless gift of space at the Sangam Residency in Tranquebar; TN Ninan, AK Bhattacharya, Kanika Datta and the Business Standard for their extraordinary kindness. Karthika, Thomas, Chiki, Meru, Gautam—thank you for your goodwill and friendship.

Every debut author should be lucky enough to have an agent as wise and generous as David Godwin, and an editor as acute and wonderfully enthusiastic as David Davidar. They took a scruffy, scrawny draft, and turned it into an actual novel. (Any errors are my fault, not theirs.) Prabha Mallya— thank you for breathing life into the wildings and their world with your artwork.

My thanks to Amanda Betts for the care and feeding of the international edition, to Louise Dennys and Anne Collins for their encouragement, to Kelly Hill for the exquisite book design, and to the team at Random House Canada.

And gratitude to Simar Puneet for all the enthusiasm and her perfectionism, to Aienla, Bena, Aruna, Varun, Ankit, Shekhar, Hina, Hohoi and the rest of the crack team at Aleph for making the business of publishing such a pleasure; Anna Watkins and the team at DGA; Kavi Bhansali for the author pictures; my Twitter feed for giving Kirri her name.

Nilanjana Roy is the author of *The Wildings*, winner of the Shakti Bhatt First Book Award. She is the editor of *A Matter of Taste: The Penguin Book of Indian Writing On Food* and is working on a collection of essays called *The Girl Who Ate Books*. Nilanjana lives in Delhi with three independent cats and her partner.

THE
HUNDRED
NAMES OF
DARKNESS

the riveting sequel and conclusion
to *The Wildings*, will be available

July 2016

Random House Canada
www.penguinrandomhouse.ca